THE WARMAKER

A BLACK SPEAR NOVEL

BENJAMIN SPADA

FROM THE TINY ACORN …
GROWS THE MIGHTY OAK

www.acornpublishingllc.com
For information, address:
Acorn Publishing, LLC
3943 Irvine Blvd. Ste. 218
Irvine, CA 92602

The Warmaker | *A Black Spear Novel*
Copyright © 2023 Benjamin Spada

Cover design by ebooklaunch.com
Interior design and formatting by Debra Cranfield Kennedy

Printed in the United States of America

ISBN-13: 979-8-88528-070-9 (hardcover)
ISBN-13: 979-8-88528-069-3 (paperback)

This book is dedicated to the Marines and Sailors of
3d Battalion, 1st Marines: The Balls of the Corps.
And for Jackie, always.
To the moon and back.

PROLOGUE

The world starts to burn the same way as everything else. All it takes is one little spark . . .

At precisely eleven o'clock the man left his office and told his secretary he was off to lunch. Despite how hectic his schedule had become over the years, he never strayed far from this routine: lunch at eleven. Period. No matter who he was expected to meet *with* or where work required him to travel, this last bit of inflexibility was all that kept him sane most days.

What was for lunch would, of course, change. Yesterday it was a grilled panini from the café two blocks away. He hated having to pay twelve dollars for what Subway charged half, but the café was locally owned and what was good for his constituents was good for him. Today, he craved something a bit more detrimental cholesterol-wise. There was usually a hotdog cart down by the courthouse, and the idea of some greasy street food had his already grumbling stomach ready to sing like a choir.

He checked his watch as he walked along the sidewalk. Just one minute to get from his desk upstairs to here, like every other day this week and every other week this month. Routine was everything, after all.

As he made his way to the hotdog cart, his mind ran a break-down of the tasks remaining for the day. Emails to send, calls to make, meetings to schedule and, at some point, he needed to find the time to see his family. He'd missed his son's most recent baseball game (much to his son's devastation). Nine-year-old kids tended to be unforgiving in that department, regardless of the importance of their dad's job.

At that precise moment, he decided to clear his weekend schedule. It had been too long since he'd given his family the attention they deserved. He'd promised his wife long ago that the job would never come before them. Clearly, he'd lost sight of his priorities. It would be good to get away for the weekend; his family was his entire world.

A smile stole across his face as his mind shifted from organizing work tasks to planning fun for the family. His wife would be prickly at first, but he would make it up to her with that necklace he'd already told her was too expensive. Their anniversary was coming up soon. And there would be plenty of time to play ball with his boys. His eldest son had a hell of an arm, and it wasn't just fatherly pride to imagine him making it to the pros one day.

But he would never take the weekend trip with his family. They would never get a chance to celebrate their anniversary, nor would his wife ever receive that pretty necklace she very much deserved. Because at precisely eleven-fifteen the man burst into flames in the middle of the crosswalk, leaving behind nothing but a blackened skeleton.

PART 1

THE BLEEDING EDGE

"I don't know what World War Three will be fought with, but World War Four will be fought with sticks and stones."

—Albert Einstein

CHAPTER 1

War. Such an ugly word. No matter how admirable or honorable the general public claims military service is, the reality of war is ugly. That ugliness takes many shapes. There's the War on Terror, which goes on and on, other countries engaged in ethnic wars as justification for committing genocide, and of course there's the ever-looming threat of traditional war with the usual suspects whose names rhyme with Shorth Shorea or Shmrussia. Maybe even Shmina. Whatever form it takes, war is something most sane people would avoid at all costs. But Black Spear is in the business of war. And business was booming in the most literal of ways.

About six months ago I was unceremoniously drafted into the Black Spear initiative, a top-tier outfit dedicated to combating terrorism of certain extreme natures. That vague mission statement was really a catch-all for anything too weird for either the traditional military or the public eye. My team, Cerberus Squad, and I dismantled a rogue veteran militia armed with an engineered chimera virus, stopped an attempted biological strike on Air Force One, and thwarted a madman's plot to launch a missile into Las Vegas that would've turned everyone into rabid psychopaths. Oh, and that was just in the first three days.

Since then, I've operated on both foreign and domestic soil and taken down two different cyberterrorist cells, both aimed at destroying Wall Street with sophisticated worm tech, a doomsday cult looking to distribute next-gen nerve agents, and a partridge in a pear tree.

In short, the bad guys were becoming more advanced.

Thankfully, so were we. Part of the reason Black Spear was so effective was due to our equipment. There's "state of the art military grade" and then there's Black Spear's state of the art. Being a part of Black Spear was like having a Disneyland FastPass to DARPA. We get all the fun toys without all the waiting.

Common Defense Industries was our primary military contractor. Nine times out of ten, a project greenlighted by the Pentagon for mass production gets turned into a cheaper version of itself to offset the costs. CDI gave us early access to their most advanced tech before that dilution and fat trimming happened.

At least, we're supposed to. Unless, of course, you're part of a military division so goddamn secret that the gate guard can't seem to find your clearance. Then you just might find yourself stuck waiting outside a security checkpoint like I was.

"I'm sorry, sir," the guard said. "You need proper identification."

I looked to the passenger seat where my boss, Captain Vaun, sat, looking strangely amused.

"Does this happen every time?" I asked.

Half a smile snuck its way to the corner of Vaun's mouth. I'd learned that he never *really* smiled. It was only ever at most that slight pull of muscle at the edge of his mouth, which I think was as close to laughter as he was capable of. He slowly reached into his pocket, pulled out his phone, and dialed a number. Putting it on speakerphone, he passed it to me to point at the guard.

"Charles, if you don't let those men through the gate, I'm putting you back on the graveyard shift until you retire," a woman said through the phone.

The guard straightened immediately, as if ratcheted back into place, and hit a switch to open the gate.

"Right away, ma'am," he stammered.

I tossed the phone back to Vaun, whose eyes glittered with far more delight than his not-smile displayed.

"It's all about who you know," he said. "Now, let's go shopping, shall we?"

I pulled our vehicle through the gate and into the CDI compound. The long driveway was lined with tall trees. Strange, I thought, that a company devoted to weapons development could have such nice greenery adorning their grounds.

We passed a large sign to our left emblazoned with the company's logo. Large red letters, each about seven feet high, displayed the abbreviated CDI name in front of a white backdrop. On the right-hand side of the sign was a golden eagle with widespread wings and outstretched talons. Across the bottom in ornate gold lettering was a line pulled right from the U.S. Constitution. *"To secure the blessings of liberty."*

"I guess subtlety goes out the window when you make billions arming America's home team," I said with a whistle.

Vaun looked unamused.

"Common Defense Industries' vehicle-reinforcing program has saved countless lives from IEDs. Most of our own team have had a bullet stopped by a CDI-developed vest that would've killed them had they been wearing different armor. I think they've earned their right to be a little patriotic."

Point taken. I guess it's a good rule of thumb not to clown on the people who kept your people alive. Unfortunately, I tend to clown and become extra sarcastic when I'm uneasy. This partic-ular case of unease went by the name of Mister Rourke. Rourke, my boss's Boss and with a very capital B, was the director of Black Spear. By decree of an executive order, the man was entrusted with unchecked authority to deploy us where we're needed.

He's not my biggest fan.

Rourke is the quintessential head honcho. When he makes a suggestion, it becomes an order. If he tells someone to jump, they don't presume to ask him how high because his word was meant to be obeyed not questioned. And, when he tells one of America's top weapons developers to hand over the good stuff, they do so with smiles on their faces.

Normally, Rourke wouldn't be in attendance on something as run of the mill as a gear acquisition, but Cerberus Squad recently earned the boss's ire. Yours truly may have accidentally exceeded his squad's monthly budget for gear allocations last month. It was an honest mistake. You add a zero or two in the wrong place and suddenly you're purchasing ten thousand rounds of specialized ammunition instead of a hundred. Can happen to anyone.

After that faux pas we were assigned a liaison with the House Committee on Armed Services, Congressman Mike Halsey. He was supposed to be another check in the box to ensure Black Spear wasn't recklessly purchasing equipment. Even a black-ops team as hidden from the record as we are couldn't escape the bureaucracy of the bean counters. Luckily for us and unluckily for Rourke, however, Congressman Halsey was frequently impossible to track down and too busy to return our calls so the big guy got to fill in for him.

"Just don't say anything when we see him," Vaun instructed.

"I wasn't going to."

"Seriously, West, this'll go a lot easier if you pretend you aren't hilarious."

"I bet you twenty bucks he's wearing that same charcoal suit and red tie. I swear his tailor stitched it to his skin."

"West . . ."

"Do you think Rourke's first name is 'Mister'? What if it's something hilarious like Earl?"

Vaun looked in my direction long and hard, making sure I took the full brunt of his displeasure. You know the expression "staring daggers"? Well, Vaun's mastered the art of staring goddamn bricks at you.

"Sorry," I mumbled as I pulled our vehicle into a parking space outside CDI's Advanced Projects hangar. "I drank a lot of coffee on the plane."

"Just look big and tough and try not to say anything."

"Damn skippy, sir. It's what I'm good at."

CHAPTER 2

Cole West. 11:40 a.m.
Common Defense Industries
Seattle, Washington

His name was Cain. With such a Biblical name, I guess he was destined to get into the war business. Samuel Cain was a dyed in the wool patriot. In 1968, when others were being drafted for Vietnam, Cain volunteered. Though he was disqualified from the military due to severe asthma, he refused to give up on the calling to serve his country. He created another way to serve when he converted his family's steel manufacturing company into weapons fabrication. Thus, Common Defense Industries was born. Over the years, it aggressively fought its way to the top of the ladder.

Defense contractors tend to get a bad rep for being so-called "war profiteers". Cain was the exception. His company devoted just as much time to making weapons as it did to humanitarian efforts. Fleets of CDI vehicles aided in recent hurricane relief in the gulf. CDI-manufactured tools and demolition charges rescued people trapped in collapsed buildings after Haiti's latest earthquake. And more often than not, Cain refused to cater to the industry standard practice of artificially inflating their prices just because the government was willing to pay for it.

In a recent interview, he said, "The cost of liberty is paid with the blood, sweat, and tears of the American serviceman, and that cost is already high enough."

The man himself warmly greeted us. His grip was iron, which caught me off guard at first, but in a weird way it felt reassuring. His handshake seemed like a testament to his equipment's reliability.

"Good to see you again, Captain," Cain said with a wide smile and a hoarse voice.

Vaun, who more often than not hid his emotions better than a pro card player, couldn't fight the return of that half-smile of his.

Cain asked, "How goes the good fight?"

"It's more easily won with the right supplier."

Cain wore a black three-piece power suit with dark gray pinstripes that looked so well-tailored, I had to remind myself how many billions more this man made than me. A small American flag pin adorned his lapel, and he had a red and white striped tie tucked behind his vest. Despite his age, he looked fit and strong. With his all-white hair combed back and thick walrus mustache, he resembled everyone's friendly grandpa. And everyone knows that grandpas give the best gifts.

The Advanced Projects division of CDI operated in a five-story reinforced warehouse. The first three floors were devoted to testing and demonstration areas; the top two were reserved for offices and the hundreds of computers required for research and development.

"The grumpy old man is upstairs waiting," Cain said. I knew he meant Rourke. "But I'm sure he wouldn't mind if we do our demonstration without him?"

Cain led us over to a small firing line. A large Smith and Wesson .500 revolver sat on a table; on the opposite end stood a dummy clad in a black tactical vest. I eyed the revolver.

Cain chuckled. "I can't hate the competition for being good at their craft." He picked up the heavy revolver, took a strong stance, and emptied five rounds center mass into the dummy. "But I'm better at mine." Cain used a red cloth to wipe off the .500, then beckoned us to follow him to the dummy.

Amazingly, the vest held up to all five of the heavy magnum rounds. The malformed bullets stuck to the front of the vest, but none had penetrated. Cain gave the dummy a few pats on the back and the .500 rounds clattered to the floor.

"Impressive," Vaun whispered and closely examined the vest.

"This is our *Fafnir Model 4*," Cain explained, "named for the dragon of Norse legend. A little much, I know, but it catches the eye of the Pentagon a little better than a boring serial number. In place of a single ballistic plate, our *Fafnir* line of armor utilizes overlapping scales of composite Kevlar and titanium fibers."

I took a closer look as Cain tried to explain the armor in more technical detail. The information reached new academic heights, and he began to sound like a Charlie Brown adult. Wonk-wonk polymer mesh this, whomp-whomp thermo-regulation that. The *Fafnir* vest resembled dragon scales, its black surface made up of dozens of small angular plates. Unlike traditional bulletproof vests with solid plates in the front, back, and sides, which leave gaps of vulnerability between and on the shoulders, the *Fafnir's* scales offered complete protection.

"The scales are interwoven with our next-gen Silk threads," Cain continued as I poked at it. "It's similar to the Army's project of harnessing spider silk for protective armor, but ours actually works. You'll be lighter, have a higher range of motion, and our vests can shrug off more hits than traditional plates."

I whistled to myself while prodding the scales a little more. As they shifted and adjusted, I thought about the past six months of sweating and chafing behind the protection of our stiff plates. This would be a welcome change. Vaun's nod of approval told me he agreed.

"This is pretty good," Vaun said, "but 'not dying' is only half the solution. What about something with a little more bang for our buck?"

"And here I thought the best offense is a good defense?" Cain's big walrus mustache curled in a funny way as he held back a smile. "Right this way, gentlemen."

He led us to another section of the warehouse where a young woman in a white lab coat stood behind a laptop. I couldn't help giving her a look over. She works in the weapons business after all, which is pretty high on my list of attractive qualities.

My attention was quickly stolen by what lay in front of her.

"Oh, now you're just showing off."

Before us stood an enormous tank, fully armored with all the bells and whistles. The main gun's bore looked like it could blow a building in half. Its secondary and tertiary machine-guns held enough bullets on their chains to mow down entire enemy brigades, and the dual missile pods on either side appeared more than sufficient to knock any air support right out of the sky. The tank's armor plating looked thick enough to eat a missile point-blank and keep on chugging.

"Meet the *ShadowCrawler Mk. III*," declared Cain with out-stretched arms. "Third in a line of tanks designed with all-terrain maneuverability in mind."

As Cain spoke I watched the tank's treads, which moments before I thought were single tracks, separated into dual front and rear sections on each side. They tilted and adjusted slightly, the front ones lifting up while the back two lowered. The *ShadowCrawler* lurched forward and back, then settled flat with a large puff of hydraulics.

"Yep," Cain said and folded his arms across his chest. "What an utter heap of rubbish."

I looked to Vaun, then to Cain, confused. But Cain only smiled, then glanced to the woman behind the laptop. I'd completely forgotten her.

"Show them what we got, Dr. Archer," Cain instructed.

The woman hit a button on the laptop. A second later, I heard hissing. The sound grew louder, and then a noxious chemical scent filled the air. It tingled the inside of my nose a little. Then, as the hissing grew louder, I watched as the *ShadowCrawler* tank dissolved before my very eyes.

At first the main gun seemed to droop, and then it fell off completely onto the training area floor. The entire tank appeared to deflate like a bounce house with a hole stuck in it as the tank's metal treads sizzled and liquefied. Within moments, the behemoth was rendered completely inoperable and disarmed.

Vaun stood silent. My jaw dropped so low, it was pretty much detached from my skull at this point.

"What . . . the hell?"

"Doctor Madison Archer is our lead on this project," Cain answered. "I think I'll let her cover this part."

At that the young woman walked towards us and extended her hand. I'm glad Vaun managed to shake it first, because I was having a bit of a staring problem now that I wasn't distracted by the tank. Before, I'd thought that working in the defense industry was high on my desirable traits list, but she definitely hit the whole top ten. It wasn't even fair. The modest lab coat utterly failed to disguise a breathtaking figure, and the conservative workplace heels only accented already shapely calves. Even her arms, which hugged the metal clipboard before her like a shield, had a respectable bulge of toned biceps that bunched her sleeves. Clearly, she was just as dedicated to keeping herself fit as she was designing cutting edge military tech.

She had sharp features with eyes so light green they looked nearly gray. Her chestnut brown hair was pulled tight into a flawless bun. She wore no makeup—not that she needed it. I wondered whether it was a deliberate choice to minimize idiots like me gawking at her in her place of work. Pouty lips curled into a frown since I was sitting there, staring like a dipshit instead of shaking her hand.

"Cole, Cole West," I said and finally shook her hand.

"Yeah, no shit," Madison said.

I instantly recognized her voice.

"Who do you think told Charlie to let you two through the gate?"

Damn. Really hitting it off well. I tried to pretend I didn't see Vaun rolling his eyes at me.

"The *ShadowCrawler* comes from the competition overseas," Madison explained, transitioning smoothly into full business mode. "All-terrain maneuverability with the firepower of a traditional tank platform. Think of these traversing the Korean mountainside. Thankfully for us, they haven't quite mastered it. The hydraulics are faulty and the separation of the tracks is prone to jamming, especially in an extremely cold environment like the Korean peninsula. Now, while the competition accepts that bigger is always better, we decided to take the opposite approach."

Madison returned to the laptop at the workstation and pressed a few keys. The screen lit up and a small image of what looked like a little bug expanded to take up the whole screen. Upon closer inspection, I saw that it wasn't a bug at all but was mechanical.

"This is our *Microswarm* tech. Nanomachines, gentlemen. Thousands of them. Each one is embedded with a corrosive payload releasable via remote activation. It doesn't matter if it's a tank, a plane, or a fleet of Humvees: our *Microswarm* can take it all down." The screen shifted to what looked to be a control display. "We can maneuver the swarm however we need. They function on a hive program that controls the entire swarm."

She entered a button sequence. I spotted a slight shimmering on the training area floor. It was strange to look at, almost like looking at the waves wafting off the asphalt on a hot day, but in reality I knew

I was watching thousands of tiny robots move around before me. With a touch of a button, Madison made the *Microswarm* take the form of a small spire, and just as quickly it collapsed back into a shimmering flat surface.

"Of course, it can be used for less dramatic purposes," she explained and turned away from the workstation. "It takes some time to get used to the control interface, but given enough practice you get the hang of it. Prep your battlefield by melting locks off doors, chew through the enemy's engine block to cut off a target's getaway, or get through safes without damaging the intel inside."

"I'm sure Tag would love this," I whispered to Vaun. He nodded.

Despite being a towering giant, Tag was our team's computer expert. The guy was a wizard with electronics and I knew he'd get a kick out of mastering these nanomachines if given the chance.

Cain thanked Madison for her assistance, and she promptly returned to her workstation to record notes from the successful demonstration.

"I think we've kept the old man waiting long enough," he said with a wink. "We'll just tell him old Charlie had you waiting outside this whole time."

More and more I liked this guy and his gear. As long as the checks cleared, Samuel Cain and CDI would stay one step ahead of the competition. At the same time, though, a worrying thought came to my mind. If Cain and CDI could get their hands on the enemy's tech, and worked around the clock to develop things that could trump it, couldn't the enemy be doing the very same thing?

CHAPTER 3

Marcus Boyd. One day ago.
The Hay-Adams Hotel
Washington D.C.

"Do you know the difference between fear and dread?"

Congressman Marcus Boyd dropped his keys on the floor when he heard the voice. This was his hotel room, which he paid good money for to be *very* private, yet at this moment somewhere in the shadows an intruder lurked. Just as he reached towards his pocket to phone his head of security, something cold pressed against his neck.

"Fear, you see, is like a knife to the throat," the voice, still on the other side of the room, stated matter-of-factly. "It's the thing right in front of you."

A lamp lit up in the corner of the room, and Boyd saw a well-dressed man sitting in one of the plush leather chairs. The man wore a black suit with a dark red tie the same color as his fiery hair. He was reading from a small leather-bound notebook in his lap, a glass of red wine on the end table next to him. He gestured to the chair across from him and smiled.

When Boyd hesitated, that cold metal pressed into his neck just a little harder, and he became acutely aware of just how sharp it was. With both his hands held in the air, Boyd eased himself into the seat.

There was a mirror on the wall behind Boyd's guest. With it,

Boyd could see the man who held the knife to his throat. He was Caucasian, lean on the side of skeletal, with a shaved head. His black turtleneck and blazer seemed to be made of the very shadows around him. A thin scar on the right corner of his mouth cut back towards his jaw and then traced down his neck. A hand, steady as a rock, held a wicked-looking, double-edged knife with a curved blade against Boyd's neck. His eyes, sunk in deep sockets, were blank vacuums that didn't register anything around them.

When Boyd opened his mouth to speak, the well-dressed man across from him simply held a single finger to his lips and shushed him. He did it in the same way a librarian would calm a noisy child. Then, he closed the leather-bound book he'd been reading, took a sip of wine, and delicately placed the book on the end table.

"I'm glad we finally have your attention," Boyd's guest said with a smile stretching ear to ear. "My employer was beginning to think you weren't taking us seriously. He is a very busy man after all, and when you stopped answering him we all got so *worried*. It didn't seem reasonable for him to fly all this way so he sent my brother and I to talk to you."

Boyd nervously licked his lips, wondering if at any second the man in the turtleneck would saw straight through to his neck bones. When he didn't say anything, the well-dressed man laughed. "Oh, you are allowed to speak now, sir."

"I . . . I don't think I can go through with this."

The well-dressed man frowned. "No, no, no, sir. When I said you could speak, I meant you could answer my earlier question. Do you know the difference between fear and dread?"

Boyd froze. The politeness of this stranger and the knife held against him had his mind racing with confusion. Unable to answer, he just sat there with wide eyes and wondered how he could get out of this mess.

"Very well, I'll tell you," the stranger said. He took another sip of wine then nodded towards the second man. "Do it, Phobos."

The second man removed the knife from Boyd's neck. For a split second Boyd felt a wave of relief, but then the knife stabbed into his side, lightning quick. Before Boyd could scream, the man in the turtleneck clamped a gloved hand over his mouth.

"Don't move, sir!" the polite stranger cautioned. "Yes, that hurts. But you see my brother is quite skilled with that knife. Right now, it's in a simple body cavity. However, any unnecessary *flinching* and you just might nick an artery or organ. And we wouldn't want that, would we? We still have a job for you to do."

Boyd screamed into the glove anyway but tried not to squirm.

"There!" the polite stranger said with wide excited eyes. "*That's* dread! That's the difference, don't you see? Fear is a reaction to something present. A knife in front of you, an oncoming car you didn't see, a rabid dog's teeth gnashing. But dread? Dread is the anxiety of some danger to come. You understand, yes? You fear a dog's bite, but you dread the infection it might cause; you fear the oncoming car but dread being paralyzed in the wreckage."

Boyd nodded frantically.

"My dear brother Phobos is the fear," the stranger said proudly.

At that Phobos removed the knife from Boyd's side. Boyd gasped in relief. Phobos placed the bloodied knife once more against his neck with one hand, while pressing what must have been a cloth bandage into his side with the other.

The polite stranger's face hardened into a frown. "However, my name is Deimos, and I am your dread."

Boyd froze.

Deimos' eyes resembled hot coals, his hair fire.

"I want you to think very carefully about your family, sir, and what I will have my brother do to them. I want you to dread looking upon your daughter Haleigh's face once her nose is cut away. I want you to think about how hard it would be to have an open-casket funeral for your wife Krista after her eyes are carved from her skull. Dementia may have addled your father's mind, but he'll be aware enough to understand the razor slicing down the length of his spine. Think about those things, sir. Make them real in your mind."

Marcus Boyd felt tears running down his face as he fell forward onto his knees in defeat. The images raced through his mind at a thousand miles an hour. The stranger took another drink of wine then picked up his leather notebook and read a page.

"Your wife will be arriving at your home, 4-7-2 Maplewood Road, in the next fifteen minutes. She'll walk the fifteen steps up the pathway towards your front door, not knowing that the fake rock with the spare key inside was found a week ago. It has since been copied and replaced. And then, once she unlocks the door and enters your home, she'll have to enter the passcode to disarm your home security system. 0-7-0-4. Your anniversary date. July fourth, yes? Very patriotic, sir."

He knew everything. Precious information that endangered his family was recorded in this man's little book as if it was something as simple as phone numbers.

Deimos smiled again and leaned forward to whisper in Boyd's ear.

"That small .38 revolver in the nightstand upstairs has had its firing pin filed down. All of the weight and comfort of a loaded firearm with none of the firepower."

Boyd swallowed back the nervous vomit that climbed his esophagus. His hand pressed to his side where the bandage was held while a soft whimper escaped his lips. There was nothing he could do.

Absolutely nothing.

"What is it you want from me?"

The stranger nodded his satisfaction. He motioned for Boyd to sit back in his chair.

Boyd complied and then promptly puked all over his shoes.

Deimos frowned and stepped back from the mess before offering Boyd a handkerchief.

"You sit on the House Committee on Armed Services," Deimos stated as Boyd wiped the bile from the corners of his mouth. "A very important vote regarding weapons acquisitions contracts is approaching this week. It's expected to be approved," he said with displeasure. "I need to ensure the committee's decision is in accordance with my employer's wishes."

"Your employer?"

Deimos smiled. "Well, *our* employer now."

What they were demanding of Boyd was nothing short of treason. If discovered, it would mean the death penalty for him and turn his family into national pariahs. But there wasn't a choice. Weakly, he nodded his head in submission.

"I'll do it. Please . . . just leave them out of it."

Deimos sighed with relief. "Very good, sir, I shall pass on your answer to our employer. One last thing before I go . . ." The man reached behind his back.

Boyd flinched, expecting a gun. But instead it was only a TV remote.

The TV behind them turned on, and Boyd craned his neck to see. The news. A reporter explained some horrific accident.

"I really do need you to understand how serious this is," Deimos said calmly, "and how far our reach is. It doesn't matter where you go or who you talk to, if you decide not to play ball this is what happens. And, as you can see, it won't be pretty."

The news was showing a story about a man whose remains were just identified. Apparently, in broad daylight the man had spontaneously burst into—no. Not possible. Not like that.

"Oh, God . . ." Boyd breathed.

Deimos chuckled and downed the remainder of his wine.

"I'll do whatever you want."

"I know you will, sir." The polite man with the red-hair then produced a small hard plastic box, no larger than what you'd store a few cigars in. Deimos undid the latches and opened it. There was a needle inside. Marcus stared at the box's contents, uncertain of what it meant. "Now, sir, there is just one more thing I need you to do before we can leave."

CHAPTER 4

"Kept me waiting long enough, Sam," grumbled the Brooklyn accented voice.

Cain led the two of us into the conference room where Mr. Rourke waited. I firmly planted my ass in the seat farthest from Rourke and did my best impersonation of a statue.

True to form, Rourke wore the exact suit I'd predicted. I flared my eyes at Vaun, but he simply shook his head.

"Oh, come on, Darren, I was just showing the kids some of the new toys I got them." Cain gave me a wink to make sure I picked up on the name drop.

I looked to Vaun, mouthing the name Darren with surprise. Vaun shrugged. Something told me he'd known Rourke's first name the entire time and thought it funny not to let me know. I'd get the last laugh, though. The captain didn't know I'd already found out from Tag that his first name was Eric. Hilarious. Darren Rourke and Eric Vaun. They sounded like '80s hair metal band members.

Rourke scowled harder than usual, which told me Cain's little reveal had gotten under his skin. I wished the salty grandpa was my boss and not the Brooklyn gorilla. Rourke reached into a pocket and pulled out what looked like a small cigarette case. Opening it, he shook out two small white pills into one of his baseball mitt-sized hands, then dry swallowed both. I still wasn't sure what the pills were, but considering how frequently I managed to upset him I figured them for strong antacids.

"We don't have time for pleasantries," Rourke said. "Every second we waste is a second *they* up their game."

Cain nodded, and his jolly grandpa smile disappeared. "What can you tell me?"

"A lot." Rourke tapped two keys on the remote that activated the projector screen on the far side of the room. Images popped up of foreign countries testing different equipment. Small arms, vehicles, missiles, and aircraft. Even the *ShadowCrawler Mk. III* from earlier. A logo of two Chinese characters sat at the top right corner of the screen, emblazoned gold over a black backdrop.

"This is the Cheng Qiang Arms Conglomerate, a foreign manufacturer rapidly gaining ground both in terms of production and development."

Cain scoffed, "I don't know if I'd say 'gaining ground'. Their tech is still years behind ours."

"Cheng Qiang is a relatively new organization, yet they've ascended the foreign market relatively unopposed. Their businesses have exploded through joint projects with state-owned defense corporations in Korea and China," Rourke continued, undeterred. "While they got their beginnings in small arms and vehicle manufacture, they've recently branched into more advanced projects like their *ShadowCrawler* tanks."

"Which don't even work . . ." Cain grumbled.

"They're getting better, Sam. There's no other way to put it."

Cain gave Rourke an unimpressed expression. I continued my statue impersonation. I didn't know we would be briefing Cain on any of the Cheng Qiang situation, and it seemed Vaun was equally surprised.

"They're accelerating production." Rourke clicked a button and showed us photos of fully staffed arms facilities busily running at breakneck speed. "They're gearing up and it can only be for one reason: war. Cheng Qiang sells to North Korea, China, they're expanding into Iran's market, and all evidence points to them supplying various terrorist networks."

"One: this is nothing new, so I don't see how this changes anything. Two: what does this have to do with me?" Cain asked.

Rourke paused for just a moment. I knew what was coming, but I also knew that it was going to hurt Cain.

"This man is what changes things," whispered Rourke. "Atharv Singh."

"Son of a bitch," Cain breathed, his hands clenched into fists.

A profile photo of a thin, balding, Indian man with small circular framed glasses appeared in the middle of the screen. Atharv Singh used to be one of the good guys. The English-born Indian had emigrated to the US of A with his family when he was sixteen, attending MIT where he earned double masters in chemical and mechanical engineering. After that, he'd come to work for Common Defense Industries. His designs were nothing short of revolutionary. Singh was brilliant and ambitious. Too ambitious, as it turned out.

Classified CDI schematics and proprietary information leaked to foreign interests was sourced back to Atharv Singh himself. He'd sold our secrets to the competition. The FBI had been moving to arrest him for treason when he'd fled the country. I knew Cain blamed himself for the loss of life Singh's actions inevitably caused, but there had been no trace of him anywhere. Until now.

"We believe Cheng Qiang's surge in development can be attributed to Atharv Singh. He's their ace in the hole and already his waves are making it back stateside."

More pictures popped up, this time of the doomsday cult we'd taken down earlier. The pictures were close-ups of their automatic rifles, another photo showed a removed magazine and the red tip on the end of one of the bullets.

"This terrorist cell was trying to manufacture nerve gas when Cerberus Squad and Hydra Squad took them out," Rourke explained. "Their rifles are standard AK's and AR-15 variants all made by different companies, most of them domestic, but the bullets were provided by Cheng Qiang. They chewed right through our vests as if they were paper. Hydra Squad took one casualty."

I remembered how awful that had been. Everyone on the squad had called the bullets firecrackers. They'd glowed red almost like standard tracer rounds but had burned right through everything in their path. Rourke flipped through a few of the photos demonstrating the damage the firecrackers had done.

Cain stroked his mustache while voicing his thoughts. "Some type of thermite-jacketed round?"

Rourke reached into his pocket, pulled out two 7.62mm firecracker rounds, and slid them across the table to Cain. "Near as we can tell. Singh is distributing Cheng Qiang's projects to terrorist groups like this for real-world R&D. It's like forcing an accelerated evolution. He's letting them test it out against us, learning its shortfalls, and every time that happens, they're refining their designs and advancing. I need you upping our game even more. I wanted you involved because of your history with Singh, and I'm sure you want him taken out just as much as we do. But I *needed* you involved because without you, Cheng Qiang will continue to gain ground. We're not dealing with terrorists hiding in Middle Eastern caves, using guerilla tactics anymore. These are near-peer threats with highly advanced capabilities."

Cain nodded. "You give me what you have of theirs, and I'll give you something to beat it. I may be in the war business, but I'm on the American side of it."

I was glad Rourke was giving Cain the full scoop. It wouldn't feel right to take all his gifts and then not be able to tell him the full truth on what we were using it for, especially when the reason would hit so close to home.

"I'll have my people send over the remainder of the recovered munitions and equipment for your and Dr. Archer's examination. You still have that *ShadowCrawler* prototype I gave you, right?"

A tight-lipped smile stretched across Cain's face, and I had to stifle my own laughter. "Oh, that thing? Yeah . . . in a manner of speaking."

Rourke's blank stare spoke volumes to his displeasure. "Sam, I'm taking a risk bringing you into the fold here. But I'm trying something new and extending Black Spear's circle of trust. Don't make me regret it."

That serious look passed across Cain's face once more, and he gave a solemn nod.

"Good." Rourke pulled his incredible weight onto his feet. "Gentlemen, finish your business and get back to the plane. We have a mission."

"And here I thought we'd get to enjoy this nice Seattle rain," I whispered just loud enough to annoy the boss. "At least we'll be back in San Diego for dinner."

"We're not going home just yet," Rourke corrected. "We need to stop in Sacramento first. Congressman Halsey has been found."

The way he said it and the look on his face gave me no illusions. Something terrible had happened to the congressman, and I think I already knew the condition in which he was found.

CHAPTER 5

The large convention center along San Diego's Embarcadero hosted several large gatherings a year. It's been home to medical conferences, technology expos and, most notably, the annual Comic-Con.

Today, however, it was home to a sniper's nest.

Kelly felt a little guilty for choosing this spot as his overwatch position. He was a huge fan of all things geek culture, and this location was practically hallowed ground. It also granted him the most unobstructed view of the Embarcadero Marina Park.

Kelly peered through his scope. Strangely, he found his thoughts circling not on their target but on how he'd never gotten the opportunity to attend Comic-Con. Maybe the Captain could pull some strings and get him tickets this year.

Even though he was Cerberus Squad's designated marksman—a damn good one—Kelly never enjoyed pulling the trigger. He understood the need for it, and he never hesitated, but it brought him no joy to take someone else's life. He would like very much to keep today's mission quiet. If he ended up receiving those tickets, it would be hard to enjoy himself knowing he'd spilled blood here.

"I've got eyes on the target," a voice reported through the earbud

Kelly wore. The voice belonged to Brandon Taggart, and Tag was posted down below at the curbside valet check-in. Tag wasn't the valet, of course. Black Spear didn't normally do costumes, but he read from an electronic tablet at the bench just behind it. There wasn't much point in donning a costume and "Bond, James Bond-ing" your way to a target. Why do that when you could just throw a bag over their head, toss them in a black site, and pull some fingernails until they told you everything you wanted to know?

Black ops. Not a pretty business.

"I still think you should be holding a newspaper," said another voice.

Billy Ho, close-quarters expert and self-appointed squad funny-man, looked upset that Tag had decided on a tablet instead of the obligatory discreet newspaper.

"That's what the guy on the bench always does in the movies."

"Nobody reads newspapers anymore," groaned the newest member of their squad, Thomas Redcloud. Thomas, recently attached to Cerberus Squad from ICE, had served among the Shadow Wolves, an elite law enforcement unit composed entirely of Native Americans. They utilized tracking skillsets passed down for generations to apprehend smugglers along the U.S. and Mexico border. These days, Thomas employed his unique skill set to ensure the Cerberus Squad never lost their enemy's trail.

"Mission is a go. Callsigns only," ordered Kelly.

"Boomerang, copy that," responded Tag.

"This is Bloodhound, copy that," answered Thomas.

"Kage, solid copy," said Billy.

Kelly was Forty-Seven, a name taken from a fictional assassin but who was arguably the closest comparison for Kelly's marksmanship skills.

Right as he considered adjusting his prone position to something a tad more comfortable, their target stepped into view. Desmond

Toole, or Des as his business associates called him, was a low-level arms dealer who had in recent weeks begun to peddle things he had no right to have his hands on. Things that nearly put them on par with Black Spear. Since he was decidedly low on the totem pole, all of Black Spear's intel had concluded he was working for a bigger fish. He appeared to be skimming gear and double-dealing under the table. For that reason, this mission was supposed to go quiet. Catch the little fish, have him lead you to the big fish. The name of said big fish? All evidence pointed to Atharv Singh.

More often than not fish don't like to be caught, but that's why Kelly had his semi-automatic Mk.12 sniper rifle handy. The Mk.12 fired 5.56 caliber bullets—the same bullet used in M-16s and most assault rifles. Normally, Kelly would've carried something that packed the whopping .50 BMG, but this was a daylight domestic mission. Much easier to suppress the sound of a 5.56 firing.

Kelly kept his reticle sighted onto Des's center mass. In the back of his head he hoped he wouldn't have to load his rifle with lethal rounds. Black Spear had access to a tranquilizer dubbed "Sandman"—a specialized nerve agent that, when administered, instantaneously blocked all the body's nervous systems function except for breathing and heart rate. Sandman worked faster than the speed of nerve impulse conduction. That meant waking up twelve hours later before you even knew you were hit in the first place. As of now his Mk.12 was loaded up with Sandman, but he had a magazine of armor-piercing rounds in case their target got froggy.

"Kage, give us some audio," Kelly instructed.

Billy sprawled on a bench near their target's rendezvous point with his buyer. Mocked up as a homeless person and smothered in dirt, he resembled someone most people try to avoid looking at. Black Spear might not do costumes, but they went to extreme measures to blend in when needed. Billy had really tried to get into character this morning when he brainstormed what to write on his cardboard panhandling sign. Underneath his filthy jacket sleeve, he held a directional mic. Handy for listening in on private conversations.

"Good for audio."

Des shook his buyer's hand. The buyer was a portly Korean man. Most likely a spy, which Kelly thought was super lame. Spies suck. They were glorified snitches, and Kelly hated the idea that someone's entire skillset was based upon abusing people's trust. If things got hot here, he would not be opposed to putting an armor-piercing round through the buyer.

At that point Billy's directional mic started feeding audio to the squad.

"Is this necessary?" the buyer asked. "A phone call would have sufficed."

Des shrugged. "Phones can be tapped. Less electronic comm the better. Call me paranoid."

That was funny. They'd already tapped Des's phone earlier this week. This little mission was put forth mostly because they'd heard nothing through his phone or email the past forty-eight hours.

"I understand, but I would have preferred not to meet unless it was to conduct our business," the spy said.

Damn, whatever Desmond was selling wasn't here. On the plus side, Kelly wouldn't need to kill anyone this afternoon. On the down side, they wouldn't be able to close the books on this mission any time soon.

"Relax. Consider this just a scheduling consult," Des said nonchalantly. "Our deal is still good. Trust me, you're going to want what we have. Those little red bullets I gave you last time were just appetizers, I'm here to give you the main course."

"You hear that?" whispered Billy. "Sounds like they got their hands on some firecrackers."

"Sounds like they have more than that," Thomas noted.

Kelly moved his hand to the top of his rifle's scope and pressed a small button. His scope was equipped with an integrated digital camera that let him snap pictures of whatever it was he had his eyes on. He wanted to know more about this buyer.

"Let's hope the Captain comes back with some goodies," Tag said.

Nobody was comfortable with the idea of getting in a shootout against firecrackers with the current body armor they were sporting. The fact that Kelly was positioned in a sniper's nest and safe from most of the gunfire brought him no comfort.

Desmond Toole shook his buyer's hand, then abruptly jerked him in close. "This deal is a big one. You know what kind of toys I have in my pockets, so don't try to fuck me on this or I'll give you and your people a very up-close demonstration."

He released the buyer's hand. The Korean tried to compose himself. That seemed to amuse Desmond, who barked a laugh before turning on his heel to leave.

"We'll see you tomorrow night. Do me a favor and don't be short on cash."

"Bloodhound," whispered Kelly into their comms, "how are we on your end?"

Thomas had been tasked with ensuring tracers were placed on both Desmond Toole's and the buyer's vehicles. A lot easier to track people when GPS pinpoints their exact location.

"Both vehicles are tagged, solid reads," answered Thomas. "Uploading to you now." A small computer attached to Kelly's wrist started to display the locations of two vehicles marked in red. Normally the honor of having the live intel feed would've been worn by the Captain, but since he was out it fell to Kelly. He watched the computer do a background check on the license plates, vehicle occupants, and known affiliates, all in real time.

Kelly snapped a few more photos and then placed the Mk.12 rifle on safe. Something big was happening, and he wished that Captain Vaun and West would hurry up and come home.

CHAPTER 6

The helipad they stood on often doubled as a sparring mat. Neither knew if it was the open ocean air or the calming breeze they both enjoyed. All they knew was it offered the perfect atmosphere for the two of them to engage in fisticuffs.

Try as he might, Deimos never could find the skill to best his brother. His brother came at him fast—as fast as always—and easily parried Deimos's chopping blow before delivering two open-handed strikes into his ribs. He followed up with a deft sweep at the back of Deimos's calf, which buckled him and sent him to one knee.

A half smile drew across the side of Phobos's face. The thin scar that traced from the corner of his mouth down to his neck resembled a question mark whenever he smiled. A glance at the scar took Deimos out of the fight for just a moment, but that was the only opening Phobos needed.

His brother lashed out with a lightning quick knee, which took both of Deimos's hands to block. Deimos responded with a round-kick that struck into the inner portion of his brother's other thigh. The blow would have sent a less agile person sprawling. His brother simply pulled back from the blow and spun his body with the balance of a ballet dancer. Whirling into the spin, Phobos whipped his leg back towards Deimos's face.

The kick missed but just barely. Deimos knew then that his brother was pulling his punches.

Right as that thought finished making its way across his mind, his brother proved how wrong he'd been. Phobos set him up with two light jabs, then rolled under Deimos's arm and ended up behind him. One of his arms wrapped around his neck while his foot kicked out Deimos's leg.

Deimos tapped before he fully blacked out, just as he always did whenever they sparred. His brother instantly released the pressure on his neck. Deimos was under no illusions of how much better a fighter his brother was; he was just glad Phobos was still willing to train with him. It felt good to know that his brother would always have his back. There was no one on earth who could stand against Phobos one-on-one, of that Deimos was sure.

"Well done, brother." Deimos clapped his brother on the shoulder.

Phobos said nothing. His brother had always been quiet. When they were younger his parents told him that Phobos hadn't so much as cried as a baby. These days Phobos never spoke, not since an interrogator had cut halfway through his tongue and down his face, his distinctive scar the result.

Eight years ago the two of them had a job go bad and were captured by a British SAS team. From there they were handed over to a covert section that was able to cross more legal lines. Their interrogator, unhappy about their unwillingness to answer his questions, had taken the knife to Phobos.

Phobos refused to talk then. Looking to his big brother with full trust, both knew they needed to remain quiet. The interrogator would have killed them both the second they'd revealed any information. All they could do was bide their time so Deimos could get them out. And he had.

While his brother might clearly be the more skilled fighter of the two, Deimos more than carried his weight when it came to planning. Deimos was the brains of the duo. His plan had led to their escape from that interrogation team, and his idea had led them to their current employer.

Working assassinations case by case was such tedious and uncertain work. It made much more sense to be fully employed by a single person. And that person had been more than generous.

Phobos cocked his head towards Deimos's phone. Deimos wiped the sweat from his face and answered it, unsurprised by the identity of the caller.

"Yes, Mister Singh?"

"Next time answer on the first ring," an Indian-accented voice instructed. Atharv Singh's somewhat high-pitched voice and his accent always made it sound like his voice was cracking.

"Of course, Mister Singh." He could practically see Singh pacing irritably regardless of his location. Deimos had found that his own overly polite nature aggravated the man more than outright rudeness would.

"I don't think we should trust Desmond Toole." Singh sighed.

Deimos tried to keep his disappointment in check. Singh clearly wanted them to pull back on this impending deal. But too many wheels were already in motion.

"I can assure you that everything will go exactly to plan, sir," Deimos said as cordially as possible.

"You can forgive me if I'm not put at ease, Deimos. Too much is riding on this for mere sentiment."

"Precisely my point, sir. I believe we are beyond that quintessential point of no return."

The man who could create a weapon solution for any problem found himself with nothing to say. Deimos waited patiently, grinning ear to ear. Phobos stood nearby, flipping his karambit knife around his finger by the ring on its handle. It was a nervous tic of his, but Deimos found it ironic that it made everyone else more nervous whenever they saw him doing it. Maybe it was the fluidity that he spun it around, or maybe they could tell just how sharp Phobos kept it. Perhaps the familiarity with which he handled the curved blade showed others his extreme skill. The certainty in his grip. Either way, it amused Deimos. Doubly so since he knew Singh was particularly put off by it.

"We proceed as planned," Singh finally said. His uncertainty clear, he still wouldn't muster the will to call the deal off entirely. Greed had a funny way of trumping fear.

Though Deimos said nothing, Phobos easily read his face and his anxious flipping of the karambit ceased. Deimos nodded reassuringly to his brother, who in turn sheathed his knife onto the back of his belt. As much as the flipping was a sign of nervousness, sheathing it was Phobos's own way of saying everything was well and there were no more concerns.

"I've received word that we've drawn the attention of some key players," said Singh. "We cannot afford mistakes."

Deimos smiled wickedly. "I dread the thought, sir."

CHAPTER 7

If you checked Congressman Mike Halsey's driver's license, you would learn he weighed one-hundred and sixty-five pounds, had light brown hair and blue eyes that many had determined to be a key factor in his trustworthy appearance. He didn't smoke, didn't drink, and the unhealthiest thing about him was that he occasionally indulged in fast food. All were factors that should have promised him a nice long life.

Of course, all that is irrelevant when you spontaneously burst into flames and leave nothing but a charred skeleton behind.

The blackened bones on the autopsy table before us weighed a grand total of nineteen point five pounds. Everything Congressman Halsey was, everything ahead of him in life, had been snuffed out in an instant and reduced to nineteen point five pounds of ashen bones. All those plans quite literally had gone up in smoke.

We'd retrieved the remains from Sacramento. Our plane barely landed for ten minutes before the black bag was loaded up by our local team on the tarmac. We took off once more for San Diego. The entire plane ride back I stared at the bag, wondering what grisly remains were inside. Rourke poured himself a drink from the onboard bar, then promised me it would all be better explained once we returned to Home Site.

If he thought seeing the congressman's body gave me any explanation, he was sorely mistaken. Our resident medical examiner, Doctor Dana Phelps, didn't have one, either. Dana's twin sister, Tanya, had also been a one-stop shop doctor for Black Spear but had sadly been killed during my very first mission. I had only met her sister very briefly, but her perpetually grumpy demeanor was the one thing that stuck out at me. Turns out it was a hereditary trait. Dana's scowl only seemed to worsen as she examined the strange remains.

"Thanks for bringing this my way, boss," Dana said sarcastically. "Next time you want to send me a confusing headache, I think you can settle for a Rubik's Cube."

Rourke in attendance further cemented my feeling that this was an unusual day.

"If you're good and ready to do your job now, doctor?" Rourke said.

Dana picked up a clipboard and began to read, "The cause of death was an instantaneous flash burn . . . though I venture to say that's fairly obvious. Check these scorch marks here." Doctor Phelps used a gloved fingertip to point at a spot on one of the femurs. I leaned in closer, as did Vaun. Rourke chose to stand back and trust the three of us to handle it.

"Whatever it was that burned the congressman, burnt straight down to the bone. Nearly all of the soft tissue was flash-burned away. Even the marrow was cooked." To prove her point she showed us a tibia that she'd previously sawed in half. Sure enough, the inner bone marrow appeared charred.

"Doc, how hot does something have to be to cause this?" asked Vaun.

Doc Phelps moved to the skull, using her thumb to touch

where an upper lip would have once been. "See the teeth?" They were mostly cracked and had a strange bluish tint to them. "Teeth are pretty resilient. It's why we use them in forensics to identify remains. For them to be affected, we're talking seriously high temperatures. This color change happens when temperatures exceed eight hundred degrees, but with the fracturing that's occurred I'd estimate we're upwards of two thousand Fahrenheit. And that's low-balling it."

A whistle sounded behind us. I turned to see the rest of the Cerberus Squad had arrived, the whistle from Billy Ho, who craned his neck to see the charred remains behind us.

"Is that the congressman?" Kelly asked.

"What's left of him."

"Shame. Heard he was a nice guy."

After the obligatory handshakes and fist bumps between squad members concluded, we quickly filled them in on what the Doc had already told us. Billy whistled again before picking up a severed ulna and radius bone from Mike Halsey's remains. He blew on it as if it was an overcooked marshmallow.

Thomas stared at the bones, then glanced at Vaun. "You show me a body and I can tell you how he died. Give me his clothes and I can figure out where he spent most of his time. But this? Yeah . . . I'm kind of empty here, Captain."

"Two thousand degrees?" murmured Kelly while leaning in close to the rib cage and prodding it. "Willy Pete grenades burn closer to five thousand. I've seen what happens when a guy takes one of those point-blank. Looks similar."

Tag gave a grunt of agreement.

None of this was sitting well with me. Members of Congress aren't supposed to up and die in broad daylight, let alone from spontaneous combustion. Between this and Atharv Singh's recent moves, I felt more and more eager to wrap things up sooner rather than later. It takes a lot to ruin my day when it starts on a high note of watching a tank melt.

"Any idea what kind of weapon could have done this?" Vaun asked.

None of us could find our tongues, let alone an answer.

"I believe I can shed some light on that," a voice said from the doorway behind us. I turned to see a short little man in a light gray suit. He wore an amused facial expression as he used a cloth to clean the lenses of his glasses. "Or is this a bad time, Mr. Rourke?"

CHAPTER 8

"How come nobody told me there was such a thing as White Shield?" I asked as we exited the elevator and walked towards the briefing room.

"Probably because you're still a rookie. We'll be here all day if we're supposed to tell you *everything*," said Billy.

As it turned out, White Shield was the intelligence-based counterpart to Black Spear's operations arm. In the past when we tried to pull up information for a mission, Vaun had assured me, "Rourke's diggers are on it." Turns out they weren't Rourke's diggers at all. Rather, they were this man's diggers.

The short man was Michael Goode. Goode was White Shield's director. As such, he possessed an almost immeasurable wealth of knowledge when it came to the happenings of the darker side of the world. From what I'd been told on the elevator ride up, White Spear's vast reach included everything from the CIA to the United Kingdom's MI6. Bottom line: if at any time a report had been filed, then White Shield had a copy of that report—somewhere. And if a device of any kind was connected to a satellite or the internet, White Shield could see it.

Goode's meek appearance was betrayed by just how much dirt he had on the entire world. The whole thing made me uneasy to be around him, despite the fact he barely stood over five-three. I doubted he weighed more than a hundred and fifteen pounds soaking wet. And yet, at this very moment, he was staring down Mr. Rourke with no sign of backing down.

Rourke looked past—well, over—Goode to where we stood. He beckoned the squad into the briefing room with his hand, and we promptly found our seats. The room housed a long dark oak table in the center, one wall lined with a series of display screens, and Black Spear's emblem painted along the back wall.

Black Spear's emblem was little more than a spearhead imposed upon the Roman omega symbol. Simple, straightforward, and resonant with the operators who performed simultaneously as the tip of the spear and the final line of defense. Black Spear didn't have an official motto that I was aware of, but it wasn't uncommon for someone to write a temporary one on a sticky note and position it beneath the emblem. The current motto read, "Breaking Necks, Cashing Checks," courtesy of Billy.

"I thought I told you the last time you should drop a line if you feel like leaving your cave and visiting mine," Rourke reminded Goode.

Goode blinked slowly and then used his finger to push his glasses further up the bridge of his nose. "Oh, please, Mr. Rourke, you needn't posture to me just because your flying monkeys are here."

"This flying monkey might just drop your ass back to kindergarten," I retorted quietly once I sat down. Nobody but the Captain had thought I could hack it with Black Spear, and I felt certain that after six months I deserved a little more credit. Rourke seemed amused enough to grin slightly, in spite of his contempt for me.

"Sergeant West, you are far from the nation's sharpest instrument for combating threats," Goode said calmly, easing himself into his own seat. "I topple dictators with a keystroke, I've dissolved terrorist finances by simply clicking my mouse. I've stopped entire wars from the comfort of my desk in the time it takes you to load a single magazine."

"If you came here to belittle my men, I assure you I'm more than capable of handling that on my own." Rourke sighed. "Why are you here?"

"As it turns out, there just happens to be a war I'm trying to stop." The intelligence director tapped a button on his watch, and the display screens along the far wall lit up.

Rourke didn't look pleased with Goode's seizure of his meeting room's equipment. When we all realized the screens displayed images of the morgue downstairs, Rourke's frown deepened.

"White Shield has eyes and ears everywhere, my friend," Goode said with a smile. "It appears that you have stumbled onto something White Shield has been looking into for months." A close-up of Congressman Mike Halsey's charred bones filled the screen, but then Goode tapped his watch and the other screens began to fill with the images of several other nearly identical skeletal remains. "We have three other reported cases of this peculiar immolation, all occurring overseas. This was the first domestic use."

Goode tapped his watch and a profile photo of a bald man with a goatee popped up. There was a collection of tattoos adorning his neck. I recognized them from Russian prison culture. "This was Piotr Bludovich, known by Interpol as Bloody Pete. Russian arms dealer who operated out of Slovakia. Four months ago, he lit up in flames in the middle of a large deal. It was a good thing for us. Unfortunately, it was also a good thing for Bloody Pete's bloodier competition."

"Singh?"

"Precisely. Nearly two months later the exact same thing happened to Orson Soung." A new picture of a well-dressed Korean man popped up. "Soung was an aspiring engineer for Cheng Qiang Arms Conglomerate. With his death, Atharv Singh's path to becoming their primary developer was secured."

After another tap of his watch, the image of a younger Korean popped up. "Lastly, we have Jun Byeong-Ho. Byeong-Ho was one of ours. We planted him into Cheng Qiang, and he warned us that Singh was planning something large. It was significant enough that Byeong-Ho blew the cover that took him two years to develop. When the CIA executed an extraction, Byeong-Ho spontaneously combusted mid-flight before a debrief could be conducted."

The blackened skeletons appeared nearly identical. And despite the considerable resources of both Black Spear and White Shield, we still had no idea how Singh was doing it. His reach had extended into home turf and the only thing we knew was that Cheng Qiang was involved somehow.

"As lead developer for Cheng Qiang, Singh has made very important friends with the Chinese and North Koreans. The tensions between our countries are already difficult enough. Any act against Singh, or Cheng Qiang, would undoubtedly bring those tensions to a head."

"He's arming gangsters and extremists on domestic soil," Rourke said.

"Things certainly look that way, but we can't confirm nor rule out that he is doing so *with* the approval of our Eastern adversaries. Whatever he's up to, targeting politicians and supplying criminal organizations, it goes far beyond real-world R&D."

"So, who do we have to shoot to figure this out?" Billy asked sarcastically. "Because I refuse to go on another mission as boring as this morning. No hobo suits for me."

"Luckily for us, Cerberus Squad is already on top of the only lead we are tracking," Goode declared. He tapped his watch and displayed the face of Desmond Toole.

"Toole is selling Cheng Qiang prototypes," Kelly said. "He must be acting as Singh's boots on the ground in the states. Whatever Singh is planning, I guarantee Toole is deeply involved."

Goode promptly scooted his chair away from the table and smiled. "Precisely. Gentlemen, the rumor mill is churning about a war Atharv Singh is gearing up to win. Desmond Toole may very well be the key to preventing that from happening. I've already taken the liberty of bringing Mr. Cain up to speed."

At that a live-feed of the weapons made grandpa himself appear. I recognized Cain's surroundings as the very office I'd stood in earlier.

"I'm having my team look into how this immolation tech works. Could be some next-gen directed energy weapons," said Cain.

"I've heard of focused microwave weapons, but this is some serious next-level shit," I said.

My evaluation seemed to amuse Cain. "Sergeant West isn't wrong. But if Dr. Archer's section can determine how it's activated, then we can hopefully create a countermeasure to stop people from popping like fireworks left and right."

At the mention of Madison Archer, I noticed Vaun glanced my way. Evidently, he was convinced I was still smitten. He wasn't completely wrong.

"Glad to have you on our team, Sam," Rourke said.

"I told you I'm normally in the business of fighting wars, not stopping them." Cain laughed. "I owe you one so I'll make an exception this time, Rourke."

Vaun now held a remote and pointed it at the screens, which in turn showed a live feed of two vehicles' locations. One was along the shipping yard of the San Diego coast, while the other was in the city. I recognized the location as one of the premiere hotels in downtown San Diego.

"My squad tagged both Toole and his buyer earlier this morning. With your permission, sir, I'd like my squad to be the ones to pull him in and get some answers."

"Of course," answered Rourke. "Hydra Squad will back you up. I'm sure they're looking for a little payback for those firecrackers."

As we watched, the vehicle parked downtown started to move. Looked like the deal was moving ahead earlier than planned. Michael Goode and Rourke seemed to size each other up again, no doubt both trying to figure out who was going to be in charge here. Surprisingly, the shorter one decided to be the bigger man.

"Whatever you need from my division is at your disposal, Mr. Rourke," Goode said and extended his hand to shake. "I do hope you pass along any information you pull from this man. And whatever happens, Captain Vaun, ensure you have a bucket of water nearby. We desperately need Desmond Toole alive."

More and more the world was beginning to feel like it was made of tinder and just waiting to explode. If it sparked anytime soon, I doubted a bucket of water would be enough to keep the whole damn thing from burning.

CHAPTER 9

As a man who was devoted to the idea of plans, Singh felt special admiration when one went exactly as it was supposed to. Whether it was a plan for a large operation or a plan for a new weapon schematic, any failures in execution were the executor's fault and not the planners. A plan is a concept. In that regard, it is perfect. It's only when someone deviates from a solid plan that it falls apart. When one little screw isn't threaded correctly, or one person isn't in their appointed place at the appointed time.

Plans were perfect. People were not.

Singh had a quiet but intense hatred for the majority of people. More than once he'd realized with great pleasure that every time he went to work, he ensured that there were less people in the world. Less chaff. Less numbers in the global population.

The world's direction had changed to such a point that intellectuals such as himself were used like tools for the inept. Most had either lucked their way into power or been born into it. Even now, at his heightened position of influence, Singh still answered to the executives who paid for his weapon designs. But really, how tenuous was their own position if they relied upon him for their success?

His intelligence was the only thing that kept his contempt for those beneath him in check. He was smart enough to know that, in the long run, he did well to hide his true feelings.

But even they had their uses. Most recently, those two animals, Deimos and Phobos, had proved useful enough. If Singh had his way he would have hired smarter help, but smart people tend to get ideas of their own and he couldn't very well have that. The only ideas he needed were his own.

Though Singh had a mind for violence, he lacked the skill for it. It was one thing to forge a new pistol but another thing entirely to wield it with accuracy. Just as he was a tool for the Arms Conglomerate, others acted as tools for him. He didn't need to have an eye for marksmanship as long as he could afford to pay someone who did.

As he watched the production floor of the factory, an amusing thought crossed his mind. He knew there were precisely ninety-two workers on the factory floor. Automation only went so far. Every single one of those ninety-two employees fully believed that once the dust finally settled, they would be on the winning side of history. They knew in their hearts that when the new era dawned, they would be among the chosen to usher it in.

How wrong they all were.

CHAPTER 10

Every time I donned my body armor and loaded up my gear, it was like flipping a switch. The civilized part of my brain was taken over by the caveman portion that was ready and willing to do some hurting. Thankfully, Black Spear provided us more than a crude wooden club to accomplish that.

I was packing a very nice assault rifle with all the fixings. Extended magazine, flash suppressor, 4x magnification sight and, best of all, instead of the standard 5.56 it was chambered in the much heavier .50 Beowulf round. An advantage of me being a regular iron addict at the gym is that I could handle the higher recoil the Beowulf spat out. Stopping power is a non-negotiable requirement in my opinion.

My sidearm was a .45 1911 by Para USA from their Black Ops line. A little on the nose, I know, but I picked one up in my first days with Black Spear and it hadn't let me down yet.

When all else fails, sharp objects never run out of ammo. If things needed to get extra personal, I kept a Pohl Force tactical Mk-9 combat knife for just the occasion. The Mk-9's generous edge had a slight curve along its length, terminated into a spearpoint, and featured a fully sharpened reverse-edge to facilitate deadly back cuts. It was forged from D2 steel, which resulted in a blade that packed enormous cutting durability. All that and in a tactical black coating. Some operators swear by sleeker folding knives, but the Mk-9's 7.87-inch blade didn't need to be opened or locked into place. One tug at its Kydex sheath, which included an insert that served a dual purpose of protecting the blade from scratches as well as silencing the draw, and it was ready. You know how in movies there's always that distinctive *shinkt* sound whenever the hero pulls his knife? Bullshit. Also, a superb way to reveal your location to an enemy.

The rest of the squad had similar carries. Most carried some special personal item for equal parts sentimental and tactical reasons. Tag always kept a devastatingly powerful snub-nosed .44 magnum tucked into the small of his back. I'd seen the thing literally take a guy's head off. Wasn't a pretty sight. Billy brought a pair of Tanto-style knives sheathed on his hip, which I'd witnessed him use with lethal efficiency. Our squad's marksman, Kelly, packed an old set of battered brass knuckles passed onto him from a demolitionist who'd given his life on my first mission. The Captain was fond of keeping a Protech Don switchblade clipped into his pocket. Our newest team member, Thomas, carried nothing extra yet.

As for myself, I'd brought a customized double-barrel snug in a shotgun scabbard over my back. The weapon was my own souvenir from our time facing off against the Terminal militia. I'd taken it from a particularly ratty bastard and used it to blow him all the way to hell. Since then, I'd had the barrels chopped down and replaced the full stock with a blackwood pistol grip. I'd dubbed it "The Boomstick" in honor of the legendary Bruce Campbell.

Our organization didn't have an official uniform or camouflage pattern, but more often than not we ended up wearing black tops and bottoms with balaclavas to hide our faces. Tonight was no different. The only thing that came close to a unit identifier was a small patch of three dog heads my team members and I wore over our left breasts. The symbol of Cerberus. I'd considered a tattoo to add to my collection of ink, but it's hard to find time to go under the needle when you're busy keeping the world from ending.

Everyone on Cerberus Squad was also decked out in our brand-new *Fafnir Model 4*'s. The guys were giddy as schoolboys once they'd tried them on and experienced the extra mobility they afforded. It was exactly that mobility which allowed us to hop the northern wall by the cargo container area near the deal's meeting spot.

"We sure these'll stand up to firecrackers?" Thomas asked as we blended into the shadows next to a long red cargo container.

"Just try to avoid getting shot, and we won't need to find out," I whispered. I slowly edged my barrel around the corner. Clear.

"It always feels ironic, don't you think?" Kelly asked.

"What?"

"Us, a bunch of warriors, off to snuff some bad guys in the name of peace."

"Hm. I guess when you put it that way it is kind of funny."

"Makes you wonder, how many people would you kill to stop a war?"

I gave him a funny look. Truth is I didn't have an answer, and I wasn't too keen on finding out tonight.

Hydra Squad was in an overwatch position in the high-rise bayfront hotel across the street. Six men, all with high-powered rifles, on the thirteenth floor with only one mission tonight: keep everyone on Cerberus Squad alive. At Vaun's behest they would keep their distance. Des's bullets had killed one of their own; shit like that tends to make even the most well-trained professionals act a bit more reckless.

"Vehicle approaching from the south," a voice said through the earbuds we each wore. The voice belonged to Hydra's leader, Major Wilcox. Callsign Slipknot. "Desmond Toole is in the open. I spot nine shooters with him. We've got beads on six." That left three for us and the simple matter of trying to stop Des from spontaneously combusting. Easy day.

"Keep an eye on Des, not a reticle," replied Vaun.

"Roger, Blackbars," said Wilcox. "Be advised, there's two vehicles at the meeting. Black Escalades."

I knew that not a single member of Hydra would hesitate to drop Des with a headshot if he made the wrong move. The deal was being held on the far dock between two rows of cargo containers stacked six high. Thankfully, that particular spot left only two routes of escape for all these cockroaches we hunted. It also gave a perfect view for our guardian angels across the street with their sniper scopes.

"Best break out that new toy of yours, Boomerang," advised the Captain.

Tag nodded and removed what looked like a silver thermos from a satchel on his hip. After opening the top, he poured out its contents then flipped up the small screen of a wrist-mounted computer. The thermos's contents made a small puddle on the ground.

The puddle was Cain's new *Microswarm*. Tag worked the controls on his wrist as if he'd been doing it for years. Each of the tiny machines also had a rudimentary camera that, when combined, provided a rough image of what the *Microswarm* collectively "saw." The picture displayed looked more like it was picking up a black and white channel with a broken antenna, but it was better than nothing.

"Should I do my taxes while I'm waiting?" Billy groaned while Tag meticulously maneuvered the *Microswarm*. It looked like tricky work, and the big man's large fingers twitched delicately.

"Not as easy as it looks . . ." grunted Tag.

"Well, hurry it up, I've got episodes of Rick and Morty to catch up on as soon as we get back. Mandatory binge watch in my room for the whole squad."

"It'll have to wait. Today's leg day," muttered Tag while directing the *Microswarm* towards the two Escalades Wilcox had spotted for us.

I tried to bite my tongue but just couldn't help myself. "Boomerang... how in the hell do you have the energy to work out after a mission?"

"Helps me calm down," Tag said. "You've got some chicken legs on you, Toxin. Maybe you should join me?"

"I like you more when you only communicate in grunts," I hissed.

"Done, swarms planted on both engine blocks," muttered Tag. With a tap of a button the swarms would release their acidic payload to cripple the vehicles.

Vaun signaled us to move up. The stack of metal containers we clung to had a ladder that led to the top. Kelly cocked his head towards it. Vaun nodded. The marksman ascended the rungs while we stalked down the line of containers to round the corner.

Overhead lights illuminated the deal area, but we stayed hidden in the shadows. Those two soon-to-be disabled Escalades were on the far side of the enclosure by an enormous tarp that covered what had to be even more cargo boxes. The tarped boxes boxed them in from the rear. All good things from where I was sitting.

We were the teeth in a bear trap, and it was ready to snap shut on our prey.

"This is Forty-Seven," Kelly said through our comm. "I'm in position. Give the word, and Des gets a dose of Sandman."

"Keep him in your sights," instructed Vaun.

I saw Des's buyer approaching with his entourage in two Porsche Cayennes. The luxury vehicles rounded a corner and then moved out of our line of sight. According to White Shield's intel, the buyer belonged to The Golden Moon, a rising Korean gang operating in Los Angeles with militaristic aspirations. The Golden Moon crew normally was on the tier of things such as low-level extortion and drugs. I wasn't exactly stoked at the idea of what they would do once they got their hands on Cheng Qiang tech.

The buyer exited his vehicle. Des greeted him. The buyer's entourage of men stood by with their weapons politely holstered while Des's men did the same.

"Forty-Seven, give us some audio," ordered Vaun.

A breath later and Kelly's directional mic began to feed us the conversation.

"—wasn't easy to get it all this quickly," the buyer was saying.

"I can assure you your investment will pay off *beautifully*," laughed Des. "With the firepower you're about to let loose, your counterparts will hear about it all the way back home."

The buyer said something in Korean and one of his men carried over two suitcases. In my head I calculated how much cash that meant, estimating it to be in the millions. Thousands can fit in a simple duffel bag or briefcase; two suitcases told me it was significantly more. That also told me The Golden Moon was purchasing some *serious* firepower. Probably enough firecracker rounds to take out every cop in L.A. and then some.

"If you'll forgive me, I just can't help myself. You won't mind a bit of showmanship, would you?" asked Des.

The buyer seemed puzzled but gestured for Des to continue. Des smiled, then spun on his heel and strode past his own men in the direction of the tarped area just out of sight. Most likely to make a dramatic show of unveiling all the ammunition they would be providing.

"Slipknot, this is our opening. As soon as the target is in the clear take your shots," Vaun commanded.

My heartbeat thumped in my ears. Bizarrely loud, but at the same time slow and calm. The stock of my rifle was hugged into my shoulder, and I was ready to take the corner at the Captain's order. As was everyone else.

"Boomerang: vehicles."

Tag tapped a button and the *Microswarm* did their work, melting through the engine blocks and fuel lines of the Escalades. No getaway for you, Des.

"On my go. Three."

I flicked my weapon off safe.

"Two."

I took one last breath and readied myself.

"One."

Here we go.

Before I even rounded the corner, Hydra Squad took their opening shots. Six of Des's crew each collapsed from a single shot to the head. The buyer and his crew stood with their backs to us, clearly puzzled for a moment. We cut them down just as quickly. A single tap to the back, and a finishing shot to the back of the head. Clean, efficient.

By the time I'd taken two steps, the combined fire of Hydra Squad and Kelly up top had eliminated the rest of Des's stunned men. In two point five seconds. We ran drills like this a thousand times in training. When we did it for real, it went flawlessly.

That entire time, the scumbag arms dealer had been out of sight. I couldn't help but grin at what the look on his face would be once he did his grand unveiling and turned, only to see all his men dead and our team of ghosts bearing down upon him.

Our squad moved quickly to reach the tarped area just as Des tore the large drop cloth free. I couldn't quite make it out in the shadows, but it didn't look like the other boxes. They looked to be stacked more in a pyramid rather than cleanly on top of each other like the rest of the containers. And much lower than the six-high cargo around us. Stranger still, Des started climbing onto the first weird box. Maybe he wanted to pull the top of the crate off?

Just then Kelly spoke up. "Hey, Blackbars, what was that Cheng

Qiang tank thing you told us about called? The *Shadowcrawler*?"

"Yeah, the Mark Three, why?"

Kelly paused for a second and his nervous gulp was so loud, I heard it through the comm channel.

"Because I'm pretty Des just climbed into a Mark Four."

CHAPTER 11

Cole West. 10:00 p.m.
Port of San Diego
San Diego, California

It was bigger than the Mk. III. That was the first thing my brain processed. The Mk. IV was a true behemoth of weaponry and steel. Its shadowy black armor plating was lined with dark red accents, Cheng Qiang's golden Chinese characters emblazoned on one side. I counted two missile pods, twin-mounted machine guns, short-range missile packs on its rear, a six-barreled minigun atop the turret, and the tank's hulking 115mm main gun. So much armament, my mind's eye was spinning trying to catalog it. In the blink of an eye, we had just become completely outgunned.

The Mk. IV's treads squealed as it pulled into full view. At the front of the tank was what resembled a large cockpit. Through a small, reinforced window I could see Des's face as he saw for the first time that all his people were dead.

"WELL, WELL, WELL . . . I WAS PLANNING ON GIVING THESE PEOPLE A LIVE DEMONSTRATION ANYWAY," Des's amplified voice declared through an on-board PA system. "LET'S MAKE THINGS A LITTLE MORE EXCITING!"

The center-mounted minigun's barrels spun. We scattered as bullets ripped through the air. I could feel their heat and see their red tinge as I rolled behind the cover of one of the shipping containers. The bullets chewed through the metal boxes around me as if they were paper, leaving small, scorched holes in their wake.

Firecrackers. The damn minigun was fully loaded with Singh's incendiary rounds.

Tag took cover with me; the rest of our squad ducked in the other direction. He stared at the burning holes in our cover for a split-second, then dropped flat on the ground as the minigun let loose another volley.

"Don't suppose you brought another thermos of little acid-filled nanites?" I asked. "I only ask because they might come in handy at the moment."

Tag rolled his eyes. "One: no. Two: it was hard enough moving those buggers into place on vehicles that weren't moving. Three: Cain used nearly a thousand times more nanites for his demonstration."

"Damn. Wishful thinking, eh?"

He grunted. We slithered like snakes away from the tank before pulling ourselves back up to our feet. When I glanced at Tag, I saw him fiddling with the wrist-mounted computer.

"Thought you were out of nanites?"

"I am. But that tank has a wireless link, and I might be able to slow it down." Tag entered a few commands and his wrist-mounted computer started transmitting. Nearby, I heard the tank's treads screech to an abrupt halt. Des's voice promised blood through the PA system. "That thing's got some serious protocols installed, it's blocking me out. Most I can do is buy us some time."

"By doing what?"

Tag turned his arm so I could see the screen on his wrist. He had access to the *ShadowCrawler*'s weapons systems. After inputting a command, Tag triggered the tank to start firing off its short-range missiles safely into the water. The tank had lost half its payload before the firewall protocols successfully blocked Tag out and re-established control.

"Gee, don't think you could've made it shoot itself?"

"Nope. Anti-suicide override, didn't have time to bypass it."

"Fantastic. Well, at least you bought us a solid ten seconds."

I looked at my vest and eyed the two grenades I had. Just as quickly I shook the idea away. Not nearly enough explosives in those to damage this monster.

"DON'T RUN AWAY SO QUICKLY!" the PA system shouted.

I heard a loud whoosh and then the wall of cargo containers blocking the Mk. IV from us exploded from two short-range missiles.

"GOT YOU!"

I pulled the pin, tossed the grenade, and ran. My throw was good, it struck right off the armored viewing window. Des flinched and then laughed, his amused cackle echoing through the PA system and bouncing off the walls all around us. But then the grenade went off, and it wasn't explosive.

Black smoke billowed out into a rapidly expanding cloud that surrounded the *ShadowCrawler* tank, blinding its driver.

"Slipknot, we need some serious firepower down here!" Vaun barked through our comm channel. His request for support was answered with nothing but silence.

"I'm not getting anyone," I heard Kelly say, "I think someone's jamming us. Moving to higher ground."

Not good. Definitely not good.

The brief reprieve my smoke-grenade had granted let us find cover in the only safe place left: right behind the tank. The smoke was clearing, the center minigun surveying left and right as it tried to spot its lost targets.

"Anyone have any ideas?!" Vaun said as he risked firing off a shot at the tank's front viewing window. The round bounced off uselessly without leaving so much as a dent. The Captain disappeared behind a stack of crates before the Mk. IV fired another string of firecrackers, disintegrating the area he'd been standing in a split-second ago.

"DON'T LEAVE!" Des shouted, "PLENTY TO GO AROUND!"

The 115mm main gun turned and raised. The barrel thundered as it destroyed one of the nearby cargo cranes. Burning metal and rubble rained to the ground. The debris sent dust up everywhere as it collapsed and cut off our escape route, trapping us in the shipyard with this war machine. Escape was no longer an option.

"For the record, I definitely don't think we're taking him alive," Billy muttered over the comms. I spotted him huddled on the back end of one of Des's Escalades. He pulled open one of the doors and looked inside, then retrieved a large black case from within.

At the same time the *ShadowCrawler*'s main gun rotated around in an effort to spot anyone. Tag and I crab-walked under its field of view and sidestepped along the tank's treads.

"Let's hope that tank wasn't the only thing Des was selling tonight worth a damn," Billy said as I saw what he'd pulled from the black case. A rocket launcher. He shouldered the massive weapon, still using the Escalade as cover, and sighted up a shot. Tag and I bailed from the spot next to the tank we'd been hiding behind.

"Go for the tracks! Disable the damn thing! Take the shot, Kage!" ordered Vaun.

"Booyah," Billy said happily. The rocket fired away. His accuracy was dead-on, and the explosion struck right in the center of the tank's right track. The beast shuddered from the hit, but then the rotating minigun returned fire and shredded the Escalade.

I didn't see if Billy had gotten away before the vehicle exploded in a ball of fire. The other two members of our squad, Vaun and Thomas, dared to take another few shots at the armored window at the front. If they could just manage to get one round through the cockpit and into Desmond Toole's face, it wouldn't matter how tough the tank was.

But instead of getting that lucky round off, they received a dual barrage from the firecracker-loaded minigun and the twin-mounted machine guns in the front of the tank. Thomas Redcloud was knocked off his feet as he took a burst right to the chest. Vaun pulled Thomas away, smoke trailing from his chest, while firing off a burst in the tank's direction.

"Bloodhound is down, I say again Bloodhound is down. If anyone has any creative ideas, now's the time."

I nudged Tag as we both stayed low to evade the searching minigun. "Give me your grenades."

"Ain't gonna dent that armor."

"It's not for the armor."

The big man squinted in confusion for just a second. I pointed to the minigun. "Every advantage is also a vulnerability. Wanna see what happens when we blow up a few thousand firecracker rounds and a couple of rockets?"

Tag nodded. "I'll draw his fire."

I gave him a fist-bump before taking his two grenades into my right hand. Considering it for a moment, I unslung my rifle and set it on the ground. For the stupid shit I was about to pull off, I didn't need any extra weight slowing me down.

I signaled Tag and then broke off into a wide-arched sprint. Tag shot burst after burst in the tank's direction, aiming for the missile pods and the minigun's mounted camera. The rounds dinged off the tank's armaments. A few punched through and the missile pods began leaking rocket fuel. I pumped my arms and forced my armor-laden body to move even faster, kicking off from the cement pavement with every step to propel myself forward.

The minigun turned away from me and spun off a dozen rounds in Tag's direction. I didn't have time to check if he was safe or not. All I could do was focus on the *ShadowCrawler* as I stepped closer still. A mere six steps away, I wrenched the pins off of Tag's two grenades, tossing them to the top of the tank. Three steps away, I pulled the pins off my own two and lobbed them up.

In my head I was counting down the fuse time as I dropped into a slide, coming to rest between the tank's tracks directly beneath it. I jammed two fingers into my ears and tucked myself into a ball.

The explosion came suddenly. The deafening roar reverberated around me until all sound became nothing but ringing. My whole body felt jumbled up from the shockwave that buffeted me. My hearing slowly came back. I grinned when I realized I wasn't hearing the scream of the minigun firing anymore. Instead, I heard the intermittent fizzing of thermite melting through steel.

Quickly crawling back out from underneath the tank, I took a moment to survey my work. The minigun had been obliterated, the steel plating atop the tank warped and melted down. One of the missile pods on the side completely detonated. Bits and pieces of metal hung off the side towards the tread track like a severed limb. The barrel on one of the front-mounted machine guns had been superheated to such a point it melted and now drooped like a wet noodle.

"You still alive, Toxin?" Vaun asked.

I thumbed my earbud radio between smoke-induced coughs. "I'm still kicking."

"Good play. You took out everything but the main gun and one of those machine guns." Risking a look over my shoulder while dragging myself behind a large crate, I saw that Vaun was telling the truth.

"Here I was hoping that would've done the trick . . ."

My eyes caught motion approaching from my right flank. I drew my sidearm in a flash and aimed but only found Tag with his hands up. Billy was still in one piece just behind him with the rocket launcher carried over one shoulder. He'd reloaded it with another rocket, two more stuck to the back of his vest.

As Tag pulled me back to my feet, I heard the hydraulic whirring of the tank's main gun rotating. The tank was still kicking and its biggest gun was pointing right at us. The large cargo containers were formed around the area in an upside-down horseshoe shape, the crane the *ShadowCrawler* had destroyed cutting off our escape from the far side. Which left us in a kill-box with this beast.

"Nowhere to run," muttered Tag.

"Who's running?" said Billy as he shouldered the rocket launcher and fired again. The rocket-propelled grenade struck the area just below the main gun's turret, exploding in a black and orange ball of fire that momentarily blocked the tank from view.

And then the smoke cleared and showed how unfazed the tank was.

"I CAN TAKE EVERYTHING YOU'VE GOT!" Des barked as the tracks on the tank lurched forward in our direction. "YOU BROUGHT GUNS TO A GODDAMN TANK FIGHT!"

The tank's cannon lowered. That pitch-dark hole at the end of the barrel looked big enough to swallow every last hope I had left.

"And he brought a tank to a crane fight," said Kelly. The crane he'd climbed into dropped its cargo. Two bulk cargo containers plummeted to the ground. They crashed down in front of us. One slammed atop Des's tank, pinning it under its tremendous weight.

Samuel Cain had briefed us on the faults of the Mk. III; the main point he'd driven across was that, although it was designed for all-terrain mobility, the *ShadowCrawler* was about as mobile as a turtle on its back. That comparison was exactly what came to mind as I saw the Mk. IV struggle to drive its treads over the giant box blocking its way. The second box atop it weighed down the tread tracks so all they could do was squeal in place.

"We drawing straws to see who gets to pry him out of there?" joked Billy as he set the rocket launcher down. Des let out a stream of curses through the tank's speakers as he tried and failed to free his armored vehicle from its makeshift cage.

I noticed Tag still holding the rifle I'd left behind, so I took it and decided to volunteer to retrieve our target. The Mk. IV continued to strain in its impromptu prison. When I was about seven paces away from the front cockpit window, the sound of the tank's engine took on a new sound. The deep roar was slowly replaced by the sounds of pistons and mechanisms shifting. Hydraulics adjusting. Weight redistributing.

I realized that the Mk. IV was moving differently than before. The tracks shifted and then separated. What once were two tracks separated, rotated, and then with a loud hiss of compressed gas and hydraulics it *extended* into six separate legs.

"You've got to be shitting me . . ." I mumbled.

The Mk. IV's three right legs dug deep into the concrete floor and then dragged the entire tank out from under the weight of the cargo containers. Metal plating shifted around and covered up where the wheel tracks had been. And then, like some horrific spider made of steel and gunpowder, it rose up to tower above us on six mechanized legs that looked anything *but* poorly designed.

"THAT WAS FUN," Desmond Toole's voice growled. When the Mk. IV shook itself, flaming debris and parts of its own fragmented armor plating fell away like a macabre lizard shedding an old skin.

"READY FOR ROUND TWO?"

CHAPTER 12

I stood frozen in disbelief as it took its first titanic step toward us. The air around us shuddered with every crash of its spider-like legs upon the concrete. My heart sounded like a taiko drum slamming in my ears. A hand suddenly gripped my shoulder, wrenching me around. I stared at Tag.

"Move! Now!"

I turned and ran. I didn't know where the hell we could go. I just ran in the direction I saw Billy headed in. The edge of the shipyard was before us; we could have jumped into the water, but then we'd be sitting ducks. We'd have a quintessential "shooting fish in a barrel" situation on our hands. Being trapped in the shipyard was a shade better.

Billy reached the end of the dock and started to ease his way onto the edge. He sidestepped around the large container at the end and inched his way further down. Tag and I both followed his lead, moving as quickly as we could without falling into the water.

I heard the sound of screeching metal and craned my neck up. Des had climbed the tank onto the stack of cargo containers behind us. Floodlights on the tank's main body shifted left and right. For the moment, we remained hidden under its blind spot.

We finished inching around the narrow ledge and found ourselves at the beginning of a long pier with a chain link door on our left and right. The door on our right led out to the pier; the door to our left would lead back through the shipyard and to the city streets beyond. Billy was reaching for the doorknob on the left when the floodlight spotted us.

"SNEAKY LITTLE SHITS! TAKE THIS!" Des bellowed. The front two legs of the spider-tank pushed one of the long metal containers from the stack. It rolled forward and came to a rest on the other side of the door, blocking it and leaving no other direction for us to go except down the pier.

Tag went to open the door on the right. He gave it a mighty kick, but its deadbolt refused to budge.

"Back!" I yelled.

Tag moved to the side.

I reached over my shoulder and drew my shotgun. Both of the Boomstick's barrels boomed as two loads of slugs obliterated the entire knob on the door.

Tag shouldered through it so hard, it came off its hinges.

Then we ran.

I heard the cannon fire before I felt it. An explosion so loud and so close, my first thought was that we were already dead. Then the shockwave from the 115mm round hit me in the back and sent me sprawling. The *Fafnir* vest absorbed the brunt of it, but I still felt dazed.

The *ShadowCrawler* descended from the stack of containers, using its two front legs to shove more debris out of its way. It stepped out onto the long pier with us, kicking up chunks of concrete with every step.

Tag pulled me to my feet once again and urged me to push on. Maybe if we could lure it out to the very edge of the pier it would be far enough from the city that Mr. Rourke could drop an air strike on it. All the firepower in Black Spear's arsenal wouldn't do us any good if it couldn't get here fast enough, though.

My two teammates and I made a mad dash for the end of the

pier. Another boom came from behind us. I saw a black blur soar by the corner of my eye. A near miss, but it was hard to feel lucky at a time like this.

The steel monstrosity took up the entire width of the narrow pier, leaving no room for us to slip by it and back to safety. The scream of its mechanics working sounded like some metal demon had crawled up from the very depths of hell.

Des apparently got fed up with the accuracy required for the tank's main gun and started using the sole remaining machine-gun to pepper the pier around us while we continued our retreat. The zip of ricocheting rounds chased after us. Chips of concrete nipped at our calves and ankles, while countless brass casings rattled to the hard ground below.

My lungs burned. My shins and calves ached from sprinting on the hard concrete. As thankful as I was for how protective our *Fafnir* vests were, I still wished I could take it off just to breathe a little easier. All the protection in the world wasn't any good to me if I couldn't breathe. A nihilistic part of me wished Des would finally clip me with one of his bursts so I wouldn't have to run anymore. God answered my morbid prayer at that moment, because right then we ran out of pier to run on.

"END OF THE LINE!" the PA declared, "NOW STAY STILL SO I CAN CRUSH YA!"

"Ah, crush this, douche," muttered Billy and brought up the rocket launcher once more. His last rocket was loaded.

"Ain't tough enough to pierce it," grunted Tag, huffing to catch his breath through his body armor's restriction.

And then my vest gave me an idea. I snatched the rocket launcher from Billy, who only mildly protested, and then I took aim.

"You're crazy," Tag said simply. "There's no way to get through that armor."

"I know," I said, then adjusted my aim. This time aiming for the already cracked concrete the *Shadow Crawler* stood on. "But sometimes even the best armor can make it hard to breathe."

I fired the rocket and destroyed the ground under the Mk. IV. Its massive legs scrambled about in an effort to find stable footing, which only caused it to unbalance worse. The heavy main turret canted to one side. Then gravity reached up its eager hands to wrench the tank off the pier and into the black water below.

The Mk. IV was instantly pulled into the murky depths, Des along with it. It looked as helpless as a spider getting washed down the drain. All of its legs splayed about in a vain attempt to grab hold of anything while the water crushed against every inch of it. I could still just barely make out Desmond Toole's panicked face illuminated in the tank's cockpit. A moment later the flooded electronics shorted out. His face disappeared.

I finally removed my ballistic vest, sucked in a huge lungful of air, and dove into the water. We were still supposed to take Des in alive. Just like I'd planned, our target ejected from the confines of his cockpit. I wouldn't have been that upset if he'd made a different choice and decided to turn that cockpit into his casket.

The man floundered in the depths. I reached him, then wrapped one of my hands around his collar and kicked for the surface. My head barely broke the surface of the water before Tag and Billy reached down to heave us out. They were much gentler helping me up than they were with him. Tag went for his jaw with a hook that sent his head whipping around; Billy decided to go for a lightning quick knee to his gut that had to have cracked at least one rib.

Our least favorite arms dealer doubled up on the pier. He retched up water and snot. What had once been a fairly nice flashy suit clung to his soaked body like fetid rags. A sleeve on his jacket had been torn completely off when he'd made his desperate escape, one shoe was missing, and blood trickled down his forehead from a deep cut.

Between fits of coughing and his pained groans, he managed to push himself up onto his knees.

"First thing I want is my lawyer," he gasped. "The second thing I want is a dry cleaner. Tailor-made and bay water don't mix well." He smiled, revealing blood in his teeth. I actually smiled back and squatted on my haunches. Then I removed my balaclava so he could see me face to face. I have a scar that cuts all the way from my eyebrow down to my cheek. I've been told on more than one occasion that it makes me look like a very hard motherfucker. Which is exactly what I wanted Des to think about the three people he was in front of.

"If you actually think you get a lawyer, then you *really* won't like how this story is going to pan out."

As if to emphasize my point, Billy kicked him in the side of the face. Des went sprawling face first onto the concrete once more. Billy is proficient in hand-to-hand to a level that could only be described as "calibrated." He knows exactly how hard he needs to kick a man in the face to knock him out, but he also knows exactly how hard he needs to kick when he just wants it to hurt. That kick was meant to be felt.

"Ugh . . . fuck," Des moaned. This time he didn't play it cocky and try to smile. He just laid on the cold end of the dock in a pathetic heap.

"You don't need to know who we are," I said. I drew my knife, the one I used when things needed to get intimate. "Whatever stateside attack you were planning on supplying ain't happening anymore. We want *your* supplier. Give us Singh."

Desmond Toole shook his head slowly from side to side. There weren't any more signs of defiance in him; he was completely and utterly defeated.

"If you actually think you've stopped anything, then *you* really won't like how this story is going to pan out," Des said as he stared at the ground. "Only reason I was having so much fun in that tank was because the second I spotted you, I already knew how this would turn out for me, win or lose. Wanted to go out with a bang. But you guys? You guys already lost. You just don't know it yet."

With that he outstretched both arms and closed his eyes.

"You can't stop him," he said.

And then right in front of us he burst into flames. The fire lit up in a flash so bright, I squeezed my eyes shut. It seemed to ignite from everywhere at once, and just as suddenly it extinguished itself. All that was left were charred bones that settled to the ground like dried leaves.

I stared at the scorch mark in front of us where a man had knelt a second ago. Nobody dared move closer to it or say anything.

Tag scanned our perimeter, trying to spot some silent figure hiding in the shadows. But there was nobody. We were completely alone on the dock.

And once again, we were left with no answers.

PART 2

ESCALATION OF FORCE

"You must not fight too often with one enemy,
or you will teach him all your art of war."

—Napoleon Bonaparte

CHAPTER 13

"Well, this certainly complicates things," Captain Vaun muttered. He squatted down next to the blackened bones on the pavement. Kelly came up behind him, helping Thomas limp along.

True to Samuel Cain's promise, our new vests had held up to the incendiary firecracker rounds. When a bulletproof vest stops a bullet, it doesn't completely erase the joules of kinetic energy. From the looks of it, Thomas was still fairly winded. I'll take a teammate with a few bruised ribs over a teammate with scorched holes through his center mass any day.

"He started monologuing pretty good right before he did his little Burning Man impersonation," Billy said. "Made it seem like whatever Singh's planning, it goes beyond just supplying some stateside Koreans. Inevitable failure, insurmountable odds, blah blah blah."

"Sounds par for the course," I said dejectedly.

We had him. We fucking *had* him. No weapons, no suicide capsule, no damn Batman smoke bomb escape up his sleeve, and yet we were ending the night empty-handed. This was on me. I'd dragged him up from the water. I think my hope was that being soaking wet would've protected him from whatever Singh was using to combust his loose ends.

"We'll get Doc Phelps to take a look." Vaun knelt closer to one of the bones. "Maybe she'll have better luck this time figuring out what the hell did this."

"Area was secured, Captain," Tag said. "Nobody else was around who could've torched him."

"If Singh's directed-energy weapons are as advanced as Cain and Goode think, then I imagine they can be fired from very far away," Vaun suggested.

"If Singh has some futuristic thermo-sniper, then why wouldn't they just use it to burn us, too?" I countered.

The Captain shrugged. More questions and less answers second after second.

"You don't think it could be satellite based . . ." whispered Kelly. "Talk about a *very* long-distance shot."

We all looked up into the blank night sky, imagining some far-off space-based weapon pointing right down at us. Billy flipped it off just in case it wasn't imaginary.

"Speaking of long-distance shots, where the hell was Hydra Squad when we needed them?" I asked aloud.

The look on Vaun's face told me he wondered the same thing.

CHAPTER 14

Cool air whistled into the room through the freshly made holes punched in the floor-to-ceiling picture window. That tell-tale low howl of wind was broken by the dying choke of the man who lay at Deimos's feet. Deimos peered down at him emotionlessly. A cluster of two-inch spikes jutted through the man's nasal cavity, and he was having a terrible go at dying.

Deimos considered putting a round between his eyes to finish the job but decided it would be a waste of a bullet. The man was dead, anyway. Deimos unscrewed the suppressor from his pistol and stowed it back inside his jacket holster.

Behind him his brother had finished the other side of the room and sheathed his karambit. His ever-silent message understood: no present threats. The sleeves of Phobos's black blazer were slick with blood. There was far more painted on the walls and floor.

"Any of those boys talk?" asked Deimos over his shoulder while looking out across the San Diego Bay. Without turning, he knew that Phobos responded with an unimpressed shrug and shake of his head.

"I figured as much. Did any of them give you much trouble?"

This time Deimos turned around as he spoke, surprised to find his brother indicating a very small cut on the back of his right wrist. Equally shocked and impressed, Deimos walked over to his brother and used his handkerchief to apply a bandage. Phobos would typically walk away completely unscathed, but no one was perfect.

"Still, I'd hate to be these other guys," whispered Deimos while examining the bloodshed adorning Phobos's side of the wall. The small team of snipers nested in this room had been literally cut to pieces. Deimos pushed a severed hand out of his way with the toe of his shoe before walking back towards the picture window.

The problem with high-powered, bolt-action rifles is that they are completely ineffective against explosives or a knife wielder up close. Deimos had kicked in the door, tossed in a new and delightfully dangerous anti-personnel bomb, and then Phobos had cut into those who'd survived like a whirlwind. It was over before they had a chance to draw their sidearms. Deimos took a moment to survey the room, wondering which had caused more bloodshed: Deimos's bomb or Phobos's karambit?

Reaching to the inner pocket of his jacket, Deimos retrieved a set of small binoculars and peered through them. Sure enough, he could see the aftermath of Desmond Toole's disaster. The shipyard was a ruin of toppled cargo containers and felled cranes. Police were arriving and establishing a perimeter, so the clean-up crew couldn't be too far behind. All to sweep this mess under the rug. "Industrial accident" he was sure they'd call it.

The man who'd been spiked through the nasal cavity finally died. Deimos purposefully knelt down and pulled a small communication earbud from the corpse's ear then put it into his own. A line remained open. The team of shooters on the ground relayed a situation report to whoever was in command regarding what they'd faced. Adjusting the binoculars, Deimos focused on Toole's remains. Burnt to a crisp.

With a smirk on his face, Deimos pulled out the earbud, then promptly stomped on it. Then, as if he had all the time in the world, he slid a cell phone out from his pocket and dialed his employer.

"Good evening, sir, I hope your morning is going well. They took Toole out as planned." He adjusted his vision to where the *ShadowCrawler Mk. IV* had sunk into the water. "No, the tank is a total loss. Its maneuverability remains its Achilles heel, unfortunately. The *other* two devices, however, continue to prove effective."

When he asked Deimos how effective, Deimos had to hold back his laughter. Once more he looked at the damage in the room he stood in, and then to Toole's incinerated remains.

"Quite effective, sir."

CHAPTER 15

It was a habit of his to replay through mission footage almost immediately after one of his teams had seen some action. After that, he'd watch it again. And again. And again and again until he knew more than his men who had been there knew. While Goode had entire sections of analysts on his staff devoted to peering over every piece of intel, in order to determine when things went awry, Rourke trusted his own judgment and that of his men on the ground over Goode's experts.

Things were brewing, and if this recent trouble was any indication, then everything would soon become very visible. Rourke hated visibility. His entire responsibility was to keep these situations from ever seeing the light of day. If Joe and Jane America could sleep at night, unaware of the danger they were continually in, then Rourke was doing his job well. Ignorance is bliss.

As it turned out, ignorance was also job security. Black Spear had very nearly been disbanded recently, and it was only a string of successful missions that had turned the tide in that fight. Currently they were on good standing, but if war broke out with China or North Korea then Rourke's accumulated brownie points wouldn't be worth shit.

"Don't suppose they'll be able to pull that tank out of the water anytime soon?" a voice said.

Rourke turned to find Cain standing in the doorway. Back on the monitor in front of him, Rourke replayed the moment when the Cheng Qiang spider-tank had crashed into the water. In Rourke's opinion, Sergeant West's strategy had been built on equal parts cleverness and blind luck. It's not like the U.S. would be combating foreign militaries exclusively near large bodies of water.

"Our cleanup crew will be onsite by morning."

Despite not receiving an invitation to do so, Cain walked into the conference room and crossed his arms before squinting at Rourke. "Yet you somehow manage to sound more grim than usual."

Rourke paused before deciding how to answer. Controlling his temper in front of Cain was never easy, and it seemed like he'd made it his life goal to push Rourke's buttons.

"We're very likely on the brink of war. Feels like building a house out of matches."

"It's nothing new."

"How many of my men will die when that war kicks off?"

"It's what they signed on to do," Cain said firmly.

Rourke scoffed. "It doesn't mean I have to like making the decisions that will cause it. You'd understand that if you'd served."

His friend was taken aback by that last biting remark.

"That's low, even for you," he said while pulling his inhaler out from his pants pocket for a puff. The room was quiet for a second. "You've got enough enemies in the world, Darren. You don't need to make me one too."

"The coming days could see us engaged in traditional warfare with a foreign nation for the first time in over twenty years," muttered Rourke. "Apologies if I seem a little agitated."

It was easier for Rourke to stare at the monitors in front of him than to look at Cain. He chose instead to watch a looped clip of the incendiary rounds the tank had fired. Those things were deadly enough when loaded into small arms; the thought of an entire fleet of armored vehicles fully loaded made Rourke's jaw ache.

"The president will want a show of force after this," sighed Rourke.

"So then let's give him one. CDI is more advanced than the Cheng Qiang Arms Conglomerate in every way but one: production. China's always had a leg up on us in that. Get me the approval, and I'll have our advanced projects division pumping out countermeasure prototypes by morning."

Rourke shook his head. History had proven that arms races never ended well, regardless of intentions on either side. If CDI increased its manufacturing, then the enemy would likely double down on their own.

"We need a response. Call the president and get the greenlight for mass production. If you're right about a war coming, then we need to get ahead of the arms race *now*," emphasized Cain.

"I just told you that it feels like everything's made of tinder, and your idea is to add some more kindling on top of it?" asked Rourke sarcastically. "You might supply us for war, but I've breathed it. Bathed in it. I know it intimately."

"Don't try to intimidate me, Rourke," said Cain, all pretense of friendliness between them quickly fading. "I won't flinch just because I know how many bodies you've buried over the years. Last time I checked, I supplied you with most of the shovels."

"If we do this, you'll be kicking a hornet's nest."

"I'm not kicking a hornet's nest!" shouted Cain. "I'm punting the goddamn thing out of our yard! I'm in the business of *war*, Rourke. And like it or not, one is at our very doorstep. I can't just stand idly by and let Singh take the advantage. If I'd had the funding, I could've supplied your men with enough *Microswarms* to easily take out that tank. I could have reverse-engineered those firecrackers and made a tank-buster that would've ended the fight in an instant." Cain snapped his fingers for effect.

Rourke took measure of the man in front of him. It was too late to try and sway him at this point. They were both devoted to their country but always found themselves at an impasse on how best to defend it.

Cain exhaled slowly. "Look, you brought me in as your expert, but it seems like all you want to do is play defense. Damage control and information obfuscation to the public. We need to go on the offensive here. Strike while the iron is hot. If you won't make the call, I'll do it myself."

Rourke stared at him, his expression cold. Perhaps describing themselves as friends after all these years had been too generous. There had always been a shadow of resentment hiding underneath their mutual professional respect. Cain resented him for being the soldier he never could be, Rourke resented him for always being able to distance himself from the hard nature of combat.

But Rourke was in denial. They both knew it. One of the oldest truths of war was that the better equipped force tended to win. As it stood, Atharv Singh had taken an edge tonight. Sometimes, in order to snuff out a fire, you have to light a bigger one nearby to suck away the oxygen.

"I'll make the call, Sam. I just hope we're making the right one."

Samuel Cain's posture softened before he gave a curt nod. "So do I. I'm flying back to our Monterey facility to get the wheels turning. Send Captain Vaun my way in the morning, and I can load him up with what I've got for him."

If anyone would have aces up his sleeve, it would be Cain. For that, Rourke would always be grateful. More than that, he was curious about exactly what Cain had in store for them.

"World wants to go to shit," muttered Rourke and extended a firm handshake to Cain who solemnly accepted, "and just the two of us to keep hell at bay."

Cain smirked. "Trust me, with what I've got we aren't going to keep hell at bay. We're going to unleash it on them."

CHAPTER 16

I don't know what it was we expected to find. Maybe we thought Hydra Squad had suffered a complete communications failure. Maybe we held out hope that we'd find all six of them drunk and the in-room minibar pilfered for an impromptu party. If only we were so lucky.

Vaun had sent Billy, Tag and I up to check on them while he and the others secured the docks. The silence on the elevator ride up to the thirteenth floor spoke volumes. Nobody made a comment on the ill-begotten luck of the thirteenth floor. Billy had remained uncharacteristically quiet; Tag dour as ever. Even when we kicked in the door to room 1308, I think there'd still been denial about what we already knew we'd find.

Hydra Squad had been completely slaughtered. I found their team leader against the far window with a collection of strange spikes punched through his face. Major Wilcox's eyes were staring lifelessly past me, his own brain blood forming a grisly red mustache across his upper lip.

I tapped my earbud. "Blackbars, this is Toxin. Slipknot is down . . . they're all down, sir."

"Roger," was all the Captain said back. No doubt he'd been

thinking how lucky we were with the only injury being Thomas, only to find out that our sister squad had been completely shwacked.

"Just what the shit happened here?" breathed Tag in a hushed bark.

The strange spikes were everywhere. Ceiling, walls, the floor. One of the bodies near my feet was so littered with them, it looked like he'd lost a fight with the world's most dangerous porcupine, another next to him had been mulched into hamburger so badly he was hardly recognizable as human.

"Almost looks like . . . like a nail bomb?" suggested Billy.

Nail bombs were especially brutal devices. A little explosive and a shit-ton of nails were all you needed to cobble together your own homemade claymore mine. Getting caught near one was like taking a swan dive through a giant cheese grater.

I knelt in the center of the entryway. Judging by the remaining spikes, this looked like ground zero. "Maybe. But not quite, check here—there should be blast residue. Charring. Anything. What's left of this guy here got the worst of it. Look how shredded he is. But no powder burns whatsoever. Also, you ever seen nails like these?"

I plucked one of the spikes out of the carpet and tossed it to Billy. It was cruciform, but twisted like a screw, no doubt designed to drill straight through its victims. Nothing over-the-counter about it.

"It's not too much better over here," Tag said from the other side of the room. He stood among the remainder of Hydra Squad. They lay in piles.

"Tag, think you can pull their security feeds?" I asked.

The big man grunted, which told me he was already hacking the hotel's security cameras with the same wrist-mounted computer he'd used for the *Microswarm*.

"West . . ." Billy beckoned me to a body he crouched over. ". . . come check these wounds out. Knifework, for sure."

The history of my teammate was wrapped in a few layers of

mystery. The few details I'd become privy to told me that before being pulled into Black Spear, Billy Ho was an assassin for the bad guys. Someone must have made him quite an enticing offer because he'd since switched sides. Billy's years of experience on the darker side of life, however, granted him an unequaled insight into certain things. Namely, unseen clues dead bodies tended to leave behind.

"Look here," he said, pointing to a deep laceration on the body's arm that had cut straight through the bicep. "Look how clean the cut is. It went damn near to the bone. And the second cut here—at the left carotid—the artery is severed perfectly." The second wound was barely a half inch long, but *perfectly* long enough and deep enough to open it up.

"What does it tell you?"

"Precision," he answered. "Our guy managed to cut deep enough into the arm to sever the bicep and immobilize the arm, yet not deep enough to nick the bone. Bone can blunt an edge. He cut exactly as deep as he wanted. And the precise small cut on the neck, the deliberateness of the wound . . . West, I've seen surgeons with scalpels that couldn't make cuts this fine."

Billy then reached next to him on the floor and found a loose hand cut from another one of Hydra Squad's members. I'd noticed that when it came to this little detective work, Billy's class clown demeanor was overtaken by a personality more akin to Sherlock Holmes. He tossed the severed appendage to me so I could take a look myself.

"One clean cut," I said.

He nodded in agreement. "Yep, cut through muscle and tendon at the wrist while avoiding the small bones. Like I said: this guy's surgical."

I looked to the other bodies. I forced myself to analyze the scene from an evidence perspective, rather than allow myself to feel the loss of more good men.

"He's deadly," Billy stated while examining a second body. "Stab wound between the ribs directly into the heart, another laceration across his femoral. West, these are nearly all kill strikes. I don't see any superficial cuts or secondary injuries."

"So our surgeon isn't just deadly but fast," I noted while glancing over a third body, whose only visible wound had been a puncture to the base of the skull at the back of the neck. "Seven shooters in a room, our mystery nail bomb takes three out, and he takes the four remaining before they could put up a fight or do so much as raise a hand to block a slash. Know anyone off the top of your head that could do this?"

Billy dusted his hands off on his pant legs, as if to shake loose any bad luck he might have picked up from touching the bodies. "Eh, yes and no. One with a penchant for obsidian knives comes to mind, but the wounds don't match up. He's more a force of nature; our guy here is laser precision. Whoever this is, let's just say I'm glad I haven't crossed paths with him yet."

Just as I was about to see if Tag had finished hacking the security cameras, something caught my eye. It was the fourth body, the farthest one into the room. Billy's cursory examination had been accurate in the sense that there weren't any superficial wounds. But what struck me was how many killing strikes were on this body.

The fourth body had been stabbed in the side of the neck, the wound puncturing both carotid arteries; two stab wounds were right over each other on his heart, together making a small x on his left breast; and a little bit lower I saw more precise stabs into both femoral arteries. Both brachial arteries on his arms had been opened. If the killer was so precise, why would he have applied more wounds than necessary?

And then I saw it. A small Spyderco folding knife had fallen to the carpet nearby, still locked open. More importantly: there was a small drop of blood staining the knife's edge. Seven men, and they'd only managed to shed one drop of blood from the enemy.

"That must've made you angry . . ." I realized while picking up the knife. We could use White Shield's database to run a DNA check once we got back to base.

Tag slapped shut his wrist-computer. "We're good. Let's go."

I radioed in to Vaun to let him know that we'd need a cleanup crew for the room once the docks were done. As I followed my two friends out of the room, I stopped short at the doorway. Turning on my heel, I took one last look at the bloody aftermath that was room 1308. I committed the image to memory. Whoever was behind this was going to pay. By God, were they going to pay . . .

CHAPTER 17

Dana Phelps. 1:57 a.m.
Home Site
San Diego, California

Being the on-hand medical examiner for the Home Site meant there was never a shortage of work. That piece of knowledge came as both a blessing and a curse for her. There were times Dana swore that the bad guys of the world had access to her bank accounts and could tell when she bought tickets to a show. Then the bastards seemed to plot their dastardly bullshit on the very night she had plans. If only they had the common decency to surrender. But no, more often than not they went and got themselves killed.

Which also brought her to Exhibit A. To be honest, everything she'd heard about Desmond Toole and his gun-running had made her eager to get his body on her table just to see his very dead smug face. As it stood she wouldn't even get that satisfaction since the only thing left of the bastard was his bones. Figured.

"Let's see what we can see," Dana muttered to herself while adjusting a microscope.

If this body proved to be anything like that of Congressman Mike Halsey, then it would provide few clues. Since they'd snatched this one up so quickly, perhaps they would have more luck this time. Try as she might, she just couldn't muster the optimism needed to hope. Optimism was perpetually in short supply in the morgue at 2:00 a.m.

Desmond Toole had been incinerated in what appeared to be the exact same way. Atharv Singh's mystery weapon had rapidly heated him to the point of immolation. Dana's earlier estimation of two thousand degrees seemed too low now, especially given that Toole had been soaking wet at the time of combustion.

Thermodynamics weren't exactly Dana's strong suit, so any guess on her part about how hot Singh's weapon was would be a complete shot in the dark. The heat needed was simply off the charts. No weapon she was familiar with could cause that and working the morgue for America's black-ops had provided her with an extensive catalog of the very cutting edge of weapons.

The other curious thing was just how complete the immolation was. A directed-energy weapon was, by its very name, directional, which meant Toole's back side should have been partially unscathed. The fact that every part of him had burned lent credence to Kelly's initially comical suggestion that it was a satellite-based weapon. She didn't even want to do the math on how powerful it would have to be to rapidly heat something that high from friggin' space.

"Source of head-to-toe immolation remains unidentified," Dana stated into her recorder. "Scorching is consistent with that of the remains of Congressman Mike Halsey. This also matches with the autopsy reports provided by White Shield on the bodies of Piotr Bludovich, Orson Soung, and Jun Byeong-Ho."

Consistency is usually good with an investigation. Unless, of course, the only consistency is that you don't know anything. She held up Toole's left ulna bone, waving it this way and that like a wand as if to conjure answers out of thin air. Unsuccessful, she set the bone back down before reaching for the recorder again.

At the last second, she froze. Something about the bone had caught her attention.

Grabbing it once more, she squinted at it under the microscope. She reached for a set of forensic tweezers.

"I really hope I'm wrong about this . . ." Dana Phelps sighed. ". . . because if I'm right, then things just got a whole lot weirder."

CHAPTER 18

Cole West. 6:30 a.m.
CDI Advanced Projects Facility
Monterey, California

Two images kept replaying in my head since last night. The first was the sudden flash of Desmond Toole's disappearing act. There one instant, skeleton the next. The second, the blood-painted walls of room 1308. I'd been wrestling all night with how unfair it was that a scumbag like Toole had gone out instantly and relatively painlessly, while good men had been slaughtered like cattle.

Cerberus Squad's personal helicopter, dubbed Charon after the Greek ferryman to the underworld, transported us from San Diego to Monterey. Cain's main headquarters facility in Seattle handled most of CDI's manufacturing, but his Monterey operation was the crown jewel in terms of weapons development. The California-based lab was where the real leaps and bounds were made.

Charon prepared to land when I noticed how uncharacteristically tired Captain Vaun looked.

"Doing alright, sir?" I asked.

After taking a long breath, he answered reluctantly, "Would it be too Danny Glover of me if I said I was getting too old for this shit?"

I shrugged. "You might have some road miles on you, but you seem to be carrying it well."

"It's not that," he said. "It's just … I mean, a goddamn Spider-Tank walking around like that? Makes me feel old when I miss taking on normal terrorists." I nodded, and he seemed more upset that I wasn't too shaken about what we faced last night. "How are you not fazed by any of this, West?"

"I dunno," I answered. "Our first mission together had a pretty strong '28 Days Later' vibe, so you can't expect me to be too surprised when things go all Shagohad from Metal Gear Solid 3."

Vaun stared into the distance. "I have no idea what the fuck you just said. Jesus Christ, I really am getting old."

Just then Charon made its rapid descent to the CDI helipad. Our ride bucked a bit, and I extended a hand to steady the Captain, who had nearly fallen out of his seat from the surprise.

"This ride ain't over yet, old man," I said, meaning the mission as much as the helicopter. "So don't go trading in your rifle for a walker just yet."

Vaun slapped my hand away before standing up once the helicopter had finished landing, "Insubordination like that's no way to get promoted, Sergeant."

"Last I checked, I still technically outrank Corporal Taggart there," I joked before stepping out of the helicopter.

Tag eyed me, muttering a signature harrumph as he hefted himself out.

CDI's Advanced Projects facility was breathtaking. The entire building was built right along the California coast, constructed atop a cliffside view of the water with sandy beaches and beautiful blue waves just below. The view from the helipad at the top of the building was so nice, I found myself wondering if I'd survive a swan dive to the waters below. Given that I was still wearing a layer of body armor under my civilian attire, which would certainly drown me even *if* I survived, I quickly decided against it. We were here on business, after all.

Samuel Cain met us at the top of a flight of stairs that led down from the helipad. Mr. Rourke would not be in attendance today, and the rumor mill hinted that he and Cain had a bit of a disagreement last night. I didn't care much for office politics as long as my boss didn't send me on a suicide mission and our outfitter continued to give us quality equipment.

As we drew closer, I saw he held a small silver rod in his hand. My mind started spinning up ideas on what new weapon he'd be demonstrating for us up here almost immediately.

"What's that?" I asked. "Laser pointer that shoots actual lasers? Exploding James Bond pen?"

"Compact dildo," Billy whispered behind me.

I tried not to let Cain see me laugh too hard.

Cain regarded me with confusion for a moment, then looked at the silver rod he held and laughed. "Oh, this? Ha, not exactly a weapon." Then he placed the small silver rod in his mouth and blew, and I realized what it was. A dog whistle.

I heard panting and heavily-padded feet running up behind me. I turned around, expecting to see a big old dog. Instead, I saw a monster. An absolute *monster*.

The thing had to be nearly a hundred and forty pounds, and over three feet tall at the shoulder. Its jet black coat made it look like a shadow as it bolted across the helipad. His large head and clipped ears made me think it was a pitbull, but I'd never seen one so damn *big*. And then I saw the monster's eyes. They glowed yellow like they'd been forged from pale gold. Needless to say, I was equal parts terrified and in love with the beast.

"Gentlemen, meet Dante."

"Lord Almighty," I breathed sharply as the beast pounded across the rooftop before stopping short by Cain's feet and sitting on its haunches. "Since when did CDI get into genetic engineering?"

"No splicing necessary," Cain answered as he put the whistle into his jacket and patted Dante on the head. "Just good breeding stock."

"He looks too big to be a pit. You been feeding that thing Tag's steroids?" Billy laughed.

Cain chuckled, but Tag seemed to take offense and only frowned. We both knew Tag was clean, but it was still fun to razz him about his size.

"He's a Canary Mastiff," explained Cain. "Out in the Canary Islands, they bred these to help herd cattle. Cattle!"

"That thing almost made me shit myself," Thomas admitted. "It could herd me if it wanted."

A nervous-looking worker appeared behind Cain, a second leashed Canary Mastiff in tow. This one had a brown brindle coat with black splotches.

Cain attached a leash to Dante's collar and handed it off to the worker. "Make sure he gets fed good. He was a good boy today. Oh, yes, he was!"

The worker reluctantly accepted the leash and led the black monster away for his chow. I assumed for a dog that large you had to feed it a stable diet of Flintstones-style Brontosaurus Burgers.

"Just between you and me, training him has been a pain in the ass," said Cain. He guided us down from the helipad. "His brother, Virgil, was easy. Dante's stubborn. Slowly but surely, he's coming along, though. My trainer tried to convince me to get a couple spaniels or bloodhounds after these two broke out of the kennels twice, but man did you *see* him running? What self-respecting war profiteer would own anything less?" Cain gave me a wink.

"I'm sorry you didn't get your man last night," he said as we entered an elevator which would take us further into the facility. "I've had Madison and her team working around the clock to figure out how to counteract Singh's weapon. And before you ask, West, no she hasn't asked about you."

Crap. You accidentally make googly eyes at a woman once and suddenly the entire world knows about it.

"I don't know what Dr. Archer could put together anyway beyond a full head-to-toe encapsulation," I said, hoping that my all-business response would redirect the conversation. "Desmond Toole was soaking wet, and it didn't slow down his incineration one bit. And the idea of walking around fully coated in fire retardant foam doesn't sound too fun."

The elevator dinged, and the doors parted to reveal a sprawling workspace. Whereas the Seattle workspace we'd seen had a more factory-like appearance, this one felt like an Apple Store. All white floors and walls with rows of computers along one wall and a large pane glass wall on the far side. I figured whatever Cain meant to demonstrate and supply us with was beyond that glass.

"Here's where we make the magic," announced Cain, spreading his arms out before him. A few lab technicians glanced over at us but then turned back to their workstations; evidently their instructions to work around the clock superseded any curiosity they might have had regarding their CEO walking in. "We have a small offshore testing facility if we need to test the more volatile aspects of a design, but for the most part our prototypes are designed, constructed, and tested right here in-house. I even installed the most advanced filtration system money could buy for the waste-water output to make sure the runoff didn't affect the bay. The Monterey Bay Aquarium people would have torn this place down if I hadn't. My grandkids love that place."

The idea of Samuel Cain designing advanced projects just a few miles from where he took his grandchildren to see the sea lions and otters amused me for some reason.

"So, what do you have for us today?" Vaun asked. "Singh's upped the ante. We really need to level the playing field here."

The smile that lit up Cain's face spoke volumes to what he intended to show us. With showmanship akin to a circus ringmaster, he beckoned us to enter the demonstration area just beyond the glass wall. There was a puff of compressed air as we entered and a pair of clean-suit technicians hurried over to us. I felt bad that I was comfortably wearing jeans and a zip-up hoodie but decided to cross my arms and try to look important so they wouldn't question it.

"A few appetizers to warm the palate," said Cain.

"You could just skip the sales presentation and let us take Dante and Virgil with us," I suggested.

"Over my dead body, Sergeant West."

He brought us over to a table with what looked like several variations of hand grenades. The first one had a purple ring around its siding. Cain picked it up and unscrewed the top. Inside was something similar to a small CO_2 cartridge.

"A cocktail of your Sandman agent and a truth serum," he explained and replaced the top. "Instant paralysis upon inhalation. Managed to retool your recipe so the eyelids are good. That way, next time you get the drop on a Toole-like character and his goons, you could just pop off one of these and start asking your questions. One blink for yes, two blinks for no. You called your bullets Sandman. I call this the Turkey Dinner because it'll knock out the whole family."

Vaun pursed his lips and nodded. An area-of-effect weapon like the Turkey would certainly work faster than Kelly with his rifle. Still, Vaun refused to look too impressed. Cain picked up on that almost immediately.

"Hmm, too quiet?" he asked rhetorically. "If you want something louder and more dramatic, I have exactly the thing." Next, he picked up what looked like a set of silver wireless earbuds, placed one snugly into each ear, and then retrieved a small remote roughly the size of a thumb drive. If this was supposed to be dramatic, it was seriously falling flat for all of us. Last night we'd seen some science fiction tech brought to life; collectively, we now hoped for something more.

"Are those Beats by Dre?" Billy joked.

"Close. More like 'Screech by Cain.'" Cain rolled his thumb along a dial on the remote and it instantly felt like someone had just driven railroad spikes into my ears. A high-pitch squeal filled my skull and drowned out all other sound. I clamped my hands on either side of my head and started to sink to one knee. As I did, I found that the very ground beneath my feet had turned to mush. I was by no means a clumsy person, yet all sense of balance had vanished. Stumbling around like a drunkard, I waved my arms wildly just to try and stabilize myself. Around me the rest of Cerberus Squad was just as incapacitated. Desperate for respite, I shot out a hand to the table in front of us and held on for dear life.

The only person not floundering about was Cain, and then I noticed those earbuds of his. They were lit up with a soft blue light, and he was standing perfectly still. After another moment of watching us suffer, he rolled back the dial on his device. Both the miserable screech and the dizzying vertigo vanished.

"Combination emitter," explained Cain while he removed the protective earbuds. "It simultaneously projects ultrasonic waves that disrupt the liquid in the inner ears, causing severe vertigo, and high-power sound waves to disrupt or destroy the eardrums. The protective buds are compatible with your current comm system, as well. By the way, it cranks up to ten—that was three."

"If you turn that thing up to one again, I'm going to find something very heavy and very expensive in here and hit you with it," I said.

"You can partially thank Dante and Virgil for giving me the idea," said Cain. "I had to install an ultrasonic fence to stop them from running wild. It didn't work so well, but this baby works just fine." Cain tapped the emitter a few times then looked to Vaun. "And . . . ?"

Vaun allowed himself half a grin. "Getting a little better. What've you got for the main course?"

That seemed to be all the encouragement Cain needed to continue. We walked away from the table with the grenades and the emitter to a small shooting gallery. A clean-suit adorned technician had just finished loading rounds into the magazine of a CDI Magnum chambered in .50 Action Express.

"Captain, if you would do the honors?" Cain said.

Vaun took the heavy weapon and gave it a once-over. "CDI Model 50s are hardly new." Undeterred, Cain gestured towards the dummy target at the twenty-yard line. I noticed the target was wearing a standard ballistic vest.

Taking a position, Vaun raised the weapon, lined up his sights, and squeezed the trigger. The captain hit dead center, the bullet punched the vest, and then I had to squint to protect my eyes from the brilliant crimson firework show that exploded out the back of the target. Smoke billowed up from the destroyed target mannequin, and the lab technician hurried over with an extinguisher in hand to put out the small fire.

"Cheng Qiang's firecrackers work. That's for sure. But nobody does fireworks like America does fireworks," Cain said.

Vaun put the weapon on safe before ejecting the magazine to inspect what he'd just shot.

At the same time Cain handed over a round to pass around for our own inspection. "I was able to rework and improve upon Singh's design. We added a delayed fragmentation once it penetrates its target. Shrapnel shredding out the exit wound at a few thousand degrees. Hit someone in the leg with Singh's firecracker, and it'll burn right through them, but it'll also cauterize the wound somewhat. Hit someone in the leg with one of *mine* and it doesn't matter what kind of armor they're wearing. They'll be the next contestant in a one-legged ass-kicking competition."

I rolled the bullet around between my thumb and forefinger. The bullet had a dark, nearly blood-red tint to it, which I assumed was due to the incendiary material it was coated in. It looked gnarly, though. It had a sharpened point and deep grooves along its sides where it was meant to fracture after impact.

"These are fresh off the line, so I haven't had the focus groups name them yet, but I'm partial to calling them Hades rounds. Seemed fitting that Cerberus would get to use them first."

I was eager to fight fire with fire and use them on Singh's men, giving them that oh so satisfying taste of their own medicine. I noticed that Thomas was reluctant to get a closer look at the Hades round; apparently, taking a few incendiary rounds to the chest last night had been a close enough look to last him a lifetime. I made a mental note to check in with him once we were done here and see how he was holding up. In all fairness he could be out on R&R, but he wasn't about to let us finish this fight without him.

"Okay, Cain, not bad," Vaun finally admitted. "But is there dessert?"

The old man raised an eyebrow as if he was considering whether or not to show off the ace tucked up his sleeve. One final Christmas gift remained in the closet. After a prolonged moment of consideration, he took us to the back of the room where a large drop-cloth covered . . . something.

"Gentlemen, in case you were ever actually concerned that the Cheng Qiang Arms Conglomerate might have gained an edge on us, I'd like to give you a reminder of why Rourke keeps me on retainer."

Cain grabbed the drop-cloth and ripped it off with a solid tug. It took approximately half a heartbeat for my jaw to unhinge from my skull and fall to the floor.

"Sweet Jesus . . . I want one."

CHAPTER 19

"I call it CHAOS," said Cain in an awe-filled declaration. "Cain's Hardened Army-of-One System."

I felt like my life had just jumped that proverbial shark. Standing before me, measuring at a solid thirteen feet tall, was an honest-to-God bipedal mech suit. It was like looking at a real-life version of the exo-suits from *Avatar*. The gunmetal surface of the CHAOS suit was streaked with black tiger stripe camouflaging, the space for the suit's wearer housed safely within the thickly armored torso behind a four-foot-wide octagonal windshield of sorts. Its arms ended in mechanical three-digit hands, and the entire mech stood atop two titanic legs like some cybernetic monster. Seemed to me that Cain was already poised to top Singh at his own game of science-fiction made reality.

"Singh's tank was impressive, but even the previous model was clumsy," said Cain. He took a puff from his inhaler. "Two legs are what evolution saw fit to deem us with. CHAOS is lighter, faster, and far more agile. But don't let the smaller frame fool you; I didn't call it the Army-of-One for nothing." With that he started a rundown of the weapons equipped to it. "Wrist-mounted 20mm autocannon on the left arm, automatic grenade launcher and laser-guided missile pack attached to the right. Currently, the twin pods on its shoulders are loaded with short-range surface-to-air missiles. However, CHAOS was designed to be modular, and we can adjust the loadout however the mission requires."

My hand reached out with a mind of its own to feel one of the 20mm autocannon's six rotary barrels. There was something about the feeling of pure firepower that was electrifying.

"Each of the hands house integrated utility tools. Flame cutter, auger drill, titanium saw. You find something with armor too thick, you can always cut a hole through it and shove a missile in there."

Vaun knocked on the armor of the mech, just outside of where the wearer's chest would be. "What's this made of?"

"The outer layer of armor is composed of depleted uranium plating three inches thick. The secondary layer of armor is assembled from larger versions of the same titanium/Kevlar weaved scales we use in our *Fafnir* vests. The windshield is cast out of our proprietary ballistic glass."

Billy looked dubious. "I bet this thing still drives like a tank."

"On the contrary," Cain answered. "The chest houses the cockpit. Within the cockpit are sensor attachments for the arms and foot pedals to maneuver the legs. The sensors apply feedback to both the hands and legs in relation to what the suit makes contact with. In essence, it allows the wearer to 'feel.' No steering wheel required, Mister Ho."

Inside the cockpit I spotted what looked like a set of boots built into the floor and a pair of sleeve-length gloves with electronic leads attached. I'd seen similar hand controls for a few prototype surgical robots. If these were even half as precise, then they'd still be far more maneuverable than a steering wheel and sets of levers.

I noticed Tag eying the electronics inside the suit's cockpit. "Any wireless backdoors? Came close to knocking out Singh's tank with a wrist computer. Hope your firewalls are better. If we get to play with this, I'd hate for it to be as vulnerable to hacking as the spider was."

"CHAOS is hardwired, closed circuit. It's impossible to hack its weapons systems. The risk of the enemy hacking a weapons platform this advanced was why I chose to make it an exo as opposed to a remote drone. The only signals even allowed in are communications signals and signals for the onboard medical protocols."

"Medical protocols?" Vaun asked with an arched eyebrow.

The weapons mastermind pressed a button on a remote and the chest of the suit opened to reveal even more secrets within the inner cockpit. "The suit has a fully functioning, automated, onboard medical bay. It can apply sutures and bandages if needed, administer painkillers or adrenaline, and can even set expedient splints if any breaks are detected. We can triage and apply first aid from up to twenty miles away."

As far as sales pitches went, Cain had effectively knocked it out of the park. I could tell from the looks on the squad's faces that everyone was just as eager as I was to take CHAOS out for a test-run.

Someone else seemed less than enthused. The sound of a slow sarcastic clap came from behind us. I turned in surprise to find Rourke and Kara Mason approaching us. Rourke's perpetual scowl deepened the closer he got to us and Cain's suit.

"That's certainly one way to put out a fire," he said, unimpressed.

"War is coming," answered Cain in a cold whisper, his friendly grandpa attitude absent now. "With all its rage, and all its fury. We can either stand still and let it wash over us, or we can fight back. I'm fighting fire with fire."

"This could be fun overseas," admitted Rourke, "but when we work domestically, our aim is decidedly more cloak and dagger."

Nothing like your boss coming in and shutting down all the fun you were having at the toy store. But I saw his point. It would be hard for Black Spear to keep a low profile if we were walking around in our very own oversized Iron Man suits.

"We'll keep this in the cupboard for a rainy day. As it turns out, the sun is shining today. And I've got work for Cerberus to do." Rourke sniffed dismissively at the CHAOS suit, then turned his back on it and us as he shook one of those white pills of his into his hand.

"What's the mission?" Vaun asked, crossing his arms.

Rourke popped the pill into his mouth. "Some cloak and dagger work."

CHAPTER 20

Atharv Singh. 11:00 p.m.
Cheng Qiang Arms Headquarters
Kaesong, North Korea

Every failure can effectively double as a lesson, given the right perspective. If a lucky shot gets through your armor, then you know where to improve it. If your battery keeps shorting out, then it's time to take a look at your wiring. All it takes is the proper mindset and emotional control not to lose sight of what the lesson is trying to show you.

Singh twisted the ring on his finger as he lost himself to his thoughts. The board of Cheng Qiang needed results from him. The longer it took to produce the leaps and bounds he was known for, the shorter their patience with his endeavors would be. As his true machinations required his own free reign, scrutiny from those appointed over him was something he simply couldn't afford at this time.

As much as his own patience for the Marstelli brothers was running thin, Singh would need to collect Deimos and Phobos's field test data for the Mk. IV if he was to make the required improvements. Toole had, ironically, been the perfect tool for that job. It was a good thing Singh's enemies weren't able to get their hands on Toole. Not in one piece, at least.

Singh smirked at the thought. One less person to contaminate the coming era of intellectuals. He wasn't sure if Toole had any children, but on the off chance he did perhaps Singh would need to send the assassin brothers to finish cleaning up that bloodline. Singh hated loose ends.

Thinking of tying up loose ends sparked a train of thought for him. He abruptly stopped twisting his ring and rose to his feet. Whenever he had made up his mind like this, it was often sudden and absolute.

As he exited his office, he was approached by a titan of a man named Min. Min had been assigned by Cheng Qiang to be Singh's shadow. Follow him, guard him, do everything in his power to ensure that the arms conglomerate's proverbial goose was still around to lay more golden eggs for them. The man was a brute—thus far a very effective brute when it came to keeping Singh alive. Min's squashed face and squinty eyes regarded Singh as he approached. The man hurried over to see what his charge needed.

"Have the plane fueled," Singh instructed. "I need to take a more hands-on approach for the next stage."

Min nodded and followed as Singh took the elevator up to the helipad. Loose ends needed to be tied up. The only logical way to do that without creating even more would be for Singh to be personally involved. Well, not personally. That's what Min was for.

Singh exited the elevator with his gigantic man in tow. The test-data needed to be collected, and he simply couldn't entrust that task to anyone else. The Cheng Qiang Arms Conglomerate had competitors, after all. If the Marstellis were so inclined, they could easily sell the data for millions.

The helicopter's rotors spun up as Singh approached. Min opened the side door before climbing in behind him. As the helicopter pulled away from the rooftop and headed in the airstrip's direction, Singh began to twist the ring on his finger once more. Plenty of his assets were already embedded stateside. Getting into the United States would be even easier than escaping it the first time.

CHAPTER 21

Mr. Rourke had grudgingly accepted Samuel Cain's offer to use his conference room to give us our mission briefing. It was the second time in as many days that we would be discussing sensitive information off Black Spear grounds, but expediency was the name of the game now. Since this was the very room Common Defense Industries used for meetings to discuss their own classified weapon tech, I trusted these walls to keep a secret.

Rourke stood at the front of the room, his right hand and bodyguard, Mason, leaning against a wall just behind him. Several images began to populate a large presentation screen on the wall next to Rourke. I could tell that most were pulled from the security feeds in the hotel Tag had hacked. Others looked to be compiled from older intel files. They were all of the same two people: the two killers who had entered room 1308 and murdered Hydra Squad.

"Our two priority targets . . . Deimos and Phobos, the Marstelli brothers," Rourke stated as two profile pictures appeared next to each other.

The man on the left had red hair and looks that should've seen him grace expensive cologne ads instead of our target list. On his right was a bald, lean-faced man with a grisly scar that cut back from the corner of his mouth and down his neck.

"Visuals were a dead ringer, but the DNA from that blood West retrieved confirms it. These two got their start carving their way up the chain as enforcers for the Veleno crime family. They got a little ambitious and decided to go freelance. Managed to climb their way to the number four and five spots on Black Spear's list of most dangerous hitmen."

"So why haven't I heard of them lately?" I asked.

"Probably because you're still a rookie, West," Mason said with an eye roll.

Rourke clicked a button, and a video file began to play. It looked to be an interrogation video. As I watched, a man ran a knife across Phobos Marstelli's face and gave him his facial scarring.

"They got a little too ambitious and wound up catching the attention of the Brits after a botched assassination attempt on a member of parliament. When captured they refused to give up the names of those who hired them, even at the point of torture. They killed seven agents making their escape. Ever since, they've been in the wind and keeping a low profile by remaining in the employ of one man."

"Let me guess: Atharv goddamn Singh," Kelly said. "That guy is really starting to get on my nerves."

Instead of responding, Rourke brought up a photo of Singh. "Indeed. According to White Shield's reports, the Marstellis have been Singh's primary enforcers while he's been stuck under Cheng Qiang's thumb. We now know that Deimos is the one who liaised the trafficking of Singh's prototypes to Desmond Toole."

"Scumbags of a feather flock together," Thomas said.

I'm pretty sure Toole's untimely death hadn't diminished the grudge Thomas was holding after being shot.

"Sir, with all due respect, we're wasting time," Vaun abruptly said. "If you have a lead on the Marstelli brothers, then let's hear it so I can get my guys out the door. We're burning daylight here."

Rourke's brow furrowed for only a moment, then he pursed his lips and nodded.

"Golden Moon," the Black Spear director stated simply. "Last night wasn't their first buy from Toole. After this latest deal went bad, most of their high-ranking members have scattered. The one we're looking for is The Babysitter. White Shield says he has his hands on a Cheng Qiang prototype, a gift of goodwill Toole gave him to open trade between The Golden Moon and Singh. We'll need that if we're going to find the Marstellis and Singh."

"Sounds simple enough," I said.

"Ms. Mason will be acting in my stead for this mission," Rourke added.

Vaun shot a confused look at Rourke, who only shook his head. "I'm being called to Washington and will be unable to monitor operations. Until I return, all comms will go directly to her. Good luck, and get it done, Captain." He turned and departed the room, leaving us alone with Kara Mason.

The woman examined all of us like a lion regarding its prey. Though she was no longer an operator, the hook-shaped scar that adorned her right eyebrow and cheek spoke volumes of the soldier she still was. Kara reluctantly handed a mission folder over to Vaun. "Hope you brought your gear in the helicopter. You're wheels-up in twenty, Captain."

We all stood at once, eager to kick things off and get another step closer to nailing the bastards who'd killed our guys. While everyone quickly filed out of the room, I hung back just a moment longer. Vaun, still in the room, stared intently at the screen we'd been briefed with.

Vaun was a leader whom I greatly admired for his ability to keep his emotions in check. The guy didn't crack under pressure. He never lashed out in anger or made rash decisions. A calculating and reserved warrior, he always managed to be a professional, and he never took personally the hardships or difficulties this life brought with it. But right now, I could tell he was barely holding all of that in order. He gripped the mission folder so tight, I thought he might tear it in half. His eyes had gone cold as he stared at the faces of the Marstelli brothers.

"I doubt you know this, but before I earned command of my own squad, I served on Hydra. Major Wilcox was my first squad leader," Vaun said, not needing to turn around to know I now stood behind him. "Wilcox is the one who vouched for me to Rourke when he thought I was ready for command."

"I had no idea. I didn't really know the Major that well, besides from reputation."

Vaun's grip on the mission folder eased, and he placed it on the table next to him. "He loved barbecue." Vaun almost smiled. Normally the most we'd ever see from the captain was a half-smile that snuck its way in from the corner of his mouth. The coldness left the captain's eyes as he continued to remember Major Wilcox. "Every Sunday, he'd fire up the grill and cook for everyone. Every Sunday. It didn't matter if we'd just wrapped up a hard mission the night before, or if we had to gear up to head overseas early the next day. He had a wife. Sarah. She made good lemonade." The twitch of muscle at his cheek where he fought back a smile faltered.

Despite his best efforts to hide them, I still caught the pangs of loss fighting their way to the surface.

"I think he might be the only man I ever met who managed to balance having a family with being part of the Spear. Even ignoring his record, he was just a decent man," Vaun said. "They all were."

I didn't know why Vaun was telling me any of this. I was still fairly new to the squad, and my teammates didn't confide in me such intimate life details. Let alone the captain himself.

"You know the only reason I'm still alive is because I've tried my damnedest to keep my emotions out of things. This job is hard enough without taking on personal baggage. Things like revenge and grudges are the easiest way to make mistakes and end up dead. It's why I promised myself to *never* take things personally."

A cold look returned to Vaun's eyes. All the joy his fond memories had given him vanished as he stepped closer to the screen with the Marstelli brothers' faces. "But for them? I'm going to make an exception to that promise."

CHAPTER 22

One thing that they don't warn you about the black-ops business is that you tend to seriously rack up frequent flyer miles. Cerberus Squad is supposed to have a more specific jurisdiction centered around the San Diego area, but until Los Angeles's Angel Site could be rebuilt and new teams formed up, we had to cover half the damn state. That's a lot of juris-goddamn-diction to cover.

Thankfully, that also meant the scenery was always changing. One second I'm at the San Diego waterfront, the next at a cliffside weapons development site in Monterey, and just a few hours later driving down the streets of suburbia in Long Beach. Our surroundings were nothing short of idyllic, but our reason for being here was far from it.

The Golden Moon crew had scuttled into their hidey-holes like cockroaches. Our good friend Goode had already located eight safe houses and filtered that information to local gangland units. We were headed to house nine.

Operating during daylight would actually be a first for me. Camouflage didn't serve much purpose as far as blending into our middle-class neighborhood environment in broad daylight. A combination of 5.11 Tactical pants and straight forward black or olive drab T-shirts under our vests would suffice. It was enough to look official but not full-Rambo and didn't risk every passerby immediately calling the police. If everything went according to plan, they wouldn't receive a single call.

Thermal imaging and our satellite feed showed that the Babysitter only had three other Golden Moon friends keeping him company in the safehouse. For six Black Spear operators, this would be a walk in the park. Considering the excitement of late, I could use an easy, by-the-books mission.

The plan was straightforward enough. The safehouse was a simple one-story with a front and back door and a basement. Tag and I would breach the front door, Vaun and Kelly would simultaneously breach from the rear, while Billy and Thomas would be posted on the left and right sides of the house in case either the Babysitter or one of his friends decided to hop out of a window. White Shield's intel reports pegged the Babysitter at roughly two-hundred seventy pounds of flab, so part of me hoped he'd get desperate enough to make an attempt.

Take the house. Smoke the Babysitter's friends if necessary. Make the Babysitter hand over the prototype and take him with us to answer any questions we had. He was a means to an end. Little more. If that meant he got a little bruised up between now and then, I didn't think anyone would be too upset.

"We're here," said Thomas.

Our vehicle lurched to a stop around the corner from the safe house.

"Weapons check," Vaun ordered.

We each packed 9mm submachineguns with suppressors attached. This was suburbia after all, no need to bring in Samuel Cain's big guns just yet. I checked the magazine on my weapon, then racked a round into the chamber. Vaun had brought one of Cain's Turkey grenades with us to breach, but I had two flashbangs on my vest in case it didn't work as promised. As much as I trusted Cain's weapons, there's a difference between testing in a lab and real-world application.

"This is Blackbars," Vaun said on the communications link to Mason. "We are awaiting greenlight."

"Blackbars, this is Sledgehammer," Mason answered.

She came in clear as day. I had to remind myself that she was monitoring us via laptop aboard Rourke's private plane. Evidently Rourke needed to prep for whatever he was being called for, and our little snatch and grab was an unneeded distraction. "You are go for mission. Bag 'em."

As soon as we heard the greenlight, we exited the vehicle. I felt exposed without a mask to hide my face. Apparently, Kelly mirrored my discomfort and decided to bring a simple black baseball cap with him. While pulling it snug onto his head, he noticed me watching and smiled. "You know I've got a spare in the backseat if you wanted to borrow one?"

"You're too kind," I declined.

The safe house was an ugly thing, coated in faded pale green paint with a deteriorated white-picket fence. The lawn was surprisingly upkept. I suppose The Golden Moon had to shell out a few bucks to keep up appearances at the safe house. Last thing they'd need was the local HOA raising a complaint. Too bad we noticed them already.

Cerberus Squad broke apart. I approached the front door with Tag.

"You want to do the honors?" he asked, gesturing towards the door.

I'm not going to lie. I got a little giddy at that moment. In six months with Black Spear, I still hadn't gotten the chance to kick in a door. It might be a Hollywood trope of having a big burly guy on the team, but they actually get it right. In our line of work, you need a big guy to do big guy things. Tag was our resident big guy, but I sat comfortably in second place.

"Turkey out," Vaun's voice chirped through our comm link.

A moment later I heard a window on the backside of the house shatter as the captain lobbed the incapacitating grenade inside. I heard the deep *poof* of the grenade expelling its contents, waited for it to go quiet, then smashed my size thirteen against the door. Truth be told, you don't necessarily need to be as big as me to successfully kick in a door. It's all about placement, right above the doorknob. Granted, having a few hundred pounds of muscle behind your boot helps, too.

The door splintered at the frame. Tag and I pushed in at the same time. On reflex we bellowed out for everyone to drop their weapons and remain on the ground, despite the fact Cain's grenade was supposed to make those commands unnecessary.

The Turkey's gas had already dissipated, but its effects took hold of the safe house's occupants. Tag and I stayed at the ready lest one of them possessed some innate tolerance. To the right of the safe house's entrance was a modest dining area with one of the Babysitter's bodyguards. He'd been helping himself to a bowl of cereal, which struck me as funny for some reason. Now he was paralyzed face-first in said bowl and on the verge of drowning in milk. I tried to keep my serious game-face on while I pulled his face out of the milk bowl.

"Where's the Babysitter?" I asked him.

The bodyguard's eyes flicked behind him in the kitchen's direction.

"Thank you." I patted the back of his head, then set it gently on the tabletop surface. No need for excessive violence. Not yet.

Beyond the kitchen was a hallway that led to the bedroom and the back door. Vaun and Kelly were already inside and met us halfway. "One bodyguard passed out in the bedroom," said Vaun. "No sign of the Babysitter."

"We had one by the kitchen. His cereal was waterboarding him. Looks like another win for Common Defense Industries."

"Blackbars, this is Bloodhound," Thomas radioed in. "Nobody got out this way. He's gotta be cooped up inside somewhere."

"Basement it is," Vaun said.

I took point. Since I didn't know the exact reach of the Turkey, I kept my weapon at the ready. But at the bottom of the stairs I found the Babysitter's third bodyguard, incapacitated. He lay with his neck awkwardly resting on the bottom step.

"Kage, pull him upstairs and put him with the others," Vaun ordered.

Billy scoffed, "Oh sure, make the smallest guy do the heavy lifting."

I passed the last bodyguard and entered the basement. Before me was a large red plush couch, our big fat target seated in the middle of it and gawking at me with a confused expression. The Babysitter's girth spilled out across the width of the couch. He wore a filthy tracksuit over a white T-shirt a size or two too small. More importantly, I saw him somehow reaching for a gun on the cushion next to him. I put a round two inches from his hand to tell him how bad an idea that was.

I glanced back at Vaun for a second. "Next time tell Cain to increase the area of effect those grenades have."

"Higher body mass index could've played a factor," said Tag as he came down the stairs.

Right around the time I was planning on hip-hip-hooraying at another successful mission, I started to notice what was behind the Babysitter. And in that soul-wrenching moment, I learned the reason for his moniker.

Kennels, the cheap type you wouldn't see in the home of anyone who actually gave a shit about their dog, lined the back of the room. There were four of them, and each one held two children. All were girls, all were malnourished, all were naked. A few shivered either from the cold of the basement or from whatever horrors they'd been subjected to, while the rest just stared dejectedly at nothing.

I'd been curious before as to why Rourke hadn't told us the backstory of the Babysitter's nickname. It dawned on me that he'd known all along and had wanted us to go in on this as levelheaded as possible. Ever the pragmatist. Not gonna lie. If he'd told me the full truth, I wouldn't have relied on tranquilizers to take care of the guys upstairs.

The Babysitter's eyes frantically darted behind him, undoubtedly realizing how dead to rights we had him. He was absolutely frozen at what was going to happen to him. It was as if he'd magically been affected by the Turkey after all. Then his eyes glanced in a different direction. To his left.

Ever so slowly, I turned to my right. I didn't want to. Lord help me, I wish I could've gone the rest of my life without looking in that direction. But I looked anyway.

Pictures. Dozens of them. They filled the wall with their wrongness. Each one was of the Babysitter with a different child. A picture says a thousand words and right now my ears heard a choir of suffering. A million filthy things that should never be but were.

I squeezed my eyes shut, eager to rid my mind of those images. Then, I turned back towards the couch and its occupant. The Babysitter was in a complete sweat now. The handgun on the cushion next to him must have felt a mile out of reach. I approached him and pulled it away.

Our resident big guy never says much, but in this moment Tag was especially quiet. Nice-guy Kelly had to take off his baseball cap as a form of silent anguish. Words like "wrong" and "abuse" just didn't do this basement justice. I had to remind myself that I stood among some of the deadliest and most experienced operators in the United States, but some types of sin you just don't build up a tolerance to.

Tag and Kelly gently opened the kennel doors and did their best to usher the girls upstairs. Hopefully to find some clothes, hopefully to try and convince them that the world wasn't complete shit. Thomas retreated back upstairs with them to a place that wasn't as tainted. That left me alone in the basement with Vaun and the Babysitter.

"Permission to get my hands dirty, sir?" I asked while I set my submachinegun aside on the table next to me. I rolled my shoulders in little circles to warm them up, eager to do some hurting whether the captain cleared me or not.

"Just don't kill him too quick," Vaun answered before casually taking a seat in one of the basement's lounge chairs.

I cracked my knuckles while stepping closer to the Babysitter. I was grateful that the son of a bitch hadn't been numbed by Vaun's knockout gas. *Now* it was time for excessive violence. And I really wanted him to feel it.

CHAPTER 23

The uptown penthouse they found themselves in belonged to Congressman Hank Cody. It served as Cody's home away from home while his family remained back in the great state of Idaho. Cody had a lovely wife and a very bright son who idolized his father. They really were a perfect little family.

The photographs Deimos had brought with him would completely shatter that.

"I will admit he is attractive, in a sort of innocent way, sir," Deimos said as he snatched the photos away from Cody's trembling hands and placed them back into a manila envelope. "Although I don't think your constituents would approve of such a relationship. Given that he has a few years before he is the legal age of consent, I imagine your constituents aren't the only ones who would disapprove. Let alone your family, sir."

Cody's face flushed a red so deep, it looked nearly purple. His shaking hands balled tightly into fists, but then Phobos stepped closer and adjusted his blazer coat. It was just enough to expose the karambit sheathed on his belt and discourage any rash action on Cody's part. Cody's hands relaxed. Deimos smiled and stood up from the table.

"I must say it's refreshing that you don't offer any excuses," Deimos stated as he walked into Cody's kitchen. The man had an exquisite selection of red wine on hand, and it would be a waste not to indulge himself. "It shows a clear understanding of things. So many people think they're safe because of the citizenship they were born with, or maybe because of the high position they've attained. They've forgotten what it means to be afraid. For some it's the money and protection it seemingly provides. But you're understanding the truth of it now, yes? No one is safe. There's plenty of things to be fearful of, sir."

Cody remained silent as Deimos examined the bottles of wine. Deimos settled for a bottle of Penfolds Grange, quite an expensive bottle indeed, and held it up so Cody could see it. "May I? I would enjoy a glass as we conclude our business."

"Help yourself."

"Why, thank you." Deimos worked the corkscrew as he continued to speak. "I assure you that if you complete your task as instructed, you will never have to see us again. Those photos will never surface, and your family will be none the wiser."

Cody's posture eased a little, which pleased Deimos. A tense man in Cody's position might be inclined to do something unwise.

Coercion for the Marstelli brothers didn't always require the edge of Phobos's knife. Intimidation was nothing more than pressure applied in the appropriate areas, and he was quite gifted at knowing exactly where those areas were. While Phobos knew where to cut a man to kill him with one stroke, Deimos knew precisely how to intimidate a man to kill his soul. Family was leverage. Livelihood was leverage. Reputation was leverage. They were all just little weights that Deimos could levy to tip the scales of coercion.

Deimos returned to the table with two glasses of wine. When he offered one to Cody, the congressman raised his eyes in surprise. Deimos gave a friendly laugh and set the glass in front of Cody. "It's your wine, after all. I do hate to drink alone, and my brother never has a drop."

Cody reluctantly lifted the glass and took a deep gulp of it. "That's it, then? Just this one-time thing? If you aim to hold that over me for my next two terms you might as well just kill me."

"Just this one thing," Deimos assured him. "One small vote on the House floor."

Cody took another gulp. "What the hell," he said with a shrug, "I was leaning that way, anyway."

"Very good, sir," Deimos said with a smile.

Phobos then stepped towards Deimos and handed him a small, hard plastic box. The same kind of box they'd presented to Marcus Boyd a few days earlier. Deimos took a sip of red wine before undoing the box's latches.

"There is one *last* thing," Deimos said slowly as he turned the box towards Cody and lifted its lid. "Just consider this our insurance policy."

Hank Cody looked at the box's contents and his body tensed once more. He then stared at the ceiling and sighed in resignation. "Just make it quick, will ya?" Cody said with a shake of his head.

Phobos reached into the box. Deimos held up the glass of wine as a toast to Cody.

"Hold still, you'll feel a slight pinch."

CHAPTER 24

I made a genuine effort to avoid breaking the Babysitter's face. We needed him to talk, and that wouldn't be too easy with a broken jaw. Instead, I focused on hitting his ribs, kidneys, and gut. Areas that really hurt. That said, I must admit I slipped up a few times.

I slipped up again and my clenched knuckles rocked into his cheekbone. The blow sent him toppling over the back of the couch where he landed flat on his back. He refused to get up; maybe he thought if he stayed there the abuse would end. There wasn't an ounce of fight in this man. Even without the Turkey's effects, he didn't put up any resistance.

"What do you want..." the Babysitter sputtered through cracked and bloody lips.

Neither Vaun nor I had said anything yet. The questioning part could wait.

With deliberate slowness I walked around the couch towards the Babysitter. I needed him to grasp that, despite how much I hated him, I wasn't acting out of anger. He needed to see me in control of the situation. I call it being professional. In my head, I channeled all the calmness that Vaun had demonstrated since I'd known him. That is, until Deimos and Phobos Marstelli murdered Hydra Squad.

When he noticed me towering over him, the Babysitter used one of the empty kennels to try and get to his feet. The sight of the kennels made me wish I had Cain's canines Dante or Virgil with us. There were few things people feared more than being torn apart by a fierce animal. Instead, the only animal the Babysitter would have to deal with was me.

"Just tell me what you want!" screamed the Babysitter.

I grabbed him by the shoulders to help him up to his feet.

The sick fuck weighed nearly three hundred pounds, but when I tightened my grip on his shoulders and threw him across the room, he didn't feel very heavy. He crashed face-first into a particularly disgusting framed photo before falling once more onto his backside. His face was crisscrossed with thin cuts, and a few fragments of glass stuck out of one trembling cheek.

"You're . . . not . . . cops!" he said. "I have drugs, money! What do you want? Guns? Girls?"

That last one was definitely the wrong thing to say. I told him as much by stomping the back of my heel down onto his elbow. His arm bent in an unnatural direction and the Babysitter's screams hit a higher pitch. Just as I was about to pull my boot back to kick him in the ribs again, I felt a hand on my shoulder.

Captain Vaun gently moved me aside and knelt next to the Babysitter's face. "Your guns. Desmond Toole gave you something, I want it. Show me or I leave you alone with Toxin here for a little longer."

To accentuate the captain's point, I twisted my heel on the Babysitter's fractured elbow. The man thrashed about for a moment before I removed my boot.

"Okay, okay!" he pleaded.

I retrieved my submachinegun from the coffee table while the Babysitter led Vaun towards a large safe hidden in a corner. I flipped my safety off just in case the Babysitter was trying something sneaky like pulling a gun from the safe.

But then the Babysitter opened the safe and stepped away. Clearly he understood that any rash action on his part would definitely lead to his death. I whistled as I saw the safe's contents.

There were several stacks of cash, bundles of cocaine, and two rifles alongside boxes of ammo. I pushed the Babysitter aside and removed one of the rifles. At first it simply resembled an AK-47 with synthetic stock and grips, but the barrel and upper receiver was encased in what looked like a long rectangular box.

"That's an SD-52," Vaun noted with a surprised squint as I slung my submachinegun over my shoulder and held the rifle in a two-handed grip. "Cheng Qiang's *Silent Dragon* line of assault rifles. The entire upper barrel assembly has an integrated suppressor that supposedly works better than any attachable suppressor. Captures all the gas created in the chamber and expels it out the front in a controlled manner. Lowers the recoil as well."

I hefted the SD-52 and gave an intrigued frown. "Quiet? How quiet?"

Vaun shrugged.

I pointed the weapon at the Babysitter's shin and squeezed the trigger. The only sound the weapon made was quiet *thup*, while the sharp crack of his tibia snapping was far louder.

"Hm, that is quiet."

"So smart, funny guy. Now you get to carry his big ass up those stairs."

"He can limp up them himself."

While the Babysitter flopped to the floor and howled with pain anew, Vaun and I continued to peruse the contents of his safe. If Vaun was familiar with the SD-52 already, then it couldn't possibly be the prototype Toole had provided to The Golden Moon. We were looking for the bleeding edge, not yesterday's news. I was right in the middle of tossing the stacks of bundled cash aside when I noticed a small, black, hard-plastic box. I tapped it and raised an eyebrow at Vaun. "Think this might be what we're looking for?"

Vaun carefully picked it up as if it would explode at the slightest touch. "I'd say so."

"Big things in little packages, eh? Something that small must pack some serious punch."

Vaun gave a gruff nod as he tucked the black box under his arm. "What's in this?" he barked at the Babysitter. Our interrogatee chose to bite his tongue. "I don't have time for this ..." Vaun sighed, "Toxin, break the rest of his arms and legs."

"Can do," I said with false glee.

"Wait, wait, wait!" the Babysitter pleaded. "I don't *know* what it is! Okay? He gave it to me and said 'have fun', but I didn't know what it was for. Two weeks later he did the same thing to another crew, and whatever he gave them must have backfired because it blew up and took out eight of their guys. I swear I don't know what it's for! I was scared to find out!"

Vaun gave me a look that asked whether I thought he was telling the truth. I nodded. Taking the risk, Vaun undid the latches and opened the small black box.

I hesitated to look at first. Maybe I was expecting an Ark of the Covenant face-melting thing to happen, or maybe I was just thinking Toole might've given the Babysitter a nicely packaged booby trap as a prank. But the lid opened safely, and we were all still alive with faces intact.

I looked inside, but what I saw only raised more questions.

CHAPTER 25

Cole West. 12:28 p.m.
Golden Moon Safe House
Long Beach, California

The Babysitter's box didn't hold a new prototype gun or advanced tech. Not that we could tell, at least. Inside, it contained a metallic vial and a small remote roughly the size of a garage door opener. There's something inherently ominous about a sealed cylinder with unknown contents. Granted, it's a thousand times more foreboding when said cylinder could trace its roots straight back to one of America's current worst traitors.

"Looks like a pipe bomb," Vaun muttered as he carefully handed it over to me. "Any ideas?"

My callsign, Toxin, is an inside joke but also harkens back to before I joined Black Spear. My specialty was chemical and biological weapons; this made me Cerberus Squad's unofficial WMD expert in the field. Cerberus tended to run afoul of some pretty terrible tech. Truth be told, there had been times that I wished I had Kelly's marksmanship specialty or Tag's knowledge of computers instead.

I studied the metal vial and worked it over in my hands. "I have just one or two thousand ideas on what could be inside this. It feels like there's liquid in there, did you feel that?" I hefted it up and down gently just to feel that slight sloshing feeling again. Whatever it was had a viscosity more akin to thick syrup than any other fluid. "But the weight's off. It's too heavy to be any chemical agent I know of. Any liquid medium you'd cultivate a virus in wouldn't be this heavy either. It's not much, but it's definitely noticeable."

Vaun cocked his head in the Babysitter's direction. "He said another crew had the same thing and it exploded."

"Right, so it might not be biological or chemical, but I'm going to keep my finger away from that remote for the time being." I returned the strange metal vial to Vaun, who resealed the box.

The Babysitter remained sprawled on the floor since I'd shot him but now seemed to know where things were headed. Vaun tapped his ear to open a channel back to Mason while I pointed the Babysitter towards the stairs with the SD-52. "I've got about twenty-nine rounds left to encourage you to start moving." He immediately shuffled as quickly as a nearly three-hundred-pound man with a gimp arm and shattered tibia could.

"Sledgehammer, this is Blackbars," Vaun said. "We've got the package. Egress to link-up, ETA thirty mikes."

"Clean it up and step it out, Blackbars. Sledgehammer out." Never one to mince words, that one.

The two of us headed for the stairs, which the Babysitter had made surprisingly remarkable progress at. He was already halfway up. Nothing like some 7.62 full metal jackets to convince you to move with a little extra speed.

Our squad was waiting upstairs for us. They'd zip-tied and gathered the Babysitter's three bodyguards in the living room. All of the gang members were still under the incapacitating effects of the Turkey. I reminded myself to thank Cain for another excellent weapon the next chance I got.

"We get it?" asked Billy, finishing the one thug's bowl of cereal from earlier. He obnoxiously slurped down another spoonful without bothering to look in our direction.

"Yep, no idea what it is, though," answered Vaun. "If we're lucky, Goode or Dr. Archer can figure out what the hell it is."

Kelly pursed his lips. "Great. Another breadcrumb." It took a lot for Kelly to be displeased.

We were trigger pullers at the end of the day, though, and an easy walk in the park mission like this was a gift, even if its success still left unanswered questions. We were more than happy to leave the detective work for more qualified individuals.

"Mount up. Load the Babysitter in the back and put a gun between his legs. Pull the trigger if he makes a move," Vaun ordered.

"What about them?" Tag asked, indicating the three zip-tied thugs. Vaun paused at the doorway just long enough to draw a line across his neck with his pointer finger.

The SD-52 *thup-thup-thupped* as three rounds popped into the backs of the thugs' heads. I didn't feel a damn thing but the recoil. Billy gave me a strange knowing look, like he would've done the same thing and was surprised I'd beat him to it.

Kelly's question of how many people I was willing to kill came to mind, and I guess I'd decided I wouldn't regret three more.

CHAPTER 26

Dana Phelps. 12:30 p.m.
Fog Site
San Francisco, California

Technically, she was AWOL. Technically, she didn't give a flying shit. She needed answers, and with Mr. Rourke and Kara Mason off in D.C. for the big funding approval vote, there was really no one left at Home Site to tell her she couldn't go.

Dana's own curiosity had taken hold. It was her job to determine cause of death, and currently there was still a huge question mark regarding that for both Desmond Toole and Mike Halsey. She didn't care that Rourke had directed CDI's top people to figure out how Singh's damn death ray thing worked. They could work the numbers and science, and Dana would work the medical angle. This was her job.

Already, she had a hunch. The clue had been found on Toole's ulna bone. It was such a small thing, she'd almost missed it. She'd had to look under a microscope just to confirm if it was even there. But it was.

A small metal fragment had been embedded in Toole's bone. After hours of looking over Congressman Halsey's bones, she'd found a similar one on his left femur. But the composition had been different. She didn't know what the fuck it meant, but she was going on about forty-eight hours without sleep now and was determined to find out.

That determination had brought her to Black Spear's San Francisco installation. The remains of Jun Byeong-Ho, the double agent who'd been sent to infiltrate the Cheng Qiang Arms Conglomerate's factory, was still in storage here. She needed a third specimen. Two instances could be a coincidence, three was confirmation.

She'd overstepped her jurisdiction about twelve hours ago, but at this point she was getting paranoid. Singh was a very dangerous man, and even in this secure building she found herself looking over her shoulder for killers hiding in the shadows.

If she was going to go straight to Rourke with what she'd put together, she needed to be sure. And for that she needed to inspect Byeong-Ho's bones. It was tediously slow work. Running solely on caffeine made her eyes swim, and staring through the microscope was giving her a headache.

Just as that headache started to graduate to full-on power drill to the skull levels, she saw it. Right along the C7 vertebrae. A faint flicker of metal.

Three fragments in three bodies. "Okay," she said aloud in the empty morgue basement, "definitely time to get the boss now."

She took a digital photo of the magnified bone and pocketed the camera. Her paranoia was hitting new heights. The last thing she thought before storming out of the basement was, the more she learned, the bigger the target on her back got.

CHAPTER 27

Our black Suburban pulled away from the unassuming safe house and the dark secrets in its basement. The rescued children had been picked up by a local Black Spear asset and were enroute to receive the help they would need. As much as I'd wished we could've driven them ourselves, counseling traumatized children was not among my skill set.

I sat in the middle row of seats, the Babysitter squeezed between me and Tag. Getting shoved between Cerberus Squad's largest members was hardly the worst punishment he would get, nor was it even close to what he deserved. Tag's favorite revolver had the honor of being pressed firmly into the Babysitter's crotch. The hammer was lowered; it would only take a flick of his finger to blast the Babysitter's nether regions to bloody chunks.

"Hey, Captain," Thomas called from the driver's seat. "Stupid question: are we expecting back-up?"

I looked over my shoulder and saw that two Land Rovers were approaching us from the rear. Both had blacked out windows, which left their occupants a mystery. Not needing an answer, Thomas gunned it and our vehicle took off.

"I really, *really* wanted today to be a by-the-books day," Billy groaned from the backseat.

Kelly nodded in agreement as he reached towards the trunk. He retrieved a FN SCAR Mk.17 with a large holographic hybrid scope. The scope offered a 15x magnification but could flip down for a simple red dot sight if needed. Kelly judged the distance then opted for the red dot sight.

"What's the call, Cap?" Kelly asked, steadying his rifle on the backrest.

Thomas hit a button from the driver's seat and the back windshield lowered. Bulletproof glass worked both ways after all.

"Sight up on the driver of the lead vehicle and standby," ordered Vaun.

"Rog," Kelly whispered quietly. His smile disappeared, the nice guy gone and the assassin awake. Kelly didn't need to be able to see the driver to know where his head would be.

Vaun tapped his earbud. "Sledgehammer, this is Blackbars. We've got two vics on our six, please advise."

"The boss might've left me in charge, but he failed to grant me the authority to scramble a drone strike in Long Beach suburbia," Mason answered drolly. "But if you really need me to hold your hand on this, I can come out there and handle this for you myself."

Vaun rolled his eyes. Everybody knew that she still missed field work. "Roger, Sledgehammer. We'll handle it."

"No license plates," noted Kelly with a frown. "Not usually a good sign."

"Stand fast," Vaun said as he adjusted his position in the front passenger seat.

"Just say the word, Cap. Course I would be kinda bummed if I punch his ticket and it turns out to be a dentist on his way back from the dealership."

"A dentist that bought *two* Land Rovers?" I asked sarcastically.

"A *very* good dentist."

Our captain seemed to mull things over for a moment, weighing the options and determining which one would be the most discreet. "Take the tire," he said.

Kelly popped off a round. The lead Land Rover's right front tire blew and went flat. The Land Rover swerved, its remaining tires squealed against the pavement, and then the tire reinflated itself. Just as quickly the Land Rover was back in control and gaining on us.

"Well, son of a bitch, that's a cool trick," Kelly said.

The first Land Rover accelerated and quickly closed the distance while the second one moved a lane over to pull up alongside us.

"Warning shot. High on the windshield," ordered Vaun.

Kelly fired again. Once more his aim was dead-on, but once more it was for naught. A slight mark on the Land Rover's blacked out windshield was the only sign Kelly had even shot it. They had bulletproof glass, too.

The vehicles pulled up onto our left and right sides. Thomas was driving like a madman and had thankfully gotten us out of the clustered suburbia. Our surroundings of white picket fences transitioned to industrial warehouses. We were well on our way to reaching the rendezvous point, but arriving with two enemy vehicles in tow wasn't a good idea.

Kelly pivoted around in his seat before aiming out the window.

"You really think they forgot to make the side windows bulletproof, too? Good luck breaking through that," Thomas scoffed.

Kelly just ejected his magazine and replaced it with another one from his vest. "Not breaking through," he murmured while lining up a shot. "Melting through."

He pulled the trigger and there was a streak of red that shot from the barrel. It hit the window, fragmented, and burned straight through to the other side. Cain's new Hades round scorched across the vehicle interior before it exploded out the other side mirror. Kelly tilted his aim down slightly and fired again, this time aiming for the right rear wheel.

The entire wheel, tire, and hubcap disappeared in a red flash of molten metal. The Land Rover trailed sparks as its weight lurched unevenly. Kelly, not satisfied that the enemy vehicle was still in motion, fired two more Hades rounds towards the front of the vehicle. They seared through the vehicle's armor and all its occupants.

This time the vehicle swerved away and reinflating tires would not save it. It hopped a curb, barreled into a lamppost, and slid for a good hundred feet before coming to a rest on its side.

"Pays to have the *best* tech," Kelly said, his signature toothy smile returning.

The second Land Rover veered away from us and decelerated. Evidently, they'd seen enough.

This was a lot of trouble over one fat child trafficker. Then again, The Golden Moon's power was supposed to be splintered, so it raised questions about who had sent the vehicles. All logic pointed in Singh's direction, but that was a red flag in and of itself. I didn't like the idea of one of America's most sought-after traitors being able to put together hit crews on home turf. Atharv Singh was a dangerously intelligent man with very powerful connections. I suppose I was kidding myself if I thought it would be hard for a man like that to find stateside shooters.

"I can still put a few rounds through the windshield on the second vic, Cap," Kelly said, then flipped up the scope on his hybrid sight.

I craned my neck around and looked out the back window. The second Land Rover was slowing to a stop, the distance between our vehicles rapidly gaining.

But then the passenger side door opened, and a man stepped out.

"Five mikes out to the rendezvous," Thomas said from the driver's seat.

The man pulled something from the vehicle and placed it into his shoulder.

"RPG! RPG!" screamed Kelly but we were in the middle of a street with no place to turn off to.

The man fired, then instantly disappeared behind a red flash as Kelly incinerated him with three rounds to the chest. Kelly emptied the magazine into the vehicle until it was nothing but a burning chassis.

But the rocket was already shooting across the street towards us. Black Spear's cars were all reinforced, but this was a goddamn missile after all.

I braced for impact, grit my teeth, and shot an angry look at the Babysitter to let him know that I hadn't forgotten whose fault this whole thing was. Just to make myself feel better, I clamped my hand onto his broken elbow and gave it an iron-tight squeeze right before the rocket hit.

Instead of a roaring boom and rocking explosion, the RPG made a strange *CLUNK* and embedded itself into the back of our car. Thomas's confused face looked back at me through the rearview mirror.

"Tracer?" Tag suggested with a frown.

"Get some distance between us. Kage, see if you can pry it off," Vaun commanded, icy calm as always.

Thomas pulled into a back alley in between two large warehouses and hit a button to lower the rear windshield for Billy. My nerves were on a hair-trigger as Billy climbed out the back of the Suburban to dislodge the rocket. All I could picture was him tapping a sensitive area by accident and the rocket going off, taking all of us with it. It took a moment before I remembered that I was still squeezing on the Babysitter's broken elbow. Oops.

"This thing's anchored in here," Billy called up from the back windshield. "Pull over. I'll knock it off in a jiffy."

Thomas glanced at Vaun first, who nodded his approval. Our Suburban slowed to a stop in the back alley, and everyone exited the vehicle. Tag roughly handled the Babysitter, hauling him out by his fractured wing then tossing him hard into a gutter.

"I'm finding less and less enthusiasm in keeping our friend here alive," I muttered.

Tag grunted in agreement. Whatever the Babysitter knew must be good, but at the moment I was having trouble thinking it was worth our efforts.

"What the hell is that thing?" Kelly asked as he handed a tire iron to Billy. The rocket hadn't just embedded itself into our ride. Three small hook-like anchors had opened from the sides of the rocket and clawed their way into our vehicle's reinforced metal. A red LED was blinking on its shell.

"No idea," Billy said as he pried the tire iron against one of the hook anchors and snapped it off. "I just hope that blinking red light means it's a tracker and not on a timer." Billy heaved again and a second anchor broke off, leaving the rocket dangling by its last anchor.

The anchors were dug in deep and weren't breaking easily. I was close enough to Billy to see the sweat building on his brow. I was close enough to see the reflected red glow from the blinking light suddenly turn green as the LED changed.

"Get back!" he yelled and dove away into a roll. There was a soft *PING* and a whoosh as the back of the Suburban disappeared in a massive ball of fire. It spread across the pavement but mostly stuck to our vehicle like napalm. The intense heat pushed me back. The Babysitter cowered deeper into the gutter nearby.

Tag groaned at this minor inconvenience and braved the flames to reach under the passenger side door for a fire extinguisher.

"Isn't napalm a war crime? I mean it seems like Singh just has no regard for any rules," I said sarcastically while dragging the Babysitter by his wounded leg away from the fire.

"Geneva Conventions, Geneva suggestions more like," said Billy.

Kelly snickered and Tag smiled as he approached the burning rear of the Suburban. Black Spear vehicles might come standard with hardened armor plating, but all the armor in the world wouldn't do you any good if napalm melted your tires.

Tag calmly pointed the fire extinguisher hose at the fire. Clearly, he was as eager to be back on the road as I was. He squeezed the handle and white suppressant foam shot out the nozzle.

And then the napalm moved.

It parted away from the spray of the extinguisher like it was alive. Thinking he might've just blasted the fire too hard, Tag backed away and tried again. Once more the inflamed napalm parted away from the spray.

"That's new . . ." he whispered.

Not knowing what else to do, I pulled the Babysitter away a little faster. And then the napalm slid off our vehicle. It puddled onto the ground like some burning, living thing. My comrades backpedaled as if at any moment it would leap up at them.

Instead, it came at me. The puddle shot in a fiery stream in my direction. The napalm was upon us. It rose up like a wave, crashing down onto both the Babysitter and me. I closed my eyes, not wanting to see my own immolation.

But when it crashed down, I felt nothing. I opened my eyes, watching the Babysitter writhe as that living fire fully engulfed him. I pulled my hand away from his ankle at the last second before it scorched my fingers.

I'm not sure which was worse, the screams or the smell. The Babysitter thrashed about on the ground, smacking his head against the concrete gutter twice in his panicked flailing. Seconds later the napalm pulled off his burned body and slipped down a drain next to the Babysitter. Its vanishing act reminded me of some magician's trick, complete with a puff of smoke. But the damage was already done. The Babysitter had second and third degree burns all over his body. Raw muscle tissue was exposed across his chest and limbs, in some areas charred bone peeked to the surface. What was left of his face was melted into a blackened mask. He managed one last weak gasp before his chest stopped moving.

Kelly ran up, three seconds too late, with a blanket to suffocate the flames. For a moment he just stood there, blanket in hand, and did a doubletake between the Babysitter's burned body and the drain that the napalm had disappeared into.

"Anyone else getting tired of not knowing what the hell's happening here?" I asked.

CHAPTER 28

As one of Common Defense Industries' top engineers, Arnold Davis understood the certainty of numbers and mathematics. There were immutable rules that came with them. They were absolute. His respect for them was why he'd risen high in CDI. Recently, he'd had the pleasure of developing the prototype for the CHAOS suit; even more recently he'd had the *displeasure* of working under Madison Archer for the deconstruction and recreation of Cheng Qiang's immolation technology.

This same respect for numbers was why Arnold had decided to finally head home and get some rest once they'd hit the forty-hour mark with no progress made. The mind could only run through so many calculations and propose so many theories before it began to run more sluggishly. At the moment, he felt beyond sluggish.

Arnold had barely taken two steps through the front door of his townhouse before his exhausted body finally gave out. He fell face-first onto his plush leather sofa and let its welcoming cushions take him in. All he needed was a little rest. Just a few hours, and then he could meet Madison back in the lab and go over the numbers again.

His cell phone vibrated in his pocket. Arnold took it out and flung it across the room. Whoever it was could wait. For God's sake, he just needed a few hours to decompress.

Unsolved problems usually had an annoying habit of keeping him from falling asleep. Today was no different. When Samuel Cain had personally assigned Arnold to designing CHAOS to one-up Cheng Qiang's *ShadowCrawler* tank, he'd had insomnia for a good three days just from trying to figure out the mechanics for the servos in its knees. It wasn't until Cain allowed him to see the *ShadowCrawler* prototype first-hand that Arnold found a solution. He'd slept like a baby that night.

But there was no prototype for Cheng Qiang's newest technology, which they planned to reverse engineer. No leaked schematics, no stolen photographs, nobody even knew what it *looked* like. Essentially, Madison and her entire detail were trying to figure out the science on a weapon purely from secondhand witnesses and its end results. It was like trying to reverse an equation based solely off the solution. There could be infinite possibilities. In order to create some sort of protection against this weapon, they first needed to understand how the weapon worked. So far, they'd struck out.

Arnold realized his mind would refuse to let him rest. With a defeated groan, he pulled himself to his feet and shuffled into the kitchen. He needed rest. If he couldn't rest, then he needed scotch.

He reached for the only bottle he had. Johnny Walker. Blue Label, too. Arnold was far from a scotch connoisseur, but he knew not to scoff at Blue Label. It was all he ever bought. Everyone working under Madison needed a way to relax. Dr. Holder, one of Arnold's fellow engineers, preferred the adrenaline rush his motorcycle gave him. Dr. Faires had a well-known cocaine habit that everyone turned a blind eye to. The assistants had their own array of vices. And Arnold had his scotch.

The bottle was even more full than he remembered, which was a welcome sight given the price it fetched. Normally he'd pour it into a nice glass and use the chilled whiskey stones he kept in the freezer. But today, he simply poured it into a coffee mug and tossed three ice cubes into it. At this point in life, he cared little what people thought about how he enjoyed his drink.

Before taking his first sip, he knocked his head against the refrigerator door a few times. The answer was right in front of his eyes like always. He just couldn't see it yet. It couldn't possibly be a satellite-based weapon, and the power source a "death ray" would require simply didn't exist yet. Not small enough that it wouldn't draw attention at least. Arnold had tried to tell Madison that the combustion weapon didn't work how they thought. If it did, it worked from science they didn't know yet. She'd shaken her head and insisted on the importance of figuring this out.

Madison Archer was a stubborn bitch. If not for her looks and CDI's generous pay scale, Arnold would have jumped ship a long time ago. Thankfully, she was as beautiful as the first day he'd met her, and CDI's paychecks always arrived on time. It was enough incentive to stay in this insomnia-inducing line of work.

He was the only one who could solve this mystery. To do that, he *needed* rest and peace of mind. Arnold did his best to shake thoughts of both Madison's legs and the unsolvable equations as he lifted the coffee mug. A workplace romance between them was about as believable as satellite-based laser rays. Her loss.

"And to think I could've worked for Tesla." He toasted himself and took a long drink from his mug. It burned as it went down, that nice little bite followed by warmth that reminded you this was the good stuff. Arnold smiled. He knew it was mostly psychological, but he already felt five shades better and more relaxed. Tomorrow. Tomorrow he would go back to work and would solve the riddle of this unknown weapon.

His throat burned a little more than usual, but he'd taken a large pull. Thinking more scotch would only numb the burn, Arnold frowned before taking another swig. It was blasphemy he knew, but he could afford to drink it without savoring every sip.

His throat burned worse, the sensation traveling down into his gut and radiating out like claws clutching at his insides.

The coffee mug fell from his hand as he doubled over from the rising pain. It shattered against the kitchen tile, that oh-so-expensive spirit splashing against his feet. He clutched at his stomach and throat. God, it burned . . .

Something was wrong. Was it even possible to get food poisoning from alcohol? He felt himself about to pass out, but he was still awake enough to dial three little numbers. Even if he blacked out before he could voice his problem, they could ping his GPS. He told himself he would be okay as he reached into his pocket to call 911.

Except his phone wasn't in his pocket. With growing panic, he remembered throwing it across the living room just a minute ago. The pain stretched from his stomach all the way through his limbs to his fingertips and toes. It was like glass running through his veins.

The last thought Arnold had before the pain finally overcame him was that his bottle of Blue Label had seemed fuller.

CHAPTER 29

Cole West. 2:50 p.m.
CDI Advanced Projects Facility
Monterey, California

Mason scrunched her nose. It was as if she could smell the horrible mixture of burnt hair and blistered human flesh through the webcam.

"He's not as burned as the others," she said. "The others were nothing but bones. Our friend here has more of a medium-rare look about him."

"It was a different weapon. Something new," Vaun explained. "Singh's developed some type of Smart Napalm. It moved like it had a mind of its own. Avoided us, moved straight for the Babysitter."

"Looks like Singh's tying up his loose ends," I added.

"Fantastic work, Captain. I knew we could count on you and your boys for something as simple as picking up a low-level gangster," Mason said.

Unfazed, Vaun only gave her a little half-smile and placed the little black box we'd retrieved onto the tabletop. "I didn't come back empty-handed, ma'am."

Mason zoomed in on the box while shooting Vaun an angry look. "Ma'am me again, Vaun. You'll be sharing a coffin with Korean Freddy Krueger there."

Seated under the display monitor's blind spot, Kelly grinned like a giddy child while Billy silently mouthed, "Oooh!"

"That Dr. Archer is one hell of a whip-cracker. She had her people going round the clock, finally gave a few of them some recovery time a few hours ago," said Mason. "You, big guy, go get one of Cain's PhD-types from downstairs and have him wrangle up the good doctor and the others. One of them needs to tell us what this is."

I did a double take because I couldn't tell if she was talking to me or Tag. Our acting supervisor only rolled her eyes. "I said big guy, not biggest guy." Tag's resting-asshole-face disappeared behind an uncharacteristic smile for a second. Just to rub it in he crossed his arms and flexed his already monstrous arms.

I rounded the corner and found a couple of vending machines. A guy was hunched over scooping a can of Coke from one of them. His lab coat marked him as just the type of person I was looking for.

I took some of the bass out of my voice and put on my softest I-Don't-Kill-People-For-A-Living smile. "Hey," I said as friendly as possible. It wasn't friendly enough because the guy nearly jumped out of his skin. He spun around and, in his panic, popped open the can of Coke, which promptly exploded in his face. As he dabbed the soda from his eyes with the back of his hand, he eyed the SD-52 over my shoulder. I'd honestly forgotten I was still carrying it.

"I swear I come in peace, dude," I said.

The man awkwardly picked up the now empty can, then tossed it into a nearby trash can. "There goes a dollar down the drain," he grumbled. "You commando guys have everybody on edge. Well, you and Dr. Archer."

"Sergeant West," I said, and bought the guy a new soda. I felt guilty that I'd spooked him.

"Thanks, I'm Tim. So, um . . . what do you need?" he asked as he warily accepted the offering. His meekness was off-putting. Not too long ago my life wasn't too different from his. Desk job. Risk adjacent more than it was on the frontline. In a word? Safe.

There it was, though. With a sniper's focus I lasered in on why Tim was rubbing me wrong. A piece of me was jealous. Operating with Black Spear had brought purpose to my life in a way I'd never thought possible, but every day I laced my boots up with the knowledge that my life expectancy was much shorter now.

Events had been transpiring at rapid-fire pace. I hadn't had time to sleep, let alone digest what was going on. Now, I couldn't stop my thoughts. One by one they blazed through my head, until a particularly devious one tickled the back of my mind. Just a whisper, but that faint sound possessed a deadly truth that I couldn't help but single out.

I didn't know if I wanted to stay with Black Spear much longer.

Fuck. That thought was a seed of pure poison, and I couldn't afford to water it right now. In typical Cole West fashion, I decided to do the healthy thing with any soul-dividing internal conflict and swallow it down deep. I'd chase it down with some tequila when I got a chance.

"Um . . . Sergeant?"

Tim's replacement soda shook in his trembling hand. I abandoned my distracted thoughts and flashed a genuine smile in his direction.

"You know if you tap the top of that it won't explode this time," I warned. "Anyway, I need you to get hold of Dr. Archer and all the other geniuses she's got on that project."

"She hasn't left this building in nearly three days, so she's *really* going to enjoy getting that call. And I'm not exactly high on her favorites list as it is. I could just give you her number if you want to call her."

"Tempting, but no. Call her up with the quickness, Doctor Tim. National security."

Being with Black Spear didn't allow for romantic entanglements. I could barely entertain the *opportunity* for said entanglements. Self-sacrifice for the greater good and all that.

Tim popped open his second can of soda, this time without the carbonated explosion, and stared up at the ceiling in defeat for a second. "You're really making my day suck here."

It occurred to me that I really *did* want to get Dr. Archer's phone number, and not for national security reasons, but I couldn't help but think that there had to be a more respectable way to obtain it. There'd be plenty of time to figure out how I'd do that if we could stop World War Three from kicking off.

By the time I returned to the conference room, the debrief was well underway. The stench from the Babysitter's corpse hit me anew. There was an acrid chemical-fire odor underlying the burnt hair, which I hadn't noticed before. I purposefully left the door open to air out the place a little.

"You're right about Singh tying up loose ends," Mason said as soon as I found a chair. "The other eight Golden Moon safehouses were all hit before authorities could make their busts. White Shield is filtering us updates now, but initial reports show the same thing across the board." Another monitor was linked to a live feed of local police reports and federal chatter provided by White Shield. "Everyone in those safehouses was already dead. Whoever Singh used were pros."

"Deimos and Phobos?" Vaun asked. The captain's calm tone belied his quiet anger.

"Doesn't look like it, not nearly as bloody as what happened to Major Wilcox's team. Single headshots, execution style. No sign of your 'Smart Napalm' yet."

"Fatboy must've known something special to get such special treatment," said Thomas.

"Maybe not something he knew, but something he had. So, what is this?" She pointed to the mysterious black box.

"West thinks it might be a biological agent," Vaun answered.

"Babysitter said another crew had one, and it blew up," I corrected. "So not biological, but an explosive of some sort. Whether blowing up was a malfunction, or if Des was just fucking with them, isn't too clear."

Mason mulled that over. "This is hardly a lead if we can't figure out what it does . . ." she muttered. "West, did you find Doctor Archer?"

As if on cue there was a weak knock on the door. Tim awkwardly peeked his head in.

"Ask him," I said, pointing in the door's direction.

Tim stood there for a moment, unsure of who exactly to look at. Cain and Rourke had done a very good job of maintaining the curtain between the Black Spear trigger-pullers and CDI's scientists. Finally, he decided that Mason's digital face looked the most important so she must be in charge.

"I, uh, called Dr. Archer like West asked," he said.

Mason gave him a blank stare.

"But . . . she didn't answer."

She pursed her lips.

Tim continued. The man looked ready to leap out of his skin. "I tried calling the chief engineer, Arnold Davis, but he didn't answer either. Neither did Dr. Holder, Dr. Faires or the three assistants I work with."

The death-stare our acting supervisor gave him had him quickly tripping over his own feet to go try again.

"What good is having brainy people on tap if they're never around when you need them," Mason lamented.

A thought came to mind. I reached across the table, swiped the monitor's keyboard and minimized Mason's face.

Her bewildered expression was no less intimidating on a small screen. "What the hell are you up to, Sergeant?"

"Playing a hunch," I said as I switched the White Shield feed from accessing Long Beach police reports to Monterey's. Sure enough, my hunch played out.

"God, I hate being right," I said, finding the names I was worried about.

Police had responded to a hit-and-run for a motorcyclist listed as Eric Holder; he'd been declared dead at the scene.

Another report was from the local hospital where the ER had failed to resuscitate a drug overdose. The victim's name: Martin Faires.

Thankfully, I didn't see Madison Archer's name among the various reports. "Singh isn't just tying up loose ends," I said. "He's cleaning out the competition as well."

CHAPTER 30

If experience had taught him anything, it was that you only survive the game by making allies with whoever you needed to. Enemies you put in the dirt; allies you inevitably made compromises with in the name of common interests. Rourke wasn't in the position to allow himself friends, but if anyone came close it would have to be Cain.

Which made this impasse they were at all the more difficult. This matter of Atharv Singh was straining what had been for years an amicable relationship between the two. For decades Cain had kept Rourke and his men well-armed so that they could be the very razor to the throats of America's enemies. Without Cain and Common Defense Industries, Black Spear would have undoubtedly been decommissioned long ago. Plenty had tried. From a particularly annoying CIA Deputy Director all the way up to the Oval Office, and yet Rourke and the Spear still stood.

Barring a complete and unprecedented shift of stances from the committee members, Rourke knew it was all but certain Cain would receive the funding approved for mass production of his advanced projects. But the entire purpose of the Black Spear initiative was to discreetly eliminate threats from the shadows. A massive surge of arms production would only escalate international tensions. On another level, it told Rourke that Cain wasn't holding out much faith that Black Spear could stamp out this mess before full-scale war was declared.

Rourke had long ago learned how to remove his personal feelings from the situation. In the end, though, he was only human and couldn't help but feel a twinge of resentment towards his old ally. Regardless of what Cain said, Singh was a blind spot for him and he was personally invested in this.

"You look like you just lost the war," a familiar voice scoffed behind Rourke, who turned to find Cain standing nearby. "Give me an hour, and I'll have won it for us." Cain wore a conservative three-piece suit and gray tie for the hearing. The briefcase he held in one hand undoubtedly contained enough reports and information to seal the deal.

"Sam, if you go through with this, you might just be guiding the direction the entire nation is forced to go down."

Cain's smile disappeared. "We have collusion between North Korean agents and organized crime within our borders. They've already forced us here. I'm just making sure we're best prepared for what comes next."

"You don't think we can stop this, do you?"

Cain paused for a moment, shifting his briefcase from one hand to the other. Then, he shook his head. "Okay, old friend. Say you do. Say you find Singh, the Marstellis, and anyone else on their payroll. Take 'em all out. Cripple the Cheng Qiang Arms Conglomerate, set North Korea's military back by a decade. A century, even. Then what? Do you really think there isn't another threat just waiting for its turn up to bat? We have to strike while the iron is hot. This is war, Darren. My projects can save *thousands* of American lives."

"And if this escalation sparks a war, you'll be putting millions at risk."

"They're already *at* risk!" Cain bellowed.

A few startled people nearby glanced in their direction, then quickly pretended to find something more interesting on their cell phones or by their feet.

Cain forced himself to regain his composure. "Our enemies are running full tilt whether I get the greenlight or not. Look at the advancements they've made through Singh alone. America's enemies aren't insurgents in caves or using box cutters on planes. We're up against near-peer adversaries. *Actual* nation states, and we've already lost the lead. If we fall too far behind in this race, then we'll lose the next war regardless of who it's with."

Rourke said nothing. The two men stared each other down, both acutely aware that the status quo of their relationship would be irrevocably altered in the coming hour. Finally, Cain broke the stare and released a long sigh. It sounded like defeat.

"If you still consider me a friend after this, I'll buy you a drink when I'm done."

"I don't have any friends, Sam."

"Keep telling yourself that," Cain said, extending his hand to Rourke.

Rourke waited just a second too long. Cain turned to step through the doors that would lead to the hearing room. He stopped, glancing over his shoulder. "You know, there is a chance it won't get approved?"

Rourke allowed himself a smirk. A snowball's chance in hell, but it was a chance nonetheless. All it would take was a majority of the committee to suddenly decide that defense spending was unpatriotic. Right.

As Rourke considered heading to his local go-to spot and getting a head start on the drink Cain would owe him, he felt a hand brush his elbow. Despite his age and long time out of the field, he was still an operator at heart. Three options popped into his head within a millisecond. His grip was still strong enough to break his aggressor's hand like dried sticks. Or he could apply a wrist lock and follow up with a quick jab to the throat. The third and simplest was to just draw the folding knife from his pocket and stick it into their heart.

But another millisecond later and all those plans of attack evaporated as the hand tugged at his elbow again, this time in a frightened manner akin to a child wanting its parent's attention.

"You're a long way from your office," Rourke said after he saw who it was.

"Can it, boss," Dana Phelps said sharply. "I've been feeling a bullseye on my back for a few days, and I'm running entirely on caffeine."

"Why is my San Diego medical examiner in Washington?"

Dana's eyes darted around as if at any moment the other people in the building would draw daggers and attack. Unconvinced at their seeming disinterest, Dana wrapped her arm around Rourke's elbow and pulled him around a corner to an empty area.

"Look, I think I found something somebody doesn't want me to find," she said in a hushed whisper.

"Not an uncommon occurrence. Get to the point, doctor."

"Most of the time other witnesses aren't bursting into flames!"

Rourke granted her that but refused to let it show on his face. Instead, he deepened his frown to show Dana just how thin his patience was running. "If you have something useful, then spill it. Look in the other room and you'll see Ms. Mason, hoping something exciting will happen, so if you're worried about one of Singh's stateside assets clipping you, rest assured we can keep you safe. Speak. Did you discover how Singh's directed-energy weapon works or not?"

Dana pursed her lips. "That's just it, boss." She looked over her shoulder before pulling a small evidence bag from her jacket pocket. "Singh's tech *isn't* a damn energy weapon or satellite cannon or any bullshit like that!" She handed the plastic bag to Rourke. He could barely see the tiny metal fragments glinting back at him. "I pulled these from their bones, boss. The scorch marks and those metal splinters indicate that those people burned from the *inside* out."

A quick flare of pain shot across Rourke's jawline. Anytime he came across unpleasant knowledge, his old wound tended to spike.

"What . . . do you mean?"

"It's hard to make out with your naked eye, but under a microscope those splinters have a certain shape. Mechanical. Boss, these were nanomachines. I've never seen anything like this."

"I have," Rourke whispered. In fact, he'd seen a demonstration of a similar nanite quite recently. The pain in his jaw radiated lightning through his skull. This was much worse than he'd thought. Singh had stolen CDI's *Microswarm*.

CHAPTER 31

The California sunset threatened to distract me as my truck careened down the road. The gods of traffic lights were generous tonight. So far, I'd only had to run two red lights. Time was not my ally at the moment, and I wasn't emotionally invested in obeying the rules of the road.

Only six of Common Defense Industries' local scientists were yet to be pronounced dead under questionable circumstances. Every second wasted was a second Singh's hit squads got to drop that number even further. In the interest of speed, Vaun divvied up the names and split us up to retrieve one of them. Cain had left the keys to the CDI garage, which thankfully held more than enough vehicles for the entire squad. As fate would have it, I was the one who would have to find the good Dr. Madison Archer.

White Shield was still tasked to support us, and it had only taken a quick phone call before one of Goode's people was pinging Madison's cell phone GPS to my car's navigation. As much as the guys on the squad wanted to razz me for my growing crush on her, my reason for driving like a bat out of hell was far simpler than attraction: she and the others were in danger. Right now, we were the only thing standing between them and a coffin. Oftentimes, we were killers. But right here and now, we had a golden opportunity to actually save people.

I ripped on the brake and screeched up to my destination. It was some hoity-toity restaurant/bar type. One look at the building told me that my current civilian attire would raise a few eyebrows. Lucky for me, I couldn't find a single fuck to give whether I was dressed to impress or not.

A valet driver in a vest tried to take my keys, but I flashed him a badge and gave him a look that said it was best not to bother asking questions. Anyone calling to verify the badge number would have their outgoing call redirected by White Shield and confirm that I was a senior detective of the Monterey P.D.

I'd barely made it two steps through the front door before the maître d's eyes tried to freeze me in place. The other male patrons were decked out in designer suits as if eating overpriced pasta required an eighty-dollar tie; my Lucky brand jeans and hoodie/leather jacket combo highlighted me worse than if I'd just walked in on fire.

As I pushed past the stuffy lobby, I glanced down at my cell phone. Madison's location was being relayed to it in real time within ten feet. Judging by the current feed she was at the bar. In the span of two seconds roughly forty different sinister possibilities began to fill my mind. A poisoned cocktail. Assassin bartender with an icepick. Given the way these missions had gone lately, at this point I honestly wouldn't be too surprised if the bad guys skipped all subtlety and sent another spider tank to blow up the entire building.

Except I found her at the back of the bar nursing a martini without a care in the world. She wore a red open-back cocktail dress that hugged her narrow waist and accented her body's curves in a way that her lab coat utterly failed to do. The dress's open back revealed a collection of Japanese-style floral tattoos that had previously been hidden. They stretched from her back and down her shoulder into a half-sleeve. A gorgeous woman with a high-paying weapons development position *and* she had tattoos? Yeah, I was in trouble.

It was a shame. She looked happy in this picturesque moment. Unbothered, even. And here I was, a living monkey wrench come to ruin it all. Then she looked over her shoulder and noticed me. I couldn't help but freeze in my tracks for a moment. It wasn't until she rolled her eyes that I found my legs moving again.

"I thought I'd find you with your nose in a book at home," I said and took an uninvited seat at the stool next to her. "Maybe hanging out with a cat or two."

"Scientists need to get laid too, Sergeant," she said without bothering to look in my direction.

"You really should've answered your phone, doctor."

"Can't a girl get a little privacy? I cut the rest of the team loose to let out a little steam, but don't worry. I told them it's a school night and to be back bright and early. We can't all be machines."

I tried to decipher if her last comment was a dig or not. She reached for her glass, but I gently stopped her. Without saying a word, I swiped a small strip of paper into her martini. I pulled it out and checked to see if the testing paper had changed pigment at all. No change, not poisoned.

I motioned for her to go ahead and down the rest of it. I figured my imminent night-ruining news would go down a little easier after one drink. Madison eyed the testing strip cautiously before hesitantly finishing the martini.

"Care to explain why you're crashing my evening? I was getting some nice glances before you scared everyone off."

I scanned the rest of the bar area. Most of the patrons had suddenly lost interest in the woman who was clearly the most attractive one present. As discreetly as possible, I did a once-over of the bartender and, satisfied that he didn't appear to have a murder-ready icepick on his person, turned my back to the bar.

"Someone's hitting your staff, doctor," I whispered. I gave Madison a hard look that left no room for questions about whether or not I was joking. "Three of your people are dead. My friends are rounding up the rest, but I need you to come with me."

Madison signaled the bartender to close out her tab. "First night off in weeks . . . terrorists are so inconsiderate," she muttered, trying to make light of the situation.

"Yeah, welcome to my life."

Madison handed a credit card to the bartender and warily eyed me. "You don't sound . . . comfortable with this."

"Surrounded by the Louis Vuitton and Armani crowd? Definitely not."

"No, I mean you don't sound nearly as comfortable saying dismissive things like 'welcome to my life' as you'd like to pretend."

I put on my best shit-eating grin. "Maybe I've been considering a career change? It'd be nice to not have to cancel a date for national security. Or have time for a date, for that matter."

"As tight-knit an outfit as Black Spear is, I would think anyone who dons the black did it for the long haul."

"Would you believe me if I said it was supposed to just be a summer gig that got out of hand?"

She smiled. It was reluctant, tight-lipped as all hell, but there nonetheless. Seeing that made me feel better about my own blossoming existential dilemma for a breath.

I opened my phone to send a text to Vaun, letting him know CDI's lead developer was still breathing. Right as I slid the phone back into my pocket, I noticed three patrons stepping closer to our side of the bar. Madison grabbed her coat from a hook on the far wall. They moved past me to come behind her. Apparently, despite my out of place attire, I looked like just another guy out for a drink.

They inched closer to Madison. I popped the catch off my hip holster. I drew my weapon and put two rounds into the floor by the closest man's foot.

"Evening." I waved Madison over to me. "I'm Doctor Archer's trigger-happy chaperone for the evening. Is there something I can help you boys with?"

The rest of the patrons of the bar were leaving in a panic, but the three men before me barely flinched. The one who'd come closest to Madison had the smile of a car salesman. He didn't seem the least bit concerned by the .45 caliber pistol pointed in his direction.

"It would've been better for you if you'd let us do this quiet," he said. He never broke his stare with Madison. It was so cold, like he was looking at scraps that needed to be run down a garbage disposal rather than a flesh and blood person.

"You boys don't look Korean, which tells me you're not with The Golden Moon. Tell me, how much is Singh paying you?"

Madison took a step behind me. I put my free hand on her wrist just in case she got jumpy and decided to do something unwise like sprint out of the building without me.

"Just walk away, we'll make it quick for her. I promise."

"Generous," I said.

I put a round between his eyes. Before his stunned partners could react, I put a double tap into both of their chests. I led Madison out of the building before they hit the floor.

"Jesus Christ, what do they want with me?!"

"You're smart, Doc. Do the math. Seems to me Singh thinks you and your team are a threat. He's fixing to eliminate Cain's golden geese."

The valet from earlier flinched when he saw me, but relaxed when he saw I was on my way out.

"Wait, did you take this from my office?" Madison asked as she climbed into the SUV.

"My car is down in San Diego so I had to borrow one of yours," I answered while opening the driver's side door. Two gunshots rang out behind us; the side-view mirror showed me that two of the gunmen were still alive.

"Vests!" Madison shouted with a point to their chest.

"Got it," I said and squeezed off another three rounds. The first shooter dropped as he took two bullets through his femoral and hip. The second shooter toppled backwards stiff as a board from a shot through the bridge of his nose. I climbed into the SUV, the engine came to life, and I pulled away from the curb.

Just because I'm a nice guy, I tossed a twenty-dollar bill out the window to the valet for damages.

"They're bound to have backup on standby," I said, "so why don't you tell me what type of James Bond crap you've got in this thing?"

"This was designed to safely transport VIPs, so no gadgets," Madison explained as we sped off back towards the CDI Advanced Projects Facility. "Armor plating reinforcing the undercarriage for IEDs and mines, tempered glass for all the windows. But we didn't get a chance to install the armor-plating to protect against aerial attacks on this one," she said.

"Not sure if that'll be needed."

"I think we're going to need it," she whispered while looking over her shoulder. I was confused for just a second, but then I checked the rearview mirror.

I was right about them having backup. In this instance, it took the form of a helicopter gunship. Lovely.

CHAPTER 32

The skin around his finger was rubbed raw, courtesy of how much he'd twisted his ring around. He'd only been faintly aware of doing it the entire flight. Singh's nerves were wound tighter than a garotte wire. Meanwhile, his man Min was completely at ease. It was possible that his bodyguard was entirely too simple to understand how high the stakes were. Maybe ignorance was truly bliss.

The hotel the Marstelli brothers decided to rendezvous in was one of the most expensive in the city. The Grand Luxury suite they rented ran over fifteen hundred a night. Usually, that hefty cost could buy discretion for any sordid activity from drugs to women. Why would their business garner any attention at all?

As the elevator carried them up to the fourteenth floor where the Marstellis waited, Singh turned to Min. "I trust you're prepared?"

Min gave a quick nod of his head then opened his jacket so that Singh could see the oversized Cheng Qiang revolver tucked in his pants. The monstrosity's eight-inch barrel was too long and its 325-grain magnum round far too powerful for any kind of practicality. But in Min's apish hands, the revolver looked more like a potato gun, so perhaps the simple giant could wield it better than others.

The elevator doors parted. Min stepped out first. Singh followed shortly behind, deep in his own thoughts. He steepled his hands, tapping his fingertips together in little claps while his mind went over all the elements present. The plan had been so meticulous. Billions of Cheng Qiang's money was on the line—as was Singh's own reliability—and he'd personally seen to emplacing numerous safeguards and redundancies.

Swing the Congressional vote by any means necessary. The Americans were monumentally stubborn and would never be beaten in a conventional kinetic war, but if you could limit their vast war machine? That would make all the difference. What good are all the fighter planes in the world if Congress couldn't afford their missiles? What use were America's tanks if there wasn't enough funding for their fuel?

That was Singh's design: defeat America through the almighty dollar. Starve their defense budget, which had never been satiated before, and relish the process as it withered.

Min used the keycard the concierge had provided to unlock the door to the suite. Singh's body man had to turn sideways just to fit through it. Deimos and Phobos were certainly deadly—that was the entire reason Singh had hired them to begin with. The mountainous Min was more than enough to handle them. Singh had once seen him cave another man's throat in with a single punch. It was supposed to be simple martial arts training. The Marstelli brothers would fare no better.

The accommodations were indeed marvelous, and more spacious than necessary. There was even a jacuzzi bubbling away inside. Judging from the type of clientele that frequented this suite, there wasn't enough bleach in this hemisphere to sanitize the jacuzzi to his standards.

"Good evening, sir," Deimos said cheerfully upon seeing Singh. The red-haired assassin drank wine from a glass. He gestured to a second glass already filled for Singh. They both knew that Singh never drank. It was the hollowest of gestures, one that they were both acutely aware of. "I hope your flight went well?"

Singh scanned the suite, looking for Phobos. The man's silence made him uncomfortable. More than once, Singh had finished entire conversations only to realize that Phobos was standing in a corner overhearing the entire thing. The upside of the man being both simple of mind and a mute was that Singh didn't have to be too concerned with what he heard.

"Where is your brother?"

"Oh, he stepped out for a moment, needed to stretch his legs. We've had a long day," Deimos answered politely.

"Yes . . ." Singh stepped behind the couch, looking at the large television mounted on the wall. "You both have been quite busy."

Deimos Marstelli finished his glass before carefully placing it on an end table with two fingers. "All has gone quite well, sir," Deimos reported. "We were able to provide the proper leverage to adequate swing voters to get the proper results."

Singh was silent. He was at a loss for words on how it had all turned out this way; and not knowing things was not in his nature. All he could do was pick up the remote control and turn on the TV, switching channels to the news, which was right in the middle of reporting on the very story that interested him.

". . . voted unanimous approval for the recently proposed defense spending bill. Several defense projects will be fast-tracked for production. This unprecedented bill is a huge step in Washington improving longstanding shortfalls in our nation's military left behind by previous administrations."

Singh's design, his entire overarching plan, was ruined by the ineptness of the Marstelli brothers.

"You had one job. One. Influence votes *away* from approval. How is this in any way the 'proper results'?" Singh, seething with rage, threw the remote at Deimos's smug face. It passed harmlessly over his shoulder and broke against the wall. "Do you have any idea what your failure means? I want you to explain this to me, Deimos. I'll even allow you to use *simple* words so you don't strain yourself. Explain how this has happened. Do you know what you have put at risk with your failure? Do you even realize the consequences? The enemies you have made for us?"

Deimos, ever the silver-tongue, was for once speechless. He looked at Singh with what had to be surprise. Or was it concern? Singh had never seen him so much as sweat, but perhaps he realized that his and Phobos's failure had just signed all of their death sentences.

Right then Singh changed his mind. He wouldn't let Min use that oversized revolver on Deimos. No, that would be far too quick. Phobos deserved a headshot before he could put that knife of his to work, but Deimos needed to be hurt. For too long he'd hid his snark behind thinly veiled incessant manners, both knowing how he truly felt. Yes, he needed to be hurt. Broken. Brought to heel and made to understand *why* Singh was to be respected. Then, and only then, would he die. Singh would even do it himself for once. He actually grew eager at the thought of sawing a knife through Deimos's neck. Especially cutting those vocal cords.

And then the red-haired man laughed. Deimos Marstelli laughed lightheartedly as if Singh had failed to get the punchline to some joke. "You, sir, are truly a source of amusement. I am genuinely going to miss our little interactions."

Singh had had enough. "Make him understand," he said over his shoulder to Min.

Deimos's smile disappeared. Singh replaced it with one of his own. He could work on damage control and ensuring his own survival after Min rearranged Deimos's smug little face. This was a long time coming.

Min didn't move.

Singh's smile slowly faded. The large man stared blankly straight ahead. Then, his head and shoulders slumped forward, revealing the second Marstelli brother behind him with his karambit knife embedded in the base of Min's skull. The giant fell forward. Nothing but dead weight crashing to the floor.

Phobos retrieved his curved blade and silently stalked towards Singh. No mystery at all to the man's murderous intent.

This wasn't supposed to happen. He'd thought of everything; his plan was supposed to be without fault. He'd thought of *everything*!

"Wait!" he pleaded. How had things fallen to such disaster? Nothing was supposed to be outside his control.

"Deimos, stop him!" Singh shouted, turning to the less blood-thirsty of the brothers. Phobos would not falter for a moment unless Deimos told him to. "Have you both lost what little mind you had?"

And then everything was replaced with white hot pain. His very vision was erased behind a blank canvas as the knife slid effortlessly into his back. A gloved hand covered Singh's mouth, smothering the scream that couldn't seem to escape his throat. Phobos shoved the full length of the curved blade into him, then wrenched it violently sideways. All feeling in his legs disappeared. He heard more than felt the pressurized spray of blood jetting out behind him.

Blood immediately soaked his trousers. Piss and shit filled his pants as his bowels emptied. His feet fumbled when he tried to back away from the two treacherous brothers. Words bubbled to his lips but refused to fully form. Finally, he fell backward and crashed into the roiling water of the jacuzzi.

The turbulent warm water instantly turned pink as it sucked down his dying body. The last thing Singh saw before bleeding out was both Marstelli brothers standing watch over his body.

"As smart as you are, you really didn't see this coming, did you?"

CHAPTER 33

There's a reason aerial superiority is a decisive factor in combat. It is the equivalent of shooting fish in a barrel. Shit, even Obi-Wan Kenobi understood that the high ground was key to victory. But this wasn't mere aerial superiority. This was complete air supremacy: Singh's gunship held uncontested control of the sky.

If Mason commandeered and scrambled DoD air assets to our location, our vehicle would still be blown to quintessential smithereens before friendly forces could reach us. Assuming Rourke had even granted her the authority to pull off that kind of power move.

All this had played through my head in the span of a heartbeat, which was also all the time it took for the helicopter to close the distance to our SUV. I floored it. Another advantage of being in the air? They didn't have to weave around other cars like I did.

"It's good to know that if they don't kill us your driving will," Madison scoffed.

I swerved around another slow-moving vehicle, missing it by mere inches. Madison maintained a death grip on the passenger side oh-shit handle.

"Not helping . . ." I grumbled. I ripped the steering wheel to the right, gave the brakes a light pump, and took a hard turn around a corner. The SUV skidded onto two wheels and threatened to roll over. I gunned it and pulled through. All I needed was a moment to lose them; the more turns and buildings I put between them and us, the better.

"We need a parking garage," I said, so tight-lipped that the words barely made it past my teeth.

"Why?"

"Can't shoot us from the sky if there's four stories of concrete between us."

The tires squealed as I whipped us around another turn. I spared a glance at the rear-view mirror but the enemy helicopter was still on us.

"Next block, take a right, then a left on Tyler."

I gave her a nod. The skin on my palms burned from white knuckling the steering wheel. At every second I expected to see the flash of a missile being fired and the orange streak as it shot across the night sky. Or maybe just the telltale red rain of tracer fire from a chain gun volley. Any of those would be a quick enough death. Fifty cal rounds would swiss cheese our truck—and us—in the blink of an eye; the blast from a missile would kill us before we would feel the heat. Quick. Painless.

But I was still on the clock, and Madison dying wasn't part of the job today. Keeping myself alive was preferable, too.

"They could've done it by now," I mused aloud as I turned onto Tyler Street.

They were more than close enough to get a target-lock. At this distance the heavy guns would still be accurate enough. Madison must have been thinking the same thing. Her curiosity had trumped her panic. She let go of the car door handle to turn around.

"What are they waiting for?" she asked. "Cheng Qiang's missile tech is on par with our own."

I slammed the pedal down so hard, I swear I nearly stomped a hole in the floor. The engine screamed as I willed it to go faster. The parking garage was in sight now, just two blocks away. All we needed was to get inside, secure a moment's respite and plenty of cover, then I could worry about reinforcements. Back-up would be more than a welcome sight at this point. Instead, I got something else.

An orange streak. The kind that usually follows right behind a missile.

I looked at Madison. Dying might not be part of the job, but in this line of work it happens all the same. But Madison was a civilian, so getting killed in the line of duty wasn't one of her regular job risks. Her eyes showed the horror of understanding, and she looked to me for some kind of comfort. She found very little.

"West . . . ?"

I leaned over in a futile effort to shield her body with my own as the missile hit our truck.

CHAPTER 34

Deimos & Phobos. 5:52 p.m.
Four Season Hotel
Los Angeles, California

He swirled the wine in his glass while staring at Atharv Singh's lifeless body floating in the water before him; the man's blood had tinted the waters a dull pink that reminded Deimos of a nice rosé. The bubbling jets billowed the corpse about like some aquatic *danse macabre*. If it wasn't for the lone wound in Singh's back, the weapons engineer would appear to just be having a nice soak.

Phobos had severed Singh's Adamkiewicz artery and cut straight through his spinal cord. The Adamkiewicz artery was located between the T-11 and T-12 vertebrae, not an easy place to deftly stick a blade. A lot of bone in the way. Unless, of course, you were Phobos Marstelli and quite experienced in placing your blade in that exact spot. Phobos dubbed that wound "The Quick Death"; once cut, death was certain. Femoral arteries could be tourniqueted, a slit carotid could be clamped down and your time extended. But a man could be on an operating table surrounded by dedicated surgeons and the Quick Death would still be a mortal wound. Phobos knew countless ways to end a man's life, but Deimos was well aware of his brother's favor for the Quick Death's certainty. It was almost a signature.

Ending their former employer and his bodyguard so quickly was a statement Deimos clearly understood: Phobos deemed neither as warriors worthy of actual combat. Despite Phobos's desire to kill Singh quickly, they were in no rush at all. His handiwork was silent as ever, and since they'd paid a week for this suite (and placed the "Do Not Disturb" placard on the door), it would be some time before anyone would come to inspect the room. By then the room would already have been sanitized and the bodies long gone.

Deimos lost himself in the view of those roiling pink waters. He finished the last of his wine without a thought. It pleasantly burned on its way down. That warmth filled his belly and radiated outwards ever so nicely. He savored the feeling. They'd crossed the point of no return in their machinations. From here on out, it would require laser focus to succeed. Thus, Deimos would reluctantly abstain from his wine until they crossed the finish line. When his empty glass *clinked* on an end table, he caught Phobos smirking on the other side of the room.

"We can't all be an impeccable monk above temptation like yourself, dear brother."

His twin scoffed, and then signed a snarky, "*Monks drink wine.*"

"Fair enough."

Behind him, Phobos finished the grisly task of cutting Min's body down to more manageable pieces. He severed all the man's limbs, cut those to two pieces each, and removed the head. After that he neatly wrapped all the pieces in butcher's paper and twine as if he'd just portioned out some choice steaks. Phobos had rolled up the sleeves of his black turtleneck in advance, yet not a single drop of blood had gotten anywhere but his latex gloves. Once he'd piled all the gory packages together, he removed his gloves, sheathed his still razor sharp karambit, and delicately dabbed the sweat from his shaved scalp with a silk handkerchief. Then he looked to Deimos and with both hands swept down and out as if clearing the air.

"*Done.*"

Though Phobos would never speak a word of it, and his face gave no clues to his mood, Deimos saw the truth behind his mask. Disappointment. Too often Phobos was not unlike a stallion eager to stretch its legs. There weren't many men that could give him a challenge in hand-to-hand, Deimos included. Even Singh's enormous body man had barely proved more than a nuisance to him.

Among the world's deadliest assassins, there were maybe a handful worthy of his skill. One was an infamous Yakuza headsman, *Mamushi*, who had disappeared entirely a couple of years ago. There was also the freelancer with a proclivity for obsidian; he'd been the Veleno crime family's go-to before the Marstelli brothers. Deimos tried not to read too much into the math of it, taking the two of them to replace one of him. Neither of those killers had so much as blipped on the radar in quite some time. In their line of work that meant they were either dead or rotting in a black site prison somewhere. Which, at the moment, made Phobos nigh uncontested at the top of the food chain. A champion, desperately in need of a title defense.

Deimos had just the salve for what pained his brother.

"Dear brother of mine," he said and pulled out his cell phone. "I'm sorry they were such . . . *unsatisfying* trifles." He unlocked the phone and pulled up a file he had just received. "However, this might just prove interesting for you."

He tossed the phone to his brother, who expertly caught it in one hand. The mute man's eyes scanned over the screen, scrolling down as he continued to read.

"According to our friend on the inside, this is the one valiantly leading the charge to stop us," Deimos said with amusement. "He particularly takes issue with your treatment of those nice fellows in the hotel. Apparently, he's got a bit of a vendetta for you. Word is, he's one of the deadliest there is."

Deimos watched his brother as he continued to read. He looked for the sign. And there it was: a little tic of his index finger against the handle of his sheathed knife. The slightest twitch at the corner of his scarred mouth. And then ever so subtly his eyebrows furrowed. It was the most excited Deimos had seen him in years.

Phobos silently mouthed the man's name, burning it to his memory: Vaun.

CHAPTER 35

Cole West. 5:55 p.m.
Downtown East Parking Garage
Monterey, California

We weren't dead. That realization struck me right as the entrance to the parking garage came up fast. Moving entirely on autopilot, my hands spun the steering wheel and our vehicle bucked as it flew over a speed bump at sixty miles per hour.

Madison was in a trance, looking like she'd had that *good ol' life flashing before her eyes* moment. Me, personally? I'd recently become sort of inoculated against that type of thing. Her eyes fluttered as she came back to reality, and then she looked to the back of the SUV.

"I knew Cheng Qiang was second-rate, but didn't think they were that bad," she said with a laugh, raising her chin to the missile that had stuck to our vehicle.

Nothing was funny about it to me. "It's not a dud, we need to get out. Now!"

I hit the brakes hard and was already out of my seat and on the other side of the car, opening Madison's door before she'd had time to unbuckle. She was still in shock, something that I had to remind myself to try to be patient with. Except keeping her alive was still more important than being patient. "Leaving. *Now.*"

I damn near pulled her arm out of the socket getting her out of the seat. My mind was too busy replaying images of the Babysitter's crispy remains after the Smart Napalm had gotten to him. I looked at the embedded missile. Its light was still blinking red Still time to get her a safe distance away.

The helicopter hovered just outside; I wasn't willing to step out from the safety of the parking garage to find out how itchy its pilot's trigger finger was. Instead, I took Madison by the hand, leading her further into the parking garage. Her heels clacked as she managed to keep pace with me. Three steps in, she paused to remove them.

"First night out in weeks . . ." she muttered and tossed the shoes aside before sprinting to catch up to me. "First time *wearing* them for that matter. Should I send you a bill for these?"

"You can add it to my tab along with the car, but hey on my paycheck it'll probably be a century or two before I can pay you back for either."

"You mean to tell me Rourke doesn't pay you lot handsomely? I figured the paycheck would have to be hefty to convince you to do what you do."

I was thinking of something quippy when the blinking LED on the missile turned green The napalm exploded outward in every direction just ten yards behind us. The flaming muck instantly collected into a puddle that flowed in our direction like some stream from hell. Patches of concrete were left blackened in its wake. Thankfully, concrete wasn't that flammable.

"Don't look back," I warned as I led her towards a door to the stairwell.

I needed to get as many barriers and levels between Madison and the Smart Napalm as possible. Also, there was still the helicopter outside. And at some point, it would be sweet if I could get just a moment to radio back to the squad.

We entered the stairwell with the napalm quite literally hot on our heels. I slammed the door shut behind Madison, who surprisingly wasn't even out of breath. "Never skip cardio day." She shrugged.

My smile was cut short when I saw that the burning napalm was slipping under the door seal. When Madison saw it, her eyes didn't go wide with surprise. Rather, they narrowed in apparent fascination.

"Maybe we'll get time to study it in a more controlled environment later," I said and pushed her up the steps. "Hope you got plenty of time on the StairMaster on cardio day."

She bounded up the stairs in her bare feet, taking them three steps at a time and using the handrail to swing herself around when she reached the top of a section. I was right behind her the entire time, only slowing to check our fiery pursuer's progress.

It was liquid with a mind of its own. With unreal speed it splashed to one wall, flowed upwards, and began to coil its way toward us. The stairwell below us had become an inferno; the noxious fumes of burning chemicals smothered us as black smoke filled the small, enclosed space. We were nearly to the top, but it would be a miracle if we didn't asphyxiate first.

"This way." I grunted and shouldered through a door that took us to the third story of the structure. I slammed it shut behind us but knew that the seal would only slow the Smart Napalm for a moment or two. Madison stood next to me, intently staring at the bottom of the door and ready to further examine the incendiary weapon.

Something about that struck me as odd. She should've been hysterical or running for her life. Here she was as if this was just another lecture at some DARPA conference.

The telltale whupping of helicopter rotors reminded me of the second threat just outside. It was on the other end of the structure from us but quickly circling around. I heard a *whoosh*, and then another two missiles struck the concrete floor. Their LED indicators were already flashing red. They detonated their fiery payload, and I pulled Madison with me in a mad dash for the opposite side stairwell.

Behind us the door to the first stairwell burned and finally gave out. The napalm slithered out, much slower than just moments ago. It dawned on me that whatever mobility this weapon worked off of couldn't possibly be limitless. There was also less of it; what had once been a wide flowing river of fire had been reduced to a much narrower trickling stream. It was burning itself out.

Unfortunately for us, the hit squad assigned to us had served up two fresh batches of it to pick up the slack. The two pools merged into one that crashed towards us like a tidal wave. It flowed past huge concrete support pillars, scorched through a few parked cars, and lit up all the refuse between us and it. There was just enough distance that I could afford to slow down to activate my earbud comm.

"Toxin to Cerberus, all points," I said, "I've got a real problem downtown. My quick pickup/drop-off ran into a few complications along the way."

"Boomerang here," Tag answered. "My guy's dead. Body looked two hours cold. I'm enroute to you now, two mikes out."

"Lab assistant Jordan Peters is deceased," Captain Vaun said. "Toxin, what's the VIP's status?"

I looked to Madison, who was hightailing it up the steps and quickly leaving me in the dust. That tight red dress of hers wasn't slowing her down one bit. "Doctor Archer is doing just fine for now, but they have an air on our ass and Smart Napalm on our heels."

"Roger, Toxin," I heard Kelly say. "Looks like you're the only one who didn't strike out yet. My guy was cooked like the Babysitter, I'll see if I can beat Boomerang to you."

"Not likely," grunted Tag.

Good. If they were this eager about being the first here, maybe there was a chance they'd get here before Madison and I were burnt to a crisp.

CHAPTER 36

If Billy had been around to make a crack about being stuck between a rock and a hard place, I would have clubbed him over the head with my gun. Back-up was a small comfort now that the Smart Napalm had entered the stairwell and cut off our escape. I had no way of knowing what other nasty goodies the helicopter kept on board, but an intel brief I'd recently sat through on the Cheng Qiang Arms Conglomerate's latest weapons didn't exactly have me feeling hopeful. A small part of me was thankful that it was just a helicopter and that Singh hadn't developed a Spider Tank that could fucking fly yet. Key word being "yet." Christ, what I wouldn't give for some wood to knock on right about now ...

I made my call and headed towards the top level of the garage with Madison in tow. I based my decision on the pretty sound logic that napalm isn't affected by bullets but men in helicopters are pretty fucking susceptible. All I'd need was one good shot.

We reached the door at the top. The chasing fire crawling up the stairwell had turned the small, enclosed space into an oven. My forehead beaded with sweat, and I cooked under my leather jacket. When I drew my sidearm, my sweaty palms threatened to fumble the weapon. Thankfully, the tacky texture of my .45's rubberized grip gripped my hand right back.

"Listen, I don't want to sound like a downer," I said to Madison as I turned the door handle and readied to shoulder through it to the roof, "but the odds *really* aren't in our favor tonight."

"You've kept me alive so far," she answered bluntly.

I frowned. "Fair enough. Let's try and keep that streak going, yeah?"

Somehow, she managed to give me a little half smile. It's the little bits of enthusiasm that can keep morale up when the situation is dire. I hoped her faith was well-founded.

I pushed through the door, my weapon up and my eyes looking down the sights. The dull black paint of the enemy helicopter was dead ahead. It encircled the parking structure but hadn't spotted us yet. Whoever was on board was no doubt juggling watching the garage's exits and covering the top level.

There wasn't a clean shot. Yet. At this angle a round would just glance off the side, which in turn would alert them to our location. I was looking to empty the magazine into the windshield and take out the pilot. I just needed the helicopter to turn a little bit in our direction.

Madison put her hand on my shoulder. I wasn't sure if it was to reassure me or herself, but it felt good all the same. Being alone in a fight is never a good feeling. Having someone at your back, even if they're just moral support, can do wonders for one's fighting spirit.

My breathing slowed as I led my weapon ahead of the helicopter's path. In that space of time, I became acutely aware of everything around me. The beads of sweat dripping down my neck. The heat of the inferno in the stairwell behind us gently licking at my calves. The weight of the trigger ever so gently resisting my finger. I could feel the tension springs stretching as I applied pressure ounce by ounce.

I told myself I had all the time in the world. My mind whispered to me that there was no need to rush that squeeze. The windshield would turn to me in due time. Just wait. Wait for that perfect opportunity to dump a few hollow points into the pilot's face. My breathing slowed. The barrel of my weapon bobbed with my breath up, then down . . . up . . . and down.

The helicopter turned to face us. I squeezed.

The .45 bucked back into my hands. I rode the kick and fired again and again, each time lining those sights dead-on to the pilot's face. The helicopter bore down on us. Still, I fired. Madison's gentle grip on my shoulder became a vise as the helicopter got closer.

And then my weapon's slide locked back on an empty chamber.

"Shit," I muttered and ejected the empty magazine, turning to pull the stairwell door open so I could reload behind some cover. But when I opened the door I was greeted by the burning napalm that had reached us from below. The sudden rush of oxygen flared it into a great fireball that shot out of the doorway. I pulled Madison out of the way at the last second and blocked her with my body, and the helicopter veered away from its gun-run as the fireball nearly hit it. The landing struts were tickled with flames that just as quickly extinguished when the helicopter banked around the back end of the garage.

"Goddamn bulletproof glass . . ." I slapped a fresh mag into my weapon, even though I knew it would do little good. Better to die giving it your all than die a coward with a saved round.

"You're on fire!" Madison hissed and slapped at my shoulder to put out the flames. I guess that fireball had been a little closer than I thought. The fire had already burned through my jacket, shirt sleeve, and onto my skin, and I hadn't even felt it yet. Adrenaline's a hell of a thing.

"This is my favorite goddamn jacket," I groaned.

Madison stared at me like I was crazy. But she probably drew a huge corporate salary and wasn't working off a measly military paycheck, so I didn't blame her for not understanding my annoyance. Leather ain't cheap, but Rourke would say my life is.

The helicopter pulled back up into view. Its side door slid open, and I stared down six rotary barrels of some type of next gen minigun. They spun with an electric whir, and I ran. The only safe haven now was under the helicopter, out of its line of fire. The napalm oozed out of the stairwell door, hungrily sliding across the garage floor after us.

The minigun fired, sounding like a swarm of hornets, and the concrete floor behind us chopped up around our feet. A few stray rounds hit the stream of chasing napalm, which kicked spats of the burning substance into the air.

We made it directly under the helicopter. I aimed straight up and fired four more rounds into the belly of the beast. At this point I was just hoping to get lucky enough to hit something really mechanically important. As it turned out, I wasn't that lucky tonight. Each and every round dinged against its armored underside; the bullets fragmented on impact and the shards ricocheted off with zero penetration.

I adjusted my aim, this time going for the tail rotor. With just three rounds left, I'd have to get really creative if my aim wasn't true. The helicopter tried to bank and turn, but we rolled and sidestepped to stay under it.

The helicopter finally steadied for a moment, which was all I needed to take my shot at the tail rotor. Sparks flew as my bullet struck true, but the rotor continued to spin, unfazed. I grit my teeth and fired again. More sparks, and still more spinning.

"Last round," I said to Madison. I went to my knee, eager for a little extra steadiness for that final bullet. My .45 rang out, the gunshot echoing off the concrete around us like a crescendo of our swan song.

And yet the helicopter's tail rotor held strong.

"Any other bright ideas?" Madison screamed.

The Smart Napalm flared again, the pilot wrenched the controls away from the momentary pyre. In that brief moment, the helicopter itself had dropped its elevation ever so slightly. Which gave me a really bad idea.

"How about a bit of a Hail Mary?" I said.

Before she could ask, I leapt at the open side-doors of the helicopter. The door gunner's face was masked behind a balaclava, but I could see his eyes go wide with surprise. He swiveled the minigun towards me, but I bashed its barrels aside and used it to haul myself aboard. I was playing entirely on instinct. Moving fast enough where I wasn't giving my mind time to ask useless questions like, *"Cole, what the fuck are you doing?"*

I wrestled with the door gunner while the pilot yelled something from the cockpit. It occurred to me that he was shouting in English. The helicopter lurched to the side and sent the gunner and me to the floor. I rolled atop him and pummeled his face with my fist. One of his hands wrenched an object from his vest and looked to the open door, readying to throw the object at Madison.

Grenade. It had to be.

My own hand clamped atop his own and kept the grenade stuck in his grip. I spared a second to take a look at it, and it didn't look anything at all like any grenade I'd seen before. It was perfectly round but pinpricked with tiny holes all over. There was a button which the gunner's thumb had already depressed. His thumb slipped off the button, but I still forced him to hold onto the strange ball. An electronic whine came from the object and began to rise in pitch.

A second later and small spikes jutted out from every tiny hole on the ball's surface. It looked like a sea urchin and was deeply embedded in the gunner's palm. He yowled in pain, and in that instant of observation my grip on his hand slacked.

The gunner thrashed away from me and frantically ripped the

sea-urchin grenade from his hand. The helicopter dipped as the pilot craned his neck around to look at what was going on. The change in level sent the grenade rolling across the floor and into the cockpit. Just as the electronic whine's pitch went to its highest point, the spikes jutting from the grenade snapped out a half-inch further, causing the ball to pop into the air. I realized I'd been counting in my head, and six seconds had passed since the gunner's thumb released the trigger button.

The high-pitched whine went dead silent, and the spike bomb burst in a smokeless explosive pulse. One-inch needles shredded the pilot. Smoke and sparks shot from the destroyed controls. The gunner put up a hand to block his face. His entire arm was pulped as the needles tore through it and pin-cushioned his face. I fell backwards, tumbling out of the helicopter's open doors. The gunner fell, screaming, with me.

The helicopter canted away from us, tearing its tail rotor off on the edge of the parking structure before plummeting to the city street. The hard concrete of the roof was just ten feet below us.

It was a hard landing but I counted my blessings, because the gunner was unlucky enough to have landed with his legs in the cooling pile of Smart Napalm. He only flailed for a second. Whether the needles through his skull had done him in or his lower half getting flambéed had done the trick was unclear.

The Smart Napalm had ceased flowing. I still kept my distance when I hauled the gunner's corpse by the collar out of it. His balaclava came off and revealed the face of a blond-haired, blue-eyed young man who would've looked right at home surfing Big Sur.

My detective hat had slipped on at some point, and I patted down his pockets. Wasn't too sure what I was looking for, some overt clues of a sort? While I didn't find a map clearly labeled "Evil Villain Secret Lair," I did find three more of the Sea-Urchins.

"At least you solve one mystery," I said, thinking back to the carnage of the Hydra Squad in Room 1308. I carefully stowed the three Sea-Urchins in my jacket pocket.

I turned around to find Madison staring at Smart Napalm that had gone still. Like cooling lava, it had finally slowed and solidified. But instead of a charred, blackened surface it was dull and flat, almost like a coat of primer paint.

What struck me was that parts of it here and there seemed to sparkle. Almost . . . metallic. The absolute weirdness of Singh's latest weapon grew and grew.

Madison studied it with great interest. The woman should've been at her wits' end or ecstatic at us beating the odds. Instead, she appeared downright intrigued. That's when I knew for sure.

"You know something," I said, grabbing her by the wrist.

Madison picked up on the difference of my grip from when I was leading her away from danger and how it was now. Hard. Not at all friendly.

"Tell me everything. Now."

She hesitated but only for a moment.

CHAPTER 37

The three men in the limousine represented a trinity of America's might. Michael Goode found the bad guys, Samuel Cain made the weapons, and Rourke took charge of using those weapons against said bad guys.

Goode had joined them outside of Capitol Hill when it became apparent that Dana Phelps was onto something. The missing piece of the puzzle she'd uncovered connected several of White Shield's dots but also raised much larger concerns. Common Defense Industries had a leak. *The* biggest provider for advanced defense projects was compromised.

For all of Cain's blustering about how they couldn't afford to lose ground in the international arms race with their enemies in Korea, this revelation had knocked him into sobering silence. Who knew how long he'd unknowingly been feeding Cheng Qiang the fruits of his own labor? The wizened old man stared out the tinted limousine windows, only half aware of Goode voicing his barely shrouded threats. Rourke let the little man continue to verbally beat down Cain. In all honesty, this was entirely on Cain's head.

"At this point we have to consider that all of your cybersecurity is compromised," declared Goode matter-of-factly. "And I can promise you this, Samuel. Heads will roll. If we don't locate the leak, someone's neck will still have to be on the chopping block. It certainly won't be mine."

Cain continued to stare dejectedly at the familiar passing landmarks. Each one was a staple of American heritage, and Rourke knew full well that Cain viewed every single one as a reminder of his failure. It's no easy thing to make a man feel like he's failed his entire country, and Rourke gauged that was precisely what was going through Cain's head at the moment.

Goode opened a ruggedized laptop. The one-of-a-kind computer allowed Goode remote access to White Shield's full database, which in turn granted him entry into quite literally every digital system in the country. When Goode saw that Cain was growing more withdrawn by the moment, he knew exactly which system to access. The Monterey police feed.

"Your own people are being executed as we speak," Goode said sharply and flipped the laptop around. The screen showed various police reports of recent deaths of CDI scientists. "The enemy has gotten the cookies from the cookie jar. Now, they're looking to take all the other bakers off the playing field. So, as sensitive as I am to how you're feeling now, we all need you to get back in this fight."

Cain pulled his inhaler from his inner jacket pocket and took a puff. "I'm in this fight, Michael . . . By God, I'm in it."

Rourke glanced to the far side of the limousine where Kara Mason sat. His assistant looked calm as glass on the surface, but Rourke could see the butt of her hand resting on her jacket at the hip. Right where her compact .45 was holstered. Even she felt nervous, which as a rule she never let happen. Next to her sat Dana Phelps, the perpetually sarcastic medical examiner who was completely out of her element in the field. While you had to notice Mason's hand readied on her gun to see she was worried, just one look at Dana's sweat-drenched blouse and erratic twitching told you that she was two seconds from having another panic attack.

White Shield's director shifted uncomfortably in his seat. As a man who never got his hands dirty, he was completely dependent on others' capability for direct violence. When those people grew nervous, then his own livelihood was less than guaranteed.

"Okay, Sam," muttered Rourke, finally fed up with the tense atmosphere permeating the limousine interior, "nobody knows your people like you. Only a handful of people could have had the access needed to steal your designs. Tell us who and we can keep that damned mustache of yours off the executioner's block."

Cain straightened as if a realization had run through him like lightning. "Rourke, there's only one person I trusted enough to—"

The window behind Samuel Cain rattled as a string of bullets struck it. The limousine's bulletproof windows held up, but Cain still huddled his head between his legs. A Land Rover pulled up alongside them with both side windows rolled down. Short-barreled sub-machineguns poked out and fired once more. Glass pockmarked but refused to shatter. The deceptively strong limousine windows might keep them from becoming bullet-riddled corpses, but it also prevented them from firing back on their attackers. That fact seemed to get under Mason's skin.

"The name, Sam!" Rourke demanded.

Cain looked to his old friend with pure bewilderment in his eyes. "Get me to my plane in one piece, and I'll serve him up on a silver platter!"

Rourke's scowl deepened for a minute, then he cocked his head towards Mason. "You heard him. Get the lead out." She spoke over her shoulder to the driver, who seemed all too pleased to no longer observe the speed limit. The driver steered away from the Land Rover, and then slammed back into it.

With all its armor plating and chassis reinforcement, the smaller limousine was denser than a wrecking ball. The definitely-not-armored Land Rover's side crunched inward like an empty soda can upon impact. One of the shooters hadn't pulled back inside in time and now the submachinegun dangled from his horribly broken arm. Mason took the opportunity to risk opening her door, snapping off three rounds in an instant. At the same time a third man in the Land Rover fired back with a shotgun. All three of Mason's rounds bulls-eyed through the Land Rover's other window, and she was rewarded with the shooter's dying yowl. Her moment of revelry was cut short when she realized she had taken some of the shotgun spray to the gut.

"You're hit!" cried Dana and moved to assist her.

Mason roughly kicked her back to her seat with the point of her stiletto heel, then opened her jacket to reveal the *Fafnir Model 4* vest underneath. With a hard look on her face, she thumped her chest twice to dislodge the shotgun pellets from her vest.

"Good shooting, soldier," commended Cain and patted her back.

She dismissively shrugged it off with an annoyed look on her face. "Not nearly out of the woods yet." With her gun still in hand, she pointed out the front windshield. Dead ahead was a roadblock made of three sedans cutting off the road. Several ski mask-clad men with automatic weapons laid across the hood and trunk, aiming in the limousine's direction.

"Oh, fuck me," breathed Dana. "I really miss my morgue right now."

"We all might end up back there, anyway," joked Mason.

Dana's unamused frown only made Mason's smile widen.

"They don't look like they're moving out of our way," muttered Rourke. "Make them."

"You got it, sir," answered their driver. The monstrous upgraded engine roared as the limousine's speedometer needle passed eighty in less than a block.

The shooters fired as one. In less than a second, hundreds of rounds streaked across the street. They all glowed red. *Firecrackers,* thought Rourke. All of the passengers dropped as low to the floor as they could.

"Please tell me your limo has the same upgrade as your vests?" Rourke asked Cain as the incendiary rounds began to pelt the front of the vehicle.

"Armor plating in the panels did," whispered Cain from the floor. "Windshield didn't."

Hot glowing red bullets sizzled through the air above them as the barrage decimated the windows. Everyone squirmed, desperately trying to get as low as possible. When he looked to the driver's seat, Rourke's frown deepened so far the very corners of his mouth seemed to drop off his face.

Where once sat a man now there was only a dried husk. The firecrackers had burned straight through him, incinerating entire chunks of flesh and taking out the seat back with it. Pretty much all that was left was his lower half, which included the foot still pressed down on the gas pedal.

Rourke tucked his chin and braced himself. The limousine rammed into the blockade with the speed of a missile and sent the shooters' vehicles flying with equivalent explosive force. The few shooters who weren't roadkill turned around and tried to shoot out the back of the limo, but the same armor plating shielded the rear as well.

Mason hurled herself over the small divider. Now in the front, she unceremoniously heaved the dead driver's bottom half out the door and replaced him. Wind rustled through the windowless vehicle, threatening to blind Mason from the shear.

"Vic still on our six," she said after glancing over her shoulder. The Land Rover, though damaged and down two of its gunners, remained in pursuit.

Rourke looked at the other two members of their self-described trinity. Cain was in a state of shock, his eyes dulled over. Goode, on the other hand, frantically typed on that laptop of his. If he was trying to relay intel of their current situation to White Shield analysts, Rourke kind of doubted they would get here in time. The strange little man's devotion to the preservation of intelligence sometimes won out over any sense of self-preservation.

"Kara, your service weapon," Rourke ordered after adjusting his position in the back of the limo. She thumbed the safety back on and tossed it in the backseat without looking. Rourke deftly caught it in one hand, half-racked it to check for that glint of brass indicating a round in the chamber, and then rose up just enough to be able to take aim through the destroyed back window.

Mason swerved all over the empty road. The Land Rover's men hadn't been loaded with firecracker rounds, but now that the limo's windows were wide open just one lucky ricochet could take one of them out. Serpentine driving was the go-to method of avoiding said ricochet. None of that made Rourke's job of aiming any easier.

He held his hands in place. Compensated for the shift of their own vehicle and that tug of gravity that pulled him slightly to and fro. He didn't adjust his aim towards the enemy vehicle, instead he kept the pistol aimed out the back window and watched as the Land Rover pulled into his shot, then out, back in, then out. In his mind he was telling himself to be patient and wait for everything to be just right.

His trigger finger was more convincing, though.

BAM. BAM.

Rourke had been out of field work for a long time now, but he was pleased to see his accuracy and shot grouping was as expert as ever. The Land Rover maintained its speed but drifted out from behind them before coming to a dead stop into a concrete divider.

"Nice shooting, boss," complimented Mason.

When Rourke was sure no one could see it, he allowed himself a brief smile.

"Take the next left for the CDI Executive Hangar," directed Cain.

Nice of him to be back in a useful mood now that the present danger is gone, Rourke thought to himself.

The limo bucked as Mason steered over a speed bump without so much as tapping the brakes. The small private air strip and hangar was dark save for a few walking security sentries with flashlights. Seeing some of Cain's armed staff still walking around gave Rourke some solace that Cheng Qiang didn't have another ambush waiting for them.

Mason pulled right up to the hangar entrance. The limo had barely stopped before she was out and opening the door to pull Rourke out. The woman was tough as nails and no matter how rattled she got, she was absolutely devoted to her one job above all others: keeping Mr. Rourke alive.

"My pilot will be here any second," said Cain as he exited the bullet-riddled limousine.

Michael Goode stepped out a second later, having taken the extra time to finish sending up whatever sitrep he had started during the ambush. He adjusted his tie before closing his White Shield laptop. "The name, Samuel. Your own resources are considerable, but Cheng Qiang is gunning for you hard now. I can have you in an off-the-books safehouse within the hour, as soon as you provide the name to Rourke's hunters."

Samuel Cain nodded, all sense of his earlier panic having disappeared and now displaying his typical confidence. He opened his mouth to speak, but then paused upon seeing someone walking out of the hangar towards them. "Ah, there's my pilot now."

Goode rolled his eyes, annoyed that Cain was holding off on releasing the one bit of information they required. Rourke felt equally aggravated, that telltale tickle of pain waking up in his jaw, but he knew that Cain would hold off as long as he could to guarantee they did everything to keep him safe.

He turned around so he could greet Cain's man. The man walking up wasn't dressed in the typical pilot attire with the stereotypical captain's hat. He wore a nice black suit with a red tie, a tie so red it matched his own fiery hair. And it only took a second for Rourke to realize who they were looking at.

"Deimos Marstelli . . ." murmured Rourke.

Mason drew her weapon but stopped short as an electric buzz rang out through the air. She fell to the ground and convulsed as her entire body was electrocuted. She became a marionette on spastic strings. Her nerves jerked and contorted with a mind of their own. One of her hands managed to reach the source of her electrocution in disbelief. Her vest. The goddamn vest was boobytrapped.

Rourke frantically looked around, then moved to pick up Mason's pistol from the ground. Before he could draw a bead on Deimos, a sharp blow struck his back and sent him sprawling. *The brother*, Rourke thought, *Phobos*.

Mason's pistol fell from Rourke's hand and clattered to the cold pavement. When he tried to reach for the pistol, Phobos placed the edge of a knife against his throat to dissuade him. The gun was just inches from Rourke's fingertips. With disbelieving eyes, he was forced to watch as someone else picked it up.

"As I was trying to tell you before, old friend," Samuel Cain said, leveling the gun at Rourke's head. "The only person I trust that much is me."

PART 3
PROXY WAR

"Mundus vult decipi, ergo decipiatur."
(The world wants to be deceived, so let it be deceived.)
—Sebastian Franck

CHAPTER 38

Cole West. 7:45 p.m.
Downtown East Parking Garage
Monterey, California

I tried to gauge the emotions playing out across Madison's face. Equal parts outrage and hurt, a touch of guilt fighting to reach the surface. She knew something, and it was clawing to get out of her. After a moment the outrage won out and she ripped her hand free from my grasp.

"Just what the hell are you getting at, Cole?"

I crossed my arms and shrugged. "Look, I've been getting my ass kicked by Singh's next-level shit all week. Cain praised you as being the preeminent mind when it came to engineering *exactly* this type of stuff. So maybe I'm just a little suspicious when you don't even flinch at something *nobody* else has ever seen before. Maybe Singh isn't the only one of Cain's employees Cheng Qiang has drawn in."

Her eyes narrowed, full of scorn. What was that old incredibly accurate saying about hell's fury? "Fuck you for even thinking that," she spat. "I've devoted my entire damn life to making sure people like you can survive. Fuck. You. *Sergeant.*"

I guess we were off the first name basis. So much for my chance at having a second date. We stood there awkwardly, both of us unhappy with what the new status quo between us meant. It made the sudden appearance of Tag arriving in a commandeered pick-up all the more welcome.

"I told Kelly I'd get here first," he said proudly.

Madison and I climbed into the back. She suddenly stopped and shot me a look that dripped with betrayal. "Do you have to put a hood over my head and zip-tie me before I get in? It's a shame I spent time on my makeup. I'm sure it'll run once the waterboarding starts."

I tried to take another look at the situation from her perspective. Despite all the advances in military technology and next-generation intelligence systems, there was still something that trumped it all: a soldier's gut instinct. And right now, mine assured me Madison Archer wasn't one of the bad guys.

At the same time it was telling me she still knew more than she was letting on.

"Doc, I'm just a lowly sergeant," I said, "they don't pay me to think. But you and I both know you know something, so do me a favor and climb aboard so you can spill it already."

Her posture softened. She seemed unsure about what to think about my change of temperament. But then she nodded, a sign of acceptance, and hopped into the back seat. I pulled myself in right behind her, keen to leave the parking garage behind.

Tag glanced at us from the rear-view mirror. "Nice dress, ma'am."

"Eyes on the road, Corporal."

"Yes, ma'am. Ten and two."

Tag raised his eyebrows, locked his gaze straight ahead, and steered the truck towards the garage exit. As we turned the corner to leave the block, we passed the wreckage of the Cheng Qiang attack helicopter. Tag eyed it and pulled out his phone. "I'll reach out to the boss and get some of our guys on clean up for that. Don't need local PD asking why a North Korean helicopter crashed here."

I nodded in agreement, but in my head I was thinking about the helicopter's gunner. He was Caucasian. I was willing to bet the helicopter wasn't of foreign make, either.

I turned to Madison. "Please just tell me what you know."

Once we were safely away from the scene, she took a deep breath and finally spoke.

"It's called *Firestorm*," she said. "Some time ago I designed it as a cleaner alternative to LZ clearing defoliants like Agent Orange. Hundreds of nanoclusters pack a proprietary CDI incendiary payload. Drop the Firestorm into a forested area and smartly burn only what you need to in order to clear a landing spot for a helicopter. It was more precise and had none of the damaging residual effects that chemical defoliants would have."

A passing fire truck with a PD patrol car escort flew by us in the opposite direction, sirens blaring. Madison watched them go past, waiting for the flashing red and blue lights to fade before continuing. She seemed wary of wolves in sheep's clothing from any direction at this point.

"How many other people were on the project?" I asked.

She bit her lip, then wrung her hands like the very thing she was about to disclose dirtied her. "That's the thing," she said slowly. "The project never got past the drawing board. Only three of us knew about it. Myself, Samuel, and a senator who was on board to fast-track its approval in the defense budget. Senator Darcy Pelletier. But even with his connections to Mr. Rourke, Samuel was wary of developing anything similar to napalm due to its international notoriety. I drew up blueprints for it, but he scrapped the entire project. It wasn't until I proposed a corrosive payload, instead of incendiary, that he approved a prototype. That prototype became *Microswarm*. But Senator Pelletier and Samuel were the only other persons who knew of *Firestorm*."

"What are you saying?" I whispered. The pieces were coming together in ways I was not okay with. It was a dumb thing to ask because I knew exactly what she was saying.

"I'm saying I think my boss is trying to start a war," Madison said, her wringing hands now clenched into fists. "I'm saying he's playing both sides."

"Why?" Tag grunted sharply from the front seat.

Madison shrugged. "Million-dollar question. Maybe one of you can get him to answer after a little of that enhanced interrogation you types like."

"That's an idea I could get behind," I said with a crack of my knuckles. "I call first dibs on the waterboarding; you can have the second round if you want?"

Somehow that managed to make her smile a little. I think she was just grateful that I was willing to believe her.

"Cole," said Tag in a low voice. "No answer from Mason about a cleanup crew."

I pondered that. "I know I'm still somewhat new, but has she ever *not* answered a call?"

"Nope. Not unless we're being jammed."

"Should we be concerned?"

"Yup."

I felt prickles spike up in my stomach. It was a weird thing that tended to happen whenever I had a bad feeling about something. After so many times of it saving my skin, I stopped thinking of it as superstitious and started accepting that it was my own guardian angel kicking me in the gut. Just a little reminder to see the danger for what it was.

"Most of the team's already at CDI Advanced Projects," Tag said. "Think we should rendezvous somewhere else?"

"Hell, no!" I laughed. "A team of black-ops operators in a facility housing state-of-the-art weapons? It would be the worst place to try and fight us."

CHAPTER 39

"I want you to know that you still have my utmost respect," Samuel Cain said softly while pouring himself and Rourke a glass of cognac. Cain swirled the rich amber liquid around, drawing its aroma through his nostrils and smiling. "Part of me is still holding out hope that you'll see my way of thinking."

He offered the second glass to Rourke.

If not for Phobos's razor sharp karambit pressed to Rourke's neck, he would consider breaking Cain's face in with the glass right then. That, and the cognac Cain had selected was Louis XIII Black Pearl, which fetched at least thirty grand a cask. Treason aside, it would be a shame to let it go to waste.

"White Shield will pinpoint our location within the hour. A Black Spear team will track the plane and deal with you not long after that," Rourke said calmly, then begrudgingly took a small taste of the Black Pearl.

Damn, so that's what thirty thousand tastes like.

"I sold you everything you have, not necessarily everything *I* have. The plane is completely undetectable. It's a moving dead spot on White Shield's radars. As for *this* little fellow," Cain said, and held up the small cell phone-like device he'd taken from Rourke's jacket. It was a failsafe Plan C bomb; it was a bit of an upgrade from Cold War era suicide pills. "We'll just keep this and your thumbprint far away from each other. By the way, the signal from the subdermal tracer embedded in your left wrist is already being rerouted. To everyone else looking at it, you're on a non-stop flight to Kaesong, North Korea. Home of Cheng Qiang's headquarters."

More misdirect and smokescreens.

"So, you're working with them after all?"

"Working with them? I *am* them, Darren. It's a shame you don't speak Chinese, perhaps you would've caught on sooner otherwise. Goode does, don't you? What does Cheng Qiang mean?"

The other Marstelli, Deimos, had kept the muzzle of a Kahr 9mm pressed to the base of Goode's neck. When Goode didn't immediately speak up, he pressed a little harder.

"Depending on the dialect it can have several possible English equivalents," he finally answered, reciting like the living encyclopedia he was. "However, the most applicable would be 'Town Wall.'"

Cain's smile stretched his thick mustache across his face. "Precisely. And what else is a town wall if not a—"

"Common Defense," Goode and Rourke said as one.

Cain spread his arms out to either side, not unlike a magician taking a bow after revealing his greatest sleight of hand.

"I've held the controlling stake of the Arms Conglomerate since its inception."

"You've been playing both sides," spat Mason. Her interruption earned her a swift kick across the ribs from Phobos.

Cain turned his nose up at Mason. "Hardly," he scoffed. "I'm a patriot, Miss Mason. I may have been fueling North Korea's war machine, but at the same time I'm the reason their ICBM program encountered problems for *years*. You're welcome, by the way."

He sipped from his glass, simply waiting for his captives'

curiosity to get the better of them and for them to ask more questions. The man was so damn proud of himself.

"Was Atharv Singh your puppet this entire time?" Goode asked.

Rourke wasn't surprised that the one whose life revolved around intelligence was the one whose interest won out.

"More of an unwilling fall guy, he never knew Cheng Qiang was mine. Can you imagine the look on my face when I discovered one of my employees trying to sell my own secrets to me? I mean, you can't even write this stuff. I actually have to thank him, though," Cain declared with a bit of a frown. "It wasn't until I discovered Singh's plans to defect that I had my moment of clarity. Why simply sabotage North Korea's progress from within, when we can take care of them for good?"

Their collective disgusted silence dissatisfied Cain. He rose from his chair and walked over to a map of the globe attached to the wall. "How many enemies does America have, Darren?"

Rourke found it increasingly difficult to speak, the worse the pain in his jawline grew. "Many."

"Precisely. And you, more than anyone, know that we have a few enemies that John and Jane America don't even know exist. How many enemies do we have waiting in the wings, though? How many terrorist cells are actively hostile against us, but on another nation's sovereign soil that we can't afford to upset? We live in a constant Cold War state globally. Nothing but conflict by proxy. Threats are in every corner of the globe, yet we can't take any action. Not until they become an *actual* threat.

"The Middle East was home to terrorism for decades. Nobody gave a shit here until they crashed planes into our buildings. Boom! Suddenly we're boots on the ground. Iraq harbored genocidal tendencies for decades, and after the first Gulf War we just left them to it. Oh, they have Weapons of Mass Destruction? Looks like we're going to Gulf War round two. You see? We're so strong, we can't even fight our enemies until the threat becomes big enough. We ignore them. Appease them. Give them a thousand UN treaties to ignore."

Despite the agony it caused him to speak, Rourke couldn't restrain his tongue any longer. "This whole thing is you? The tensions escalating, arms production accelerating, the assassinations? All just to start a war? You don't even have a clue of just how fucking insane you sound."

The warmth left Cain's eyes. He finally saw that Rourke wasn't buying what he was selling. "Fine, then," he said, coldly. "We've been hard at work getting the tinder and kindling for the world just right. It's almost fitting that we'll use you to set this great pyre ablaze. I've already got a crew and a camera ready."

Rourke didn't flinch. He stared Cain down, rudely finished the rest of the Black Pearl without so much as tasting it, then pushed the empty glass towards Cain's side of the table. "Why don't you be a sport and top me off while I'm waiting."

From the corner of his eye Rourke saw Mason's smirk. A strong sense of humor had never been a quality Rourke was known for, but this was far from the first death an enemy promised him. In his experience, defiance was always the most infuriating response to his would-be killers. And a furious captor was a sloppy captor.

The corner of Cain's mustache twitched. Whether that was a tell of his building anger, or a quirk of finding Rourke's attitude amusing, was still unknown. He obliged Rourke with another pour from the expensive cask.

"Oh, don't worry about me. My coffers are filled to overflowing now that the funding bill has been pushed through," bragged Cain.

"I could care less about your money or your pricey hooch," groaned Rourke. "Hearing your bullshit just makes my jaw ache. The least you could do is offer Michael a drink."

Goode sat like a gargoyle in the corner. Rourke was certain this was the closest Goode had ever come in his career to real danger. Its mere presence had seemingly sucked all the fight from him. At the end of the day, he was the world's most knowledgeable analyst, but analysts don't fight on the frontline. If he had Rourke or Mason's mind for tactics, he would've known that not having eyes on him created the perfect opportunity. Except Goode had the mind of Goode, which meant that the only thing on his mind was analyzing and recording every detail of their situation. Intel gathering was ingrained into his very soul. It looked like it would be up to Rourke's side to get hands-on. When the time came for it.

Phobos moved the edge of his knife from Rourke's throat to the base of his skull as if he could sense the brewing plot in Rourke's head. It might be possible to aggravate Cain into slipping up but not this one. Phobos Marstelli had the emotional capacity of a lizard. If Rourke was going to make a move, it would preferably have to wait until Phobos's karambit tip wasn't ready at his brain stem.

Although, if he made Phobos kill him here and now, then Cain wouldn't be able to manipulate his death into more propaganda. The mere idea of deliberately going out in such a "fuck you" kind of way made Rourke smile. The sight of Rourke's defiant grin seemed to finally set Cain's anger to rage. He violently lashed out and threw Rourke's drink at the wall.

"What a waste . . ." Rourke muttered.

Cain stood and glared at him. "You know the funny thing about all this? You've spent your entire life fighting the secret wars, keeping the country safe. And now before you die, which by the way is one hundred percent happening in case we weren't clear, you are going to help me drag us into our next glorious conflict."

"Not the word I'd use."

"But it will be. Glorious. Despite our calls to higher morals the only thing—the *only* thing—that has ever galvanized the entire country is war. The next generation will sleep easier knowing its enemies overseas were truly brought to heel, and not by an embargo or sanction but by the edge of a sword. They will live in a time of prosperity not seen in a generation, brought on by an economy driven by singular purpose. We're saving America, Darren. The only difference between us is that only one of us is going to be there to see it."

Rourke's eyes fluttered as his chronic pain spiked again. He wholeheartedly agreed with Cain on one matter; one of them would save the country before the night's end. The other one wouldn't live to see the dawn.

CHAPTER 40

"Favorite goddamn jacket . . ." I muttered as I stared at the scorched sleeve. I drew my Mk-9 knife and cut along the shoulder seams of both sleeves to convert my favorite hooded leather jacket into my new favorite leather vest. I threw it back on, gingerly pulling it over the shoulder that'd been burned when I'd blocked Madison from the Smart Napalm. She'd found me a first aid kit when we got back to CDI Advanced Projects, hooking me up with some burn ointment and a bandage. It'd do for now.

Relaying to the rest of Cerberus Squad the truth about Cain's betrayal had been a straightforward matter. It's not every day that you find out the surrogate grandfather, who had been supplying you for years, is really a madman bent on inciting war. Accepting it was easy for me. I was still new and hadn't even known Samuel Cain that long. The others had known him for years. Their skin had been saved more times than they could count by his equipment. They took the news surprisingly well.

And then there was Vaun.

A beast had been brewing in him since we'd found Major Wilcox and Hydra Squad pin-cushioned by a spike grenade. Finding out that the mad dogs who'd murdered Vaun's mentor were really on Cain's leash had thrown gasoline onto a grease fire. Vaun's fury roiled just beneath the surface; more than once I thought he would snap and put his fist through the wall. Instead, he managed to keep the rage in check. Somehow his restraint seemed even more frightening. It was like watching a man hold back the fury of a hurricane.

"Man . . . I really liked the old man," Billy whispered, then enthusiastically slapped a fresh mag into his handgun. "Whelp, let's go bag us a grandpa!"

"Easier said than done," Tag grunted. He tapped a few keystrokes onto a laptop; a moment later it showed a map of the United States. "See anything missing?"

"Don't we usually have a really convenient blinking red dot or something showing us where we can go shoot bad guys?" Kelly asked with an arched eyebrow.

"Yup," Tag answered.

"I miss the little red dot . . ." Billy sighed.

"Usually, you have White Shield as support," Madison added. "When the most sophisticated satellite imaging, cell phone location pinging systems, and facial recognition software were at your disposal, you could find any target within seconds."

Vaun paced around the room, his patience growing thin. "Cain wrote himself a blind spot into all of the systems he sold us. He's a total ghost."

Intel drives all operations. Without actionable intel, even an outfit as experienced as ours would be no better than a gang off the streets. Well-armed, yes, but directionless.

Thomas inhaled sharply. "Show me a broken blade of grass or some scuffed dirt, and I can track anyone. But he literally has an entire planet to hide in right now."

It dawned on me that the former ICE Shadow Wolf was taking

it personally that we didn't even know a starting point to begin tracking Cain.

"I'm still confused," I said, never afraid to be the one to admit I was fuzzy on something. "What's the connection between the *Firestorm* prototype napalm and the random peeps spontaneously combusting?"

"They are one and the same," said Madison. She held up the cylinder we'd retrieved from the Babysitter's safehouse. "The same incendiary nanites injected straight into the bloodstream. Coursing around a person's circulatory system, programmed to stay dormant until ignited with the press of a button. They were basically turned into freely walking hostages. Cain could track the nanites' location from anywhere in the world. The trigger could be remote or time-based. He watches the nanites' GPS, waits until the CIA picks up that Cheng Qiang double-agent, then roast him on the helicopter. Or wait until a congressman is in broad daylight to incinerate him on his afternoon walk to lunch."

"They're all smoking guns. Clues to make the West afraid of the East, getting their hands on technology that puts ours to shame. Just a fucking excuse to get Congress to write him a blank check and ramp up his own production," Kelly added. "Cain just went full Lex Luthor."

My temples throbbed. A whole week of close calls was beginning to take its long overdue toll on my nerves. When things kicked off with spontaneous combustion and a mechanized giant spider, I should have known it was just going to go off the rails from there.

"If we're going to stop a war tonight, I'm going to need some more caffeine," I said and moved towards an espresso machine in the corner. The thing looked like it cost more than my salary and a headache started to form at the realization that this thing might be too complicated for me to figure out. Give me a good old Mr. Coffee any day.

"Sugar is in the left cabinet," a familiar voice laughed through an intercom speaker in the wall. Cain's voice.

I drew my sidearm and aimed at the speaker on reflex. My comrades readied their own and faced about, expecting danger from any angle at any moment.

"You can put that down, Sergeant. I'm not *in* the wall."

I turned about, seeing for the first time three other identical speakers on each of the walls. Cain's voice came from each one. It really gets under my skin when I have a full mag and no idea where to put the bullets.

"I'm glad you're all still comfortable with my accommodations," Cain's voice said.

"My compliments to management," I responded. "Why don't you tell us where you are so we can thank you in person?"

Cain's hearty chuckle echoed off the walls. "Tempting. But tell you what, I'll make you this one-time offer. Do nothing," the warmaker said. "Twenty-four hours. That's all it'll take. In just one day, we will be irreversibly gearing towards full mobilization against our enemy. China will be drawn in and we will crush them as well. It's the easiest thing in the world: do nothing. Go home, boys. Have a night on the town, Madison here can charge it to the company card."

Vaun scoffed, "Why the hell would we do that?"

His response was met with silence from Cain. Then, with a voice that dripped poisonous promise, Cain spoke.

"Because if you don't, I'll oust you all as traitors." The large display screen on the far wall lit up and began to display several lines of accounting. They were all alien to me. All but one. The only reason I recognized it was because it was the account and routing number to my personal checking account. Except its balance had about seven zeroes more than it should have.

"All of you have received some *very* sizable deposits from a

Chinese holding company on behalf of Cheng Qiang. They've been backdated going back six months; more than long enough to establish a history of collusion with a foreign entity. Everyone from Homeland Security to the FBI will be hunting you down come sunrise. Black Spear operators don't show up on any other federal database, so good luck convincing anyone you're anything other than a band of domestic terrorists."

More photos popped up on the monitor. This time of our activities at the Babysitter's safehouse. Somehow, Cain had even managed to secretly capture footage of me executing the last of the Babysitter's thugs in the kitchen. Another video clip showed us hauling the large pedophile out of the house and into the back of our vehicle. To anyone other than us, it would look like we'd shot up a house and kidnapped a random civilian.

"We might not be that convincing," said Vaun, unimpressed, "but Mr. Rourke's word is better than gold to Washington. One word from him and every single one of your assets will be frozen and seized; I think we'll be just fine."

"Oh, that's the other half of my offer. Do nothing, or I oust you all as traitors *and* I execute your boss."

Vaun's eyes narrowed. That prickly thing happened to my stomach right as the ground beneath my feet seemed to disappear. I looked at Tag.

He shook his head. "I never could get a line through to Mason or Mr. Rourke. Thought we were just getting jammed at the time."

"They're a bit tied up, but I assure you they're still in one piece at the moment," Cain warned. "But that could change if Phobos gets a little bored."

The thought of the Marstelli assassin butchering our comrades had my already uneasy stomach doing somersaults. I noticed the twitch of a muscle along Vaun's jawline and knew his thoughts were on the Hydra Squad massacre. Cain's threat filled the room like thick smoke; we all found ourselves at a loss for words as we choked on it. Any action we took would be a death sentence upon our allies. And our inaction would lead to the deaths of potential millions. Not for the first time I found myself grateful that I wasn't in charge of our ragtag little outfit. The collective quiet told me the rest of the squad felt a similar sentiment.

Vaun finally broke the silence. He looked down at the floor when he spoke. "We're assassins. Killers. Saboteurs," Vaun whispered. "Everything we do is illegal. Any damn day we could be locked away as war criminals. We stopped being afraid of prison the day we started this job." Vaun had been hesitant to look in our eyes. He could have just damned us all to a life perpetually on the run.

"They'll hunt you," Cain answered, his voice sounding far less sure than it had seconds before.

"They will. But they won't get to us before we get to you." Vaun's temper finally flared. He snapped off four shots, bulls-eyeing the four speakers on each of the walls.

Cain had been right about one thing. No turning back now.

I squared my jaw. So be it. Next to me, my teammates wore similar expressions. Resolved. Certain. Ready. Of the lot of us, Billy was the only one bearing a wicked smile.

Cain wanted to dissuade us, threaten us into silence. Instead, he'd just made Cerberus Squad more dangerous than ever by taking away the one thing that had held us back before: something to lose.

CHAPTER 41

Fools. Stubborn damn fools, the lot of them. They all clung to their ideals like an infant did a security blanket. For Rourke it was his misguided belief of patriotism, that hypocritical desire to protect America yet not willing to take the full measure against her enemies. For the entire cadre of Rourke's soldiers, it was their frustrating sense of supposed honor: a refusal to accept what they saw as a wrong, regardless of how righteous the reasons were. Christ! Even the poor dead Atharv had been convinced of the need for a global geniocracy and his place at the top of that intellectual ladder. He'd been blind to the chess pieces maneuvering against him. Every single one of them were prisoners chained to their beliefs.

He was no different than them. In the Bible, Cain was the first man to kill another. It was the original Cain who'd birthed murder to the world. Invented it. Without that first act of bloodshed, would David not have slain Goliath? Would Jesus not have died upon the cross? It was the death of Abel, an innocent, which had made it all happen.

That was what Cain believed in. The responsibility to usher in a new world, brimming with possibilities, and bear the burden of the hard choices it took to get there. Nobody would ever learn of the necessary sins he would forever live with, but that did nothing to lessen their weight. Speaking of which . . .

Cain used the on-board phone to dial Senator Pelletier.

"Is it wise to be calling right now?" she asked.

"CDI literally wrote the standard on what constitutes a 'secure line'," Cain answered. "This far exceeds it."

"Well then, if things are moving along on your end, I can all but guarantee my part will be easier," said the senator. "Honestly, you send that snowball downhill and my work will practically be done by default. Even as divided as politics are these days, it'd be career suicide to stand in the way of this coming storm. Regardless of which side of the aisle they are."

Cain nodded to himself. "Good, good. Rourke's headhunters might not be so keen to roll over so easily, by the way. Such is their wont."

"We talked about this. I'll have everyone from the U.S. Marshals to the Boy Scouts of America gunning for them come morning. All in all, Sam, this time next week they'll either be getting fitted for prison jumpsuits or sized for their coffins. Meanwhile, we'll be witnessing history whilst reaping the benefits of CDI's skyrocketing stock prices."

"It's not about the money, Darcy."

"Of course not. But it does make the treason more palatable, no?"

Her haughty laugh felt like worms under his skin. Cain hung up the phone and pondered the senator's words. There was a dry itch at the back of his throat that threatened to send him into a coughing fit. He took a puff from his inhaler before beckoning Deimos to him.

"What do you believe in, Deimos?"

For the first time in their long relationship, Deimos was at a loss for words.

"Sir?"

"Money. Infamy. The sense of power that comes with dominating another's life. Men of your profession must believe in something, so what is it that drives you?"

Rather than answer, Deimos walked to Cain's wet bar and helped himself to a generous glass of fine red wine.

"It's funny, sir. You know in all the time you had us doubling for Mr. Singh, he never once asked anything as personal as that? To be seen and used as mere tools is just . . . well, it's downright unsavory, sir. Not at all a pleasant sensation, if I'm being honest."

"What is it, Deimos? Let's be curt. Recognition? Appreciation?"

Deimos stifled a laugh that caused him to sputter a bit of his wine, "Nothing of the sort. I care not—nor does Phobos—for your war, or for Mr. Singh's new world order, or even for how much you've exceeded our retainer fee. Though I do appreciate it, just to be clear. Life became rather complicated when my dear brother and I ran afoul of British intelligence. I would never insult Phobos by implying we needed protection, but remaining under your employ does have the advantage of a certain level of . . . guaranteed survivability."

They both chewed on that for a moment. Cain sipped from his cognac, Deimos his wine.

"We're at the five-yard line here, Deimos," said Cain. "You might not believe in my mission, but I don't need you to. Because the things that drive us, however different, are both balanced upon a house of cards right now. You and I? Our interests are in singular alignment. If another card alongside our own were to have . . . different priorities? Different motivations?"

Deimos settled his empty wine glass on the table between them. His eyebrow arched in curiosity, and then he looked at Cain's cell phone and no doubt thought of the caller that had been on the other end. Cain's eyes narrowed to emotionless slits. No words were needed, all Cain did was give Deimos a nod.

"I do this not for the money, Deimos. Greed is dangerous. Anyone guided by that is likely to topple our cards."

A sly grin escaped Deimos as he pulled that leather notebook of his from his jacket. It dripped with secrets, and he opened it purposefully. "I might have a note or two that could help."

CHAPTER 42

Cole West. 8:50 p.m.
CDI Advanced Projects Facility
Monterey, California

Drumsticks rattled against a snare drum. The tempo sped up gradually, and then a voice was crying out asking the age-old question of what war is good for.

We were just about ready to find that answer. Billy eagerly played "War" by Edwin Starr over the PA system as we raided Cain's precious facility of anything and everything that might come in handy.

In a sense it was poetic that we'd be using CDI tech to take down its founder. We took weapons. We took prototype equipment. We took as much ammunition as we could cram into Charon. Kelly and Billy were both visibly disappointed that we couldn't find the giant CHAOS mech. I explained it wouldn't have fit in the helicopter anyway, but they didn't seem convinced. All in all, we were packing enough firepower to legitimately start a war. Unfortunately, we didn't know where we were going just yet.

"Two more cans of five-five-six, Captain," I said as I loaded the last of the bullets onto Charon.

Tag and Kelly sat up front as pilot and co-pilot. Vaun loaded magazines next to Thomas. Strangely, he didn't seem too concerned about not having a lead to follow yet. Maybe the menial repetitive task of pushing rounds into magazines gave him a sense of calm.

"West brought little bang-bangs, I brought big boom-booms," scoffed Billy. He shoved a small crate into the little space remaining within Charon. "Short-range missiles and plastique. Now we've really got a party."

"Low on space. We really need to bring her?" I asked Vaun, cocking my head in Madison's direction. She'd since switched from her dress into a pair of cargo pants, sneakers, and a white blouse.

"All the other lead scientists Cain was knocking off were done very discreetly," answered Vaun. He thumbed a final round into a magazine before sliding it into a pocket on his vest. "They sent three shooters. A helicopter. Incendiary nanites. You didn't stop to ask yourself why the special treatment for her?"

"Gee, I thought she was just a special lady deserving of some extra attention," I joked.

Madison rolled her eyes, but I still saw the little smile that escaped before she hid it.

"She knows something important," I said more seriously. She looked at me, eyebrows furrowing in confusion. "She might not know what it is, but clearly Cain thinks it's worth going the extra mile to make sure she's dead."

"Exactly. You're still in charge of keeping her alive, West."

"Roger."

I tried to give her a reassuring look but given the fact that by morning every federal agency would be hunting the seven of us down, I doubted it looked convincing. Vaun extended his arm towards me, handing over four filled magazines for my SD-52. I'd grown rather partial to the silenced weapon and, now that I knew the design was actually by an American, I didn't have as many qualms over its reliability.

"Is there something you're not telling me?" I asked the captain, who for some reason was still looking a few shades more relaxed than he had in the conference room earlier. "You seem pretty confident, considering we don't know where we're going."

"We know *exactly* where we're going," he said.

He turned around the tablet he held, and I looked at the screen. Satellite imaging. Thermal scans highlighting security patrols. The works. More importantly, and alarmingly, I recognized the photo of the target that was pinned in the corner of the screen. The good news was that, if this worked, we'd have our lead to Cain's cozy hidey-hole. If it didn't? Well, words like "treason" had already been thrown around enough this evening.

I nodded and closed Charon's door behind me.

"In for a penny, in for a pound."

CHAPTER 43

She hated company. Privacy was one of those privileges you gave up once you're forever in the public eye as an elected official. Still, something as simple as the solitude of one's own home shouldn't have been too bold a request. Unfortunately for Darcy, her personal security attaché was practically grafted onto her like a pair of conjoined twins.

There was Mark, whom Darcy had now paid twice to be tailored for new suits when his shoulders had become broader than an armoire. Mark was more bear than man, and Darcy was certain he indulged in performance-enhancing drugs, but his mere presence had deterred countless aggressions.

Next in the guardian hierarchy was Jameson, a former Delta operator Darcy had grudgingly taken on as a favor to the man's father. Said father happened to be one of Darcy's largest donors and had been eager to find a home for Jameson's skillset when he'd been ousted from the service due to some particularly colorful accusations from a seven-year-old Sudanese girl.

Mark and Jameson were the heavy hitters, but there were a handful of others whose names Darcy never bothered to learn. They did their job, rotated in and out, and remained faceless and indistinguishable in her memory.

"Mark, it's been a long day, I'm jet-lagged, and I'm going to sleep," Darcy said as she yawned.

She ascended the stairs, but rather than falling immediately into her bed, she instead drew the curtains and looked out at the water beyond the seaside cliffs just below her home. Her good for nothing husband, Andrew, was thankfully not home to ruin her small moment of Zen. He was most likely too busy fucking that little boy-toy of his down at the Ritz-Carlton and couldn't be bothered to remember she'd flown home today. Less he was around, the better.

Darcy couldn't help but wonder when would be a good time to cut her losses with him. It would be preferable to sever things before the impending CDI windfall. Divorces for politicians were especially messy, and Andrew would leech whatever he could from her. Of course, you don't have to pay alimony to a corpse. Too many decisions to think of on too few hours of sleep . . . but it was an enjoyable mental exercise, nonetheless.

She smiled at the enticing thought of being a very rich single woman once more. Or an even richer widow. She turned away from the window, failing to see the twelve black-garbed men approaching from the cliffs.

CHAPTER 44

Gremlin. Jackal. Zombie. Three teams of four and no names given. That's the way he liked to work. For this hit he was running as Gremlin-1, the nameless overall mission lead. Fine by him. In his opinion, you don't sign up to be a merc in the hopes of earning the accolades. Recognition was for the friggin' birds. You do it for a paycheck. Anonymity was kind of a requirement when you took stateside jobs, or any job that the news circuits would consider "distasteful."

Damn hypocritical sycophants, preaching from their soap-boxes to the masses all their bullshit moral posturing, while simultaneously bending over to take it up the ass for their corporate sponsors. Gremlin-1 would off every last one of them if only he could find somebody to pay him to do the job. Stateside work was a premium, and political targets pricier by an order of magnitude. He'd do the job if the check cleared. He considered that professionalism. And this job warranted quite a heavy paycheck, indeed.

"Jackal-1," said the team lead for the section going up the south side of the senator's lavish home grounds, "I've got eyes on one sentry on the balcony, stationary camera observing Zombie's approach. Ninety-eight-degree FOV."

Despite not revealing their names, Gremlin-1 was familiar with Jackal-1. He had an intricate tattoo of a lion on his shoulder that had its claw reaching across his neck to his face. Gremlin-1 remembered seeing it when they'd worked a hit in Turkey a few years back. He'd watched Jackal-1 crater a man's face with a steel collapsible baton. Now, as then, the shooter was operating as fluidly as the best seasoned vet. Professionals. Goddamn, Gremlin-1 loved working with them.

"This is Zombie-1," radioed the third team leader. "Making entry now."

Their employer had hooked them up with all the doodads. Normally, Gremlin-1 had no issue running low-key Russian surplus Kalashnikovs and over-the-counter body armor. That being said, he wasn't about to look a gift horse in the mouth, especially when said gift horse came in the form of state-of-the-art stealth suits and rifles so slick, they looked straight out of an Apple Store. Even the small piece Zombie-1 used to hack the electronic lock on Senator Pelletier's basement side door was like some kind of wizardry.

The stealth suit ran cool. It used some type of thermo-regulating mesh that hid their heat signature from any infrared scopes. A little overkill for a hit mission like this, but Gremlin-1 wasn't ignorant to the fact that this job doubled for field evaluation of the tech. Two birds, one stone.

A quick check of the wrist-mounted computer he wore showed a three-dimensional schematic of the house. Four dots of Zombie team's transmitters displayed them in real time as they moved through the basement.

"Gremlin-1 to Jackal, take the sentry."

There was no "roger" or "affirmative." Although Gremlin-1 did not hear the gunshot, he did hear the telltale sound of a body slumping over a balcony handrail. The senator's security detail was running light this evening. With the balcony man gone, only two others remained. As an afterthought, Gremlin-1 used his wrist-computer to access Senator Pelletier's car. On the off chance the teams dropped the ball and she slipped away, then she would find all the electronic systems uncooperative as hell.

"Gremlin-1, moving up," he said.

His team entered through the kitchen side door. A second bodyguard was face-down in the hallway, a barely noticeable entry wound at the base of his skull courtesy of Zombie team. Zombie-1 waited for him at the bottom of the stairs. Gremlin-1 gave Zombie-1 a fist bump as he took point up the steps. The bodyguards worked a two-on, one-off rotation, which meant the sole remaining man would be snoozing in the guest room outside the master bedroom.

Some mercs would be disappointed with this all going by the numbers. Twelve guys to off three bodyguards and a senator who should've been put out to pasture decades ago? Where was the challenge? Most of them wouldn't even have to pull a trigger. Gremlin-1 wasn't most mercs. He didn't have a fragile ego that needed to get his gun off just to prove his worth. When he eased the guest room door open to ghost the bodyguard, he instead signaled Gremlin-2 to take the shot.

Gremlin-2's weapon made three quiet puffs—no louder than a schoolkid hocking spitballs through a straw—and the sleeping man's slowly rising chest stilled. There was a pause as Gremlin-1 waited to see if the slight noise had stirred their actual target. Nothing. He smiled underneath his balaclava.

He and his three team members stepped into the master bedroom. He flicked a flashlight on and cast its blinding beam onto the senator.

"Wakey, wakey," he said. It wasn't a whisper.

The senator's eyes fluttered open. There was a stretch of a good ten seconds before the hamster wheel inside her head kicked into motion. Her panicked gaze darted around the room as she squinted against the bright light. Gremlin-1 sighed, comfortably sitting down on the bed near her feet.

"What is—"

"Shhh," he said. "Martyr or overdose?"

The glazed sleepy look in her eyes cleared. "What?"

"You have two options," Gremlin-1 said and procured a small remote device. "Option one: I use this cool gizmo on you and you burst into flames. I'm told it's an instantaneous combustion deal, but lady, just between you and me, I've watched a lot of people burn alive and even when it's fast it's not pretty."

The senator eyed the remote device. "I'm familiar with how Sam's weapon works."

"Gross, I don't like names. Anyway, on the other hand, we have option two. You swallow down a handful of those sleeping pills on the bed table there and go back to nighty-nighty time. I've taken the liberty of slipping a couple extra in there that'll carry an extra kick. Don't worry, don't worry. They won't show on a tox report. Arguably less painful than burning alive, but then the media's going to blast about how either you're a drug addict or careless with your meds."

"I doubt there will be any room in the news for me with everything about to happen tomorrow," Senator Pelletier said.

"The pills then? Cool. Think it's a better choice. And, just me personally, I could go without having that burnt hair and scorched flesh smell in my nostrils."

"I have money, I could pay you to—"

The collective laughter of the four shooters in the room cut her off. Gremlin-1 silenced them with a wave of his hand, then removed his balaclava to show her his face. She tried to avert her eyes.

"You know why I'm okay with you seeing me? Because there's a thousand percent certainty of me doing my job tonight. Now, you've had a good run, and you've ended up further along in this great old rat race than most, but it was always going to come to an end. That end just happens to be here, and it just happens to be with me. So . . . martyr or overdose?"

Before she could answer a voice squawked across his radio.

"Jackal-1 to Gremlin-1, we've got a problem out here."

Gremlin-1 hissed through his teeth, then gestured encouragingly to her and her sleeping pills before thumbing his radio. "You go ahead. I'll get back to you in a second. Jackal-1, I was just finishing up here. If you're bothering me about the husband coming home, I am quite sure you can handle one old man."

Senator Pelletier had become utterly detached. She refused to look at any of the men in her room as her shaking hand found its way to the pill bottle and unscrewed the top. Gremlin-1 flashed her a smile full of yellow teeth and gave her a thumbs up of approval.

"It's not the husband, we've got—"

Through the bedroom blinds Gremlin-1 saw a helicopter swoop in from the night sky. His balaclava slipped back down over his face before the helicopter finished touching down and taking off again.

Interesting . . .

He turned slowly to the despondent woman in the bed, his voice as cold and empty as a graveyard wind. "Be a good girl and take your medicine now."

He signaled his team downstairs. Gremlin-4 would stay with the senator to see the job done. They'd been briefed on the possibility of running into some opposition, but Gremlin-1 hadn't expected outright military aircraft.

Still, this would be enjoyable. Whoever they were didn't know who they were fucking with. This merc outfit was manned by the best. Stone-cold killers each and every one. Then you give them advanced weapon and armor prototypes? This wouldn't be shooting fish in a barrel. More like dropping a C4 block in a goldfish bowl.

Gremlin-1 readied his rifle and admired the overwhelmingly favorable odds. He posted at a window with one of his men, giddy at the idea of getting some serious field research for their employer. He was thinking about how intimidating the enemy would find them when their bullets just bounced off of Gremlin-1's men's armor, or how frantic they would be when incendiary bullets scorched right through their own. He thought of what a surprising delight this job was turning out to be.

He was still thinking that when the sniper round blew through his head and pelted his brain matter onto the far wall.

CHAPTER 45

Cole West. 10:20 p.m.
Half Moon Bay, California

"Bit of backsplash on that one," I said to Kelly.

He worked the bolt on the rifle and pursed his lips. "I'm not going to play the game of seeing if Cain's special bullets are strong enough to punch through Cain's special vests. They're all getting facelifts tonight."

"Fuckin' rah," I said as he sighted up on another target, exhaled, then blew him away.

Whatever they wore hid them from both the thermal binos I looked through and Kelly's scope. It was like looking at gray silhouettes standing in front of a gray backdrop. As it turns out, spotting those proverbial well-armed needles in this haystack was not beyond Kelly's skill. I felt entirely useless as his spotter and couldn't tell what I was looking at until the interior of their skulls exploded into the air.

"Toxin to Blackbars," I said into the radio. "Still have one warm body upstairs in the master bedroom."

"Keep them pinned," the captain answered. "Bloodhound, Boomerang, and I are moving in. We need her alive, Forty-Seven."

That we did. Madison had prepped some of Cain's Sandman/

Turkey Dinner sedative so we could get our questions answered. There hadn't been enough on site for a gas grenade like we'd used in the Babysitter's safe house, but she was able to load what we had into a small aerosol device the size of an inhaler.

It had been my idea. For the part the senator had played in Cain's plot, Vaun had promised to get very hands-on in a very Guantanamo Bay kind of way until she spilled her secrets. I'd seen his handiwork before and wasn't convinced it would work best in this situation. Instead, she'd get a quick puff and we'd extract her to have a little chat elsewhere. All that covert gadgetry had seemed like a good idea at the time before we knew Cain had already sent a crew of assassins. Now, it seemed unnecessarily discreet.

Back in the fight, the shooters inside were escaping Kelly's discerning eye. Wherever they were, they were being very still, which gave us both a hard time.

"Kage, give me a real dramatic flyby, would you?" I said into the radio.

"All this firepower onboard and the best I can do to help is be a big bright distracting light . . ." groaned Billy from Charon's cockpit. "Alright then. Look at the birdie, dipshits!"

Billy piloted the helicopter into a low sweep, nosediving down to a mere ten feet above the lawn before buzzing right by the front windows. A few spooked shooters took potshots at the banking aircraft. Kelly returned in kind with much more effective fire.

"Yippee-ki-yay, am I right?" laughed Billy.

I was just about to give Kelly an encouraging punch to the shoulder when a shadow separated itself from the bushes next to us. The shadow split into four separate men who wrenched Kelly's rifle from his hands and started laying into the both of us. The fuckers had flanked us. Whether there'd been a rear team outside that had circled around us, or if they'd slipped out of the house when we weren't looking, I didn't know. All I knew was that the taste of a rubber boot tip kicking into my mouth was a rather unwelcome feeling.

If they were smart, they would've just shot us both before we'd realized they were there. Maybe they didn't know where we were until they'd practically walked up on us. Either way, getting up close like this even in an ambush wasn't the smart play. It was two-on-one for both Kelly and me. They'd decided to kick and beat at us rather than draw a knife and slip it between our ribs.

Like I was about to do.

One of the masked men was winding up another kick when I rolled over like a log, drew my Mk-9 knife, and slashed it across his knee. The tendon separated with a wet squelching snap. The cut went deep, nearly severing the lower leg entirely but for a bit of tissue and tendon. He howled and fell forward, but my blade-tip was right there to catch him under his chin as he went down. The downward pull of his own body weight and gravity did all the work for me. There was a *pop* that I felt more than heard as the steel spiked up into his skull.

Kelly was too busy wrestling with two of his own assailants to lend a hand. Less than five seconds passed since they'd jumped us and I'd killed the first. I'd only just pulled my knife from his head when my second attacker realized what had happened. There was a *click-clack* as he swung out a collapsible baton.

For some reason or another—I'd never know and didn't care if I was being honest—he tore the facemask from his head to reveal a snarling face with a fierce tattoo of a lion tearing its claw up his cheek. Maybe he was so confident that he'd cave my skull in, he wasn't afraid of identifying himself. I don't know; all I know is that baton hurt like a sonuvabitch when I took a hit to my shoulder. My arm dropped dead and my knife with it, but my reflexes were fast enough to catch it with my other hand. Then I was on my feet, which was very bad for him.

"Gonna fuck you up, man," he threatened and swung the baton again. This time he went for the head. I backstepped, but rather than let my heel touch the deck I used my leg like a coiled spring to shoot back forward once his attack missed. I drove the point of my knife into his chest with all my momentum. We both tumbled to the ground. I wound up straddling him, but my knife hadn't gone in. Fucking armor. Kelly had said earlier that he wasn't taking chances with anything less than a headshot. I was kicking myself for not doing the same.

The mercenary whipped the baton across my face. I managed to get an arm up to take the brunt of it, but it knocked me off him all the same. He dove at me, and we wrestled with our weapons. I kept my knife up with its clip pointed towards his eye. He pressed the baton lengthwise across my throat, trying to crush my windpipe.

Somehow I willed my dead arm back to life. With numb fingers, I reached for my pocket, while pressing with all my might to keep him from killing me. I found the Sea-Urchin I was looking for as he heaved all of his body weight down on me again. I jammed a thumb into its button and readied to shove it into his mouth.

Instead, I caught a second hit from the baton that thumped into my chest so hard, the activated Sea-Urchin slipped from my hand and rolled along the ground. A third horizontal strike knocked my knife from my grip. Then he bore down on me, gritting his teeth as he lay the length of the baton across my windpipe again.

From behind us the Sea-Urchin's electronics whined as its six-second digital fuse counted down. One second passed, and I heard a click as the first-stage spikes jutted out. Five seconds until the second stage popped it into the air and detonated it.

Of course, it wouldn't matter if he crushed my larynx first. The pressure in my head felt like it was bound to pop like a blister. My eardrums felt like they were going to burst.

Ears . . .

As a last Hail Mary, I stuck a hand in my pocket and felt for the device. Cain's Screech dual emitter device. Cain had subjected us to level three as a demonstration. I didn't have time to fuck around and thumbed the dial on the remote up to ten. Our integrated comm headsets kept Kelly and me safe, but the effect was immediate on him. I could see the blood spurt from both of his ears as his eardrums ruptured like grapes. He arched backwards and straightened upwards to his knees. In that perfect moment where his inertia was moving backwards, I bucked him back and booted him in the chest with a double-footed donkey kick. He landed on the Sea-Urchin.

And then the electronic fuse hit six seconds.

The *pop* of the spikes extending out in an effort to launch itself into the air and finding only Mr. Baton's backside changed the pitch of his screams. An instant later the man was gone. In his place was a splash of minced red flesh and small missiles of razored steel hurtling outwards into the sky. As I held up a hand as a shield against the gore-shower, I turned to check on Kelly.

His two assailants were down but alive. They both writhed about with hands clenched to their ears. Blood leaked between their fingers. Kelly drew his sidearm and finished them both off with a clean shot to the head each.

From surprise attack to bloody finish, our little scuffle had lasted all of thirty seconds. That was still enough time for things to go wrong for our friends in the house. I fiddled with my comm piece to make sure the Screech hadn't ruined it, then opened a line to Vaun.

"Toxin to Blackbars, four tangos down over here." I rubbed my neck at the spot where the baton had nearly crushed my windpipe. "Moving to another location, then resuming overwatch."

"Negative," he answered. "We're done in here. Everyone's dead, come on down."

Kelly retrieved his sniper rifle from the deck, and we cut across Senator Pelletier's extensive front greenbelt. The side door was open.

We hurried inside and found the rest of our team waiting upstairs.

It was only when we got to the master bedroom that Vaun's words rang through my head again. *Everyone's* dead. By the time I walked through the doorway, I already knew what was waiting for us. Senator Pelletier lay on the bed. Her soul, and all of Cain's secrets it held, were long gone.

"Grab her phone," Vaun said to Tag. "Her computer. Her ereader. Her car's goddamned GPS. I don't care, find me something that points us in the right direction."

He pushed out of the room to the entryway downstairs. I followed him, hoping to maybe reel him back from losing his shit. We stood there silently for a second. The tension emanating off him had the very air feeling taut as a rubber band.

And then that rubber band snapped, and I utterly failed at keeping him from losing his shit. He whirled and kicked one of the mercenaries' corpses square in the nose. He put everything he had behind it. All that barely bottled rage, all the impotent frustration, and all the accumulated hurt of the week's betrayals were loaded like gunpowder into that kick. The steel-toe completely caved in the dead body's face and nasal cavity like something out of a grotesque Loony Toon.

If the image of my boss crushing in a man's head in such a barbaric way was unsettling, the sound of him *squelching* his boot out of it was worse.

"Boss, if you—"

"Don't," he said. "Just don't, West. I told you I was making an exception to my promise."

"That exception is going to get you killed," I said.

The Captain looked taken aback.

"You know why you've survived in this game as long as you have? By being that goddamn frustratingly robotic, stoic bastard the squad looks up to. Nobody's seen you so much as actually smile beyond that half-a-smile thing you sometimes do, or seen you get angry, but right now you're scaring a lot of us. Because this isn't you."

Vaun held his hands out as if feeling the weight of the entire room. "Look around, West. This isn't me because this isn't us. Yesterday it was us against rogue terrorist cells, tomorrow it'll be us against every law enforcement agency there is. Local, state, federal, random Paul Blart types on Segways. If I'm more on edge than my typical baseline, perhaps ask yourself if it's because there are mere hours left for the six of us to stop a catastrophic loss of life and an event that could change the course of history."

"Seven," I corrected. "There's seven of us. Madison is in this, too."

Vaun took a moment to wipe the tip of his boot clean on the carpet. "Well, we'll certainly need all the help we can get."

A buzzing from another one of the dead bodies had Vaun drawing his sidearm on reflex. The sound came from a corpse that was sans head, and I remembered it as the first merc Kelly had taken out. Vaun fished through the headless man's pocket and retrieved a cell phone. He arched an eyebrow at me before answering the call and hitting speakerphone.

The caller was blocked, but I recognized Cain's voice immediately.

"Is it done?"

"In a manner of speaking," said Vaun.

There was a deep sigh from the other end. "Oh Captain, my Captain … Whatever am I to do with you and your bunch? Or, better question, what am I to do with your boss? Was my threat against their lives too … lenient? That's it, I shouldn't let Phobos have all the fun. Matter of fact, Virgil and Dante are a little hungry. I think I'll carve a piece or two off one of your people as a mid-flight snack for them."

The thought of Cain's oversized dogs tearing into Rourke and

Mason made my already uneasy stomach contort into all kinds of fun shapes. I didn't doubt for a second that Cain would be willing to do something so brutal, but it was the savagery of it that got to me. There was something primal and terrifying about being mauled by an animal. No advanced incendiary nanite could ever capture that.

I thought Cain's threat would send Vaun into a renewed rage. Instead, he went cold. A familiar sense of calm returned to him. Then, ever so slightly, there was that memorable twitch at the corner of his mouth. The ghost of a half-smile.

It was the happiest I'd seen him all week.

"We'll see you soon, Cain," Vaun promised.

PART 4
FIRESTORM

"What fire does not destroy, it hardens."

—Oscar Wilde

CHAPTER 46

Cole West. 10:45 p.m.
Half Moon Bay, California

Billy landed Charon in the grass right outside the late senator's home. Madison swung the side door open as we ran to it.

"Don't ever leave me alone with this guy behind the wheel again," she groaned.

Billy leered back at us from the cockpit, the light from the instruments casting his shit-eating grin into a green hue. "Just showing the lady a good time. The captain never lets me fly anymore!"

"There are reasons for that . . ." Vaun said as he slid the door shut behind him.

I waited until we were all seated before tapping Vaun on the knee.

"You want to fill me in, boss? Where the fuck are we going now?"

Like a poker player revealing a trump card in his hand, he smiled and leaned his head back. "You didn't catch it?"

I shrugged. I had no idea what he meant. Vaun looked to Madison and raised an eyebrow, making sure she was listening too.

"He said 'mid-flight snack.' That tells us two things: one, they're in the air; two, his damn dogs are with him."

"And that helps us how?" Kelly asked from the co-pilot seat. "Last time I checked, him being airborne kind of does the opposite of narrowing our search. He could be anywhere."

"Samuel's plane might be ghosted to us, but his dogs aren't," Madison said. "After they escaped their kennel for the second time last month, I had them microchipped. Couldn't have the boss's precious pooches running off just any tracking system, so I made a dedicated one just for them. I was planning on surprising Samuel with it the next time Virgil or Dante ran off."

Charon's rotors got up to speed and lifted off the senator's lawn. I slammed the side-door shut, invigorated by the thought that we had a line on Cain after all.

"Keep to the coastline," Vaun ordered.

Kelly gave him a thumbs up and followed along the seaside cliffs, headed south. Not headed in any particular direction except for as far from the latest bloodbath as we could get.

"So where is he?" I asked, more than a little anxious to get some payback.

"If I activate the tracer too early, then Samuel might ping it before he gets to where he's going," Madison explained.

Great. The waiting game. It was literally my least favorite aspect of military life. Knowing that every second I was forced to wait was another second Cain got closer to his endgame didn't make it any easier.

"Cain has a lot of shooters on his payroll," Billy said. "Combine that with whatever assets Cheng Qiang's providing, and the numbers are even less in our favor than usual. Not that I'm going to want to share any of the shenanigans we're about to get into. Having a few other squads might come in handy, don't you think?"

Vaun nodded. "Minotaur and Demon Squad were out on assignment last I checked. Grendel and Valkyrie might be available."

Good, they all had excellent track records in the shit-hitting-the-fan department. Vaun tapped his earbud to open up the channel to all frequencies. "All points, all points. This is Blackbars. Code Orphan. I say again, Code Orphan."

Less than a breath later a flustered voice responded. "Wizard for Valkyrie here," the man on the other end said. "This for real?"

"Affirmative, Wizard. Father is taken."

"Roger. En route now," Wizard said.

"Minotaur here," said a gruff voice over a background of automatic gunfire. "We've got our hands full with a bit of a situation." Another death cry accented his statement. "We'll rendezvous with you as soon as we wrap this up."

Both Demon Squad and Grendel Squad were silent. All it meant was that they were busy with a fight of their own at that moment. Vaun adjusted his comms for a direct line to Demon Squad; rescuing Rourke took priority over all else. The call went out, Vaun tapped his foot on the floor of Charon while he waited.

"Captain Vaun . . ." a voice murmured on the line.

Vaun's face scrunched up into confusion. The voice did *not* belong to Demon Squad's leader.

"I gave you the chance to sit out this whole mess," the voice continued, and its familiarity became apparent. Cain. "It looks like you've made your choice."

"You made it for us, you son of a bitch."

"Temper, temper, son. Not good of you to be so angry with that much sophisticated weaponry on board. Who knows what could happen."

My eyes went wide. I looked to Madison, who immediately raised her hands. "He can't remotely detonate bullets, or the guns."

Cain sighed through the radio. "No, Doctor Archer, I can't. But there is a much simpler weapon you might have overlooked. Gravity."

All at once the lights in the helicopter cabin went black. Our comms system died. The rotors stopped. And then we plummeted out of the sky.

CHAPTER 47

Men aren't meant to fly. We all know this, but our arrogance as a species and determination to conquer the laws of nature try to convince us otherwise. It's not until gravity reaches out to put you back where you belong that you realize just how naïve you are. It's the simplest rule. What goes up must come down. And we went down hard.

Our stockpile of commandeered weaponry bludgeoned us as Charon descended into a spin. That's the thing about any kind of crash or rollover. Literally anything not strapped down turns into a dangerous projectile. That includes human beings, which I discovered when one of my teammates collided with my chest. It was pitch black inside so I couldn't see who it was. All I knew was that the point of one of his elbows nailed me in the temple before he was flung away.

The side door flew open from the centrifugal force and more equipment flew out behind it. My neck strained as my head was pulled back against the headrest by the g-forces. I tried to scream but my jaw was clenched too tightly. Beyond the gaping door, I could see the ground coming up fast. I did what little I could to brace myself, and then the scream finally escaped my throat.

I don't remember the moment of impact. I just remember the moment right before when a blackness swallowed me up. The pain that wracked my body when I came to made me wish that same blackness would take me again.

Occasional sparks showered down from above, the only source of light in an otherwise suffocating darkness. The moans and gasps of pain around me let me know that at least I wasn't the only one to survive our crash landing. It also meant they might need me, and I couldn't lay here any longer. I sat up, every single one of my ribs screaming in protest and feeling ready to snap like brittle twigs, but I seemed to be in one piece. Relative term, mind you. My body armor had held up well from the impact. Cain might be a traitorous son of a bitch, but I'll give credit to his designs when it's due.

There was a distinctive stink of oil in the air. It was all the incentive I needed to get a move on before yours truly got the extra crispy treatment.

It took me another moment to steady myself and get to my feet. As I stood, I felt something warm trickling down the side of my neck. Delicately, I patted at the area and found a nasty gash by my right ear that cut down my jawline to my neck. My good looks were gradually being diminished, scar by scar. Still, I was grateful the wound didn't go deep enough into my neck to cause some real bleeding.

"Oof, that's going to be a nice memento, bud," Kelly said from his seat in the front of the wreckage. The man looked absolutely chipper given the circumstances.

"It'll be a nice addition to the collection I've been building." I groaned and tried to find my way towards the side door. Loose bullets were spilled all over. It felt like I was shambling across a floor made of marbles.

"Everyone okay in there?" I heard Vaun shout. "Sound off if you're dead." His voice came from outside, so he must've been thrown clear from Charon during our landing.

"I'm good," I answered.

The side door had flown open during the crash but was now stuck on jammed hinges halfway open. I shoved into it a little harder and the whole damn thing fell off the hinges and collapsed to the dirt outside. With our exit clear, I turned back inside to pull Madison out.

"Two helicopter crashes in two hours," she said. "You must be going for a record."

"I wasn't in the first one when it hit the ground at least," I countered with an unconvincing grin. She returned it, but then grimaced and nearly fell to the floor. I caught her and helped her out of the rumpled metal helicopter.

"You okay?"

"My head . . ."

"You and me both," someone said.

Billy came out of the shadows behind us. His uniform was tattered and scratches crisscrossed his arms and legs, but he was still among the living. He helped her sit down and started shining a small pen light in her eyes. Billy's extensive knowledge of how to kill a man occasionally assisted in triaging someone we didn't want to die. "Your pupils are constricting unevenly. You've got what we in the industry call a little bit of drain bamage. Hopefully it's just a concussion. That's minimal, so you're still smarter than Cole here."

I flipped him off and walked around the helicopter to the other side. I stopped short and got a sudden case of vertigo when I realized how close we'd come to careening right off a cliff. The helicopter had landed in a hard slide along its belly, coming to a rest just five feet from the edge of a sheer drop to crashing waters below.

"Solid piloting, Kage," Vaun said to Billy as he helped pull Kelly from the cockpit. If it wasn't for Billy, the crash could've been far worse, and we could all be far more dead.

"It wasn't flying, it was falling with style," laughed Billy.

Tag's massive body squeezed out of the cockpit and lumbered

over to us. I wondered for a moment if he'd been the one who'd cannonballed into me when we were going down, then decided there's no way I'd be alive if that boulder of a man had been hurled at me. Something about his gait seemed even angrier than usual.

"You alright, big guy?"

He responded by holding up his left hand and showing us his last two fingers. They were both horribly bent at a nearly right angle. "I think they're broke."

Kelly pulled out two ballpoint pens from his pocket to apply a field expedient splint. "I'm going to have to straighten them. Please don't hit me."

Tag's tight-lipped stare gave Kelly pause, but then the towering giant forced a smile that was somehow worse. "Just do it."

I moved over to where Vaun stood. The captain was scanning the nighttime horizon, trying to piece together where we were. With CDI equipment as compromised as it was, he didn't dare to so much as open up a GPS right now. At this point we couldn't trust anything with Cain's stamp on it.

"Any idea where we are, sir?" I asked, hoping beyond hope that the simple formality of a "sir" would help the captain find his bearings.

"Somewhere north of Garrapata. It's a state park. Not much there, nobody to call this into the FAA."

"We're nowhere. Good. Hey, Thomas is probably stoked. We're finally in his element, he can get his tracking on and find our way back to civilization."

Vaun smiled, but then it quickly turned to ash. "Thomas. Where's Thomas?"

I spun, looking back into the ruined helicopter interior. I scanned the toppled weapons crates, checked under the destroyed side benches, and around the immediate vicinity of the helicopter. But Thomas Redcloud was nowhere to be found.

"Does anyone have eyes on Bloodhound?" Vaun bellowed.

The emptiness of the open area around us swallowed his voice. We started our frantic search, even Madison back on her feet and eager to help us locate our comrade.

A swath of tall grass was nearby. I sprinted towards it, pulling a flashlight from my vest and shooting its beam into the field. I shouted Thomas's callsign. Met with silence, I more fearfully called out his given name. Ten feet into the tall grass, I heard him groaning.

"Over here! Over here!" I repeated, waving my arm in the air for the others once I'd found him. I knelt down and used my flashlight to look him over top to bottom.

Head: good.

Chest: fine.

Arms: good.

Legs . . . *not* good.

The *Fafnir* vest had done its job, it had kept Thomas's core and vital organs protected. But a vest did little to protect the extremities. Sharp white bone gleamed through punctures on the thigh of his right leg. More bone stabbed out horribly from lower on his shin. The left leg was even worse. It was broken so badly at the knee that his pant leg had sheared cleanly. It looked like it was kept on by a few thin flaps of sinew and tendon. A wet feeling in my knee let me know I'd knelt in his pooling blood and hadn't realized it.

"Stay with me, Bloodhound," I said sternly while pulling a tourniquet from the med-pouch on his hip. Thank God it was intact. Thomas was shaking, shock already setting in. His breathing was growing sharp and shallow, quickly turning into little more than gasps. The seasoned tracker's normally dark skin grew paler by the second.

The rest of the Cerberus Squad encircled us. I looked to Billy, waiting for him to guide me in whatever I could do to help him stabilize Thomas. My teammate was bleeding out in front of me, and I wanted Billy to fix him. It took Billy all of three seconds to analyze

Thomas's wounds. The grim expression painted on Billy's face said it all, though. Slowly, he lowered himself to one knee next to Thomas and held one of his hands tight. "It's okay, brother."

"Cap . . . Captain . . ." Thomas sputtered through graying lips.

Vaun placed one of his hands on the back of Thomas's neck, gently tilting his head forward. "I'm here. We're all right here."

Tremors ran through Thomas's body. The blood we all knelt in spread out further into the bed of tall grass surrounding us. With his eyes fluttering, barely able to stay open any longer, he whispered to Vaun, "I'm gonna sit this one out . . ."

Thomas's eyes rolled into the back of his head. His breathing slowed. "Just promise me you'll do it. You can stop it . . ."

Vaun lowered Thomas's head back to the ground.

"I promise," he whispered.

We were quiet for a moment. The only sound was the wind blowing in from the ocean and howling against the sea cliffs nearby. That wind carried Thomas Redcloud's soul away to whatever awaited him on the other side.

"Where is he?" Vaun demanded in a harsh whisper.

Nobody said anything at first. I think we were all confused about who he meant. But then Vaun rose, whirling around and grabbing Madison's shoulders so fast and so violently, she choked on her own gasp. "Where!"

Madison backpedaled, nearly tripping over the overgrown grass and her own shoelaces. Vaun's grip on her tightened, the cloth of her sleeves bunching in his fists.

A rage had been building in Vaun for days now. So far it seemed as if I was the only one who'd seen it simmering just beneath the surface. That fire hiding behind those gray eyes of his. But this? None of that fury was hidden anymore. It was all laid bare for the entire squad to witness.

I moved up and raised my hands in the air to try and calm him down. Kelly seemingly appeared from nowhere to stand next to me. Unfazed by both of us, Vaun stepped towards Madison once more. I outweighed him by at least forty pounds. Taller by inches. And still he shouldered me aside like I was nothing. It wasn't until Tag placed a single powerful hand lightly upon Vaun's shoulder from behind that our leader paused.

"She didn't do this to us," Tag said. The man was built large enough that he could break any one of us in half without so much as breaking a sweat, but right now he was practically begging Vaun. "Ease down. Please."

He slowed. The hands that had been clenched so tightly into fists gradually loosened. Then, as if a switch had been flipped, Vaun's entire posture changed. Swallowing down his rage once more, he breathed all the fire out in a long sigh before stomping away from us.

When I looked to the others to see who would finally go after him, I was met with uncertain stares. It wasn't just that I was newer. This was a Vaun *none* of them had ever seen before. He was the one that was supposed to be the immovable rock.

If nobody was willing to speak to him, then I guess it would be up to me. I found him ten paces off with his gaze fixed upon the seaside horizon. He heard me coming and didn't bother looking over his shoulder before speaking.

"Don't worry, I'm not jumping off this cliff just yet."

"Nah, not worried about that," I said. "You've got a bit of a vendetta to settle up first. We're still with you."

Vaun exhaled sharply. "Loyalty can be as much a shackle as a virtue, West."

"It does bring new meaning to the term 'chain of command'," I joked. "But . . . permission to speak freely?"

He turned away from the cliff and the way his eyes locked onto me had me feeling very small, but I had to speak. Vaun nodded for me to proceed.

"I don't think you've been in a rage off Major Wilcox dying just out of mere loyalty," I said. "Far as I can tell, old Slipknot did what everyone else has told me is impossible: he had a family outside of all this. He had a wife. Shit, you said he used to do regular Sunday barbecues like he was some regular Blue-Collar Joe. Maybe, maybe we all hope for a life like that one day. The happy ending. But then to have his life snuffed out? Maybe it shows us that it really is impossible, and this path is all we've got."

"Strong words from someone who's already talking about walking away, West," said Vaun. "Oh, don't act surprised. I know you've been talking with the boys about hanging up your guns. A career change for us tends to be directed rather than elective. Guys get hurt and end up in administrative roles or they get broken in other ways and get shown the door. I don't know of anyone who walked away of their own accord."

"I could be the first," I said. For some reason, the words came out sadder than I intended. Maybe it was because I felt like I'd be letting him down if I resigned once we closed this case. More likely it was because saying it out loud made what I'd been feeling for a while now more certain.

But Vaun gave me a sorrowful look and did that little half-smile of his. "No, I don't think you will be." He let that hang in there as we both simmered on what had been said. Perhaps happy endings aren't in the cards for guys like us. And maybe I really was destined to roll with Black Spear until my final days. All that still required me surviving past tonight and us ghosting Cain.

Vaun finally nodded a slow nod. "We're burning moonlight here," he muttered. "The closer we get to daybreak, the closer we get to a Homeland Security strike team taking us out. We're still on the clock."

"We'll pull what we can from the wreckage and find somewhere to hole up for now. Once we get our bearings, we'll figure out our next play."

When I turned to scavenge what I could from the helicopter, I was surprised to see Madison approaching us. She wore an uncomfortable expression like she knew she was still an outsider to Vaun's circle, and being an outsider meant she wasn't yet fully trusted. But I knew there had to be a reason she would approach Vaun so soon.

"I know where he is, Captain."

CHAPTER 48

Darren Rourke. 11:20 p.m.
The Platform
Pacific Ocean

The cordialities quickly expired once Cain saw Rourke had no intention of being anything but difficult. Hoods had been pulled over his and the rest of the hostages' faces, zip-ties cinched tightly around their wrists. Rourke had initially thought to track their destination by feeling the shift in the plane's weight. The hum of the engines could help determine speed, the shift in balance direction. But Phobos Marstelli was disinclined to allow such behavior and struck him hard across the jaw.

The spike of pain that leapt across his jawline like a bolt of lightning had completely whited out all his senses. It took a solid seven count before Rourke was able to force his screaming pain receptors into silence. Even then his entire skull felt like a hot coal plucked from a dying campfire.

What he wouldn't give for one of his pills...

Once their plane had landed at their unknown destination, they'd been corralled into a small space. The sound of helicopter rotors speeding up let Rourke know that their trip wasn't quite over yet. Inching his feet sideways, he could feel the toe of his shoe tapping against the narrow heel of a stiletto shoe. That meant Mason was seated to his left. When a gust of wind caused the helicopter to lurch, Rourke rode that momentum and used it to lean his weight slightly to his right. A shoulder bumped low on his arm, near the elbow. It could only belong to Goode. Rourke memorized the seating arrangement, aware that any piece of information could prove vital in the coming moments.

Rourke felt the helicopter lowering, then heard the metallic creak of the landing struts meeting the ground and taking on the helicopter's weight. The side door slid open and a harsh breeze blew into the helicopter cabin. Rourke sniffed the air, tasting the salt on his tongue. They were somewhere out at sea, yet the sound of waves rocking against something sounded far *below* him.

"Watch your step, sir," Deimos instructed politely, pulling Rourke out of the cabin by his tie. "It is a long way down from here."

Rourke felt Deimos at his back, prodding him forward. He could easily turn around and lunge into the man; if he was lucky and Deimos wasn't lying then he might be able to send the red-headed bastard into a fall to his death. But that wouldn't stop Phobos from eviscerating him and the others, and it certainly wouldn't stop Cain's war from starting.

Rourke allowed himself to be guided along his unseen path. The surface beneath him was metallic. It clanked and echoed with every step their group took. It must have been some kind of catwalk overlooking the rest of wherever they were. Eventually he was led inside; he surmised as much from the now absent salty wind.

He tried to count his steps. If he could map out the path they'd taken then he might be able to backtrack to the helipad if he was given an opportunity. But the pain across his jawline was only growing worse the longer he went without one of his pills. Soon it became difficult to even think about anything other than the hurt.

Rourke became like a zombie, shambling around with barely a mind of his own. Finally, Cain commanded him to sit. And Rourke, dog-tired and wracked with agony, obeyed. He lowered himself into the chair that was placed behind him and hung his head. He told himself it wasn't defeat, told himself that he was simply conserving his strength. But even from where he sat, the distinction between the two was hard to see.

When the hood was jerked from his head, the sudden blinding light added a new layer to his agony. Gradually his eyes adjusted to the bright environment. Cain stood in front of him, leaning forward at the waist to meet him at eye-level and tilting his head. He looked at Rourke as if examining some grotesque display.

"Look at you," Cain growled. "Look at how the mighty *Mister* Rourke has fallen so easily."

As much as he wanted to give some threatening response, Rourke's jaw was clenched too tightly to let words escape.

Cain straightened and looked down his nose at Rourke. "And to think the safety of our nation rested in the hands of someone as fragile as you."

Mason howled some muffled obscenity through her gag. Deimos, none too pleased with her rude outburst, struck her at the base of her skull with the butt of his handgun. She slumped over, unconscious.

Rourke pulled his wits together and tried to get a better lay of the land. The fluorescent lights above were relentless, but the rest of the room sat even worse with him. On the far side was a full gamut of professional camera equipment and what looked like a set pulled right from a Hollywood studio. North Korea's flag was emblazoned across the wall. Rourke had watched more than enough execution videos to know exactly the purpose of this mock set-up. More smoke and mirrors for the greatest con in history.

"All this to kill me on camera?" Rourke managed to ask. Despite how much it hurt he managed to give Cain a smug grin. "I'm honored you think me that important."

Cain's bemused frown gave Rourke pause. Then the frown gave way to a smile of his own. "You pompous bastard," he said with a shake of his head. "You really think this was all about you? You're a good prize, but you're just sprinkles on the cupcake." Cain's grin stretched wider as his eyes bore through Rourke. "You were never my main target." Then, slowly, his gaze shifted from Rourke to the one on his left. To Goode.

Phobos appeared behind him to remove the hood and place his blade to Goode's neck. Meanwhile, Deimos set up a small table and set a laptop in front of him. It was Goode's own. The one-of-a-kind system with a direct link to White Shield's entire intelligence network. Puzzle pieces of Cain's intricate plot began to fit together as it dawned on Rourke exactly what his former friend intended.

Goode's personal computer gave him access to quite literally every system connected to so much as a phone line or Wi-Fi connection. He could read any piece of intel from any level of the government, from a lowly analyst in the CIA all the way up to the Joint Chiefs' emails. That unrestrained authority to read also granted a secondary feature: it could write.

Through Goode's computer Cain could fabricate any piece of intelligence he wanted. Satellite imaging could be faked to show mobilizing enemy forces. Hacked emails of foreign military personnel could be rewritten to say exactly what he wanted. It would all be transmitted, become real, and would disseminate throughout the government like a virus.

"Okay, then," Cain said and placed his heavy handgun on the table across from Goode. "Let's send some smoke signals, shall we?"

CHAPTER 49

We'd been forced to leave Thomas's body behind in that cold empty field. It didn't feel honorable, but it was necessary. He would've understood if he'd been in our shoes. That pill was sour, nonetheless.

Refuge had taken the form of an old boarded-up gas station on the side of a back road. The accumulated dust on the fuel pumps was a solid sign that there wouldn't be any customers, and the long since discontinued Mountain Dew Supernova cans I spotted in a refrigerator were a clear enough indicator that the owners had packed up shop years ago.

We took the time to lick our wounds. Billy found an old first aid kit under a counter and went about rationing its contents where it was needed most. A few pills from a travel-size Tylenol bottle were all Madison needed to take the edge away from her banged-up head. As delicately as he could, Kelly helped Billy apply a more proper splint and bandage to Tag's hand. Vaun stood to the side, still processing all his thoughts.

Madison retrieved a small tube of burn ointment from the kit and tossed it over to me. "For your shoulder," she indicated.

I eyed my shoulder, registered that my bandage needed to be

replaced, and that it was starting to hurt like a son of a bitch again. Too much adrenaline and too little down time had kept me from even thinking about it. I unzipped my newly cut favorite hooded leather vest, exhaling sharply as the leather slid over the raw red skin.

Madison abruptly averted her eyes.

"You don't have to make this weird . . ." I muttered. "My friend's blood is still on my pants. Not exactly a romantic situation?" I tried to give her a smile, but she saw right through it to the grief I was still avoiding.

When she looked at me again it was like she was examining an intriguing painting. She wasn't looking at my body so much as the scars. "How did . . . how did you get all of them?"

After I finished smearing the ointment on my burned shoulder, I pointed to the jagged scar on the opposite shoulder. "This one was from a spear. Crazy asshole tried to kill the president with a bioweapon. He also gave me this one." I indicated the thin scar that cut from my eyebrow across to my cheek.

"Wait . . . a spear?"

"Yeah, well this one was a spear. He used a knife on my face."

She fought back a smile. No doubt amused by the weirdness, yet not wanting to offend me by laughing at previous injuries.

"Hey, it's cool. I mean, I'm still here and he got it way worse."

Madison pointed at a spot low on my side just below the ribs. "Another knife?"

It took a second before I remembered. "No, that was a really big shard of glass. Took a swan dive through a skylight. The landing was a bit rough."

"Have you been shot . . . ?"

"Not yet." Ever the superstitious one, I took the time to knock on the wooden counter. Things were bad enough without having to add bad luck into the mix. "I almost did on day one, but Kelly over there took it for me."

Without a word Kelly waved at us with a smile and pulled his shirt collar over to show the circular entry-wound scar from a 9mm. "Didn't feel a thing, bud."

Billy walked over to us, noticed the gash I'd gotten in the crash, and prepped to stitch me up.

"Another one for the collection?" Madison asked.

"Each one a story. We might not have a long life expectancy, but at least it's an interesting one."

Billy's hands were steady as a rock as he started sewing up my wound. "I could've just left it to you, ma'am, if you wanted to play doctor with West."

"Not that kind of doctor," she sighed.

I winced as the needle and thread was worked through my neck. Any other normal day we'd be operating with bleeding edge military technology in advanced facilities worth millions. Tonight, we were sharing an eight-dollar first aid kit to pull ourselves together and using a cheap plastic jug of warm vodka for antiseptic. Taking another look at our surroundings put into perspective how far we'd fallen.

Kelly seemed to read my mind from across the counter and made a show of pilfering a small bag of dusty Doritos from a shelf. "Fugitive life may not have the best digs, but it still has its perks, West." He started munching from the bag. Meanwhile, Madison used a laptop to begin her show and tell now that everyone was patched up as best we could.

"I pinged the dog tracker, and it gave us this location." Her screen displayed a map of the western hemisphere, a red dot blinking off the west coast.

"Hell, yeah! We got our little red dot back!" Kelly said through a mouthful of orange Dorito mush.

"Missed you, buddy," added Billy.

I looked at the screen and arched an eyebrow. "Cool. So he's in the middle of the ocean . . . what, did his plane crash?"

Kelly and Billy's excitement broke as they saw the truth to my words. The dog tracker showed a location nearly eighty miles from the nearest land.

"Or he chucked one of the pooches out of the plane . . ." groaned Kelly. "Treason is one thing, but we're going to have to go John Wick on his ass if he killed the dog."

"There's *not* nothing there," Madison cut in sharply. When all eyes fell on her once again, she opened a file from her desktop. "This is the location of CDI's off-shore testing facility. We call it The Platform."

Madison's computer screen was filled with what at first appeared to be a vast oil rig. Its hexagonal superstructure rose from the ocean atop six massive tower-like legs. The facility sprawled out over the water, smaller platforms extending out from the center and connecting via metal catwalks gave it an almost spidery appearance.

"Samuel constructed the Platform supposedly for safety and security reasons with our more volatile prototypes," Madison explained. "That far out into the water there was little risk of endangering civilians and even less concern for industrial spying from competitors. I always suspected the truth to be that he simply needed a facility in international waters to sidestep some of the more problematic laws that come with weapons development."

Vaun turned the screen towards himself, examining the Platform more closely. "Only two helipads. Not good odds for an aerial insertion."

"The lower helipad is meant to be for medevacs and occasional prototype pickup/drop-off," she explained. "The executive helipad is for Samuel's private use and when he wants to bring in VIPs for a prototype demonstration."

"How does the rest of the staff get to and from work?" asked Tag.

Madison blew up a section of one of the legs that rose out of the water. "Platform staff work in three-week stints. They're brought in by boat to a small dock here where a cargo elevator brings them up. The central hexagonal core of the Platform is broken into six sections. This one here by the cargo elevator is dedicated to personnel. Living quarters, mess hall, basic necessities."

I could tell Vaun was piecing together a plan of sorts. On a typical mission we would have air assets available that would allow us to parachute in. Mr. Rourke could make some calls to someone in the Navy to put us aboard a submarine, hook us up with some scuba tanks and a manned submersible, and shoot us out for an amphibious insertion. But as it was, we didn't even have a set of flippers or a snorkel to share among the six of us.

"Any chance Valkyrie Squad makes this party?" I spoke quietly to Vaun while the rest of the squad continued to look over the Platform's schematics.

"No way to tell," he answered with a slow shake of his head. "All our channels are bugged. For all I know, they could be like us and Cain sabotaged their ride over to the rendezvous. Unlike us, they might not have walked away as intact."

His grim analysis hammered home just how alone we were in this. I tried instead to focus on the advantages that our position might provide. Strangely, for some reason the first thing that came to mind was Kelly's bag of Doritos. But it was exactly what I needed to think about.

"Maybe we have more than we think we do, Cap," I said.

He looked over in my direction with an arched eyebrow.

"Right now, we're fugitives. Maybe we should start acting like it."

CHAPTER 50

Ralph Olson. 12:15 a.m.
Los Angeles Air Force Base
California

Staff Sergeant Ralph Olson had no illusions about himself. He knew he had one of those jobs that looked exciting on paper but was dreadfully mundane. "Space Systems Operations" sounded like he'd be deploying to the planet Klendathu to go toe-to-toe with the Arachnids from *Starship Troopers*. In truth, his entire career had been centered around monitoring computer screens. Seated at his honorable post, i.e. his computer station, it was upon Olson to faithfully watch satellite feeds for any threats.

Five years of service later, the most exciting thing he'd seen was when a computer glitch momentarily erased the entire Seventh Fleet from Olson's screen. The most heroic moment of Olson's career was rebooting his computer and presto: America's Naval presence in the Korean Peninsula returned. Once again the South China Sea was deterred from any aggression. Not exactly a crowning achievement in military history.

Being an avid fan of most pop culture, Olson tried to draw connections between his own perpetual watch and that of the sworn brothers of the Night's Watch atop their Wall from *Game of Thrones*. They were both dedicated to their duty, even if it meant years of nothing happening. Truth be told, he was jealous of Jon Snow since his watch was actually met with some excitement. If the enemy showed up at Olson's "wall," it would take much more than arrows and swords to repel them. He knew it was a shitty thing to wish for a little excitement, but he secretly wished it all the same.

Olson went through his dull daily tasks with robotic precision that could only be formed from years of repetition. One by one he checked things off his mental To-Do List. It was routine, and routine was never exciting. When your job is to ensure China or North Korea don't do something stupid, eventually even the most level-headed person will find themselves wishing something stupid would happen just to break up the monotony.

Nearing the end of his nightly routine, Olson leaned back in his chair and stretched his stiff arms out to the sky. His shoulders popped. That smidgen of skeletal release was a welcome sensation in the latest of a long line of unremarkable days. It dawned on Olson just how sad his life was when something as simple as a shoulder pop was the most enjoyable part of his shift.

He rubbed his tired eyes. After a yawn, he looked back to his screen.

Something had changed. Olson sat forward in his chair so quickly and violently, the edge of his station slammed into his gut. Heat signatures on the satellite feeds indicated a large-scale mobilization from the Korean Peninsula. A *very* large mobilization.

Olson grabbed for the phone next to his computer. His hands shook so badly, he fumbled it twice before successfully bringing it to his ear. His officer on the other end answered immediately.

"Sir, we have a situation."

Everything his officer was saying on the other end was drowned out in Olson's own frantic thoughts and booming heartbeat. All hell broke loose on the watch floor as other alarms started firing off, one after another.

Excitement was what he'd wished for a thousand times before. One thought fought its way to the surface atop all of the hysterical ones. Be careful what you wish for.

CHAPTER 51

Darren Rourke. 12:30 a.m.
The Platform
Pacific Ocean

On one hand, he could forgive Goode. White Shield's director had never been close to the frontlines; any actual danger was only perceived behind a keyboard and computer screen. And the Marstelli brothers certainly had a way of convincing even the hardest of men to comply with their wishes. Goode had even put up a respectable amount of resistance until they started breaking his fingers. All in all, Rourke could reasonably find a way to forgive Goode.

On the other hand, Michael Goode was going to be directly responsible for Cain's plan succeeding. Now *that* Rourke couldn't forgive.

"Eyes, sir," Deimos requested.

Goode was already leaning towards the laptop's small but sophisticated retinal scanner when Phobos wrenched his head forward. The computer checked Goode's eyes, completed a temperature check at the same time to ensure that the eyes were still attached to a living person, and then the laptop's touchpad lit up.

"Fingers, if you please." Phobos straightened Goode's broken fingers, then pressed them against the touchpad. When he grimaced, Deimos looked at him with a pained frown. "A touch indelicate, I'm afraid, but we'll be through soon enough."

With the security checks passed, the laptop extended the login for another thirty minutes. Thirty minutes. It didn't sound like a considerable amount of time, but by Rourke's calculations that was eighteen hundred seconds worth of disaster. Intel passed in an instant. Conversations between Joint Chiefs might only take moments. Thirty minutes more . . . there might not be enough time left after to reverse what Cain had already done.

"How's it coming along?" Cain asked from the pseudo movie set. He took a puff from his inhaler then stowed it back in his jacket pocket. Rourke wondered if that meant his old friend was less composed than he let on.

"Swimmingly, sir," answered Deimos with a cheerful smile as his fingers flew across the laptop's keyboard.

Cain nodded, lost in his own mysterious thoughts. What Rourke wouldn't give to be able to crack Cain's skull in two and take a peek at what those thoughts might be. All he could do now was bide his time. Hope for a slip up. An opportunity would eventually present itself, of that Rourke had no doubt.

Rourke was abruptly pulled from his own plotting by the familiar sound of a bolt being racked back and a live round sliding into a chamber. Cain had just readied a Cheng Qiang assault rifle.

"That's a tad underwhelming," Rourke said. "All the weapons at your disposal, and you're going to execute us with that?"

"Oh, believe me there are some *very* fun ways I could go about it," Cain answered. "I mean this place is Candyland in terms of weapons. Just between you and me, I was brainstorming the entire trip over on what to use. We've got this prototype in one of the labs here that uses sonic waves to breach through concrete; I thought it would be interesting to see what it would do to your skeleton. Then again, we've been having recent breakthroughs with our automated surgical bots. I imagine it would be quite a spectacle watching it dissect you alive with absolute surgical precision. So many ways, Darren. So many deaths."

"And you decided on that, a bullet to the head? A little lackluster for your recent showmanship."

"True, as Americans we have a strange fascination with the sensational. But the simplest solutions are still usually the best. Yes. A bullet to the head. *Firecracker* straight to the brain. It's almost poetic . . . the shot heard round the world and the literal final spark to light the fires of war."

Rourke's face tightened into a deeper scowl. "Just don't miss."

His resolve was like glass under Cain's skin. Even now Rourke refused to break. Although given how long it had been since he had taken one of his pills, it might be just a matter of time until he was reduced to a fetal position on the floor. Currently, he was doing his damnedest to channel his pain into anger, focusing that anger into determination.

So far, so good.

Undeterred by Rourke's resistance, Cain instead made a show of hitting a page button on one of the walls to make an outgoing call.

"Security Chief Mosley," a voice answered.

"Mosley, it's Cain. Bring in our cast, please."

After that, Cain stared at Rourke.

Rourke stared back.

Neither blinked as a full minute passed in utter silence. Then, the door opened and a tall, somewhat portly man in black fatigues and tactical vest, who Rourke could only surmise was Chief Mosley, strode in.

Rourke had seen many men of his build before. Once upon a time, he must've been all muscle but now the years and pounds had layered upon themselves. There were still clues to his long-lost physique; his arms were still wrapped with corded muscle, and he was as barrel-chested as a bear. But the gut that bulged out from the bottom of his vest and the jowls on either side of his face both said that those golden years of youthful athleticism were long past.

Mosley considered Rourke and the other captives with an upturned nose. "About time," he said. "Our guests were beginning to grow impatient."

Behind Mosley followed three men in full military uniform. Their brownish dark olive jackets and trousers indicated NKSOF, the Korean People's Army Special Operation Force. The red stripes on the shoulders of the first two marked them as a Sergeant and a Sergeant First Class. Rourke chalked them up to paid expats for more of Cain's charade. But the one that brought up the rear wore stars on either shoulder, which identified him as a Major General. Even worse, Rourke recognized him. Major General Bahk, legitimate North Korean and all around dirtbag.

"Had him flown in this morning," Cain said proudly. "He's not too keen on being shackled to the regime any longer."

Bahk walked over to the movie set, his hands clasped behind his back. The Sergeant began to examine the loaded assault rifle while the Sergeant First Class saw fit to adjust his uniform in a mirror to make sure it was just right. Evidently squared away uniforms were a must even on the eve of mass conflict.

"You crazy bastard," spat Dana, who'd finally managed to work her gag off. "Pull your Houdini shit on our intelligence network, trick our satellites into seeing an attack coming, use North Korean military to execute American VIPs. It won't change anything. When the dust settles and your trick is played out, everyone will see this for the sham it is. America won't go to war and retaliate over a fake attack that never happened!"

Cain's lips parted, revealing both sets of capped pearly whites. "My dear Doctor Phelps, who said anything about *faking* an attack?"

CHAPTER 52

There's a certain freedom that comes from knowing the odds are stacked against you and you are completely fucked. In its own strange way, it becomes a relief. If your death is certain, then the moment you accept it is the moment you find yourself capable of incredible things. Dangerous, reckless . . . but incredible, nonetheless.

"This plan of yours sure is something," Vaun said to me as our boat rocked over rolling waves.

We'd stolen it from a marina. Hey, if you're wanted for treason, what's a little grand theft on top of it?

"It's a damn long shot," muttered Tag from behind the steering wheel.

"A long shot is better than no shot," I said. "It'll work. Or it won't, and we'll all die. Either way, we won't have to worry about it come tomorrow."

A large wave splashed over the side of the boat and drenched Billy's obscenely colorful Hawaiian shirt. "This is my favorite shirt, Tag!"

"Better a little saltwater than blood . . ." Kelly said.

Given the dire straits we'd found ourselves in, we hadn't found the opportunity to change from our casual civilian clothing. Between Billy's Hawaiian attire, my now cut-sleeve leather jacket, and Kelly's Deadpool T-shirt, we really did resemble a motley crew. Captain Vaun, ever the professional among us, still wore his 5.11 collared t-shirt and tactical pants. Thankfully, we still had our body armor so we wouldn't look completely unprepared. Which, admittedly, we still were.

Tag checked our bearings, then conferred with Madison. "Five mikes out."

I donned my body armor, being careful not to rub my shoulder burn wrong as I slid my arms through the vest. My comrades did the same. With each rock of the waves, the nervous lump in my throat bobbed a little higher. I tried to focus on our final prep to stay grounded. I chambered a round into my .45 sidearm before holstering it, patted the hilt on my Mk-9 knife sheathed at my hip for reassurance, and finally adjusted the sling on my SD-52.

All around me Cerberus Squad members were in their own little worlds, going through the same process. Tag had a CDI rocket launcher on his back and a half dozen additional rockets in a satchel over his shoulder; they were one of the few things to have survived our crash landing.

Kelly thumbed at his sniper scope to ensure it hadn't loosened. Billy finished strapping his twin Tanto knives to his belt, then gave me an enthusiastic thumbs-up. Vaun ran his thumb along the edge of his own knife, ensuring it was sharp enough to drive it through Phobos's heart. We were ready to go to war . . . all to stop one from ever happening.

"Hey, Doctor Archer," Tag said, squinting through the water-streaked windshield, "I think your intel might have been a tad outdated."

I peered ahead and saw the Platform looming before us, but more importantly I also knew exactly what Tag was referring to. In her little show and tell earlier, she'd shown us schematics that indicated the Platform only had two helipads. Which made the small new flight deck jutting out from one portion of the Platform a bit of a surprise.

"Jesus . . . I see over a dozen jets," said Kelly, taking a closer look through his scope. "Fast movers, rocking some pretty snazzy North Korean markers."

The wheels in my head turned a little faster to account for this new addition to the scenario. The possibilities dwindled down to the sole realization that Cain wouldn't have brought the aircraft here, of all places, so close to the west coast, if he didn't plan to use them.

Billy held up a set of binoculars. "They're rocking more than markers. They're loaded for bear; they could level a few cities with that squadron."

That settled it.

"We're going to have to split up, Cap," I said to Vaun. "Half of us look for Rourke, the others cripple the flight line."

It took all of three seconds for Vaun to think it over before he nodded his agreement. He'd already lost one man in this mission, and while splitting up his squad was never something he was comfortable with, it was the only option on the table.

"Fine. We close enough yet, Doc?" he asked Madison.

Madison's fingers were a blur across the keyboard of her laptop. "Just now," she said and connected to the Platform's wireless network. Now was the moment of truth. We had to get close enough to access the Platform's network but not close enough to be detected. "But Samuel has probably revoked my access already."

"Yeah, about that . . ." mumbled Tag and gently took the laptop from her.

Billy took the wheel. The big computer wiz started inputting commands; his typing speed made Madison look like a beginner. Within moments he was in. He gave a signature grunt of victory, not stopping his speed for a moment. "We've got a window. Cameras and motion are down. Maybe twenty seconds before we're locked out and they're back up."

Billy gunned the engine, and we shot straight for the cargo elevator. I counted the seconds down in my head, at the same time watching Tag try to keep the CDI firewall from blocking us out. The spotlights on the Platform's perimeter went dead as we got closer. Eight hundred meters, fifteen seconds.

The boat bucked with every wave, each time slowing our gain just a bit and causing me no shortage of anxiety.

"Come on, come on . . ." I muttered, thumping my fist against the windshield.

Five hundred meters, ten seconds.

One by one, windows on the laptop that had shown Tag's breached access to the Platform started closing. The system was fighting back. And winning. Security lights, gone. East side cameras, gone. Three hundred meters, five seconds.

The floodlights lit back up, bathing the Platform's surroundings in light. Motion detectors monitoring the Platform's outside perimeter came back to life. The system finished blocking out Tag and the laptop went completely black as the cameras booted back up.

But we were already past all the Platform's defenses and riding into the cargo elevator dock hard. Billy spun the wheel to bring our boat alongside it. Kelly used the momentum to roll out, firing a single shot to take out the security camera watching the dock. All before anyone had a chance to see what had happened.

We piled out of our commandeered vessel. Billy tied it off to the dock while the rest of us took up positions at the elevator. Madison stayed at the very rear, a pistol we'd provided her at the ready.

Vaun tapped the button to call the elevator. In that final calm before all hell broke loose, we looked at one another. Brothers all finding some modicum of comfort in each other's eyes. Just the six of us against all the technological might Samuel Cain brought to bear.

Us against the odds. Us against the storm. Us alone to hold back the fury and horror of war.

"Kelly, earlier you asked how many people would you kill to stop a war," Vaun said. He gave each of us a hard look, then charged his rifle. "As many as it takes."

And then the cargo elevator doors opened.

Game on, motherfucker.

CHAPTER 53

Samuel Cain. 12:48 a.m.
The Platform
Pacific Ocean

There was a clock on the nearby wall. With each tick of its second hand, Cain could feel his anticipation rising. He tried to tell himself that the feeling he had growing within him wasn't giddiness; that was far too low an emotion for an undertaking such as this. But he had to admit, there was an element of pride tied to his accomplishment. How many years did it take to sow the right seeds? How many months of setting the stage, only inching forward when the conditions of the world grew unstable enough that his own progress blended and became hidden? All of it—all of the work and all of the patience— just for this day.

"Stay with us," he said and rudely slapped Rourke across the cheek. His old friend was so incapacitated with his own pain, he barely registered the blow. Cain followed up with an even sharper backhand. "I said, wake up!"

Rourke's pupils narrowed with focus upon Cain but his face refused to express any feeling, despite the reddening marks across both cheeks.

"It's not too late to stop this, Sam," Rourke muttered. His deep Brooklyn voice was little more than a murmur now. There was so much weakness in that small sentence. Almost all resemblance of the imposing enigma that was the legendary *Mister* Rourke was evaporating by the second. "You can stop it all."

Cain exhaled sharply; a laugh caught short by the hilarity of how pathetic Rourke had become. "No, no . . . I don't think I will. It's too late to turn back and believe me when I say that the consequences for my failure at this point would be far worse than any prison."

Just as his old friend was readying to say something else, he paused. His eyebrows furrowed as he thought about what Cain had just said. Cain realized he'd just said too much, and worst of all Rourke had caught it. Rourke's eyes lit up as he connected the dots. Ignoring how much it must have hurt, Rourke actually smiled a ghastly smile at him. "That's it, isn't it? Why you can't stop. This isn't *your* war. You're working for someone else. You couldn't stop this even if you wanted to."

"Shut up."

"Tell me: who commands America's would-be savior? Who are you afraid of failing? Samuel Cain, the great weapons maker . . . in reality, just someone else's weapon. Someone else's finger is pulling your trigger."

Cain's nostrils flared. His hands balled into fists. They clenched tighter when he saw that everyone in the room, even those on his own payroll, now looked at him with suspect expressions. For a moment, his eyes flashed to the loaded weapon on the table behind him. He considered ending Rourke right then and there. Rourke's mocking smile nearly finished convincing him to just fucking do it.

Instead, Cain's hands circled Rourke's throat. He squeezed with maddened strength. Rourke barely squirmed, just continued to stare hard back at Cain while his throat closed within Cain's grasp.

"You think you know what power is?" he snarled, shaking Rourke's head as he squeezed even harder. "You have no idea. You think Black Spear is something to be afraid of? What criminals and terrorists tell ghost stories to each other about late at night? Your band of misfits is nothing but a laughing-stock. Amateurs. You have no idea what *real* power is." He violently throttled Rourke's neck, then punched him with a wide overhand. "You have no idea. Black Spear's nothing but a cheap joke."

Cain pulled his hand back to strike Rourke again when he felt a gentle touch at his wrist. Deimos.

"If I may, sir," he said politely as he pushed Cain's hand back down to his side. "This gentleman still has a role to play. As it stands, he *does* still need to be recognizable for that." Deimos's pleasant smile somehow managed to disarm Cain and give him pause.

Cain tried to walk it off. His shoulders heaved with every breath, and his chest felt tight around his lungs. As if to seal the envelope on his little outburst, he took a puff from his inhaler. Half physiological, half psychological, the stilling effect took hold.

"Enough waiting, then. Let's get this show on the road. General?"

Bahk was looking over the printed script they'd provided him. He'd already had plenty of time to rehearse and practice his lines, but still he mouthed them to himself one last time before setting the script on the table. He gave Cain a nod before summoning the other uniformed stand-ins, who dragged Rourke onto the set and set him on his knees.

Deimos signaled the cameraman, who started rolling. The Sergeant First Class held the loaded Cheng Qiang assault rifle to the back of Rourke's head. Cain stood next to the camera with his arms crossed, eagerly awaiting Rourke's execution.

Chief Mosley positioned himself behind Cain. Cain was annoyed to find Mosley mumbling something into his walkie and absolutely spoiling Cain's perfect moment of final victory. He turned to look at Mosley while Major General Bahk's speech was just gearing up. He didn't bother speaking, but his eyes screamed, *"Do you mind shutting the fuck up?"*

Apparently, Mosley understood because he pulled his face away from the walkie on his shoulder and gave Cain a shrug. "Having a few glitches in the perimeter grid, sir. But it looks like it's all up and running again."

Cain squinted. "Define glitches?"

Before the security chief could answer, all the lights in the room went dead. The cameraman stopped filming; he didn't have a low-light setting on his camera so he held up a hand to pause Bahk, who groaned angrily. The Sergeant looked around the room, wondering if he should bolt for the exit. The Sergeant First Class shifted uneasily, the assault rifle in his hands beginning to sway just a bit.

Meanwhile, Rourke's smile returned to his face. "I'd pay attention, Sam. That 'cheap joke' of mine is about to make one hell of a punchline."

CHAPTER 54

My knife slid out from the base of the security guard's neck so smoothly, you'd think I'd greased the blade. The only other guard in the security office was busy having his windpipe crushed behind Tag's meaty forearm. When the second man's eyes rolled up into the back of his skull, Tag twisted his head until it gave a wet snap for good measure.

"This will only work for so long," Madison said with a sharp exhale. She started sabotaging as much of the Platform's infrastructure as she could. Each of the Platform's six sections had their own security station with limited access to the various systems, but to truly cripple it we still had to reach the central hub at the heart of the facility. "They're going to lock this station out soon."

"Misdirection is the entire name of the game right now," Vaun reassured her, making sure I noticed him glancing my way. This long shot was still my plan after all. "Forty-Seven, Kage, how far to the flight deck?"

"Forty-Seven here," Kelly answered from somewhere else in the facility. "Only about fifty meters to go, but there's a lot of tight quarters to clear through first. If we can keep from raising the alarm, then Cain's crew will be like fish in a barrel."

For the time being quiet was *also* the name of the game. Since we were outgunned about a hundred to one, we needed to maintain the element of surprise for as long as possible. Thus, the stabbing and snapping of necks.

"Lights and cameras are out for now," said Madison while Tag edged the door open to verify that the corridor outside was dark. "Captain, the second they lock this station out, they'll know where we are."

"Which is why we're moving," I said, pulling her chair away from the desk.

Tag cleared left outside the door, Vaun right. With the coast clear we pushed on from the security station.

The Platform was divided into six sections: Administration, Living Quarters, Fabrication, Testing, Storage, and Engineering, all of which surrounded the central portion known as the Executive Center. Administration contained all the hardcopy and digital records on-hand; everything from weapons schematics and financial dossiers to the Platform's employees' medical records. The Living Quarters were exactly that, but they also were home to the medical wing, a well-stocked gym, and the mess deck.

The cargo elevator we'd ridden up had led to the Living Quarters section. Small-scale manufacturing was conducted within the Fabrication section via a collection of advanced 3d printers, industrial assembly robots, and a staff of technicians. This section lay adjacent to Testing where CDI put all their prototypes to play. Those that proved successful enough were transferred to the Storage section to either be sent to the Advanced Projects Facility in Monterey or the Headquarters factory in Seattle. Or, apparently, shipped overseas where they slapped a fresh Cheng Qiang Arms Conglomerate label on it.

While each section had its own limited emergency power

supply, Engineering housed the massive generators that powered the enormous facility. So, if a few very angry commandos were to say, fuck with said Engineering section? Yeah. It could prove to be a serious pain in the ass for anyone interested in keeping the Platform fully operational.

"Through this doorway and across the catwalk," Madison instructed.

She swiped her access card in the reader next to a heavy steel door that led outside. It beeped green and the door opened outward. I was never officially relieved of bodyguard duty, so I slid in front of her to ensure there wasn't a guard taking his smoke break on the catwalk.

"Clear," I whispered over my shoulder.

I stalked across to the Engineering section with my rifle at the ready. Despite my delicate, careful steps, the walkway beneath my boots still made tinny clanging sounds with each step. I stacked up against the door to Engineering and hugged my body against the threshold as close as I could get; the idea of getting caught in the open made me especially uneasy. I kept expecting a punch in the gut from a sniper's round or blinding floodlights to suddenly spotlight my position. Instead, there was only the wind howling up at me from the ocean below.

Madison came across the catwalk towards me, pistol held low and keycard at the ready.

"Don't like being out in the open like this," I said and shifted out of the way of the card reader so she could scan us in. She swiped her card wordlessly and bit her lip while the scanner blinked.

And then it lit up red.

"Shit!" She swiped it again.

Vaun and Tag had moved up to join us.

"What's the hold up?" Tag asked.

"I think they're onto us," I answered when Madison's card swipe resulted in a second red light.

Tag rudely pushed both Madison and I out of the way, "Lemme try mine."

If this was a clichéd action movie moment, Tag would've shot the reader and, in the face of all electronics logic, it would have miraculously unlocked for us. Thankfully, this was reality and Tag wasn't the boneheaded lug others mistook him to be. From a pouch on his belt he withdrew a small tablet. Then he did smash the side of the card reader but only to expose some of the internal components.

"Hurry it up, Boomerang," Vaun ordered.

Behind us the lights in the Living Quarters section corridor came back to life. The rest of the security systems, including the cameras and motion sensors, would quickly follow.

"Hurry it *way* the fuck up, dude." I aimed my rifle back across the catwalk, fully prepared for a security strike team to mob through the doorway at any moment. Both the green and red lights on the scanner alternated lighting up as Tag did his damnedest to work around CDI's advanced system. The two lights flashed back and forth as if competing for whether the door would stay locked or give in.

The green light won the fight.

Hydraulics hissed and the door to the Engineering section slid out of our way. Tag took point, Vaun behind, Madison third, and I brought up the rear. The door was just closing behind me when I heard the first gunshot from the catwalk.

It zipped past my shoulder, missing my flesh by mere millimeters but clipping the fabric at my hip. I dropped to a knee and spun around while shouting, "Contact, rear!"

A security team scrambled through the Living Quarters doorway and onto the catwalk. The narrow exit bottlenecked them, but three had already made it through and were laying down fire in our direction. It was a good thing we were already doing the same, and much more effectively.

The three guards on the catwalk went down as Vaun and I picked them off with a center mass double tap each. They squirmed on the ground, and I noticed there weren't any entry or exit wounds. It looked like Cain had ponied up to supply his security goons with decent body armor so I adjusted my aim and put a round in two of the guards' heads. The third guard tried to draw a sidearm but was cut short as Vaun shot him through the eye.

More guards squeezed through the doorway onto the catwalk. Bullets snapped by as I clung to the wall behind the Engineering doorway. Before the number of guards on the catwalk got too high, Tag decided to thin their numbers. His belt-fed machine gun opened up with a great and unending *Buddabuddabuddabuddabuddabudda*. A veritable storm of lead chewed into the security team. Cain's state of the art body armor protected the guards' center mass. The same could not be said for their limbs or heads. I watched as Tag's fire literally tore the enemy to pieces.

The catwalk became a charnel house of red chunks and strewn body parts. And still Tag fired. With the initial crowd cut down, he took to unleashing more controlled bursts. *Buddabuddabudda. Buddabuddabudda.*

"Find some important shit to break," Tag said tersely. "I'm good here."

I considered asking if he was sure, but the big man's scowl was more than convincing. We had all come on this mission expecting some payback both for Cain's betrayal and Thomas's death. The way Thomas had died, broken and bleeding out helplessly? There was a lot of payback owed. And right here, right now, Tag was cashing in. All I could do was give my comrade a pat on the shoulder as I moved deeper into the generator areas.

CHAPTER 55

Kelly and Billy moved with such fluidity, you would think they were twins. If they weren't twins, then you'd swear they must have shared a psychic link of some sort. Kelly would cover a doorway, Billy would bound past. Kelly would bring up the rear and then move past Billy, who then covered him. Rinse and repeat, smooth as glass. Not a word spoken nor a hand signal given. The two had fought together long enough that relying on the other was muscle memory. To say they were connected psychically wouldn't be a far stretch of the truth.

"Getting close now," Kelly said, finally breaking the silence.

Halfway down the corridor were two doors—both open—on opposite sides of the hall from each other. When Kelly took a lightning-quick pivoting step to aim into the left doorway and clear the room, Billy moved at the exact same time to clear the right door. They stood back-to-back, looking at two different empty rooms.

"Good," Billy answered. "Things were a little quiet for my taste."

Kelly could feel the shift in weight at his back as Billy turned to advance down the hallway. That slight change in physical contact was the only signal Kelly needed to know he had to turn to cover their rear.

They'd cut through the Administration section to get to Testing;

the newly constructed flight line was an extension built off of the Testing section. So far, they'd managed to evade detection through two of the Platform's sections. Hugging walls, ducking into shadows, and silently rounding corners were all simple enough. Being quick enough to take a shot at the security cameras they spotted with his silenced 9mm was a bit more challenging. But not challenging enough to slow them down.

Both of their pasts were steeped in shadow by design. Neither needed the rest of Cerberus Squad to know the full details of how they earned their skills. At the end of the day, Vaun was a soldier. But Kelly and Billy were assassins. Quiet was how they liked to work. The shadows were home.

Only once so far had evasion not been an option. On the exterior catwalk connecting Administration to Testing, they'd come across a pair of technicians out for what must have been a smoke break. There were no shadows to hide in. Billy made quick and quiet work of one by sticking one of his tanto knives through his throat and sweeping him to the ground. While the other technician gaped at the surprise attack, Kelly opted for a much simpler solution and gave him a sharp crack across the jaw with the buttstock of his weapon. The second technician toppled back over the guardrail and plummeted to the waters far below.

It had only been a few minutes since then, but Kelly felt like their lucky streak was bound to run out. The thought came contrary to Kelly's typical optimistic views, but even an optimist needs to be realistic on occasion. If there was going to be a significant enemy presence, it would assuredly be near the flight line.

Kelly expected to find technicians refueling the jets, security patrolling the area, and flight crews gearing up for their impending mass murder. Their numbers would be significant, but the pair knew only about twenty needed to die: the pilots. No pilots, no faux surprise attack.

Conversely, if they could disable the launching catapult, then Cain's squadron wouldn't be able to make takeoff speed. The catapult along the flight deck accelerated aircraft to over one hundred and fifty miles per hour. Without that boost, they'd simply plunge off the edge of the flight deck and into the waters below. Which would also be a desired outcome.

"Blackbars to Forty-Seven," Vaun's voice echoed through Kelly's earbud. "We're taking fire in Engineering."

"Need backup?"

"Negative," answered Vaun and Kelly could hear rapid gunfire. "Security will be converging on us. It might clear your path."

"Roger. I'll let you know when we're done here."

That was Kelly. Not "I'll let you know *if* we can do this," or "I'll let you know how close we get." There was hope in the way he expressed his certainty, and he wished his brothers could feel it. The guys often said that though Vaun was the leader of the squad, Kelly was its heart.

Kelly tapped his earbud to close the line, then gave Billy a reassuring nod before stacking up against the last door between them and the flight deck. Time to make good on his word to Vaun.

CHAPTER 56

They kept coming. From the sound of Tag's belt-fed monster and the resounding death cries, it was clear that Cain's stock of cannon fodder wasn't running low. The same wasn't necessarily true for his ammo count. Tag had the one catwalk covered. Unfortunately, it wasn't the only entrance into the generator area. Vaun knelt behind a workbench with his aim set upon the other doorway, leaving myself and Madison to sabotage the power systems.

"Place the charge there," she instructed.

I stuck the remote charge against a portion of the wall that didn't look particularly important. Hey, I'm no engineer but I trusted the good doctor to not lead me astray with our limited explosives. We only had three plastique blocks.

"Only two explosives left, don't you think we should place them *on* one of these generators?"

"We don't need to destroy all of the generators," she answered. "Just their connection to the rest of the Platform. Place the next one there." I did as she directed and stuck the charge onto a panel on the floor. "Blow those sections, and we sever the power lines. Last charge there."

I emplaced the final explosive and couldn't help the surge of optimism I felt in my gut. I swallowed it back down with the clarity that the mission was far from over.

"We done?" Vaun called from his corner.

"Just now," I answered and tossed him the clicker detonator. The captain caught it one handed without so much as glancing in my direction. That spark of hope was definitely taking hold despite my best efforts.

So it was a little surprising when I saw *actual* sparks coming from Vaun's chest. All at once a lightning bolt shot through my own body. By the time I toppled over onto my locked knees, Vaun was already convulsing violently on the ground.

The shock wracked my body without end. My jaw slammed shut with a mind of its own so suddenly, I feared I'd bite my tongue off. Fingers that had been trained through years of discipline squeezed tight along the grip and trigger of my rifle. Bullets sputtered out of the suppressed rifle. The only silver lining in my utter helplessness was that when I collapsed my barrel ended in a direction other than Madison's face. Rounds dinged off the metallic floor and far wall, only ceasing when the firing pin struck on an empty magazine.

Madison gaped at the both of us. Panicked, she checked the other corner where Tag had been posted with his machine gun. The big man was similarly incapacitated. Spasms jerked his body around like a drunken puppeteer. He fought against it with everything he had, but his arm refused to reach out.

I'm sure Madison must have considered trading up her pistol in exchange for Tag's belt-fed heavier automatic weapon. If only the security team that stormed in from Vaun's door had given her time to make a decision.

A flash grenade bounced into the room and in my electrocuted helplessness, I couldn't even do so much as cover my ears. The deafening blast hit me full force. Madison, barely four feet away, was hit with a concussive wave that knocked the wind out of her. And, just like that, our crack team of renegade war-stoppers was taken down.

CHAPTER 57

There were an infinite number of reasons for him to be awakened at this hour, and the president was fairly sure not one of them was due to anything good. Uneasy lies the head that wears the crown, and right now the president's brow was quite troubled indeed. He sat up and rubbed his eyes, allowing himself a precious three seconds before he would don the weight of the world.

"How bad is it?"

Gary Bell, his Chief of Staff, paused for a moment. He looked at the two Secret Service agents to either side of him, as if either of them would have an answer. He swallowed nervously. It was only when the president's tired eyes focused on the lights that he saw Bell was slick with sweat.

"Gary, out with it. What's going on?"

"We . . . we may be under attack, Mr. President."

The president leapt out of his bed, whipped a robe off a nearby hook, and strode out of his bedroom within half a heartbeat. Politics were a headache of schmoozing and bullshitting. Policy was always a pursuit of a no-win scenario where inevitably someone was going to have a gripe with whatever decision was made. He'd made peace with that some time ago. You can't make it far in American government without first accepting that fact. But an attack? That transcended the day-to-day bullshit of the American political system. That unified everyone across the aisle. It was a sad fact of life that the only thing the left and the right agreed on was that dead Americans by foreign hands could not go unpunished.

"Okay, first thing," he said as he walked into the Oval Office. Several of his Cabinet members were already present, as well as some of the Joint Chiefs. "What do you mean attack? Terrorist threat? Mass shooting by a foreign national? Someone sending white powder through the mail accidentally getting flagged again?"

The last one was meant as a joke. He even offered a half-hearted smile to make sure everyone in the room knew it. No one laughed. It dawned on him that everyone in the room wore the same grave expression as Bell. The president suddenly felt very underdressed and stupid in his bathrobe.

"How . . . how bad is it?" he asked. He couldn't pick his eyes up from the carpet.

General Robert Wainwright of the United States Army, chairman of the Joint Chiefs of Staff, stepped up. "Mister President, as we speak our satellites are detecting a large number of North Korean fighter planes approaching U.S. airspace." A thirty-pound ball of lead hit the bottom of the president's stomach. "We're also seeing heavy mobilization of an as-of-yet unforeseen North Korean fleet advancing into the Pacific."

The president ran his fingers through his thinning hair, feeling the first beads of nervous sweat already spotting up across his scalp. "Don't we have eyes on their fleet . . . twenty-four seven? What do you mean, unforeseen?"

Bell answered. "This fleet is consistent with intelligence reports that assessed North Korea having several hidden docks and shipyards, sir. Subterranean. Our satellites couldn't spot them until they'd crossed into open water."

The world was perpetually doused in kerosene and the president did his best day by day to swat as many matches as he could away from it. Today, one hell of a match had slipped under his radar. Right now he wanted to slap his entire intelligence community for not bringing these reports to his attention sooner. Or maybe himself for not remembering that they'd already done so.

"What the hell is going on?! Is China pushing them to this? I've never been briefed on anything *close* to this. Where, why... I don't... Wait. Give me timelines," he said. "How long before our Navy will have to engage? More importantly, how long before their assault reaches U.S. airspace?"

General Wainwright gave him a stony stare. The old soldier was never one to mince words or beat around the bush. Wainwright always took a moment before speaking. His way of being absolutely sure he meant what he said. It was one of the reasons the president liked him so much.

"The North Korean fleet will be within striking distance of the Seventh Fleet within two hours."

The president breathed. Still time to make a decision. Acts of war and retaliation were better made when given time to think. Wainwright saw this and his grave expression never faltered. It gave the president pause. "Sir, at their current trajectory and speed, their jets will be entering our airspace in the next thirty minutes. After that, they'll be able to attack any of the major West Coast hubs within five minutes."

Though he didn't need him to, Wainwright began to list the possible cities. "San Diego, Los Angeles, San Francisco, for starters. If they adjust their flight path, Seattle is a possibility."

"Can't we scramble a few of our jets and... I don't know, intercept them or whatever?"

Wainwright slowly stood, and then handed him a picture. He immediately recognized it as a satellite imagery printout. Such a weightless thing seemed to weigh a ton when the president saw the sheer number of Korean aircraft on it.

"Mister President, this is a *massive* aerial assault," he said bluntly. "This is not some international posturing or show of power. This is an act of war. We need to act before it's too late."

"Where is Mr. Rourke?" the president asked. He'd come to appreciate the necessity of a man such as Rourke, who scared the shit out of him. If anyone had some sort of Hail Mary solution for this type of nightmare, it would be him.

"We haven't been able to reach him," the secretary of defense stated. "Hopefully that means he's working on something, as well."

The president nodded. He'd already learned his lesson about the capabilities of the Black Spear initiative. Underestimating it was a mistake only a fool would make twice. Still . . . this was full-scale war. Black Spear was geared towards terrorism in extreme circumstances.

"Mister President, we don't have time to wait," Wainwright said. It wasn't exactly a secret that the General didn't approve of Black Spear. Though that didn't change the fact the man was right. The president couldn't stand by, waiting for word from Rourke that he may or may not be working some black-ops angle to solve this.

The president sank into his chair. Again, he felt completely underdressed for the gravity of the situation. "What are our options . . ."

"With this scale of attack, it is unlikely that we'll be able to stop all of the aircraft. We will likely still suffer heavy casualties; between the hundreds and thousands depending on their final destination. Retaliation will be necessary. Ground troops from Mujuk can be ready within hours. Our forces in Japan can begin to mobilize. And, of course, the second we take action against North Korea, their allies will be sure to join their efforts against us."

"China," the president said bluntly.

The General pursed his lips and nodded. "This is going to be a war, sir. This isn't some skirmish that's going to be settled overnight."

"Years . . ." the president breathed. "This will take years. My God . . ." His legacy would be marked by the start of a conflict with a foreign nation. Not against an insurgency, not against rogue terrorist cells, but against an actual sovereign state. A world power. It would lead to conflict on a scale the planet had not seen for the better part of a century.

Over thirty-six thousand American men had given their lives the last time their countries had been at war. This time would be worse. Technological advances would now cause twice that number. *Ten* times that number!

"There's no way to stop this, is there?"

General Wainwright read the president's mind and considered what to say. Everything in him screamed not to say it, but his job was to inform the president of the reality, not to play to ideals. And the reality was that it was entirely possible to stop this war overnight. To completely cripple and punish Korea for this brazen attack and to deter her allies from so much as raising a fist against America.

"There is the nuclear option."

The president's face fell into his own hands, which barely managed to keep it from slipping to the desktop beneath.

Jesus Christ. Oh, Jesus fucking Christ . . .

CHAPTER 58

Cole West. 1:05 a.m.
The Platform
Pacific Ocean

The shocks ceased as CDI security filled the room, but my nervous system had called it quits on me a few thousand volts ago. A particularly portly man sauntered in once all the other guards had secured the generator room. The nametag on his uniform said "Mosley"; and if that wasn't enough then the way he shouldered through his men to get to center stage definitely told us he thought himself in charge. As self-important as the prick came off, something else caught my eye. The small remote in his hand.

"Check 'em," he ordered.

Two men set about pilfering through my pockets in ways I could only describe as thorough. Every hidden goodie and secret stash was snatched away. One of the security guards found the Screech emitter, but Mosley warned him away from fiddling too much. Another one found the Turkey Dinner aerosol sedative and looked at it curiously.

"Give me that shit," said Mosley and stuffed both in a cargo pocket. "Promise you it isn't perfume."

I was a prisoner in my own body. None of my limbs wanted to move. My skin felt burnt, the veins running down my arms like charged cables. If I could find a mirror, I was certain there would be smoke billowing from my ears Loony Toons style. Glancing at Vaun, I saw him manage to shift his bodyweight just enough so that the detonator slid underneath a workbench behind him.

"The big one's still moving, chief," one of the guards near Tag said.

Mosley frowned and pointed the remote in Tag's direction. When he pressed the button, Tag was hit with another dose of electricity.

"Bring him over here," Mosley ordered.

"Guy weighs a ton . . ." the guard muttered.

Two more stepped up to help him pull Tag's body over, each grabbing an arm while the first pulled from the shoulder straps of his *Fafnir* vest. Mosley wrenched Madison's head around by her hair, then shoved her to the floor near me.

"It's the vests . . ." she whispered. "Samuel planted some kind of boobytrap in them."

"I gathered as much," I said through rubbery, limp lips. All our communication gear and network capabilities with CDI components had been scrapped already, but we should've counted on the clever son of a bitch finding a way to sabotage equipment that didn't even have electronic components.

"We're three short here," Mosley said. He looked around the room with outstretched arms, frowning at his men. "What the fuck is this? Mister Cain said there were six on Cerberus Squad plus the doctor."

"No one else here, chief," answered a guard from the far side of the room.

"Yeah, I can see that, dipshit! So, where are they?"

None of his men spoke. Mosley turned in a slow circle, waiting for an answer. Fed up, he pulled a compact Glock from his belt and placed it against Madison's temple. "Look, I'm pretty sure I'd just waste my time threatening these black-ops fellas, so I'm going to threaten you instead, *capisce?*"

Madison winced away from the Glock's barrel, yet her eyes showed no fear. "Chief Mosley, I've had a very interesting day. That gun isn't the first I've had put in my face tonight. And to be perfectly honest, I'd say so far it's the smallest."

Even though it hurt my fried chest like hell to do so, I couldn't help but laugh. Vaun let out a quiet pained snicker as well.

"It's not the size but how you use it," Mosley said. He fired three rounds in the air then stuck the hot barrel against Madison's temple.

The skin seared, and she screamed.

"Where. Are. They?"

With each word he gave a harder jab of the gun. A circular welt rose from her temple.

"Dead," mumbled Vaun.

Mosley whirled on him. His Glock snapped to Vaun's face, which was pretty unnecessary since he was still limply sprawled out facedown.

"Dead?" Mosley asked. He cocked his head towards two of his men, who lifted Vaun up to his knees by his arms.

"Cain crashed our helicopter. Three of my men didn't walk away."

Mosley sneered at that. He messed Madison's face back into the ground like a schoolyard bully and strode across the generator room.

"Fancy that," he said and laughed. The rest of his men gradually joined in. The combined amusement rebounded off of the walls around us and turned into a mocking cacophony.

Somehow a spark of life found its way to my fingertips. Any other day, and I'd use it to flip Mosley the bird. But I didn't. For some odd reason I decided to use it to tap Madison's elbow. Just the lightest of reassurances that it was going to be okay. Which, if I couldn't get the rest of my body to move sometime soon, was probably the biggest load of bullshit I'd shoveled in a while. I don't know if he caught it or if he was just that much of an asshole, but Mosley decided to kick me in the ribs all the same.

"Those friends of yours?" he asked and kicked me again, this time in the back. "The ones who died in the crash? I hope you got a good look at their mangled bodies." A stomp to the gut this time. My mind was too busy remembering a comrade bleeding out in the tall grass to feel it. "How broken their bodies were. I hope that image is *really* vivid." He placed his boot on my hand—the one I'd barely been able to move a second ago—and ground his heel in. All I felt was the warm pool of Thomas's blood I'd knelt in. All I could hear was the last promise he asked us to make.

You can stop it . . .

"I remember it," I said and gritted my teeth. I'd die before I gave this son of a bitch the satisfaction of hearing me cry out in pain.

"Good . . ." he said, drawing out the word with sick pleasure. "Because how they died in that crash? However horrible it was? I promise you, we are going to do *so* much worse to you." Mosley pulled back his boot to stomp my face this time.

And that was when Tag stood up. Maybe his higher muscle mass was able to absorb the shocks easier. Maybe his adrenaline fought off the effects a little better. Personally? I think he was just too damn angry to have something as simple as electricity keep him down. I don't know how he got up. I certainly knew why, though. Tag was a complicated guy to like, but there was one absolute rule with him: you don't fuck with his friends.

He stood up so explosively and suddenly, the two men who'd held his arms were thrown to either side. The scream that came forth from his lips was so primal, so goddamned pure in its hate, the other guards in the room looked taken aback. It was only for a second, which was enough to even the odds.

The closest man to Tag took a punch to the throat that instantly caved in his windpipe. Before he could cough up blood and die, Tag had already launched himself at the next man and delivered a powerful kick to his chest that sent him flying. It also tossed his rifle into the air, which Tag promptly caught. He let loose with a stream of bullets in a wide arc. Three more went down.

Mosley panicked. He fumbled the remote to our vests and ducked behind cover as the last of Tag's bullets chased after him. Mosley's men were caught between taking care of their wounded and returning fire. That same confusion only added more wounded.

"Shake it off, boys!" Tag roared. He scooped up one of the dead guards' sidearms, emptying the magazine as he hugged a corner behind one of the enormous generators. I watched Mosley make a break for it. The security chief ran past me, taking the closest exit and leaving eight of his men behind.

Tag's words got to me. Somehow, I found the strength to shake it off. I pulled myself up onto phantom limbs, stripping off my vest as I stood. The thought of catching a bullet unprotected came in second behind the thought of riding that lightning again.

A hand slammed onto my shoulder. I drew my sidearm with speed that surprised even me, but it was only Vaun. The salty captain was already up and looking a few shades better than me. We both helped Madison to her feet. There was a wild look in her eye. When she pulled her pistol and fired in my direction, I thought she'd snapped. The guard who fell behind us clutching at the bullet-hole in his carotid cleared up my confusion.

"Move your ass, Boomerang!" Vaun ordered. Mosley's goons were caught between us, but their numbers kept Tag from regrouping with us.

"Just blow it!" he said. He pulled his trusty .44 from the small of his back and took a single shot. Vaun glanced at the detonator, his finger hovering over the button. I pulled him by the shoulder towards the second exit. Madison was already moving.

"I said blow it!"

Tag backed out the way we'd come. More gunfire chased after him, each round daring him to move just a little slower. He squeezed off another shot and was rewarded with a guard slumping over.

"He'll be fine," I said. "Do it."

Vaun waited until he could see Tag had made it to the far catwalk, then he hit the button. The explosion licked at our heels before we dove out to the second exit walkway. The remaining security team disappeared behind the blast. Strangely, the explosion seemed to do very little to affect the generators. The lights on our walkway didn't so much as flicker.

Right as I was about to scratch my head over Madison's precise placement of the explosives, the Engineering section let out a large groan. The entire structure shuddered. The edge of the walkway we stood on bent and then snapped free entirely from the doorway to the generator room. Then, swaying like a felled tree, the Engineering section tore away from the rest of the Platform and crashed into the dark waters below.

Hundreds of gallons of fuel stored in the section ignited as it fell. The resulting fireball flung the burning fuel out in every direction. Adjacent sections of the Platform caught flame and the waters below became a lake of fire. The roiling inferno beneath us reached up its fiery tendrils, hungrily licking at the enormous support pillars of the other Platform sections.

A low *Hoooommm* echoed throughout the Platform. And then all the lights went black, leaving us alone, in the dark, out in the middle of nowhere as the fires rose.

CHAPTER 59

His previous life of agency-sanctioned assassinations often saw him all on his own with nothing but a well-hidden blade, but those days were long gone. Kelly couldn't recall a time he'd been so outnumbered. None of it mattered. The only thing on his mind was disabling the launch catapult in time.

That Billy was alongside him made death's inevitability that much harder. Knowing his own ticket might get punched tonight was one thing, but thinking his friend was also on the line was strangely more sobering.

All around them their enemy scrambled. Roughly fifty men in all, each moving at breakneck speed to mitigate the fire creeping up from the waters below. Kelly peered through his thermal scope and tried to single out the pilots. Billy was hunkered down next to him with a rifle of his own, deciding on his first target on the other side of the flight deck.

"We wait any longer and we're going to be aiming at nothing but taillights," Billy said.

"They're jumpy. Jumpy guys can kickstart some serious shitstorms, bud."

"Jumpy people make mistakes. Easier picking."

"Jumping the gun is also a mistake."

Billy's forehand impatiently tapped the handrail of his weapon. "Call the play then, dude."

Kelly evaluated the playing field once more. There had to be a way to level it.

And there it was. A technician on the far end of the flight-line was rigging up a battery-powered floodlight to help illuminate the darkened runway. And he was quite close to the edge.

"Man overboard," Kelly whispered and fired. The sea winds swallowed up the sound of his suppressed shot. To everyone else it looked like the technician had simply fallen off into the fire below. Nearby crew and security rushed over. A few squinted into the blaze but there was no sign of their lost crewmember.

Two pilots that had joined the crowd suddenly followed the technician and plummeted down. In that half-second of confusion, when everyone was wondering why everyone else had lost their footing so easily, another pilot and security goon were picked off. Somebody had spotted the blood splatter and spun around.

Three pilots down, about seventeen to go. And thirty or so armed guards determined to keep that from happening.

"Go for the pilots," reminded Kelly.

"They aren't the ones shooting at us."

A guard with a machine-pistol rushed their position, then fell flat on his face when Kelly's bullet punched an apple-sized hole through his forehead.

"Don't worry, they won't get close."

Billy sighted in on two clambering up a ladder towards an open cockpit. They never reached the top. With every person Billy took down, Kelly felt like they were winning back time on the doomsday clock; every two guards Kelly took out bought Billy time to sight in on another. Kelly took no satisfaction in what they had to do. All he felt was a minor sense of pride that, at the end of the day, live or die, he'd done all he could to save thousands.

Billy missed a shot. Just one, but it allowed two to climb aboard and seal themselves in. In his haste to correct his mistake three more pairs loaded into their own cockpits.

"Getting to be a lot of targets here," Billy muttered, risking a shot at a pilot through the windshield then scowling when it bounced off.

"Still just the one that matters."

Billy risked taking his eye away from his scope to look at Kelly, and he immediately understood. The catapult.

"I knew there was a good reason I brought this," Billy said and turned around for a second. When he turned back towards Kelly, he had the rocket launcher across his lap. "One shot. Just give me an opening, yeah?"

Kelly gave him a solemn nod, then promptly squeezed off two rounds. Two more headshots. The advancing security forces took cover behind crates or the fighter jets themselves; the jet's turbine engines were already roaring. They could roar all they wanted in a few more moments.

"Any day," Kelly shouted, firing his magazine's three last rounds to keep the enemy behind cover. He swapped it out for a fresh mag, firing again as Billy leaned out from behind the other side of the cargo box they hid behind.

The tip of Billy's rocket peaked out, and Kelly could hear one of the guards shout "RPG! RPG!" over the screaming engines as Billy fired. His aim was true, and the rocket went right to the middle of the flight-line where the catapult track lay on the deck's surface. It struck, and the dark flight deck was basked in light as the rocket exploded. Four men were too close to find safety and were instantly turned to chunks, two more were thrown back by the tremendous blast, and one was unlucky enough to be thrown clear over the edge where he fell into the arms of the ever-hungry fire. When the smoke cleared there was a deep jagged crater where the start of the catapult launcher should have been.

Billy discarded the spent rocket launcher, ducked back behind cover, and retrieved his rifle.

"Go ahead and check 'Save America' off the To-Do List. You're welcome."

Kelly didn't bother fighting the huge smile that stretched from ear to ear. But then Billy was looking past him, well *over* him really. He was looking towards the squadron of jets. Even though the launcher was destroyed, their turbines were still going. In fact, they were speeding up. There was a mechanical whirring as something within one of the fighter planes shifted.

Then, impossibly, the first jet *rose*. It hovered in the air for a moment before gradually rising more and more. The entire squadron were VTOL jump jets, capable of vertical takeoff and landing. Meaning they'd never needed the catapult launcher to begin with. One by one the jets lifted off the ground, then they shot off towards the horizon as one.

Kelly and Billy stared at the aircraft, horrified. They'd stopped nothing.

CHAPTER 60

Moment by moment, the man she respected most in the world slipped deeper and deeper into pain-induced shock. Mr. Rourke's suit, which was always impeccably pressed and clean, was soaked through with sweat. Those hard-squinted eyes that so many men found difficult to meet directly were fighting hard not to roll into the back of his skull. Darren Rourke was already broken; the only thing Mason still wondered was how long before the remaining pieces of the man crumbled into dust.

The silver lining at the moment was that Cain's smug confidence had been falling apart almost as quickly. His little home movie execution was halted when the lights had momentarily been deactivated; but whatever antics Cerberus Squad had gotten into had since knocked them out a second time. They had yet to turn back on. The same explosion that had caused the blackout rocked the entire Platform so violently, Cain's video camera tripod toppled over, the high-definition lens shattering on impact.

Emergency lights on the walls pulsed weakly with the last remnants of their reserve power, bathing the entire room in a dull red every two seconds. The tint painted across Cain's face perfectly captured his escalating rage.

"What's the matter, don't have a spare camera in the closet?"

At that moment one of the doors opened. For about half a second Mason actually expected it to be some CDI technician with three spare cameras in tow, but it was only Phobos Marstelli returning. Cain's bald enforcer had since changed from his slim-fitting blazer and dress slacks into more appropriate combat dress. Tactical fatigue pants and a *Fafnir* vest—that Mason assumed didn't hide a secret taser—with a dark turtleneck. Phobos's actual business attire.

The lower half of the thin scar trailing from the corner of Phobos's mouth was hidden underneath the turtleneck's collar. It seemed strange for such a cold-blooded killer to be self-conscious about a scar, but Mason wasn't too keen about the one on her own face, either. A muscle tensed along his cheekbone. His fingertips rolled anxiously along the large karambit on his belt.

He's dressed for war and antsy for it, Mason thought, *but dressed for war with who exactly?*

"The air strike is right on schedule, sir," Deimos said from behind the White Shield laptop. "Estimated arrival to Los Angeles and San Diego is fifteen minutes, five more for San Francisco."

The update lifted an invisible weight from Cain's shoulders. He stood a little straighter, frowned a little less, and his back and forth pacing around the room slowed from its manic rate.

Phobos, however, was not as elated. He drew and flipped his karambit around by its ring. Incessantly.

Deimos noticed Phobos and gave him a gentle smile. "Soon, dear brother. Soon. He is still on his way."

Phobos's hand froze on the knife, then he returned it to its sheath.

A door crashed open, and Chief Mosley stumbled in, the man visibly shaken. He held his pistol in one trembling hand while his eyes darted around the room in bewilderment.

"Mosley . . ." Cain said through tight lips. "Status?"

"They're here. Look, the bastards even brought some of your own stuff back."

Cain took two small devices from Mosley and glared at Rourke. "Ungrateful little shits still using my things, huh? Fancy that, Rourke." He stowed both items inside his jacket and shook his head. "I'll be sure and confiscate whatever remaining CDI property they have from their cold bodies."

"Sir, you're not listening," Mosley stammered. "Engineering . . . they just blew up all of Engineering!"

Cain's mustache twitched. He ran a hand through his white hair and turned his back to the room. Mason took the brief distraction to start working at the rope around her wrists again.

Major General Bahk shifted uneasily on the execution set, as did the rest of his fellow stand-ins. "This isn't what we agreed on, Cain."

He said nothing. Meanwhile, Mason felt her binding give just a little.

"We need to get out of here. The place is burning!" Mosley shouted.

All eyes fell on him.

Mosley continued. "That much fuel? It's going to do more than melt some steel beams here. We have to get out *now*."

"I still expect payment," Bahk said, although Cain ignored him. "You aren't the only one who's put a lot at risk here. Where's my damned money?!"

Cain turned around and shot Bahk through the eye. "Given recent changes, I regrettably no longer require your services."

The Sergeant and Sergeant First Class actors balked as the General fell to the floor. Deimos calmly drew his sidearm and shot them. The expression the fiery-haired man wore was one of surprise. He acted without question, following Cain's lead, but clearly felt unsure where things would go from here.

With her wrists now freed, Mason reached down towards her shoe.

"We're not leaving yet, Mosley," Cain said, deliberately wiping off the barrel of his pistol. "You know how much this facility means. Gather your men, get back out there, and *finish* them!"

Mosley did a double-take on the dead Koreans. He took a moment to compose himself, then that cocksure look returned to his face. "You can count on me, sir. They just proved a bit of a surprise is all. But they're just a handful of men, all alone. We'll take them out."

His smug look vanished as a nearby explosion rocked the entire room. It was far too devastating to be an after-effect of the Engineering section. The others in the room were in a panic, but Mason, all too familiar with the sound of an air attack, immediately recognized it.

"Who said they're alone?" Mason snarled and leapt out of her chair.

Mosley turned towards her and drew his gun, too late, as Mason used the broken off heel of her stiletto shoe as a shiv, spiking it into his neck again and again. In the blink of an eye, she had pierced his throat nearly a dozen times, leaving a ruined mess of blood and holes. The Glock slipped from his dying hands, and Mason scooped it up before it hit the ground. She spun in the direction of the room's gravest threat, Phobos, and emptied the magazine. A red-haired blur dove through the air and tackled Phobos to the ground before a single round could graze him.

The Marstelli brothers retreated through the back door, abandoning Cain to his hostages. Mason knelt by Mosley's still warm body and snagged a spare magazine from his belt. By the time she'd reloaded, Cain too had slipped away unseen.

"Slippery bastard . . ."

Mason turned her attention to loosening the restraints from her other fellow hostages. Rourke was too far gone to notice when his wrists were freed. That perpetually sarcastic coroner, Dr. Phelps, was bug-eyed and practically glued to her chair. Poor girl was too scared to move without a word from Mason first. Rather than reassuring her that they were still going to make it out alive, Mason moved to release Goode from his chair. She wasn't a babysitter. If Phelps was too shell-shocked to move her ass when the fire got to the room, it was her problem.

Except Goode was no longer in the room with them. Cain had taken the White Shield director with him.

"Fucking slippery *bastard*!"

CHAPTER 61

Being the back-up on a mission meant they had the pleasure of coming in hard once Cerberus had done their part to black out the Platform's defenses. No anti-air meant that Valkyrie could bring plenty of shock and more than enough awe. They'd arrived as quickly as they could; a Code Orphan was no small thing. Every one of them were betting it all on Sergeant West's gambit.

Their pilot, Zorro, brought the helicopter in for another strafing run. Twin Gatling guns and a battery of short-range missiles slammed into the north side of the Platform's Executive Center. The Platform might masquerade as a weapons testing facility, but it was absolutely built for war. It shuddered as chunks of reinforced structure were blown away. Nearby guards and fleeing workers caught in the blast disappeared in the smoke, but still the Platform stood.

"Drop us off at the helipad," Valkyrie's squad leader, Magdalena "Magnum" Cruz, ordered.

Zorro gave her a thumbs up from the cockpit.

"Got two runners making a break for it from the helipad," Magnum said.

The squad sharpshooter, Wizard, leaned out of the open side doors. His rifle cracked twice, and then the runners were no longer running. "Presto."

Half of the helipad was taken up by a CDI executive helicopter. Magnum considered spending some of their ordinance blowing it to hell, but she decided there were other more important targets. Their own helicopter touched down, and Valkyrie Squad was boots on the ground.

Magnum jumped out first, as always, and took the point. Wizard was right behind her, his high-powered rifle slung across his back and swapped out for an AA-12 shotgun. The man had a gift when it came to accuracy at long distance, but in close quarters he leaned on the spread of buckshot. Valkyrie Squad's demo-man, Matchbox, brought up the rear with his personal bag of goodies in tow.

"Zorro, keep giving 'em hell. I want them bundled up inside watching the air and not in the hallways," Magnum ordered.

"Got it, Mags."

Valkyrie Squad advanced from the helipad down an ominously long walkway that led to the central core of the Platform structure. Sure, they were doing this to rescue Mr. Rourke. Sure, failure most assuredly meant the complete erasure of the Black Spear initiative and prison time for all parties involved. And, yeah, there was that other part of World War Three breaking out in less than an hour if they couldn't stop this. But none of those had truly been the reason Magnum had moved heaven and earth to get her team here in time. What it really came down to was that Rourke wasn't the only hostage, and quite frankly Magnum couldn't wait to see Mason's face when she realized who had come to rescue *her*.

The thought of her rival's scorn spurred her on as she led her squad into the eye of the storm.

CHAPTER 62

Phobos had no trouble hauling his brother down the hallway. Despite being the leaner of the two, his strength betrayed his size. The entire time Deimos tried to push him away, insisting that he was more than capable of escaping on his own, but Phobos's protective instinct was in full gear. He refused to give up on the half-carry he had around Deimos's waist.

Kara Mason's bullets had been too damned close to them both and the only thing currently on Phobos's mind was getting them away. Pull back, regroup. Gain the advantage. Then they could return and Phobos could finally claim his prize: Captain Eric Vaun. That opportunity to face his promised opponent had been ripped from his hands by a handful of 9mm bullets.

"Let me go, I said."

They'd covered enough distance that Phobos felt it was safe to stop for a breath or two. He let go of Deimos's belt and pushed him around a corner while he watched the way they'd come. So far, no one had followed them. Phobos nodded to himself then moved to pull his brother further along the corridor.

Except his brother had fallen to the ground. His breathing was shallow and quick. The woman's shots hadn't just been close after all. Red stains were spreading out from Deimos's shoulder, gut, and thigh. Phobos froze.

"I will be … quite alright," Deimos managed to say between breaths. "If I could trouble you for your belt, though?"

Phobos removed his belt and used it to tourniquet Deimos's leg. A sharp gasp escaped his brother's lips as he cinched it down tight. Then he moved to apply pressure to the gunshot wound on Deimos's stomach.

Deimos pushed him away.

"I believe I can manage," he said, clamping one of his hands onto the wound.

Phobos tried not to stare too long at the growing amount of red on the wall behind Deimos.

"But we're still on the clock, dear brother … take this." With his free hand he pushed the White Shield laptop towards him. "You keep that close, and he'll come right to you."

Phobos's eyes pleaded with him, but Deimos simply rested his head against the wall. Phobos gestured down the hallway. *We could just go?*

Deimos shook his head, "We have a reputation to uphold, and our word to live by."

Phobos used two fingers to point to Deimos, then both hands to motion towards himself. *You're my responsibility.* The woman had been aiming at him. If Phobos had reacted more quickly, then Deimos wouldn't have had to save him. He wouldn't be bleeding out.

He saw the pained look in his brother's eyes, eyes that so rarely betrayed any emotion at all. Deimos smiled, then signed back to his silent brother: *Not your fault.* Deimos gave his brother one last solemn nod. "Go."

Phobos stood, laptop in hand, and left his brother behind.

CHAPTER 63

It was getting hot. A hopeful part of my mind made the case that with the power out, so was the A.C., and all the trapped air was just gradually warming up. The more reasonable section of my mind was too busy screaming that the whole place was burning down and us with it.

"When you told me where to place the explosives, did you know this would happen?" I asked.

Madison gave a nervous laugh. "Fight fire with fire, right? Samuel's been playing with it for so long, it's time he got burned."

"If you utter one more fire-related metaphor, I'm tossing you overboard."

"Fair. But no, I didn't know for sure that we'd cause a chain reaction. I was just trying to detach the Engineering section."

"Really not complaining with the results."

"Can it," Vaun barked.

My jaw slammed shut like a mousetrap. The captain was on edge again, growing more tense the closer we got to the Executive Center. I could lie and say it was because our window of opportunity to save the day was closing, but I knew the real reason. The closer we got to the Executive Center, the closer we got to the Marstelli brothers. The closer Vaun got to getting even for Major Wilcox's death. I'd thought that the rage inside him had settled; turns out he was only playing it quiet.

I barely recognized him. Vaun was moving quicker than we should be, passing doorways without fully clearing them, and straight-up ignoring the fact that two other people were with him. All he cared about was getting to the end of the corridor and reaching the hostages.

Madison noticed the shift in our fearless leader's demeanor. Having such a seasoned operator lose his disciplined edge in front of you was not unlike losing your sense of balance. It was like all the lights suddenly going out and you losing the handrail you were using as an anchor point. It was made worse by the realization that I'd have to step up even more and keep all three of us safe if he couldn't. I'd stopped being the squad rookie a long time ago, but there was a difference between being capable of surviving and being capable of filling the gap Vaun left.

"Pick it up," Vaun said sharply.

I finished clearing a doorway he hadn't seen.

"Roger."

I eyed Madison and waved my hand towards the ground, urging her to calm down. It was advice intended as much for me as for her. We reached the doorway to the Executive Center. I gave Vaun a quick shoulder pat. It was to tell him I was ready to breach, but I was also hoping it would pull him back into disciplined muscle memory. We needed him to be calm and focused. Anything else, and he would get Mr. Rourke and the others killed.

But just like that I saw his posture change. It was like he'd shrugged out of the skin of that angry stranger and suddenly the stoic Captain I respected so much returned. I just needed him to stick around this time.

"On your go, Toxin," he said, shifting out of the way of the door so I could kick it in. He was letting me go in first. A good sign.

"Rah, Blackbars." I booted the door hard right above the handle. I must've given it a little too much oomph because the damn thing flew off the frame and into the room. We barreled in. I immediately cleared the blind spot to our left while Vaun covered our twelve o'clock. But the room was already clear.

"Nice of you to show up," Mason said. "Don't take it personally, but I got tired of waiting for you to come rescue us. I don't really do the damsel in distress thing. No, offense, Doc."

Madison was taken aback. "I'll have you know I've been on the other side doing *plenty* of the distressing so far."

"Oh, didn't see you there. Glad you decided to join us! Wasn't even talking to you, Other Doc," Mason said. "Previous comment would be directed at contestant number three." She gestured towards Dana Phelps, who was glued to her chair in full-on panic mode.

I spotted Rourke, the great Black Spear titan, looking in a bad way. Mason shoved two of those white pills of his into his mouth and forced him to swallow.

Vaun knelt near a twitching body, pleased that it was only Security Chief Mosley. He pulled a spike out of Mosley's throat, and upon realizing what it was, returned the shoe heel to Mason. She used it to pin her hair up into a tight bun, not even bothering to wipe the blood off first.

"Cain?" I asked.

"Gone, he took Goode with him. The Marstellis took the laptop."

We were going to need both intact if we had any hope of undoing Cain's machinations.

"Who'd you bring in for backup?" Mason asked. "Their little diversion is what got me the opening to get us free."

"Valkyrie Squad," I answered.

"Oh, for fuck's sake . . ." Mason groaned. "Is it too late to tell them to turn back?"

"About that, we're right here," a voice said as three soldiers entered the room. Magnum, Wizard, and Matchbox. I knew them by reputation but had yet to work alongside them.

"We brought goodies," Wizard said and passed two earbud communicators to me and Vaun. "Non-CDI tech. Won't reach across the country, but they'll do fine here."

Mason shook her head upon seeing Valkyrie Squad's leader, "Goddamn it, Mags . . ."

"You miss me?" Magnum said, blowing a playful kiss to her. "Boy, this is embarrassing. The legendary Sledgehammer getting rescued by little old me?"

"I guess that makes us even for the oh, I don't know, thirty or so times I pulled your ass out of the fire."

Magnum beamed. It would have been entertaining, if not for the more pressing business at hand.

I clapped my hands to get the ladies' attention. "Fucking newsflash. The whole place is on fire and the whole world will be tomorrow if we don't unfuck this. Get the hostages the fuck out of here, and we'll handle Cain."

Magnum's eyebrows lifted in mock shock. "Sheesh, say it, don't spray it, kid. But the big guy's right. The whole fleet of fighter jets is already on its way to carpet bomb the West Coast."

A stone hit my stomach. The countdown to zero was closer than I'd thought. If Cain's aerial raid had left the Platform, it raised questions as to the condition of Billy and Kelly. I put the thoughts out of my mind and focused instead on what I could actually control.

Matchbox hauled Rourke to his feet while Wizard gently took Doc Phelps by the hand to escort her from the room. Magnum then turned to Mason, fighting to hold back her smile and utterly failing. "Ma'am, I'm going to need you to come with me. You heard the man. All hostages need to be evac'd."

". . . I still have one good heel, bitch."

Magnum looked to me confused but I just shook my head. "You don't want to know. Get them out of here." Mason removed her shoes and reluctantly followed Matchbox and Wizard back to the helipad.

Free from distractions, I turned back to Madison. "Okay, I'm really running low on leadership energy, so I need you to point us in some kind of direction here." She took off towards one of the doorways so fast, I grabbed her shoulder. "I said point us, not take the point. Still on bodyguard duty here."

Vaun silently took up the rear as we left Cain's mock studio and climbed a flight of stairs. The dull red emergency lights disappeared, replaced instead by blinding white fluorescents.

"This is the central security hub," Madison explained.

The fully illuminated room was filled with screens that should have displayed live-feed from security cameras, but instead all but four of them showed static. Two showed separate helipads, a third a large server room, and the fourth was what looked to be one of the facility's storage warehouses. A large monitor on one of the walls listed all of the systems that were down, blinking in red LED letters. "Samuel has nearly all of the emergency power rerouting to this hub for some reason. What good is a security station if none of the systems are online?"

I pondered that while looking around the rest of the room. A computer station in the corner caught my eye. I didn't know much about computers, but judging by its size and how many connections it was being fed through the wall, it was clear it had cost a fortune.

"Say, doc, is this important?"

Madison arched an eyebrow, then sat in the chair and started to move the mouse. I hadn't the slightest clue what she was doing, but her eyes lit up with recognition. She carefully moved the cursor across the screen, as if scared of what the computer might do. Then her eyes went wide, and she held a hand to her mouth.

"Cole . . . I know why Samuel wanted to kill me."

CHAPTER 64

The flames rising up from the waters climbed higher. The closer they got, the more they distorted Kelly's thermal scope. His view flooded with white blooms that masked the crowd of advancing enemies. Fed up, he hit the quick-detach lever and switched to the flip-up iron sights.

"Running low," Billy said.

Bullets snapped into the crate they hid behind, so near that splinters puffed into the air and momentarily blinded him. Billy's rifle had run dry a few minutes ago, and he was down to his twin Glocks. Two quick shots later and one of the slides locked back on an empty chamber.

"You and me both." They were boxed in and being overrun. The only thing keeping the enemy at a distance was their own accuracy. That would be a different conversation the second they ran out of ammo. Only six rounds remained in his sniper. Not nearly enough.

"Turning into a real bad day here..." Billy muttered. He squeezed off another shot and a CDI guard fell over the side of the flight deck. Kelly considered the options, what few there were, and came to a hard conclusion. Both of them would not make it out alive.

There was a door across the flight deck that led back into the Platform interior, but there was too much open ground. Somebody would have to stay at the crate and cover the other; that somebody wouldn't have time to make it to the door before he'd be overrun. But Kelly had already made his mind up.

"Two rounds in the mag, one in the pipe . . ." hissed Billy.

"Give me your sidearm, fast," Kelly said.

Billy tossed his Glock and its three remaining bullets in Kelly's lap. While Billy was too busy looking over the crate, Kelly cycled the pistol and nodded to himself as the barrel snapped forward.

"Here's the deal, bud, I'm going to burn my mag and you're going to Usain Bolt your ass to that door. Just run. Don't stop, don't shoot. Just fucking get there in one piece, then you scratch my back and we beat feet the fuck through the door."

Billy looked to the marksman. His friend. There was a grimness to Kelly now that Billy had only glimpsed on rare occasions.

"Hey," Kelly said, his expression softening, "we're gonna be alright, man."

Billy nodded, took a breath. "How much do you have left?" he asked Kelly.

"Enough." He took a deep breath. "Go on three. One, two, three!"

Billy took off in a dead sprint for the door. Kelly leveled his weapon across the crate and took his last shots. The buttstock kicked into his shoulder. As much as he wanted to glance to his side, Kelly refused to look in Billy's direction. All he could do was buckle down, ride out these last shots, and hope Billy made it to the door. The rifle went empty, and he transitioned in a blur to his sidearm and burned three rounds.

And then it was done. The rifle and pistol, finally empty, were left atop the crate as Kelly knelt back down. Only then did he allow himself to make sure his friend had made it. And he had, which brought a smile to Kelly's face he couldn't hold back.

Billy's eyes met his own and he posted up with the pistol Kelly had reloaded. He sighted on an enemy closing on Kelly's crate, then pulled the trigger. Even over the rampant automatic fire from the other shooters, he still heard the hammer fall upon an empty chamber.

Kelly had taken the three bullets from his Glock and loaded an empty mag into Billy's pistol. He'd left himself high and dry just to make sure Billy had enough covering fire to make it to the door.

Conflicting emotions flew across Billy's face. Kelly knew he'd hate him for the trick he'd pulled, knew he'd stupidly beat himself up about how Kelly died saving him. But Billy would still be alive. That would be worth the hate and gave him solace enough.

Billy stood in the door frame, shoving against the door with everything he had. It didn't budge. Again, he slammed his weight into it to no avail.

"Come on, bud, get that damn door open . . ." Kelly muttered as he heard footsteps closing in on him. He slipped a set of brass knuckles over his fingers. He'd go down swinging, by God.

As Billy pulled back to slam his shoulder into the door one last time, it flung open from the inside. Billy stared down the barrel of a gun.

Thankfully, it was on their side.

Tag pulled Billy in with one hand while stepping out and using the other to spray the flight deck with bullets. "Let's go!"

Kelly was already running, and yes, the smile was definitely on his face now. He dropped into a slide for the last four feet like a runner stealing home. Rounds bounced off the floor and walls around them.

Billy bent over to help him off the ground. "Not cool, dude. We're going to have a talk when this is all over."

"Don't know what you're talking about, bud."

Tag slammed the door shut.

"Can't leave you two alone for a minute," he grunted.

"Weren't you supposed to have three other people with you?" Kelly asked.

"Long story." Tag inspected his weapon, which had been fully expended, then jammed it against the door handle. He gave the two of them a queer look and his frown deepened. "Ditch the vests. They're boobytrapped."

"Don't gotta tell me twice," Billy said. "It was wrinkling my favorite shirt, anyway. I guess it was too much to hope you were carrying a few hundred extra bullets for us to borrow?"

Tag drew his .44 revolver. "I've got four rounds."

Billy blew out his cheeks, then unsheathed one of the Tanto blades on his hip. "Like to keep these handy for close encounters, anyway."

Being the senior man, it was on Kelly to call their next move. His signature optimism made a return when he saw a sign on the wall. "If I was a betting man, I'd say that there might be something down that-a-way we could use."

He pointed to the placard. The hallway they were in led directly to the Testing section.

CHAPTER 65

Cole West. 1:45 a.m.
Central Security
The Platform

"*This* is why he's after my head!" Madison shouted.

I looked at the computer screen filled with data but drew a blank. "You're going to have to break it down for me, because I don't know what I'm looking at."

Madison opened a tab on the screen and hundreds of what appeared to be serial numbers were listed.

"These serial numbers are all sequential. You get it? That's how he's gotten so many people to go along with this scheme. They're all implanted with *Firestorm* nanites."

"Get back to the part where you said this is why you're important."

"This iteration has very few deviations from the prototype I designed. I wrote the original programming: I can disable the triggering mechanisms."

I felt hope rise, so close I could grab for it but far enough away that I was scared to reach out. Then Vaun swatted it to the ground. "There's no time. Disarming it won't stop that fleet from bombing the West Coast," he said. Then, he released a long exhale. "But arming it might."

"What are you talking about?"

"The pilots," Vaun said.

The words were uttered so coldly, I felt my heart ice over.

"They have the *Firestorm* in them, as well. They *have* to . . . how else could they agree to this? Hit the button, burn them, and we stop this war right here."

Madison gaped at the captain. He refused to look at her. Instead, his eyes were fixed on the screen, at all of the numbers. People's lives reduced to mere digits.

"Captain, it's not that simple . . ." she said.

"No, doctor, it is. We torch the pilots or thousands die today. Then millions die tomorrow."

"Damn it, listen to me!" she yelled and clicked another tab on the screen. The list of numbers displayed more than tripled. "There are over a *thousand* sets here! Do you have any idea how long it will take to go through each one and determine which belongs to a pilot and which doesn't just belong to one of the security teams here? Or just another hostage under Cain's thumb?"

We all stared at the numbers. It made me dizzy. The numbers seemed to dance on the screen and meld, making it impossible to tell where one sequence ended and another began.

"Samuel will know," she finally said. "Get him, get the pilots' numbers. And this ends today."

I looked to my leader to see if he was on board. Vaun was too busy looking somewhere else.

"Where is this?" he asked, pointing to one of the few security screens that was active. It showed a large room filled with rows of servers. There was a small table in the center of the room and carefully placed upon it was the White Shield laptop. Phobos stood calmly next to it. His karambit in hand, he used its ring to flip it around his hand, back and forth. Forward grip, reverse grip.

The gaunt man stared up at the camera patiently. Waiting.

"Where?!"

"D-digital records," Madison stammered. "It's in the adjacent Administration section."

That feverish look overcame Vaun once more. If he went off half-cocked like this, he'd only get himself killed, but we still needed the White Shield computer Phobos had commandeered. The only option was for me to take care of Phobos myself.

"I'll handle him. What's the fastest way there?"

"Back the way we came, follow the green lines. Half of those hallways are already burning."

She pulled up a digital map of the Platform, the fire alarms and smoke detectors still active. Judging by the display, nearly three quarters of the station was aflame. I was planning my route when Madison blew up one of the other security feeds. "It's Samuel. I found him!"

The feed was from one of the elevators. Both Cain and Goode were inside. The warmaker himself had the White Shield director at gunpoint. "The executive elevator. It leads to the helipad."

"Can you stop that remotely?"

"Of course." She hit a button and both men stumbled as the elevator abruptly halted.

Cain looked around, then reached up and opened the service hatch on the ceiling. Before goading Goode through it, he shot out the security camera.

"Okay, I'll take Phobos and get the laptop. Cap, you get this son of a bitch and make sure he doesn't get away."

I turned away from the computer screen to ensure Vaun was on the same page as me. Except he was no longer in the room. The man had already gone off following the green lines, too lost in vengeance.

"Never mind that," Madison hissed and grabbed my wrist. "Get Samuel. Get those *Firestorm* codes. Otherwise, he wins, Cole. And *everyone* loses."

I nodded. It was down to me. No pressure, right?

CHAPTER 66

Just put one foot in front of the other. That's all he had to do for a little while longer. Deimos didn't have to worry about balance, which was quickly fading, anyway. The wall he leaned on kept him upright well enough. He limped down the hallway. A long red smear along the wall marked his grim progress.

"Almost there," he said as he pushed on. The blood kept leaking out of him in a constant drip that had soaked through his jacket to the sleeve. More of it trickled down the back of his hand. It rolled down his fingertips, then to the floor, leaving red drops in his path like little breadcrumbs. His vision grew hazy, and his legs felt weaker with every step. Blood loss would soon take him.

The Platform's medical wing was clear on the other side of the facility. Deimos would never make it there before he bled out. That was only if the fires hadn't consumed that portion of the Platform yet. Given the current state of affairs, that was a fairly large "if."

No, the medical wing was very much out of reach. But Deimos was not yet without options.

He gritted his teeth and shuffled on. As he reached the end of the hallway, he pressed his hand harder onto the gunshot wound in his gut. It gave a persistent spurt for a moment and then the flow stemmed. But it didn't stop.

At the threshold of the large room he neared, and with no more wall to support him, Deimos's legs finally gave out and he fell forward onto his stomach. He was so close now.

"Not . . . quite yet," he promised himself.

He dragged himself across the floor, hand over bloody hand. He felt that mortal coil slip a little looser with every motion. As death approached Deimos, his thoughts fell upon his brother. Would Phobos get his reward? God, nothing seemed to be going right. His brother deserved at least that.

The enormous room he found himself in was lined with large cargo containers and a few target mannequins. Deimos's salvation lay at the very end of the room. He didn't bother applying pressure to his wounds. It would take both of his arms to make it in time, or he would bleed out regardless. Like some hellish slug, he left a trail of dark red behind him.

His enemies wouldn't be long now. Captain Vaun or one of his merry bunch, to be sure. Deimos would welcome their arrival if he could just make it a little further, just another meter or two.

Blackness swam in his vision. Everything got cold so fast, he started to shake. Still, he crawled on. He fought with everything he had against his body's instinctive call to slip into shock. A bad cough came up his throat, bringing more blood with it. Another followed right behind, triggering a fit that threatened to sap the last of his will.

But he managed to fight through and reach his last hope of survival. His hand brushed against the cold steel, and he couldn't help but smile. Despite the pain, despite his own looming death, he might delay the reaper a bit longer.

Mustering the last reserves of his strength, Deimos pulled himself into the CHAOS armor prototype. The cockpit sealed him in with a hiss of compressed air. His vision started to fail, but he had enough life in him yet to activate the proper sequences.

"MEDICAL DIAGNOSTICS ONLINE," a commanding robotic voice boomed through the onboard speakers.

Deimos went numb as the automated medical protocols activated. His head fell forward and his tired eyes closed, but he still heard, "MULTIPLE TRAUMAS DETECTED."

"Bit of an understatement, my friend . . ."

Small robotic hands went to work stitching him up, one gunshot wound after another, and then tightly applied a bandage across his chest. And then the larger needles came. Two of them jabbed into his neck. Immediately Deimos's eyes shot open, his pupils contracting to mere pinpricks.

CHAOS had just pumped him up with enough fentanyl to numb his wounds and a strong enough adrenaline amphetamine cocktail to effectively wake the dead. And he felt very, very awake. Deimos flexed his hands with renewed vigor. The sheer intensity of what he felt flowing through his veins astounded him. His heart throttled against his ribcage like a battering ram. Another needle hooked to a blood bag went into his arm to begin a blood transfusion.

"Why, thank you," Deimos said. "I felt about a quart low."

Where moments before they moved sluggishly, now his hands fired off lightning quick. He flipped switches and hit buttons to fully activate the CHAOS armor. Electronic systems lit up. Weapons systems armed. A loud whirring sounded as the internal servos and hydraulics powered on. This was the Testing Area, after all. This particular piece of machinery was overdue for more intensive trials.

"CHAOS: ONLINE," the robotic voice declared. The behemoth was alive. And it was ready to hunt.

CHAPTER 67

Eric Vaun. 1:50 a.m.
Digital Records
The Platform

"I've been waiting for this," Vaun said.

Phobos returned Vaun's words with a silent nod that seemed to mirror the sentiment. The fires hadn't reached this area yet, but they would soon. Somehow Vaun knew Phobos was aware of that. It was as if—win, lose, or draw—he intended this location to be both men's final stand.

"You know me?" Vaun asked.

Phobos graciously waved his hand at him, gesturing that Vaun's reputation preceded him.

"No way out from here."

The mute shrugged, utterly unconcerned with the nearing danger.

Vaun slowly circled the room. He never broke his gaze off from Phobos, but he got the lay of the land as he walked. Seeing angles. Measuring the battleground. A thought came to Vaun's mind. "Where's your brother?"

Phobos inhaled sharply. That reaction pleased Vaun. Hopefully, it meant Deimos was already dead or dying. But no matter how bad that hurt Phobos, it wouldn't be enough to sate Vaun. He undid his gun belt and slung it over one of the server towers. From his pocket he withdrew his ProTech Don switchblade, then pressed the button.

"I tell all my men that, as a rule, revenge is an unprofessional pursuit," Vaun said. The four-and-a-half-inch blade locked open in his hand. "But you know what they say. Rules are meant to be broken, aren't they?"

Phobos extended his hand towards Vaun, palm up, and then beckoned Vaun closer.

Come get some.

Vaun didn't care that Phobos was unarmed. It wasn't going to stop him from driving steel through his heart. He took a quick step towards Phobos while slashing diagonally for his neck. Phobos, still waving Vaun towards him, spun under Vaun's arm, drew his karambit, and finished his spin by slashing his knife across the side of Vaun's hip.

Fucking Christ, he was fast. Vaun patted a hand down at his hip, but the cut was shallow. It had barely broken the skin. Lucky.

Phobos feinted, stepped to the left, then flipped his knife to a reverse grip and stabbed upward for Vaun's face. Vaun saw the attack coming, managing to parry it away from him before following up with a downward slash of his own at Phobos's leg. With the amount of force Vaun was pushing behind his blade, it would shear down to Phobos's femur.

If only Phobos hadn't skillfully pivoted his leg clear of the swipe. He was agile in a way that Vaun hadn't expected. Over the course of his career, Vaun had reluctantly ended up crossing blades with an opponent nearly a dozen times. It was never like the movies; these real duels would last all of five seconds before Vaun delivered a killing strike. Which was precisely the reason Vaun grew nervous when ten seconds had already passed.

Phobos came at him again. This time with a furious cut at Vaun's chest. Vaun caught Phobos's wrist and stabbed with the point of his own knife for Phobos's gut. But Phobos dropped his karambit to his free hand and in one motion slashed at both Vaun's belly and forearm.

Vaun winced and pushed away from Phobos. A hot red line was drawn up the middle of his arm; a similar one ran horizontally across his navel. Small cuts. Again, Phobos had come just shy of what could have been a more grievous injury.

That's when it dawned on Vaun what was happening. Like a shark taking nipping bites, Phobos was testing his prey. He was bleeding him just a little. Sizing him up. Any one of the three cuts he'd dealt could have been lethal. Phobos was coming up short on purpose.

Vaun switched his knife to his uninjured arm and lashed out with a lightning-fast cut. The lunge caught his enemy by surprise, and he backpedaled. The mute's hand snapped backwards like a child withdrawing from a hot stove. Holding out the underside of his hand for Vaun to see, Phobos let two drops of blood well up and patter to the floor.

And he smiled.

Phobos unleashed a flurry of cuts as if the slight wound had energized him. Vaun blocked and parried, again and again. The only sounds in the room were the whistle of blades in the air and the meaty slap of hands deflecting or redirecting attacks.

Warmth spread across Vaun's thigh, and he realized he'd missed one of Phobos's slashes. He hadn't noticed it until the blood stained his pant leg.

When he stumbled back, he felt it. This cut was much deeper than the others. Every step sent waves of shattered glass down through his leg all the way to the heel. Phobos saw the opening that presented itself from Vaun's backwards limp. He cut the distance between them in two quick steps. His footfalls landed feather soft—and just as quiet—as he closed. With one fell swoop he pushed Vaun's blade out of the way then slashed *deep* at Vaun's exposed chest. The wickedly sharp karambit lacerated him from shoulder to opposite hip.

One hand clutching at his chest, Vaun roared as he thrusted upward. At the last second, he twisted his knife and cut horizontally. He was rewarded with the wet sound of steel parting flesh.

Phobos sidestepped away, one hand reaching up towards his face. Vaun's knife had cut through the corner of Phobos's mouth, giving him a mirror-image wound to the scar he already had on the opposite side. His eyes flared with rage as he gingerly pawed at it.

Vaun seized the opportunity and stepped in, aiming the tip of his knife for the soft palate of Phobos's skull.

But the agile killer deftly caught Vaun's wrist, pivoted around to lock out Vaun's outstretched arm, and then drove his curved blade deep into his bicep. Vaun's own knife clattered to the floor. The karambit stabbed through muscle, bone, and artery. Blood spurted as Phobos forced the blade deep. Vaun cried out, no reason to hold back anymore. Phobos pulled him in close, then gave the knife another thrust. The end of the knife pierced all the way through his arm and out the other side. A glint of blood-soaked metal pushed towards Vaun's eye.

The entire time he held Vaun there, he didn't say a word. Didn't so much as huff or sound out of breath. He just stared at Vaun as blood dripped from the corner of his own mouth. Then, his head tilted slightly. Like a bird of prey watching its food, or perhaps a praying mantis in the middle of devouring a meal.

Vaun realized that Phobos was finished testing him. The killer was done playing. The shark was done with its nibbling bites. He'd finished his assessment and was clearly through with the opening pleasantries. He wasn't even fighting Vaun anymore: Phobos was just killing him.

CHAPTER 68

Daniel Kelly. 11: 50 p.m.
Testing Area
The Platform

"You hear that?" Kelly asked.

Tag scowled. A deep groaning sound like some awakening monster had come from nearby. He and Kelly's eyes met, and the same thought went through their heads. Tag's four bullets would not be enough for whatever it was.

"Find something that looks useful and violent," Kelly instructed.

They spread out into the large open testing area. Various prototypes of anonymous purpose surrounded them. A nearby target mannequin clad in a *Fafnir* vest caught Billy's eye. He had no interest in the armor itself, but the semi-auto shotgun that had been used to test its durability was much more enticing.

"Eight shells left," he noted, discarding an empty box of ammunition.

Tag found his way over to a large hardshell case. It was nearly six feet long by two feet, and two feet deep. He undid the latches and flipped the lid up.

"Anything good?" Kelly asked, so far coming up empty himself.

Tag's face was blank. Then, the man looked at him. His perpetually grumpy expression was replaced by an ecstatic smile that stretched from ear to ear.

"Oh, yeah."

Tag unloaded what looked like sets of rotary barrels, a heavy-duty tripod, several belts of ammunition, and a turret base. Finally, he picked up a thick three-ring binder and began leafing through it.

"It's called a Hydra. Says it's a man-portable sentry gun proto-type," Tag explained. His eyes darted from the binder to the disassembled pieces as he figured out how to put it together. "Testing notes say that everything worked perfectly. Firing rate. Barrel heat. Only issue was its weight. Too heavy."

"Think that'll be a problem for you?"

Tag's frown returned. "I'll manage."

A thing of beauty behind Tag grabbed Kelly's attention. He eagerly ran over to the table and grabbed it with both hands. The bolt-action rifle was an Intervention, chambered in .408. It was one of the most powerful and accurate rifles one could hope for. But it was made by CheyTac, not Common Defense Industries, which struck Kelly as interesting. When he brought the weapon to his shoulder and looked through the sight, he realized that the scope was anything *but* standard.

Kelly found himself looking at a strange, light blue, cutaway world. Tag, still assembling the Hydra, was at the edge of Kelly's field of vision. Except all Kelly could see was an x-ray of his skeleton.

"Just like Superman," Kelly said, looking around the room and through its walls. There were knobs on the side of the scope that adjusted how the scope penetrated. Kelly was trying to get the hang of it when he saw another skeleton on the far side of the room. It didn't belong to either of his teammates. A quick glance with his naked eye showed that this one was behind a shutter. But it was moving closer.

Curious, Kelly adjusted the knobs again to try to get a better look. The impulse to just pull the trigger was snuffed out by the thought that it could very well be another member of Cerberus Squad. Stranger still was that the approaching figure seemed to be walking a few feet *above* the ground.

"Hey . . . guys?"

The skeleton reached the shutter, and then the enormous mech armor punched through the wall. Giant hands gripped the metal shutter and peeled it open like it was tin foil.

Deimos Marstelli, adorned in the CHAOS armor prototype, thundered into the room. Kelly had a half-second before it began its slaughter. Left arm 20mm autocannon, right arm belt-fed 40mm grenade launcher and laser-guided missile, and SAM packs on its shoulders. All that firepower bearing down on him . . . and all he had was seven shots to his rifle.

But to call it just a rifle was a bit of an understatement. The Intervention wasn't a mere sniper rifle. It was officially deemed an anti-materiel rifle because it was supposed to be used on vehicles and equipment instead of people. The brutality with which the .408 round decimated a human body was considered too cruel. Right now, Kelly was counting on that same power.

Kelly tried to steady his heart as the CHAOS stomped towards him. It was something he'd done a thousand times before. Shoulder the rifle, acquire the shot, take it. Nothing to it. One good shot was all he'd need. If only the madman in the machine was generous enough to give him an opportunity.

Deimos raised the CHAOS's left arm and Kelly lost his shot. The 20mm autocannon spun up, made a sound like a swarm of angry hornets, and the room filled with bullets. So many bullets. Kelly could feel the very air grow hot with the sheer volume. A Hawaiian shirt-clad missile slammed into him from the side, and then both Kelly and Billy were tumbling like logs out of the line of fire.

"Always saving your ass . . ." Billy groaned.

They crawled on their hands and knees behind a large bulk container. The heavy anti-materiel rifle proved to be a pain in the ass to crawl with.

"Need a second favor," Kelly said as he pulled up into a crouch.

The CHAOS trampled along the Testing Area but hadn't spotted the two of them yet. To say it was like a bull in a China shop wasn't too far from the truth.

"I need you to distract him."

Billy looked at him as if he'd cracked a terrible joke. "Oh, yeah. Buckshot against a titanium-plated, goddamn Hulkbuster armor. That'll end well," he scoffed.

"To be fair, it's more like the War Machine armor . . ."

"Not helping!"

The two dodged around a corner right as Deimos nearly spotted them. Kelly looked back to his friend, a more serious look upon his face. "Do you trust me?"

Billy swallowed and nodded. It was a question Billy didn't even need to answer.

"I just need one shot, bud," Kelly said with a faint smile.

He exhaled slowly and readied himself. "Don't worry. I'll make sure you get it."

Billy popped out to the left of their cover and fired at the behemoth. The buckshot hit the CHAOS's black tiger-stripe emblazoned armor, and the pellets rebounded as if they were made of rubber. Deimos responded by pumping off grenades in his direction.

The chain explosions buckled the large container and sent it hurtling backwards. Billy aimed for the CHAOS's cockpit window and wasted another two shells. Deimos oriented on him once more and brought both of his weaponized arms to bear.

That buzz-saw hornet sound came again, but this time the storm of lead hit Deimos's backside. The sheer number of bullets, though not enough to pierce the armor, was enough to push the mechanized suit off-balance.

Tag, ever the quiet one, now bellowed a mighty war cry while emptying his reassembled Hydra cannon. The big man had no issue wielding its considerable weight. The fact that every second the weapon got a few hundred bullets lighter certainly helped. Billy used Tag's distraction to tuck tail and run.

Kelly watched his two comrades from the opposite end of the large warehouse. Deimos turned to the left and right, switching his focus from Tag to Billy as they both retreated. Each time Deimos's angle adjusted, Kelly lost his shot. His view of the cockpit window appeared and disappeared, again and again. He just needed the one shot.

And then it was there.

That perfect moment presented itself. He took it. As it was a thousand times before, Kelly's aim was true. The Intervention's heavy .408 round, powerful enough to punch through concrete barricades and steel plating, hit the windshield right between Deimos's eyes.

And the glass didn't even crack.

CHAPTER 69

The only way out was up, and up took me by way of one frustratingly long-ass ladder. I lost count of how many rungs I'd passed after the first two hundred. Add "Disabling The Other Elevator" to the list of things I was going to kill Cain for. Just as soon as I got those damned codes from him.

"Keep going, Cole," Madison urged through his earbud. "Cain and Goode just reached the top."

"Not. Exactly. Taking. The scenic route," I managed to say between huffing and puffing. A guy my size is a lot of weight to pull up a vertical climb. Just sayin'. The SD-52 rifle across my back that swayed after every rung wasn't exactly helping either.

"You have fifteen feet to go."

"Easy for you to say."

Every time one of my sweat-slicked palms hit a rung, it threatened to slip off. I screamed at myself to just keep climbing. That primal, desperate cry echoed off the shaft walls and drove me to push even harder. I needed to move faster, and that was only happening if I shed weight. I spared just a second to shrug off my rifle.

Shame. It was a good piece of gear.

That bit of relief felt like I'd shed fifty pounds. I flew up the last section of the ladder and heaved myself out of the shaft. Gassed, I fell to one knee for a single breath. I convinced myself there would be plenty of time to be exhausted after I'd gotten my hands on Cain. It made it easier to get to my feet.

I drew my Boomstick from over my shoulder and walked away from the elevator shaft. Before me was a short catwalk to Cain's private helipad, but I was too busy focusing on the hellscape that surrounded us. The entire Platform was ablaze.

The inferno at the waters below had eagerly spread and climbed until the whole structure had become one enormous pyre. The tops of the flames were just thirty feet below the catwalk and the temperature was already unbearable. I stood atop a personal roasting grill. My view across the catwalk to the helicopter shimmered from the heat. Squinting through the haze, I could just make out Cain shuffling across the walkway with his hostage in tow.

I still had time.

I ran for the helipad with my double-barrel at the ready when Cain whirled around. He used Goode as a human shield, sticking the barrel of his gun hard into his ear.

"Not another step!"

I took another two anyway, stepping off the catwalk to the helipad. I tried not to think about the fact that I could feel it swaying beneath us. The waves in the air played tricks on my eyes, and the groaning sound from the metal walkway supports warping in the heat made me question my accuracy. My feet cooked inside my boots. Cain scowled and put his back to the helicopter.

Sweat stung my eyes. I swiped it away with a thumb and took another cautious step towards Cain. "The three of us are going back downstairs and undoing all this bullshit you pulled, and we're going to do it lickity-goddamn split. This whole place is coming crashing down!"

"All the more reason to leave before that happens."

I felt the walkway wobble slightly underfoot. A large section from the adjacent Administration area gave way and fell to the burning sea below. Every ounce of me wanted to take the shot and put a round through Cain's face, but I still needed the codes in his head. Which meant kill shots were a no-no.

"You picked the wrong weapon today, Sergeant," Cain said, inching towards his escape. "If you want to keep me from blowing his head off, you'll have to take mine. Of course, with a sawn-off like that you'll end up killing Mr. Goode here, too. And *then* there's the little problem about still needing me alive, right? Put the gun down, son. I could use a man like you."

"Oh, yeah? How long before you inject me with a bunch of flammable nanites?"

"That's only for the drones. The worker bees. A real hornet like you would be too valuable. Come with us!"

I felt my sweaty palms threaten to fumble my weapon. If this outdoor sauna I found myself in got any hotter, my soles would melt to the floor.

"What do you say, son?"

"Hard pass." I switched my aim, firing both barrels over Cain's shoulder. Right at his helicopter. Earlier tonight I'd tried, and failed, to shoot out a helicopter's tail rotor. It was a good thing I'd had the foresight to load my Boomstick up with Cain's own incendiary Hades rounds.

The Hades rounds chewed off the tail section. Sparks showered down and the rotor blade dangled like a broken tree limb before the molten metal gave out. Cain's eyes went wide with rage.

I couldn't help but smile. "Now that your ride's busted, why don't we readdress that whole 'go back downstairs' conversation we were having?"

Cain threw Goode to the ground and aimed his weapon at me.

"That was stupid," he said. "You're empty."

Goode screamed and charged Cain like a bull. Cain turned, managed to squeeze off one shot that hit Goode in the side. I was already there knocking the gun from his hand before he could finish the job. It slid across the helipad and stopped just short of falling over the edge to the fire below. Goode wheezed on the ground with both hands clutching tightly to his gut, but I didn't take the time to worry about him.

The old man looked at me, the expression on his face showing he clearly understood how fucked he was now. My fist knocked that expression off his face so hard, I thought I'd broken his neck. The blow whipped him around in a full circle. The lights in his eyes flickered for a moment before he fell flat on his ass.

Despite everything on the line, despite how close the countdown was to zero, I was really tempted to just throw him over the edge right then and there. The satisfaction of hearing him fall and burn might have made up for the thousands that would die.

Cain crawled backwards from me. One of his hands reached inside his jacket. For a second, I thought he might pull another gun. Instead, he produced a small rod the size of a pen.

"One last gadget to save your hide?" I asked, shaking my head. "I don't give a shit if that's a blowgun or Voldemort's magic wand. You're coming with me, you son of a bitch."

Cain smiled. "Hard pass."

He put the rod to his lips and I gave him a confused look. Was it a straw? But then I heard the helicopter side door crash open behind me. The sound of panting breath and padded feet sprinting towards me confirmed my suspicions as to what Cain's last Hail Mary was.

A dog whistle.

Now, I was fucked.

CHAPTER 70

Daniel Kelly. 1:53 a.m.
Testing Area
The Platform

"What the shit is that made of?" Kelly muttered as he worked the bolt. Three times he'd hit his mark on the CHAOS windshield; not once did it go through.

The CHAOS on-board threat detection system tracked his shots. The armored mech's right arm reached out in Kelly's direction, marking his position for one of its missiles. Kelly had just enough time to take four running steps before it hit. He was flung through the air and landed at the bottom of a set of stairs. His ears rang, and he was pretty sure patches of his hair had been singed off. He wrote it off as just another occupational hazard.

With nowhere else to go, Kelly scrambled up the stairs and found himself in an observation booth overlooking the entire testing warehouse. Movement in the corner caught his eye. Kelly sighted in and nearly took Tag's head off.

"Get your own hiding spot," Kelly said.

"I was here first."

Tag hunched over a laptop, fingers flying across the keys in a blur.

"Not exactly the time to be checking your Facebook, bud."

"You tried your way," Tag replied, indicating Kelly's Intervention. "Let me try mine."

There was a screeching sound of speaker feedback as Deimos accessed the CHAOS's PA system. "USUALLY, I LEAVE THIS TYPE OF HANDS-ON WORK TO MY BROTHER," Deimos said. "BUT I'LL ADMIT, THIS IS QUITE AN *EXHILARATING* EXPERIENCE!" He picked up a nearby mock Humvee and threw it clear across the training area. It crumpled against the concrete wall as if made of tin. The autocannon rattled off another burst, and the wrecked Humvee's fuel tank blew.

It didn't seem like Deimos aimed for anyone, just letting loose for the hell of it. Bullets ricocheted off the walls while 40mm grenades arched across the testing area, obliterating everything in their path.

Kelly considered that the suit's power had made Deimos snap.

"MISTER CAIN REALLY BROKE THE MOLD WITH THIS ONE. I IMAGINE YOUR MILITARY WILL PURCHASE DOZENS FOR THE COMING WAR."

Deimos fired a second rocket with a great *WHOOSH*. The doorway from which the three of them had come was destroyed. No way out now. From his vantage point Kelly surveyed their private little battlefield. Their third teammate was still nowhere to be seen. Deimos stood in the center of the area, smashing nearby equipment to pieces and shooting wildly with the autocannon any time he thought he caught movement. For the time being, the CHAOS's tracking systems were having trouble spotting them.

Kelly adjusted his x-ray scope while aiming at the CHAOS. There had to be some type of weak point. There always was. Even the Deathstar had that damn Exhaust Port. If not the windshield, then maybe an exposed power source of some sort. But even with a cutaway view of the CHAOS armor he was coming up empty. Nothing important-looking stuck out of that hardened carapace.

The CHAOS suit continued its rampage. Even if Kelly had a hundred rounds for his Intervention, it wouldn't be enough. It would be just as effective if Kelly was throwing water balloons at it. He racked his brain, trying to think of a way to stop it.

"Every strength can be a weakness, right?" he asked aloud, for himself as much as Tag. Tag grunted. "That's what Cole said at the docks the other night. An advantage can just as easily be a disadvantage. So how do we play an unstoppable fucking Gundam suit's strengths against itself?"

Tag's gaze didn't leave the laptop. "Dunno. Convince him to shoot himself?"

Right as Kelly was thinking of a witty response, he stopped short. The CHAOS had stopped flailing around wildly and had oriented itself on something.

Billy.

"FOUND YOU!"

The autocannon arm aimed at him. Kelly emptied all but one shot into the CHAOS's back in a desperate and failed attempt to draw its attention. Deimos was so focused on his prey, he didn't bother tracking where the shots came from. Billy was caught like a deer in headlights. Freezing was uncharacteristic for him, but then again how often does a guy come face to face with a murderous robot suit?

But their luck hadn't run out just yet. Deimos attempted to turn Billy to pink mist with a heavy burst, but the autocannon had run dry. The CHAOS must have only been minimally loaded for testing purposes. By the time Deimos raised the grenade launcher arm, Billy had already run in the direction of the observation booth.

Deimos screamed incoherent curses and unloaded with the 40mm as he gave chase. The grenades exploded on Billy's heels, seemingly propelling him forward even faster.

Deimos adjusted his aim, led his target, and fired the last round.

This time it exploded at ground level ahead of Billy. The blast flung him backwards, flipping him head over heels. When he came to a rest near the CHAOS's feet, there were jagged pieces of shrapnel sticking out of his leg and side.

He gave a pained moan and rolled weakly on the ground. One of the CHAOS's enormous hands slammed to the floor to pin Billy in place. The other hovered in the air. The autocannon rotated out of place, the armor plating unfolded, and a large auger drill flipped into view. Cain had explained that the CHAOS was also equipped with utility tools for humanitarian operations, though this isn't what Kelly had expected.

"IF YOU DON'T WANT TO SHOW YOURSELVES, THEN YOU CAN AT LEAST HELP ME DECIDE WHICH TOOL TO USE," Deimos boomed. The enormous drill spun with a large whine. Deimos tested it on the ground next to Billy's body and it eagerly dug down four feet in an instant. "NOT PLEASED WITH THIS ONE? I ADMIT I WOULD BE PARTIAL TO SOMETHING A BIT MORE EXCITING."

The drill retracted into the CHAOS's hand and was replaced by an enormous titanium bladed concrete saw. Deimos lowered the spinning blade towards the floor.

"Whatever strength you plan on hacking and turning into a weakness, you better do it quick . . ." Kelly muttered.

"Mobility and weapons are completely hardwired," Tag explained. "Cain didn't want anyone wirelessly hijacking the suit . . ."

The industrial saw easily chewed right through the concrete floor by Billy's head. It kicked up sparks and chunks into the side of Billy's face. Deimos dragged it closer. Kelly considered risking his last shot to destroy the saw blade, but quickly realized it would make no difference. Without the use of the saw, Deimos could just smash Billy with a flick of his wrist.

"Don't worry," Tag grunted. "I'm almost in."

Kelly arched an eyebrow. "How are you going to shut it down if all the systems are on a hardline?"

Tag shrugged, refusing to answer. Kelly turned back to the observation window as the screaming saw inched closer to Billy's neck. Whatever scheme Tag had better be damned quick, or they'd be bringing Billy home as mulch.

"ANY LAST WORDS, MY FRIEND?" Deimos asked.

The blade was so close, Billy must have felt the heat coming from it.

"I've got one," Tag screamed. He stood before the large observation window so Deimos could see him. Deimos pulled up the saw-blade and turned to look at him. Tag smiled. He hadn't lied to Kelly; all of the CHAOS weapon and mobility systems were impossible to access remotely. But its medical systems weren't.

"Clear."

Tag pressed the button and activated the defibrillator inside the cockpit. Maximum charge. Through the windshield they watched Deimos violently thrash. His arms, still connected to the controls, caused the mech's limbs to flail around violently as it mimicked its pilot's spasms. Deimos's lock-jawed scream was cut short as the shock shut down his heart. The charge kept going. Sparks flew from his clothes. What had once been a suit of armor now became his electric chair. The CHAOS slumped over, smoke escaping the cockpit from its electrocuted occupant, then fell to the floor in a mighty crash.

Billy, bloodied but still alive, managed to sit up and give his friends a shaky thumbs-up. Kelly exhaled slowly, realizing only then that he'd been holding his breath for the last minute.

"Remind me never to make fun of you and your computer ever again," Kelly said.

"You never have."

"You know what I mean."

"That's not the only thing this laptop had," Tag said, his brow furrowed. He hit another few keys and turned the screen to face Kelly. There was an emergency evacuation map blinking on it. "I found us a way out."

CHAPTER 71

It had been far too long since he'd fought someone capable of truly testing his skill. He had been patient, obeying every instruction from both Mr. Cain and his brother. When the time had come to finally face Captain Vaun, he had been ecstatic at the opportunity. But now, standing before his prize, Phobos was completely underwhelmed.

Vaun was fast, skilled, and as experienced as Phobos was. The ugly cut he'd marked Phobos's face with was a testament to his skill. It was the best wound anyone had ever scored against him in a duel. Unfortunately, Vaun was fighting mad. Anger made one sloppy. Phobos knew the fight was his within their first exchange of attacks.

His opponent could barely stand. He'd grown ghostly pale, and Phobos knew it wouldn't be long before blood loss took its toll. It was . . . disappointing. One arm hung limply by his side, the entire sleeve stained all the way to his red-soaked hand, while the other was clamped down on the deep wound Phobos had inflicted to his bicep.

Phobos approached his quarry. Vaun's knife lay on the floor. As a show of good faith, Phobos kicked it across the floor to him. He made a pained grunt as he bent to retrieve it, nearly collapsing from the effort, then stood once more with the blade in his blood-slick hand. Vaun took a weak step forward, arcing a sluggish slash that Phobos merely turned away from. There was no strength left in him at all. No speed. No challenge.

And where there was no challenge, there was no need to delay. Phobos was not a cruel man, after all.

Phobos calmly walked towards him and used his karambit's ring to flip it into a reverse grip: time to end this bout. Two thrusts delivered in a flash. The knife tip pierced both of Vaun's shoulders. Both arms fell limp. Vaun's knife dropped once more, this time its handle landing in Phobos's open palm. Phobos finished with a spinning lunge, dropping low as he turned like a whirlwind of steel with both blades out, and sliced Vaun to ribbons from belly to legs.

Small intestine peeked through a deep laceration along his gut. Blood gushed from a slash that ran from one thigh clear to the other. At the last portion of Phobos's spin, he'd run Vaun's own blade against the bottom of his right kneecap. The severed ligaments parted away with a wet elastic snap.

The captain went down onto his one good leg in defeat. His hands moved to apply pressure to the worst of his wounds, but there were too many for just two hands. After a second he even gave up on trying. It was over.

With a quick flick of his wrists, Phobos flipped the knives around, flinging little drops of blood from the blades as he moved to Vaun's back. Vaun knew he was finished. He wasn't going to beg or shy away from what was coming. Instead, he used one of the nearby server towers to pull himself back up and stood as tall as his one good leg would allow. There was still enough life and honor in him for that.

Phobos admired that. Rather than let his challenger simply succumb to his wounds, he would hasten his departure.

He would grant him the Quick Death.

The knife hovered millimeters from Vaun's skin as he traced a line from the base of Vaun's neck down his spine. He found the spot. Right between the T-11 and T-12. Phobos gave Vaun a cordial pat on the shoulder as he readied his blade for the kill.

His brother was dead.

The thought came from nowhere and froze him in his tracks. No, it wasn't a mere thought. It was a realization. Deimos was dead, and somehow Phobos knew that. It washed over him so completely and suddenly that, at first, Phobos couldn't make sense of it. They had always shared a connection. Now, it was simply gone. It was as distinct a stoppage as severing a phone line.

There was a great void in the world where his brother should be. That emptiness swallowed everything. His obligation to their employer, his own desire for victory, even his sense of self-preservation. In that absence, none of it seemed to matter. He'd been holding out hope that dear Deimos had reached the medical bay, but now Phobos knew in his heart that he hadn't. He'd left his mortally wounded twin brother behind, willingly, because Deimos wanted him to face Vaun. This moment—this entire encounter—was a gift.

But... Phobos struggled with the weight of that. Wouldn't Deimos have known that Phobos would've preferred to decline this gift in favor of being there for his last moments? Especially since their duel had turned out to be so underwhelming for him.

Vaun spared a look over his shoulder, no doubt wondering why Phobos hadn't ended him yet. He just as easily still could, but it hardly seemed important at this point. Phobos turned around and punched a button on the wall. The captain was very nearly crushed flat by the emergency fire escape ladder that descended from a hatch in the ceiling.

Phobos grabbed Vaun around the shoulders and pushed him towards it. Vaun hesitated, unsure of why he was being let go. To be honest, even Phobos wasn't completely sure why he felt compelled to spare him.

Vaun leaned against the ladder for support as Phobos took two steps away. He returned with the White Shield computer and tucked it under Vaun's arm. Then, as an afterthought, he took the time to loop an expedient tourniquet around the worst cut on Vaun's thigh. Whether Vaun would make it out or not would be up to his own resolve now.

Before he could begin his difficult climb, Phobos handed over his karambit. Handle first. An offering. But, more importantly, it would serve as a reminder of the one man who had beaten him. If Vaun survived, then he'd carry that memory forever. That was reason enough for Phobos to allow himself a rare smile. It physically pained him to do so. Both the old scar that graced the corner of his mouth, which had never truly healed, and the new cut Vaun honored him with bled down his face. And still he smiled.

Despite how much it hurt his scarred and underused vocal cords, Phobos managed to croak out one word. "Go."

Vaun slowly ascended the ladder with blood-slicked hands. He disappeared through the ceiling hatch without so much as looking back once.

The fires were getting close now, but Phobos had no intention of leaving. There was nowhere else for him to go. No one to escape to or with, either. This . . . this *was* his happy ending. He could die, knowing that he'd faced the best there was and proved himself better. He was retiring undefeated.

Phobos sat cross-legged on the floor and waited for the fires to come.

CHAPTER 72

Nearly three hundred pounds of fur and teeth slammed into my backside. Cain's favorite pooches, Virgil and Dante, had been waiting patiently in the helicopter, and I was too focused on their owner to see them. That oversight was quite literally biting me in the ass.

Both Canary Mastiffs viciously gnashed their teeth and bit me where they could. I swung my arms around to keep them back and protect my face but Virgil, the one with the brown brindle coat, locked his jaws around my shoulder and wrenched me about. Dante, the younger jet black one, stayed back, letting his big brother do all the hard work. Not that Virgil needed any help.

All the weapons and training in the world and here I was being mauled to death by dogs.

"It's funny, America's always been fascinated with more and more advanced weapons of war. But it's always the simplest ways that end up being the best," Cain said.

Virgil stopped pulling me around. He kept me pinned to the ground. Every time I tried to move, he bit down deeper onto my arm. If he bit any harder, he would take the whole thing off.

Cain reached inside his jacket pocket and retrieved a worn-down set of brass knuckles. He slipped his fingers through it with a smile. "Like I said, the simple tools."

He punched me across the jaw, and I swear he nearly took my face off. Blood welled up around my teeth. It was a wonder they were still there at all. When I fell over, Virgil pounced and sank his teeth into my shoulder. Dante encouraged his brother with a few barks before joining in himself. Fangs latched onto my ankle and pulled my leg out from under me. The only thing keeping Dante's powerful bite from tearing through my ACL was the leather of my combat boot. It occurred to me that Cain could have easily told either of the hounds to simply tear out my throat and be done with it. But, no, he wanted to drag this out as painfully as possible.

Cain watched carefully. He waited for an opening when he wouldn't accidentally strike his prized dogs. When he saw it, he took it. His brass knuckles cracked two ribs in that second punch. I used my forearm to block a third going for my face and my arm went dead instantly. The rising fires below us cast wicked shadows across his face. Jesus, all the industrialist sophistication was stripped away and the true psychopath beneath was revealed. He enjoyed the brutality.

I kicked my ankle free of Dante and booted the black dog in the side. Virgil barked loudly in my face and attacked my thigh. One of the support struts below us gave out in the fire, the walkway buckled and shifted under us. Cain, off-balance, threw another brass-topped punch my way. This time I managed to parry it out of the way. The punch rolled over my shoulder, where it smacked Dante across the face. He let out a pained whoof and kept away.

Cain shouted a command at Dante to maul me some more, but Dante just whimpered and hid his face. A faint memory deep in my head remembered Cain telling us how much harder Dante had been to train than Virgil. Right now, I was pretty damn glad Dante had been a slow study.

Virgil let go of my thigh long enough to try and find another tasty part of my anatomy. I wasn't ready to be puppy chow just yet. I like dogs. Oftentimes, I find their company easier than a lot of people, but I have my limits. Unlike Dante, Virgil had no problem tearing me to pieces. Some bad dogs just need to be put down. I curled my fingers along his collar, turned my hip, and threw him behind me with all my strength. The giant dog slammed into and over the handrail. I could hear its last angry yelp as it fell to the burning waves. No, I didn't feel good about what I'd had to do. But dog teeth in your femoral artery feel a lot worse.

I rose to my feet. Bloodied, beaten, but not yet broken enough to give up. Every breath sent white-hot stabs through my cracked ribs. I swallowed that fiery pain down and felt it course through my fingertips.

Dante cowered and nursed his hurt snout.

"Stay," I said to the dog, then turned my attention to its master. "The pilots' codes. Now."

Cain looked at me like I was some sort of monster. Right then I was sort of feeling like one.

The helipad swayed again as more of the supports gave out. The metal groaned. Bolts the size of my torso snapped off in the heat. Cain stumbled back and nearly fell. I merely took two steps closer to him. My hands twitched with promise for the hurt I had in store for Cain.

"No... no!" Cain stammered. His eyes, moments before overflowing with rage, now filled with fear. "We can't stop it."

I stomped towards him. My ravaged thigh hurt like hell, but I refused to limp. Blood ran hot from the bite on my shoulder and trailed down to my balled fists. When he looked at me, he would see nothing but conviction. I was too fucking angry to let something as trivial as blood loss slow me down.

"You're all too small to understand," Cain said. "If you stop this, they'll just find another way. And you can't stop them. They're everywhere. They are *legion*."

I realized then when I looked in his eyes, pupils constricted in terror, that it wasn't me he was afraid of. It was his employers. The puppet masters who'd been pulling the strings had him more scared than I did, and I can be pretty damn scary when I need to.

"I don't have a choice!" he screamed and threw a wild haymaker.

I parried out with my elbow pointed at his forearm, wrapped my arm over his elbow joint, and broke his arm. Hard. I could actually feel the jagged point of his snapped humerus, causing his skin to bulge out unnaturally. When his scream wasn't satisfying enough, I wrenched on the limb again just to raise it a few octaves.

The brass knuckles fell from his limp hand, and I slipped it onto my fingers. I didn't bother asking him for the codes a third time. I just laid into him. His ribs cracked, his nose flattened, teeth were knocked out, and on the last blow to the body I'm pretty sure I felt a kidney burst. I stopped short just long enough for him to remember that there was still a reason I was keeping him alive.

Instead, he spat blood and teeth in my face and pushed away from me. Before I could finish beating him to death, a loud groan came from the catwalk. The last support finally buckled, and the end of the walkway collapsed beneath us. The entire helipad went down into the roiling inferno below and the walkway itself canted downwards. I found myself hanging by my fingertips at the end of it. Any second longer and the walkway would break free from the Platform. Blood from the bite on my shoulder had already drenched my arm and made my grip slick. The blast furnace below opened its hungry mouth for me. It dared me to lose my grip just a little more.

Cain balanced on the swaying catwalk four feet away from where I hung on for dear life. He hocked up blood in between coughing up a storm. The noxious smoke would've been over-whelming for any asthmatic, let alone one who'd just been beaten within an inch of his life. He held his broken wing and just stood there, wheezing and watching me.

Then, he knelt down. For just a second I thought he was reaching down to help me up. Mind you I'd just been attacked by dogs and most likely had a fracture in my skull, so that would explain why I thought his actions might be benevolent.

Then he stood back up with his retrieved pistol in hand. The act of bending over sent a fresh coughing fit through him. I tried to pull myself up over the edge while he struggled to catch his breath, but my own effort was too much and all I managed was hauling myself up to my elbows.

"You . . ." he sputtered between wheezes, "don't know . . . who you're . . . fucking with."

The man aimed his gun at me with one tottering hand. The cough that seized him came on even stronger. This time I think I saw it bring blood to his lips. And, unable to breathe, he finally opted to tuck the pistol under his shoulder, then reached into his jacket for his inhaler.

He took a quick puff, sucking in a lungful of it. He was eager to breathe again, eager to finally punch my ticket and send me down to the flames. But the second he inhaled, he knew something was wrong. Even there, with my feet dangling over the fiery depths, I knew what had happened. Samuel Cain had just fucked up. The inhaler he'd used wasn't his. It was mine. The one that had been loaded with the aerosolized Sandman sedative.

The effect was instant. His limbs went limp, the handgun slipped from where he'd tucked it, and Cain fell face-first onto the catwalk. If he was capable of screaming, I'm sure he would have as his wrinkled face sizzled against the searing hot metal. And I'm more than certain he would have screamed even louder as the downward angle sent his limp body sliding towards the edge.

But all he could do was blink at me. Cain was utterly helpless as he slipped inch by agonizing inch along the ground. The entire time his skin bubbled and burned. I was just as helpless, though. Unable to spare a hand and grab him to stop his descent. I tried anyway, risking it all and stretching my blood-soaked hand out.

Cain was inches out of reach. I was powerless to do anything but watch as the warmaker slid right on past me. My own grip on the handrail was failing and for a second I thought I would be following suit. Then Goode was there to help pull me up. He was pale from blood loss but alive nonetheless.

I finished hauling myself over the ledge just in time to see the end of Cain's plummet into the pyre. I imagined the drawn-out horrified scream locked within his own mind as he took that plunge. The fires below eagerly welcomed him. A pillar of flame rose as he disappeared below the blazing surface.

And then he was gone, taking any chance of finding the pilots' codes with him.

CHAPTER 73

When the elevator doors parted, Madison smiled upon seeing me and Goode. That optimism disappeared when she saw how wounded I was. Vicious dog bites to my leg and shoulder. A swollen and potentially shattered eye socket. Blood leaking out the corner of my mouth from a few teeth that might not be tenants in my gums for much longer. Let's not even mention the *other* shoulder and a definitely-going-to-get-infected burn. Picture of fucking health, this guy.

"I made a few additions to the collection," I said.

She read the expression on my face but asked anyway. "The codes . . ."

I didn't answer. I just limped over to the chair next to the *Firestorm* computer and collapsed into its welcoming plush leather. A loud banging at the door caught my attention, and I looked to Madison with a raised eyebrow.

"The rest of Mosley's security forces," she said quietly. "Thirty or so. The only safe way off the Platform is via the cargo elevator we first took, and I've locked down the door to it. They've been trying to break in here and unlock it, but it's held up so far."

I nodded. Either we were going to burn to death, or drown when the Platform finally collapsed, but that was only if the last of Cain's security didn't just kill us first. I wasn't exactly in any condition to put up a fight anymore. From over my shoulder I drew my Boomstick, breaking it open and shaking the empty shells out so Madison could see.

Fresh out, nothing left.

"Cole . . . the codes?"

I shook my head slowly. She looked at Goode, but he couldn't seem to pick his eyes up from the floor. Madison sat in front of the *Firestorm* computer and stared blankly at the screen. After everything we'd gone through, Cain was going to get his war after all. Knowing he was too busy being a crispy skeleton to see it was a poor consolation prize.

"How many possible? How many are carrying the *Firestorm* nanites?" I asked.

"Two thousand four hundred twenty-eight. We'll never figure out which ones are the pilots." We were just close enough to the goal line to watch it all burn. Within minutes some of the most populated cities in the country would be reduced to rubble.

Or maybe not. I knew what had to be done, and quite frankly I wished that literally anyone else in the world but me could've been here to make the call. I looked Madison dead in her eyes.

"Burn them all."

She gaped at me for a second. Just one. Then she closed her eyes hard, shook her head once, and began to select all of the serial numbers on the computer. She knew what was on the line here, and I think knowing *Firestorm* was based on her design gave her some sense of responsibility in ending it.

The codes filled the entire screen. Line after line of digits, each one representing some poor soul who'd been roped into Cain's operation. Scientists. Workers. Politicians. Two-thousand four-hundred and twenty-eight cogs in a war machine. Them being injected with *Firestorm* meant that likely they'd never been true believers in Cain's plan. Only those who'd resisted it were doped with his little incendiary insurance policy. We would have no way of knowing just how far Cain's conspiracy reached until we swept up their ashes.

Madison hit the button to activate the incendiary nanites embedded in all of the carriers. A dialogue box popped up on the screen: *Confirm?*

Her finger hovered over the mouse. One click, and she could end the war. One click, and she would murder thousands. It wasn't the cost of war. This . . . this was the cost of peace. In her own way this was the cost of redemption for the small part she'd played in unknowingly furthering Cain's agenda.

A tremor ran through Madison's hand. The weight of what I was asking of her was too much. It was too much for anyone, really. Even if we had an hour for her to think it over instead of precious seconds, it still wouldn't be enough. At the end of the day, she was a scientist who'd gotten in way over her head. An innocent. Someone like her, from that world of good people I used to be a part of, could never hit that button.

But I could.

I hit the button. For her, for our country, for this whole world, I hit that damn button.

God help me, I did it. I watched as, one by one, the *Firestorm* nanites were activated. The banging on the door was replaced by startled gasps, then begging screams, and the tell-tale sound of flash ignition. Unseen, one by one their panicked cries went quiet. Smoke roiled underneath the doorway. The silence that came after was the most terrible thing I'd ever heard in my life.

We left the Central Security area for the cargo elevator. I moved completely on autopilot. The charred bones of the security team awaited us in the hallway. That smell of cooked flesh etched itself into my memory, and I fought back the gag clawing at the back of my throat. The next thing I knew, we were riding the cargo elevator to the second helipad. I was walking in a fugue state and found myself stepping towards one of the helicopters. Its rotors were already spinning, and it was ready to take off.

My legs gave out. Maybe it was the blood loss, maybe it was the shock of what I'd just done. Hands gripped under my arms and hoisted me to my feet. I thought it was surprising that Goode and Madison were strong enough to carry me, but when I lifted my head I was even more surprised at who had actually done it. Tag and Kelly. I looked to the helicopter once more and saw Billy and Vaun, both wounded, were already loaded up.

"How?"

"We all made it," Kelly told me. "We're all here."

They loaded me up in the back. The Platform groaned its last death-rattle as it went down, but we were already in the air, pulling away. I suppose I finally had an answer to Kelly's question.

"How many people would you kill to stop a war?" I said with a sad smile to no one in particular. My face was already buried in my hands before the first tears came.

EPILOGUE

I

The clock on the wall ticked the minutes away. Rourke finished reading the last of the prepared documents while his guest squirmed uncomfortably in the seat across from him. He and White Shield had worked around the clock, cleaning up Cain's conspiracy. The attack squadron's bombing run had been cut short just twelve miles from the coastline.

How close the world came to World War Three would only be known by a few. For everyone else, including the public, the impending attack that had the president's finger ready on the nuclear button was caused by a simple glitch. A zero in the code where a one should have been. The talking heads blamed the usual suspects, but it's not like anyone possessed the attention span to keep track. This time next week, there would be a new scandal to serve as the nation's latest lightning rod.

All of Common Defense Industries' defense contracts were indefinitely frozen, barring a congressional inquiry into how their system had been so flawed. Samuel Cain was subpoenaed but, unfortunately, had perished two days prior in an industrial accident in one of his facilities. Tragic.

By Rourke's estimate, CDI would finish imploding within two months' time. In the twenty-four hours since their contracts had been unofficially dissolved, nearly a dozen other weapons manufacturers ponied up to take over. War was an opportunity, after all. Like vultures to the carcass, they flocked the second CDI's power waned.

Thanks to Sergeant West, most of the conspirators were incinerated, but there were still others who lived. Still more were those who needed to be vetted to determine whether their part in it all had been willing or unwilling, complicit or ignorant.

A one-time steep upgrade of Rourke's regular medication had killed off most of the pain that had nearly crippled him, but the dull ache lingered. Once he was done dealing with this last loose end, the pain in his jaw might finally go quiet. For now.

Rourke set the documents aside and sized up his guest. Dr. Madison Archer. She was scared, but that was understandable. She was a key contributor to Samuel Cain's attempted war. Even a generous court would have burned her at the stake. He could understand why the thought would make a person nervous. That, and Mason stood behind her with a pistol at the ready.

"I suppose it goes without saying that this is entirely off the record?" Rourke asked.

Madison bit her lip. Mason nudged the back of her head with the barrel of her gun. She recoiled, remembering similar treatment by the late Security Chief Moseley.

"This is off the record because, well, the types of prisons I send people to don't leave a record. You understand? The hole I could put you in is the sort of place terms like 'cruel and unusual punishment' were written for."

"I understand."

"Good. That hole is already getting some new visitors. White Shield has had a field day with Sam's computers and turned up plenty of intel. None of the people identified as having been complicit were extended the courtesy of a conversation like this. Their reception has been decidedly more . . . explicit."

Madison remained quiet.

"Without you, Sam would never have come as close as he did to accomplishing his goal. That's not something I need to argue. It's a fact." Rourke's words hit the woman like a slap. It was precisely the effect he'd intended and expected. "Something as quick as a bullet would be preferable when compared to the hole. A gift, really. By the way, were the Hades incendiary rounds a product of your mind or Sam's? I only ask, though I couldn't care less, because Kara here felt the need to point out to me the poetic justice of using one to burn through your skull."

At that Mason lowered the hammer on her .45 and adjusted her grip. This time Madison didn't flinch, she was ready. More than that, she'd accepted that the judgment was deserved. The bill had come due. That also was Rourke's intention. If he were a lesser man, he would've let himself smile.

"On the other hand . . ." he began, and Mason's finger froze along the trigger, "I can think of an alternative form of payment for your dues."

Madison's gaze met his. "What do you want?"

Rourke's mouth curled into a tight-lipped frown. "Much was lost when Sam's Platform burned down, but we've still pulled whole terabytes of weapons schematics from CDI's networks. Some of it may be repurposed to more beneficial purposes. Others could potentially be advanced even further." He nodded to Mason, who lowered her weapon. "My best weapons designer currently has a bad case of being dead. Thankfully for you, that means there's an opening. I'm here to offer you a job, Dr. Archer."

II

It's not easy to see your heroes broken. We'd all been at Captain Vaun's bedside after the Platform, but the crowd slowly faded until I was the only one stubborn enough to stay. The others had eased up on their vigil when it became clear he wouldn't die. They'd resolved that he'd been hurt before and bounced back before, and this time would be no different.

I didn't share their optimism.

Even when his blood count was back to normal and his multiple lacerations healed, he would not be the same man. Nerve damage to his arm meant he'd never have full mobility again. The knee injury was the worst of it; the doctors told us as gently as possible that he would never walk without a cane. Billy tried to make a joke about how thanks to Cain he'd need a cane, but it fell on deaf ears. We were all coping in our own ways.

This case had taken a lot out of Vaun, body *and* soul. He and I both knew it. His rage and sorrow at Major Wilcox's death had compromised him more than he'd been willing to admit, more than anyone else but me had been willing to see.

"I think I need a vacation," Vaun murmured as he woke from his latest painkiller-induced sleep.

"After that loose-cannon shit you pulled, I believe the term 'administrative leave' would apply more. Sir."

Vaun was quiet. It was low of me to hit him while he was already down, but at the same time there were some *very* sore feelings between us. His norm of calm and collected had always been the example I'd looked up to. It had been an anchor for the whole squad. For him to fly off the handle and get himself inches from death felt like some sort of betrayal. The sheer number of knife wounds he'd suffered made it extremely difficult to hold a grudge, though.

"They told me what you did." He sighed. "What you *had* to do."

"Yup."

"Cole . . . I swear to God I wish I would've been there to hit that button for you."

"Cards on the table? I kind of wished you had, too," I said, then forced a smile. "It's done, though. Rourke is mandating I see a counselor before I'm cleared for duty. Again. I'll manage."

"Don't be so eager to jump back in that fire. And you're wrong about one thing," Vaun said more slowly. "It's not done. Not yet. Samuel Cain may have been the warmaker, but someone else was orchestrating this."

One of the last things Cain had said came back to me. *They are everywhere. They are legion.*

A man says something like that to you, it makes a guy feel mighty paranoid.

"I don't think I'll be taking a vacation," whispered Vaun. He stared out the window by his bedside for a long moment. "No administrative leave, either. No . . . Cole, I think it's time to retire."

"No," I said bluntly.

"It's not up to you," he said with a pained laugh. He grimaced and a hand went to the sutures on his stomach. "Hell, it's not up to me. Phobos could've killed me, I suppose he meant this as a mercy of sorts. But look at me. I can't lead the squad anymore. I've lost that right."

"You recruited me yourself and not once have I questioned you. Sir . . . if you'd asked, I would've followed you to Phobos and gladly died by your side."

"I *never* recruited you to just follow me," Vaun said. He placed something in my hand. A bundled-up cloth handkerchief. I opened it up to see what was wrapped within. It was his black set of captain's bars. "I was training you to lead."

I immediately tried to hand them back. "Sir, the rest of the squad has been with—"

"The rest of the squad will follow my last command," he said. "Billy is the most capable fighter I've come across, but he doesn't have the desire for leadership. He thrives on being the lone wolf out on the frontline, plays the wildcard role, but what he really needs is someone to bring him into the pack. Tag is the most loyal brother you could ever ask for, but that same loyalty is why he can't command the squad. He'll devoutly follow orders, but he will hesitate every time giving them if it means putting one of us in danger. And then there's Kelly. You'll never find a more accurate marksman than him. He's at his best from a distance, but a leader needs to be on the ground. You're it, Cole."

A moment ago, I grappled with the thought of a Cerberus Squad without Vaun. Now, I was getting sized up to fill his boots.

"It was your plan that got us onto the Platform," said Vaun. "It's all been you. You stopped Des at the docks. You got Valkyrie Squad aboard and Rourke out. You."

The small piece of black metal in my palm weighed a hundred pounds. "I'm not as good as you are. I'm not as good as . . . as any of them."

"Not *yet*. But you could be better than us all. You're already on that path. You just keep going, Cole, because you're on your way. You're on your way."

I closed my fist around the captain's insignia. I told myself before that this could be my last hurrah with Black Spear, but . . . but the die was cast.

"The Cerberus of legend wasn't just some mad beast from hell. It was a guardian. It kept the true horrors from reaching the world of man," Vaun said. "I need you to lead that dog now."

I pocketed the black bars. "And what'll you do, sir? While I'm . . . dog-sitting?"

His eyes narrowed. "Just because I'm retiring from Black Spear doesn't mean I'm hanging up my gun belt just yet. Something's been moving in the shadows . . . It's time someone shined a light on them. I'll have a lot of spare time on my hands. Plenty of time to travel. Think I might go shadow hunting."

"If something comes up, I hope you'll be smart enough to call for backup this time."

Vaun gave me that half-smile of his. "I know who I can count on, Captain."

III

"Is this all of it?" I asked.

Goode's assistants finished bringing in the last cardboard box and placed it on the long conference table next to the others. The table's entire length was covered in boxes, each stack two boxes high.

"The very last," Goode said. "As dedicated as I am to the pursuit of information, I can't help but question the necessity of this."

I pulled the lid off the closest box. It was filled with tightly packed folders. I riffled through the files with my fingertip like a deck of cards. At random I pulled one of the folders out and began to read. "These people, all of them, were hostages. Some more complicit than others, but they were hardly sympathizers to Cain. It could've easily been any one of us in one of these boxes."

I stopped reading as I got to a picture of a young man. He was younger than me by at least five years and his eyes shone with optimism. And he, like all the other people in all the folders in all these boxes, was dead. Because of me. "Let's just call this closure."

"You actually think this will help?"

I stared at the picture of the young man. The memory of scorched flesh and burnt hair stung at my nose. Images of those charred skeletons from the Platform flashed in my eyes. In my head I heard the guards' desperate screams for mercy while the men around them immolated one after another. Those screams and those smells had kept me from getting a wink of sleep for a few days now. I choked back that memory, along with the sob that threatened to come with it.

"I hope to God it does."

Goode surveyed the long expanse of boxes, waiting for his assistants to leave the room before speaking again. "I never got a chance to thank you for saving my life."

"You took a bullet meant for me. We can call it even."

"I seem to recall taking a bullet *and* pulling you up from a ledge," he said. "By my count, I think that means you still owe me, Sergeant."

I tapped the new rank pinned to my collar. "Captain, Mr. Goode. Captain."

He smiled and nodded. Despite our earlier animosity, things had changed between us. Maybe not friends yet, but there was a newfound respect.

"I suppose a man with a gun does still have his uses," Goode said with a sly smile.

"And I guess a man hidden away behind a computer can put up a fight when he needs to." I offered my hand, and we shook on it. A simple unspoken agreement that, while we may be fighting two very different fronts, we were still fighting against the same evils.

Director Goode turned to walk away but stopped short and gave me a queer look. "That other item you requested? It's downstairs. I still don't understand why you insisted on bringing it back. It makes even less sense than forcing yourself to read all these."

Instead of giving him an answer, I headed for the elevator.

"Be careful, West," Goode called. "It's dangerous. Some weapons can't be repurposed."

I thought about his warning on the long elevator ride to the bottom. It ended in the armory where the man on duty indicated a back room with a lift of his chin. He looked nervous at what Goode had left for me. That struck me as funny considering how many explosives the armorer regularly accounted for.

"Hey there," I whispered, approaching the dog crate in the back room. Cain's surviving Mastiff, Dante, cowered inside. He whimpered and huddled away from the front grate of his shelter. I held out my hand, and he hesitantly gave it a sniff. "That's it, boy."

Dante looked at me. Not a weapon, just a poor animal scared to death of what it'd gone through. What he had very nearly been made into. Those big wet eyes of his recognized me. They looked sad. I'd never thought dogs were capable of regret before, but those eyes of his had me convinced otherwise. We'd both hurt each other. And we both hated ourselves for it.

"My bosses don't think you can be saved," I said as he nuzzled my hand through the grate and gave it a lick. "But I'm getting pretty good at proving them wrong."

I let him out of the crate and sat on the floor with him. When that oversized dog rested his head on me, the weight of the world felt just a little lighter.

In Alighieri's epic poem, Dante had to go through the inferno before he could reach salvation. I found that thought encouraging. Maybe, there was still time for us both to be saved.

ACKNOWLEDGMENTS

Though this book and all its characters are a work of fiction, it wouldn't have been possible without the very real men and women in uniform who I've had the pleasure of crossing paths with. The stories, experiences, and expertise of too many incredible people to possibly list every single one was a vital foundation for this latest Black Spear adventure. I am truly indebted to the experts who shared their insights and give some direction in the development of these fictional weapons. Let's just keep our fingers crossed that even in this crazy world, we can keep these things firmly entrenched in the "fiction" category! So, here's to all of you that wore the uniform and signed on the dotted line to do your duty honorably, whatever that job may be. I owe you animals a drink next time we meet.

A special thank you to knifemaker extraordinaire Dietmar Pohl for graciously allowing me to equip Cole with one of his absolutely badass knives. As much as I have fun making things up, it's even cooler to inject something from the real world onto the page. If it's good enough for Rambo, it's good enough for Cole!

To Scott Snyder and the entire Best Jackett team behind the Comic Writing 101/201 class. I had a blast translating the lessons of pacing, emotionality, and structure from the comic medium into this format. Just as every comic issue should leave readers anxious for next month's issue, I hope readers of this book feel the same way at the end of each chapter leading into the next.

I would be remiss if I did not take the time to thank my family, and while anyone who knows me knows that I'm blessed with the most amazing partner who's given us four beautiful children, I really have to thank my *entire* family. My wife has been right there by my side this entire time. I could write entire bookshelves of autobiographical novels solely revolving around her love and dedication, but it was the outpouring of support from siblings, cousins, aunts, uncles, and even family of bond rather than blood which I was truly touched by. The entire extended Spada Clan is indeed a tight-knit unit.

Lastly, if you made it this far into this book, I want to thank you, the reader. There are so many brilliant writers in this genre. It is my sincere pleasure that you chose this one. It's hard to believe we're already two books into this wild Black Spear world, and I am so grateful you've joined me on this journey so far, but all I can say is this: the best is yet to come.

ABOUT THE AUTHOR

Born and raised in California, Benjamin Spada has had a lifelong passion for storytelling. Benjamin is a dedicated taco aficionado, self-described "Professor of Batmanology," proud Fil-Am and lumpia enthusiast, and has made a career in the United States Marine Corps. He has been a Martial Arts Instructor, been assigned as a Section Leader in the Wounded Warrior Battalion for our nation's wounded, ill, and injured, and served overseas to help train our foreign military allies in defense against chemical, biological, and nuclear weapons. He has trained Marines, Sailors, Federal Agents, and other friendly forces in individual survival measures for everything from nuclear attacks to deadly nerve agents. Despite these grim assignments, he has carried on with equal amounts of sarcasm and stoicism. When out of uniform, Benjamin is an avid sci-fi and horror movie fan, tattoo collector, comic enthusiast, and two-time holder of the Platinum Trophy in Elder Scrolls: Skyrim. *The Warmaker* is Benjamin's second novel in the *Black Spear* series.

Benjamin lives with his wife, Jacqueline, and their four daughters in Oceanside, California.